D0453883

CUT HER DEAD

Also by Iain McDowall

A Study in Death
Making a Killing
Perfectly Dead
Killing For England

Cut Her Dead

Iain McDowall

PIATKUS

PIATKUS

First published in Great Britain in 2007 by Piatkus Books
This paperback edition published in 2007 by Piatkus Books

Copyright © 2007 by Iain McDowall

The moral right of the author has been asserted

*All characters and events in this publication, other than
those clearly in the public domain, are fictitious
and any resemblance to real persons,
living or dead, is purely coincidental*

All rights reserved
No part of this publication may be reproduced, stored in a retrieval
system, or transmitted in any form or by any means, without the prior
permission in writing of the publisher, nor be otherwise circulated in
any form of binding or cover other than that in which it is published
and without a similar condition including this condition being
imposed on the subsequent purchaser

A CIP catalogue record for this book
is available from the British Library

ISBN 978-0-7499-3841-3

Papers used by Piatkus are natural, recyclable products made from
wood grown in sustainable forests and certified in accordance with
the rules of the Forest Stewardship Council

Typeset in Times by Palimpsest Book Production Limited,
Grangemouth, Stirlingshire
Printed and bound by Clays Ltd, St Ives plc

Piatkus Books
An imprint of
Little, Brown Book Group
100 Victoria Embankment
London EC4Y 0DY

An Hachette Livre UK Company

www.piatkus.co.uk

For my mother, Nancy, and to the memory of my father, John.

'Our chief business, then, must be to prove that all objects to which we ascribe identity, without observing their invariableness and uninterruptedness, are such as consist of a succession of related objects.' David Hume, *A Treatise Of Human Nature,* 1739

Part One:

Art Never Sleeps

Chapter One

Brady knew the girl was the one the moment he saw her walk into the bar. Precisely the kind of girl he would enjoy hurting, enjoy terrifying. She was blonde and pretty in such an ordinary-looking way. Something about how she wore her clothes told him that she was wearing one of her best outfits, that she'd made an *effort* to come to a place as tedious as everyday as this. She was looking for something special to happen. And Brady would ensure that it would, would guarantee it personally.

He took another sip from his glass. Maria and Annabel were both drinking what passed for margaritas in a provincial town. Brady was sticking to unsullied mineral water, discarding the shabby slither of lime that came with the new glass every time they re-ordered their round.

Maria wasn't so sure and neither was Annabel.

'She's got a boyfriend with her, Brady,' Maria objected. 'We don't want complications.'

Brady sneered pleasantly.

'She's got a *drunk* with her, Maria,' he replied, 'the way he's sinking back the beers. Probably dropped something as well – or will before the night's out. The boyfriend isn't a problem, believe me.'

They stopped arguing with him after that. It was his show after all – it was always his show and he hadn't messed up yet.

Two margaritas later, Annabel announced that she was getting bored, that at this rate she'd end up pulling some local or other, end up screwing him in the toilets, just to stop from nodding off. Brady sneered again. Once you'd selected your target, he reminded her, it was all about watching and waiting for your opportunity. Then it was all about grabbing it.

Casper hadn't risked taking the stolen any further into town than Mill Street, never drove inside the CCTV circuit unless he had to. He'd parked it up not far from the bail hostel, scraping the tyres on the kerb as he did so. The stolen in question was an old-style Beetle but re-sprayed and customised: a nicely polished engine, everything inside gleaming – and dayglo decals all over the shop, even a Greenpeace sticker in the rear window. Some wanky student's shagging wagon without a doubt. All paid for by Daddy most probably.

'This is it, girl, we cab it from here,' he said, clambering out, pushing the driver's door wide, regardless of the passing traffic.

Tracey shot him a sulky look but complied. She stepped out on the passenger side, banged the door shut. There had been an anti-theft device fitted to the steering wheel. The old-fashioned bar type that was supposed to make the vehicle impossible to steer. Except that it had been kitted out with an even older-fashioned lock that a half-blind granny could have picked in her sleep. Casper had brought it out of the Beetle with him. As soon as they were clear of the scene by a good ten yards or so, he lobbed it casually behind him, shattered the fucker's windscreen right the way across. Now anybody who could be arsed to could help themselves to the cd player or anything else inside that took their fancy. Stuff 'em, he thought, tossers who drove cars like that. Tossers who lived like that. Deserved all they had coming to them.

They nipped in to the Bricklayer's Arms and Casper told Tracey to call up a cab on her mobile. In the end, of course, she had to let three cabs come and go while Casper got embroiled in a complicated sequence of pool games – and lost every single one. It was pushing ten thirty by the time the fourth cab whisked them towards the town centre and dropped them off outside Club Zoo on Holt's Way. Casper hated the place. Straight city – and poncy with it. He'd only gone along with the idea to keep her off his case, mollify her a little. He was still uneasy about yesterday, still hedging his bets about whether he'd finally been caught out or not. He paid the driver with a tenner, acting flash, giving a tip bigger than the fare. There was a female bouncer on the door doing the weapons search. A complete and utter fucking joke to Casper's way of thinking – although, to be fair, there were two proper gorillas just behind her, standing next to the ticket booth. One of them was idling, adjusting his shirt cuffs. The other one was posing, poncing it loudly into the mouthpiece clamped to the side of his chubby, fatboy head. The Zoo comprised the dance floor room itself plus a big, neony bar and a couple of smaller chill-out rooms. This early in the evening, only the bar had any real life in it. Casper got another lager in for himself and a Red Bull with vodka for Tracey. *That's right, mate, make it a double.*

Tracey found a table, sat down and lit a Lambert & Butler while she waited. It was just as well the lying toad was flush, she thought, otherwise she'd have chucked him last night. He could deny it all he liked but she knew where he'd really been yesterday afternoon when he'd claimed he'd been off the estate, working cash-in-hand. *Something came up at the last minute, girl.* The lying, two-faced toad. Something had come up all right. Tracey's mother had seem him herself – and he'd seen Tracey's mother seeing him. Half past three, according to her mum: Casper emerging from a front door in Shelley Court. And not just any front door. Of course not. Casper emerging from Number 29 to be precise. Her place: Dirty Laura's – the same old cow he always went back to in the end, as if he just wasn't capable of keeping away, as

5

if she'd had a homing device fitted to the end of his big, stupid cock. He'd tried to laugh his way out of it of course, had said her mum must've been mistaken. But her mum was in no need of a pair of glasses yet and Tracey had never known her to lie to her about anything important. She took a deep puff, clocked him heading back over with the drinks. Dirty Laura was welcome to him really. Good flaming riddance. But Tracey wanted to enjoy the weekend first, to be out and about in town, not cooped up on the Woodlands in front of her telly, trying not to listen to her mother having disgusting parent-sex in the very next, too thinly-walled room.

She lit him a cigarette as well when he sat down, sipped at her drink, only half-listening to his usual bollocks: scores that had gone well, bigger scores that might be possible, the bright, shiny future he had planned for both of them. Tracey had plans too – or one plan anyway, scheduled for immediate implementation: let Casper spend his cash until maybe midnight, say, and then dump him for a better offer.

'I told you I ain't seen her,' Casper tried again, 'whatever your old dear says, it ain't true.'

Tracey didn't bother to answer. Let him read her non-response anyway he liked. Most probably, six beers in, he'd think she was getting over it, letting him away with it even – it wouldn't be the first time after all. But Tracey's mind had moved on. She was watching a guy in the far corner. Fit. Spelled F-I-T. His hair cut a bit like the singer in Coldplay. Too bad he wasn't on his own. Although there were two girls with him not just one. So maybe neither had their claws all the way in. Both of them were hanging on his every word though. He'd say something and they'd both laugh. You couldn't hear any of it from over here – but you could still see it, still follow the body language. All three of them were well dressed of course. It was only the smart crowd you got in here. Which had been the point of coming really: ditch waste-of-space Casper and walk out with something decent.

And she didn't just mean to look at. Casper was good to look at – and look where that had got her. What she wanted now, she'd decided, was some upmarket bloke with a non-stolen car and non-stolen credit cards. Well why not? Just because she'd grown up on the Woodlands didn't mean she had to live there for ever. She was only eighteen, her entire life didn't *have* to be a flaming life sentence.

They drank on. And the place filled up, turned noisy, busy. She took to glancing over that way every now and again, whenever she was sure Casper wouldn't notice. But quickly, casually, just in case he did. They were still there each time. Still just the three of them. And she knew the guy had seen her, spotted her, knew he was smiling at her each time she looked. Just *knew* it.

Chapter Two

Around midnight, on his tenth pint and started – well started – on to the Bacardi chasers, Casper did finally notice.

'What you keep looking at, girl?' he asked her. 'That ponce in the corner? Looks like a flaming estate agent. Why don't you shag him if you're so keen? Probably got a knob the size of a fag end.'

Casper laughed at his own joke, feeling relaxed by now, confident that it had been another false alarm. Even if she *did* know about Laura, so flaming what? It wasn't as if the pair of them, Tracey and him, were married or engaged or joined at the hip. There wasn't even a kiddie involved, thank fuck. Plus you couldn't take Laura seriously anyway, could you? Mean to say: Laura was just a laugh, a randy old cow, something to do on a wet Friday afternoon.

'You're the one I take seriously, girl,' he said out loud, risking something close to a confession.

I am so over you, Tracey thought, but there was something inside that still stabbed, still hurt. He was as good as admitting it. And he was laughing about it. Like it was a joke. Like it was funny.

He moved his chair closer, stretching his arm around her shoulders. She thought she might gag in his late-night odours: beer, nicotine, Bacardi and CK One, the latter most probably boosted – nicked – from Boots by his light-fingered kid brother.

'Don't worry about it, Trace,' she heard him say, more or

8

less bragging about it now. 'I've told her no way, never again. I promise I have.'

With his free arm he lifted up his pint glass, held it halfway towards his mouth.

'Sides, it's like being in bed with a bouncy castle, I swear to God it is.'

For the last hour, Tracey had been wondering precisely how she would actually end it, what she would actually say or do. And suddenly she saw that this was as good an opportunity as any. It was more dramatic than she'd planned. But it was no more than he deserved. In fact it was quite a lot less. Cheating was one thing, cheating with an addled old sow, turning your real girlfriend into a laughing stock, was another thing altogether. Plus, thinking practically, Casper had been wolfing down the benzos on the drive into town. The way he liked to do if they went boozing or clubbing on a Saturday night, getting himself well and truly wasted. His eyes were pill-dead and already he was slumping in his seat – his reactions, right now, would be slower than a tortoise.

She slid his arm off her shoulders, waited until he'd put his glass back down. Then she was on her feet – and the remaining three quarters of Casper's chilled pint of Foster's lager were torrenting down over his head and his face and then continuing further downwards: splashing all over the front of the Tommy Hilfiger jacket she'd told him to wear since they were going somewhere half-decent for a change.

'Bye, Casper,' Tracey said quietly.

A cheer went up from the nearby tables. Tracey slipped through the crowds milling in front of the Zoo's faux-retro long bar. She made for the Ladies, needing to be somewhere less totally public until she could think what to do next. It was one thing taking revenge on Casper, it was another thing altogether ruining her own night by going home early. She came back out five minutes later: in time to catch a glimpse of Casper struggling ineffectually as two bouncers – one male, one female – propelled him towards the exit.

Maria insinuated herself next to the girl where she was standing – right at the far end of the bar. Quite a performance, she'd thought. So had Brady and Annabel. They'd worried for a moment that the bouncers would go after her too. But either they didn't know what she looked like – they'd arrived at the scene of the incident several seconds too late, attracted by the sudden uproar – or they didn't much care. They'd chucked out the boyfriend and no one seemed to be causing any more trouble after all. So why would they? Job done in their book, she supposed.

'That was brave of you,' she said, smiling.

'He had it coming,' Tracey replied, clocking that this was one of the two who were with *him*.

Up close, Tracey realised, she was wearing some kind of wig. Long and black, vaguely Gothy. But she was attractive all the same. Slim and medium height like herself. A nice smile. Nice white teeth.

Maria insisted straightforwardly on including the girl's drink in her own round, suggested that she was welcome to join them if she liked. Better than being there on her own surely? The girl hesitated for a minute and then said yes, OK, fine. It was as easy as that. Simple. As simple, Maria conceded to herself, as Brady, sending her over to the bar, had told her that it would be.

Chapter Three

Brady's place was in the old Hat Factory, he announced. Right at the top of the building. Tracey had nodded, had said she'd heard the flats there were really cool, had said this nonchalantly – implying it was the kind of place she might live in herself if she had a mind to. As if. The closest she'd come so far was scanning the property supplement in the *Argus* now and again, day-dreaming idly about being rich – or at least about not being dirt-poor. All over the centre of town, she knew, neglected Victorian buildings were being gutted and yuppified, turned into smart living spaces for the new century. Brady had only just moved in, he'd said. Up from London. Annabel was his sister and Maria was her flat-mate down that way. Putney, he told her, lying about nearly everything. They'd come up for the weekend, were helping him get the place sorted. Plus tonight there was going to be a party. A late-night bash. Not too many people though. He didn't know too many people in the area yet. But a small gathering all the same, sort of a housewarming. She was welcome to come with them, if it didn't sound too boring. Tracey had swallowed her nerves, answering him. No, she'd said, it didn't sound boring at all.

The car pulled away smoothly into the night. A BMW. Tracey had taken in the make at once, saw that it was new-looking, more or less pristine. She sat in the front, watching Brady drive, liking the confident way his forearm moved when he shifted up through the gears. There was an expensive-looking watch on his left wrist, glistening in the semi-darkness. His sister, Annabel, and her friend, Maria, were in the back. Maria was building a joint. 'Do you smoke, Tracey?' she'd asked her in her soft, polite accent. *Yeah, 'course*, Tracey had answered. Though in fact she rarely did. Dope was what her mother had always been into, something old and boring. Coke and speed were more her thing, though not so much as they'd used to be. In the case of tonight, being pissed off with Casper, getting ready to dump him at long last, she'd preferred to keep a clear head.

Brady shoved some music on the in-car. Mozart, he'd decided. The piano concerto number 24 in C minor. Just to be a little devilish, just to play her something she'd never have heard, enjoy watching her pretend to like it. He turned it up loud as the car cruised through the lights at the Flowers Street junction and headed across town. The Hat Factory development had secure, underground parking. Brady punched in an entry code at the barrier and drove smoothly down the ramp to a numbered parking space.

He fob-locked the car and led the way to the lift entrance. Annabel and Maria fell into step behind Tracey, Maria passing the joint, now lit, to Annabel while Brady pressed the button to call the lift.

Brady's big, spacious apartment was on the top floor. Minimalist plush. Tracey admired the view through the floor-to-ceiling window while Brady fixed drinks and Annabel and Maria disappeared together into one of the bathrooms, saying they wanted to freshen up a little for the party. It seemed as if the whole of Crowby was below her, spread out at her feet. The late-night geography of a thousand street lights and headlamps. She watched the cars speeding through the streets. Boy racers mainly. Although their thumping, thrumming sound systems didn't really carry at this height. Brady was at her side after a moment, proffering a crystal glass.

'Champagne,' he said, 'cheers.'

'Cheers,' Tracey replied, taking the drink from him.

She'd barely registered that Annabel and Maria had made themselves scarce, along with their joint. But now she commented on it.

'Those minxes,' Brady replied glibly, 'I think my sister could be – well, gay.'

Tracey smiled – but suddenly thinking that Brady was nothing but a smoothie, a smug, middle-class smoothie. Casper had been right for once. Brady was the real yuppie type after all, well used to money, always expecting his own way. And he was older too, up close, than he'd looked from across the bar. Pushing twenty-five, she thought, or maybe even already pushed it. She could sleep with him all right, he'd given her all the signals. But then what? Nothing in all probability, just an insincere see-you when she left in the morning. She sipped the champagne anyway, the bubbles tickling the back of her throat. No real harm done, girl. Just drink the booze, have a laugh. Then call a cab later, leg it back home.

Brady was standing really close to her now, his arm, she was certain, about to shoot around her shoulder. She stepped away from him, pretended an interest in the interior decor. The entry phone chimed but she didn't look around to see who had appeared on the tiny video screen. *Sure, come on up*, she heard Brady saying. There was a set of framed photographs in a recess near the window. Parks, fountains, street scenes. Paris maybe, she thought, or Rome. Not flaming Crowby anyway. She took a good, long look at them. Brady had made himself scarce too by the time she'd finished. She'd heard the sound of the main door opening and closing out in the hall and now she could hear voices from another room – the kitchen maybe. She decided she might as well join them through there, see what was what.

The door which led to the kitchen opened when she was halfway towards it. Brady then Annabel and Maria. Then a newcomer she hadn't seen before. Tall. Probably male.

Although it was hard to tell since he was cloaked and hooded from head to toe, was looming up behind the others like a mad monk in a horror flick.

'Nobody mentioned fancy dress,' Tracey said uncertainly.

She noticed that the others were carrying similar costumes, were pulling them on now, over their normal clothes.

'This her, Brady?' the newcomer asked, his voice unmistakably male.

Brady pulled the cloak on, adjusted the hood over his head, before he answered. Then: 'This is indeed her. The sacrificial lamb.'

Brady took a step towards her and Tracey understood at once that she'd made a bad mistake coming here. Though exactly what kind of mistake still wasn't clear. She darted around a long, white sofa – away from Brady and towards the door to the hall. But the newcomer was waiting there for her. She aimed a hard kick at his shin bone and ran past him. Maria and Annabel barred her path. She lunged at them but one of them – Maria she thought – grabbed her by the hair, really pulling at her scalp. The other one was suddenly holding something small and shiny in her hand. A spray can of some kind.

'Fuck off,' Tracey shouted, trying to kick Maria, trying to stay out of Annabel's reach. Too little, too late. Tracey's vision blurred and there was a searing pain in her eyes. Hot, unbearable. Somebody caught her from behind then – Brady or the newcomer, she didn't know which – and she felt her hands being shoved together, something like cuffs being applied.

Somebody slapped her face. Hard.

'Don't tell me to fuck off, you pathetic little slapper.'

Tracey spat in the direction of the voice – Annabel, she guessed, her vision still a red, painful blur.

Another slap. Even harder this time.

'Not if you know what's good for you. Not if you want to get out of here alive.'

14

Chapter Four

It wasn't mainly a physical thing. Anything but. You needed
to take physical control obviously, to get them quickly and
exactly to the helpless place where you wanted them to be,
needed them to be. But that was only the preamble. Only a
necessary prior condition before the real fun could be begin.
As soon as they had the handcuffs on her and had shut up
her shouting and cursing mouth with a generous slice of
masking tape, they frogmarched her over to the sofa, shoved
her down into it. Annabel held her there while, very nearly
gently, Maria bathed her eyes, got most of the gunk out.

The minute she could see again, the girl struggled to stand
up. Brady shoved her back on to the sofa.

'I don't think you understand yet, Tracey,' he said. 'Your
only chance of long-term survival is to *behave* – to do exactly
what we tell you to and nothing else.'

'Don't lie to her, Brady,' the newcomer said. 'She's dead
meat and we all know it. No more life for you, darling,' he
said, adopting a comic tone, '*your* time's up.'

Brady leant closer to her so that she could stare into the
pinhead irises in his blue eyes. It wasn't obvious otherwise
but his eyes gave it away – he was *on* something now, she
realised.

'My colleague has a tendency to overdramatise, Tracey.
But I'm afraid he's right all the same. Very soon, we're going
to bury you alive, dear girl. Then listen to your last gasps
for air. It's going to be such fun, isn't it, friends?'

His voice, the way he was speaking, had changed too,

something over-the-top about it all, like a bad actor on the telly.

'Such fun,' Annabel said, stepping forward, brushing her hand lightly down the front of the girl's top.

'Tsk, tsk,' Brady said, shoving her hand away, 'We're here to murder her, not to molest her.'

Tracey kicked out again, aiming for Annabel and then for Brady but failing to connect either time.

Brady smiled like a master of ceremonies introducing the next act.

'Time for a little more bondage, I feel,' he said, nodding to the newcomer.

Tracey watched the newcomer walk back into the kitchen and come back with a length of rope.

Brady and Annabel held her legs while the newcomer tied them together at the ankles.

Tracey studied her captors, her mind trying hard to stay with anger but filling up with unwanted fear. Each of them was fully cloaked now, making their respective heights the easiest way to tell them apart visually. The second tallest one – Brady – picked up a TV remote from the arm of the sofa. In a distant corner of the room, a large-size plasma screen clicked itself to life. Tracey gaped at the image: it was herself, here and now, bound and gagged.

'Pity you can't smile for the camera, Tracey,' Brady said, 'but the main thing is we've got you on record. Every little flicker of fear on your face, dear girl.'

'Isn't it time yet?' the newcomer asked, a hint of annoyance in his voice, a suggestion that Brady was making too much of a meal of it.

'Why, Adrian, I do believe it *is* time,' Brady said.

So he has got a name, Tracey thought. Adrian. Adrian and Brady. Annabel and Maria. Brady has blond hair, poofy-looking on a bloke really, Annabel's hair is black. Maria might be a redhead under the wig. The car reg was S-something for the last three letters. SGN maybe. It would be important to remember as much as she could later. There would be a later, she told herself, trying to take deep breaths, willing herself to be calm. She had to believe that, had to.

Casper was well hacked off. He'd hung around across the way from Club Zoo for a good half-hour or so after they'd ejected him. He'd thought about trying to force his way back in. But each time he'd thought better of it. In the end he'd wandered back through town and down towards the Bricklayer's, which stayed open till two on Friday and Saturday nights. From there, he'd teamed up with Mad Billy Briers and his mates. Billy had liberated a Megane, had a plan to drive over to a club near Coventry. But there turned out to be something seriously wrong with it – gear or clutch trouble, Mad Billy said – and in the end they'd abandoned the fucker on the approach road to the North Crowby bypass and walked – bleeding, bastarding *walked* – all the way back to the Woodlands. Casper had thought about calling in on Dirty Laura when they'd got back and then had thought better of that too. Tracey was a good lass, he'd realised, the best he'd had to be honest. Maybe if he stayed away from Laura, made it clear that he was staying away from her, she'd come round again in a day or two. It had worried him though, leaving Tracey in the Zoo on her own, prey to some big-money yuppie flashing smarmy cash to get into her knickers. But it was his own fault he realised – and there was no way, realistically, that he could've fought or snuck his way back in to the Zoo anyway – not without getting lifted. And getting lifted again meant a stretch, the court had made that all too clear the last time. So here he was, his cash all spent, letting himself into his ma's place, no girlfriend – and no action – on a Saturday night. He was more or less straight and sober now as well, no longer off his face. He switched on the light in the kitchen, mooched in the fridge for something to snack on. He'd call round in the morning, he decided, check that she'd got home all right. Not that there was anything really to worry about, was there? Mean to say: Tracey had grown up on the Woodlands, for fuck's sake, same as he had himself. She knew how to look after herself if anyone did, didn't she? Of course she flaming did. He extracted a couple of rashers of bargain-pack bacon and looked around for an egg, decided a fry-up might put him in a better mood.

Brady and Adrian carried the coffin in from one of the bedrooms. It was relatively lightweight, the do-it-yourself kind. But it still took the two of them to carry it through neatly. They set it down in the centre of the lounge with an air of ceremony. Brady lifted back the lid, pointed to the semi-circle of tiny holes he'd carefully drilled out earlier in the day.

'Breathing holes, Tracey. You'll die deliberately at the appointed time. Not before. Not accidentally.'

Tracey struggled to her feet somehow but Annabel, who'd been standing over her, pushed her back onto the sofa.

'I don't think the slapper wants to die.'

'She should have thought of that before,' Maria commented.

'Enough, ladies,' Brady said, 'let's get the jack into the box.'

Brady and the newcomer called Adrian lifted her up by the shoulders and Annabel and Maria took her feet. Slowly, they carried her towards the coffin and placed her inside. She struggled futilely, tried to prise herself up with her elbows. But then one of them – she didn't notice which one – slid the lid across the top of the coffin. She heard the sound of bolts sliding into place, of locks clicking shut. She could still hear all right. But, apart from the miniscule shafts of more-or-less worthless light finding their way to her through the air holes, she couldn't see. Not anything, she realised, total panic finding her at last, finally overwhelming her. Not anything at all.

Chapter Five

Jim Hallam parked his Vectra in the car park at the foot of Crow Hill. At 7.30 AM on a Sunday morning, there were no other vehicles in sight. Hallam was a bulky man, near enough forty. But bulky from muscle not fat. He spent a lot of his weekends well away from Crowby, fell-running whenever he could over in Wales or up in the Lake District. He'd taken the sport up when he'd been at college and had never let it drop. Outside of his job, which he was fortunate enough to like, and his marriage, which was fortunate enough to be happy, running was his passion, his main interest in life. But there were family reasons why he'd had to be here on this particular weekend. Specifically, his sister's wedding – her third – had taken up all of yesterday afternoon and then the reception had taken up all of last night. The proverbial triumph of hope over experience, he'd thought, but he wasn't the kind of man to let his family or his relatives down. His own wife, Diane, had suggested he should have a lie-in this morning – they'd not got home till gone two after all – but Hallam had resisted the temptation. There was a big competition event coming up in the Brecons at the end of the month and he wanted to maintain his peak fitness if he possibly could.

He got out of the Vectra and locked it, securing his keys in a section of the mini rucksack he liked to wear for a training run like this one. He could keep everything he needed inside it – the stuff he'd ordinarily carry in his jacket or trouser pockets – his wallet and his mobile especially.

Plus a litre of water to ward off dehydration, which was probably a higher risk than usual this morning. He wasn't much of a drinker ordinarily – but Diane had coaxed him into the party spirit for once and he'd woken up the worse for wear. Champagne, beer, even a couple of large brandies. He walked across the car park to the start of the waymarked trail which led up to the summit of the hill. Crow Hill was high ground by local standards and the car park had been clawed out of the woodland that surrounded it at its foot. There were trails through the woods too, even the occasional bench and picnic table. All in all, it was nature over-tamed for Hallam's taste but the climb up to the top was steep enough to give your legs a basic workout if you set yourself a fast enough pace. He stopped for a moment, did a bit of trunk bending and leg-stretching to get himself properly warmed up. He was thinking that he was just about ready for the off when he heard the first, unexpected footfall. *Crack.* Something moving wildly amongst the nearby trees. *Crack.* Crashing around by the sounds of it. *Crack.* And maybe too big, certainly too clumsy, to be any of the animal life you might be likely to find out this way – rabbits, foxes, or very, very rarely, a deer.

He stood still and waited. And then there she was, running out into the clearing. A girl. Or, to be more precise, a young woman. Medium height, slim, blonde. Also naked. Also caked in mud and dirt. Also cut and bruised, bleeding in places. When she saw him, she froze in her tracks. *Help me*, she said softly. She said it like a fearful question, her intonation rising on the second syllable. As if help might be the last thing he had on his mind.

He walked back to his car, found the Halfords tartan rug in the boot that Diane liked to keep there for picnics. *You're all right, lass, you're all right*, he said to her, not really sure that she was. He offered her the rug but now that she'd ended her wild run, her limbs seemed paralysed, inert. She'd covered her arms across her breasts but she seemed unable – unwilling

– to make any other movement. Seeing this, he wrapped the rug slowly around her himself with a big man's lumbering gentleness. It came to him that she might be hungry or thirsty. He took his water bottle out of his day pack, held it open to her lips. She drank at it greedily, the water spilling down her chin. When she stopped for a moment, he took his mobile out and called for the cavalry. *That's right, love, an ambulance. And I think we'd better have the police as well.*

Chapter Six

DC Emma Smith was 50 per cent of the understaffed Sunday morning duty CID. The other half was DC Ray Williams. Not the best combination from her point of view since the demise of their short-lived affair. But shifts and work patterns couldn't accommodate every delicate, inter-personal issue on the force. You put up or shut up. And Emma at least had it clear that she wasn't going to let her lapse of judgement over Williams get in the way of her career. They were sitting in the rape suite's admin office, waiting for Carole Briggs, the Victim Support stroke Family Liaison officer, to give them the all-clear. Weekends were a busy time for Victim Support so it was fortunate that Briggs had been available. Emma had worked with her before, respected her as one of the VS officers most capable of walking the fine line between the interests of the victim and the operational demands of a police inquiry.

'You don't think we should call in Jacobson, then, Emma?' Williams asked.

Emma reminded him that it wasn't possible anyway. Jacobson didn't only have this weekend off, he'd arranged to spend it on a weekend break in Paris with his girlfriend.

'Oh yeah. Course,' Williams replied, 'I keep forgetting the chief's got a life these days. What about DS Kerr then?'

'Maybe we should. But let's see how the interview goes first, eh? No need to pass things up if we can handle it ourselves.'

'Yeah, I guess not,' Williams agreed.

Emma poured herself a plastic cupful of over-chilled water from the water cooler and hoped they'd made the right decisions. They'd left the uniformed patrol – two officers – up on Crow Hill to keep a guard on the cordoned-off area until the duty SOCOs could get there. Plus the police surgeon – sorry, the forensic medical examiner – was with the girl right now. Everything was unfolding exactly as per the text book, so why disturb Kerr and his missus under the sheets if there was no immediately urgent need to do so? No real reason, she supposed. Except that if even half of what the girl had garbled to the ambulance crew and to the uniformeds was true then they were dealing with a distinctly nasty set of bastards. The kind that you definitely didn't want pulling a fast one in court just because of some sloppy procedure or unforeseen minor omission on CID's part.

The rape suite, less than three years old, lived at the end of a back corridor on the second floor of the Divisional building. There were medical facilities, an interview room that looked more like a lounge and an actual lounge where a victim could sit with friends or relatives between seeing the doctor or the counsellor and talking to whoever – meaning police – was really dealing with the case. Emma had suggested it was the best bet under the circumstances and Williams had agreed, hadn't been able to see any grounds not to. He usually made an effort to be ultra-amenable around the lovely Emma these days, didn't need a resumption of hostilities between them. In any case, he'd thought, she was the one who'd taken the Advanced Rape Investigation course, not him. Not that this was a rape case. Not exactly. Not in the normal sense of the word. But whatever you wanted to call it, you were still left with a young woman in a traumatised state – and in clear need of the type of medical attention that didn't just treat wounds but looked at them as potential *evidence*.

They were expecting Carole Briggs but in the event it was the FME himself who stuck his head around the door. Dr

Colin Naylor. Young-ish. Unmarried. Newly appointed. Keen.

'The nurse is helping her clean up now. Carole's still with her too,' he said. 'She's hoping that she can sit in on your interview, hold her hand when she needs it.'

'Good idea,' Emma said.

Everything – warrants, arrests, bringing charges – depended on an accurate statement from the girl of everything she claimed had happened. Without that, they were in limbo, unable to act.

Williams dutifully nodded his agreement.

'So what can you tell us, Doc?' he asked.

Naylor entered fully into the room, pulled the door shut behind him.

'She's in pretty good shape considering. Physically at any rate. Most of the cuts and injuries are actually pretty minor. And a lot of them are probably self-sustained – branches catching at her while she was running through the woods for instance. That kind of thing. The only exception I'd mention is the bruising on her wrists – which *is* pretty bad. They were taking a big risk, cuffing her like that and then confining her on her back in a small space. Even for a healthy young woman, there's always the risk of an embolism.'

Emma finished her cup of water, tried not to see herself in the girl's place, tried not to see herself enduring what the girl said she'd been through. Not even for a second.

'She gave her consent for an intimate examination then?' she asked.

'Yep, she did. *Anything that will do for them*, she said.'

Naylor glanced at his clipboard, and pulled at the lobe of his left ear. A nervous tic which he didn't seem to know he had.

'Bears out her story as far as I can see. No conventional sexual assault. Nothing vaginal or anal. But I've followed the standard rape procedures anyway – I've taken a full set

24

of body samples for the lab if they turn out to be needed.'

The girl's claims were so bizarre they'd wondered whether she hadn't just been conventionally attacked – and then gone into some strange kind of denial. Naylor had drug-tested her too, had wanted to establish the state of mind she'd been in.

'And you're happy she's ready to talk again?' Williams asked.

'As long as you take it easy. Let her have as many breaks as she likes, let her set the pace.'

They found Tracey Heald hunched on a yellow sofa in the interview room, ignoring the mug of tea which sat in front of her on a low, pine table. She was wearing a loose pale blue tracksuit that Carole Briggs had looked out for her. There was a stock of them – in the full range of standard sizes – in the cupboard in the admin room. Usually they were swapped for the victim's own clothes which were bagged as soon as possible and sent on for forensic examination. Carole Briggs sat alongside her. Whenever Tracey asked for a cigarette, which seemed to be about every two seconds, Carole found one in her bag, lit it and passed it to her. The room had discreet video resources. Anyone on the sofa was automatically inside camera range. Williams checked for a clean tape, pressed the relevant button.

'Whenever you're ready,' Emma said, 'just take us through it from Club Zoo again. You went there with your boyfriend, but you had an argument, right?'

Tracey tried the tea at last. Not enough sugar. But at least it was hot. She took a couple of sips, drew on her latest cigarette – some kind of useless, low-tar brand – and looked at them. Two detectives – a man and a woman. The woman not looking too much older than herself. Still in her twenties anyway. Plus the motherly cow, Carole, who you didn't know what she was supposed to be really. A kind of professional mother-hen, fussing and smiling, always seeming to get in the flaming way. All the while they were sat here nattering, she thought, Brady and his slimy crew could've taken off anywhere. She'd told them this before. Now she tried to tell them again.

'How many times do you need to hear it? Have you sent someone round there yet?'

'Just as soon as we've got a clear statement of what you're saying, Tracey,' the woman cop answered, 'then we can take the appropriate action.'

'They stuck me in a frigging box. They said they was going to kill me. What else do you need to know?'

'We want to catch whoever did this, Tracey, believe me. Send them down. That means going by the book, I'm afraid. Now if you could just talk us through from when you were in Club Zoo with – with Casper wasn't it?'

She didn't know how long she'd been in the coffin. The plain fact was that she'd lost it in there. Completely lost it. Her mind tripping out everywhere and anywhere. Places she'd been, places she'd never been. Things that happened years ago, things that had never happened. Anything to blank out where she was, to shut out the pain that had spread to every inch of her body. She couldn't even scream with the tape tight across her mouth. She'd banged her head hopelessly against the lid for a while. Until the ache in her neck and her shoulders became more than she could stand. When her mind wasn't drifting – in odd, floating moments when she seemed to go beyond panic, beyond terror – she could hear them moving around near her, could hear them speaking together all at once – like it was a frigging chant or something. And weird music in the background. Not modern weird, but old-fashioned weird. Like nothing she'd ever heard before, hoped she'd never hear again.

And then the light flooding in, blinding her so that she had to squeeze her eyes shut. When they'd lifted her out, she couldn't stand, had collapsed on to the floor and one of them had thrown cold water over her, bringing her round. They were in their ordinary clothes again and she could get a good look at the new one's — Adrian's — face at last. He's not bad looking, she'd thought, though it had seemed like a daft thing to be thinking. None of the four of them had looked like monsters. Then from somewhere, some TV show or movie, she'd remembered that if you were kidnapped, snatched, it was always bad news if you were allowed to see your captors. If they were going to kill you, they didn't have to worry about you identifying them. She'd looked away when she'd thought that, tried to avoid any of their faces for a while. Maria had leant over her then, the one who'd seemed so nice, so friendly, when they'd first met at the bar. She was holding a sharp-looking kitchen knife in her hand. The blade looked big and shiny.

'That was just a little taster, Tracey. The kind of thing that happens to bad girls who don't do exactly as they're told. Understand?'

Tracey had nodded — or tried to nod — her eyes blinking submission. It was somewhere else entirely, not even in the room — but somewhere that didn't seem only to exist in her imagination, where she saw herself with her hands free, grabbing hold of the handle of the knife, grabbing the cow by the hair and slitting her throat wide open. They'd removed the tape from her mouth after that, but had warned her to keep quiet, not to utter a single word or sound. Or else. She'd winced while they'd pulled at the tape and the other bitch, Annabel, had slapped her for it, had slapped her hard across her face.

'And that was when the drive out to Crow Hill was first mentioned?' the woman cop was asking.

'That was when a drive was mentioned,' Tracey corrected her, accepting a new cigarette from Carole Briggs. 'They didn't say where to. Only that I had to act normal on the way down to where their car was. If they ran into anybody, I wasn't to try anything. There was four of them and there was just one of me, Brady said. *Don't say a fucking word if you know what's good for you.*'

'And that was what you did? You didn't try to get help?'

'I never got the flaming chance, did I?' Tracey replied. 'There wasn't anyone about from when we left the flat. Straight down in the lift and straight into Brady's car. Not a soul. Lucky for them I suppose.'

She took two drags in quick succession. One of the worst things was that she'd never know if she would have tried if there'd been a chance, if she would've found the courage or not.

'You didn't see an opportunity just to make a run for it?'

Only the woman seemed to ask anything. The man just sat there. Like a useless waste of space.

'If only. I couldn't hardly walk after – after being inside. Brady went in front and his mate was at the back. In between, it was me in the middle and Annabel and Maria either side. Propping me up. If somebody had seen us, they'd most probably have just thought I was pissed.'

'And they kept you handcuffed the whole time?'

At last the man had asked a question. His accent sounded Welsh or something. Not local anyway. They moved around all over, coppers did. Or so she'd heard. Made it easier for them to keep their distance, she supposed, easier for them to stitch you up in the normal run of things. Which this wasn't. Not normal at all.

'No, not the whole time. Uncuffed me in the flat, cuffed me again in the car. I expect they thought it would look less suspicious that way.'

Tracey had rode in the back the second time, tall Adrian on one side of her, the bitch Annabel on the other. She'd tried to reason with them, thinking it might be safe to talk now they were cocooned from the outside world inside the car. She didn't know what they had against her, she told them, she'd never done anything to them, she didn't even know them. But if they'd just let her out, just let her go, she'd go home and forget about it, wouldn't say a word to anyone, she swore she wouldn't. Brady had glanced at her via the

*driver's mirror, had replied in more or less his normal voice
this time. 'This isn't about you, Tracey. It's about us. Now
shut it or the tape goes back on over your pretty little mouth.'
She'd said nothing after that, just kept an eye on the route
they were taking. Brady had avoided the car park when they
reached Crow Hill. Probably because it was a popular spot
as a lover's lane, especially at weekends. Probably because
there would still have been a dozen or so vehicles parked
up there. It was just after four AM, according to the dashboard clock. Although clocks were easily adjusted, she'd
thought, easily altered to fuck with your mind and confuse
you. Instead Brady had just driven off the road at a quiet
spot he seemed to know, had seemed to be looking out for.
There had been a gap between the trees just about big enough
to squeeze the car through, conceal it from any passing
traffic. Tracey thought she had a memory that he'd scraped
the sides, forcing it in. She had tried to run this time, the
very first minute she was out in the open. But her legs were
still like rubber and Annabel and Maria had easily caught
her. Maria had held her by the hair again while Annabel
had slapped her. It was about then that Tracey had started
to notice the video camera which always seemed to be around.
All of them had taken turns to use it, depending on what
was happening, depending on who was doing what. Except
that after they'd reached the pre-dug grave, she thought she'd
only seen Adrian with it, seeming to film the others as much
as he was filming her.*

'And you think it was about three feet deep?'

The woman cop was asking the questions again.

Tracey had asked for another cup of tea and they'd stopped
the interview while Carole Briggs had gone off and fetched
it. Plus a couple of digestive biscuits which so far Tracey
had ignored.

'I think so. It came up above my waist when they made
me stand in it. All the earth and stuff was piled up on the
side.'

'They made you get in – then lie down?'

Tracey felt the skin on her cheeks reddening. Embarrassment. Anger. And the memory of the fear she'd felt.

'That was after Annabel and Maria stripped me. Maria held the knife to my throat. Annabel did it – apart from when Maria had to cut my sleeves off around the cuffs.'

'You weren't taped up though at that time. You didn't think about calling out for help?'

Tracey looked straight at her. A smug cow on her police salary. A smug cow who'd never been scared witless.

'Of course I thought about it. But who would've heard? And would anyone have frigging come?'

'This getting you naked, Tracey. You're sure they didn't do anything sexual?'

'No. Apart from all of them gaping at me – and filming me. Annabel pawed at my tits a bit but Brady told her to stop it.'

'And she did?'

'Whatever Brady told them to do, they did. Like he was Lord God all flaming mighty or something.'

They'd made her lie down on the cold soil, had retied the rope around her ankles. Brady had picked up a spade – she supposed it must have been there already, she hadn't seen them bringing it from the car – and had started shovelling earth over her.

'Keep the spiders off you, Tracey – for a while anyway.' She'd lost it again then, crying and whimpering, begging them anything to just let her go. Brady hadn't seemed bothered by the noise this time, had just carried on covering her while the two women stood and watched. And while Adrian went on filming. Brady had been methodical, careful to leave her head and face clear. But eventually the rest of her body was completely covered over. Whatever kind of movement she attempted, the weight of the earth bore down on her, trapping her where she lay.

'Who wants a coffin anyway?' Brady had asked, as if to nobody in particular. 'Far better to let nature take its course. Make direct contact with Mother Earth. More honest that way. Flesh and muck. Filth on filth.'

He'd leant down over her then, peering in close, Adrian moving in very nearly as close with the camera.

'The thing is this, Tracey. I really am about to put a foot of earth over your head. Earth with worms in it for all I know. Then you're going to suffocate and die, I'm afraid. So, my dear girl, any famous last words for the camera?'

Tracey had struggled one last time, had tried to roll on her ankles, had tried to arch her back, maybe get some momentum started that way. Nothing. Completely nothing. She'd looked straight into his face, glib in the pale moonlight. This was what hopeless was, what hopeless really meant, how hopeless really felt.

'My mum,' she'd said quietly, very nearly whispering, 'tell my mum I love her.'

Chapter Seven

They left Carole Briggs to deal with Tracey Heald, to drive her home, to talk to her mother, to set up whatever ongoing support could be quickly arranged. Naylor had offered her a sedative but she'd said no. She didn't want to blank it out, what had happened to her, she'd said. She needed to face up to it, deal with it, she didn't need flaming zombiefying. Brave girl, Emma Smith had thought. Or maybe just reckless. They drove over to the Hat Factory in an unmarked Astra, parked on the other side of the street, a little way down. It was a good vantage point. You could see all the way into the main entrance and you could see both the exit and entrance ramps to the car park underneath the building. They were waiting for two uniformed patrol cars to reach them, two plods in each. Initial back-up. They were also waiting for a phone call from the control room detailing the emergency service's entry code which would get them into the building without disturbing – or alerting – the inhabitants.

In the passenger seat, DC Williams fidgeted with his mobile, anxious for the call to come through.

'Here come the plods,' he said, catching sight of the first patrol car looming up in the wing mirror.

Emma Smith flashed the rear lights, watched the patrol vehicle pull in smoothly behind them. A minute passed. Then two. Then three. No one entered the building or left it. The second patrol car finally turned up. In the next second, William's phone finally buzzed. He repeated the entry code out loud so they could both memorise it.

Two of the uniformeds stayed where they were: ready and available if needed. The other two followed Williams and Smith across the street towards the broad, stone steps which, once upon a time, would have led to the Victorian-era factory's main offices. They took the lift up instead of walking. It turned out to be fast but more cramped than they'd expected for a 'luxury' development. One of the plods was tall, six four, maybe six five, had to duck his head the whole way up. There only seemed to be three apartments on the top floor. Thirty-two, thirty-three and, the one that interested them, number thirty-four. The tall plod checked out the terrain before they went any further. Other than the lifts and the stairs which doubled as a fire escape there were no other exits, no other ways down. There was no bell or knocker on the door. Most visitors would gain access via the entryphone – and in any case this wasn't the kind of place where the neighbours called round to borrow a bowl of sugar. They noticed the fish-eye lens – an extra security precaution, presumably – so Williams and the two plods held back, leaving only Emma Smith in the line of sight. A woman on her own always looked less threatening, less instantly suspicious, less obviously official. She knocked briskly. Then knocked again. Then again. No answer – and nothing to see when she peered through the letter box except a firmly-closed inner door. She tried a fourth time, tried shouting through:

'Police – we need a word.'

Silence – until the door to number thirty-two opened behind them. A bloke in his thirties, coffee cup in hand, overloud Sunday morning dressing gown exposing his spindly legs below the knees. DC Williams showed his ID, said they needed to speak to his neighbours in number thirty-four, asked when he'd last seen them.

'There's been no one there since August, as far as I know. A guy on his own, an architect. He's left the country, gone to work in Australia. Good for him if you ask me – some partnership in Sydney, I think.'

Williams exchanged a glance with Emma Smith. It would soon be October.

'You're sure about this? Mr, er—'

The neighbour volunteered his details, reiterated that the flat had been empty for the last five or six weeks. The guy who'd gone to Australia had been called Marshall, he thought. Or something along those lines. Definitely started with an M anyway.

'And you've not seen or heard anyone coming or going in that time?'

The neighbour hadn't. Although he hadn't been here all that time himself. And the building had good soundproofing, which it should do at that kind of asking price: it was possible, he supposed, that someone new had moved in, and he'd just never bumped into them yet.

The door to number thirty-three opened while he was talking. Another thirty-plus upmarket town-dweller. But female this time and fully dressed, looking like she was on her way out to somewhere nice – somewhere not usually involving crime, criminals or Crowby CID. She was definite about the name – Ben Marshall – and definite about the gone-to-Australia theory. He'd bequeathed her some plants and she was fairly hopeless about looking after them. They were in touch by email about watering and nutrition. She even found them a postcard of the Sydney Opera House that he'd sent her, dated 31 August.

'It's possible somebody's moved in since then – but I haven't noticed them myself if they have.'

'The place is for sale then?' Williams asked.

'I wouldn't think so. The owners are a retired couple, as far as I know, living over in Spain.'

'Malaga,' her neighbour agreed. 'They were still here when I moved in but they've been renting their place out for the last couple of years.'

All right for some, Williams thought. But did he know which letting agency they'd used? No, he didn't, he said, but the property management company who maintained the building probably would.

Williams asked if there had been any disturbances last night, any noise, anything unusual of any kind. The neighbour in the loud dressing gown shook his head – no, not that he'd heard. A sleepy-looking woman appeared in the doorway behind him. A silk kimono this time – subtle, quiet colours – and a glass of orange juice in place of coffee. She'd heard nothing either, she didn't think there was anyone living there right now. The woman from number thirty-three said she'd been out at a party in Wynarth: *a bit boring really, work-colleagues, you know?* She'd left after midnight, got back here probably around one o'clock. The place had been as quiet as a mouse. Loud Dressing Gown mentioned the excellent soundproofing again. Apparently it was a selling point.

DC Williams frowned. There were no warrants yet – warrants required names, identities, and Tracey Heald's four first names hadn't got them very far in that direction. But the alleged incident was definitely classifiable as serious: the standard Powers of Search would probably cover their backs – or just about.

'Stand back please, if you don't mind,' Emma Smith advised the three neighbours, reaching the operational decision a second before Williams did.

The tall plod stepped forward. Door-kicking-in was pretty much a professional sport for the uniformed branch. It was evident from the first kick that the doors in the Hat Factory were top-of-the-range. Solid, chunky, dead-locked. But they were still *civilian*, constructed for law-abiding citizens not crack dealers. The second and third kicks shook the hinges. The fourth kick sent the door flying open.

Williams asked the tall plod, who was looking quietly pleased with himself, to stay where he was, guard the entrance. For the time being, number thirty-four was a potential crime scene, off-limits to anyone unofficial. He

35

asked the other plod to check out the car parking level, see if any vehicles down there matched Tracey Heald's description: a BMW saloon, black, last three letters possibly SGN. Emma Smith pacified the audience. The police contractor would repair the door as soon as they were finished, they were investigating a serious incident but there was nothing to be alarmed about. She handed out two cards. If any of them did remember anything later on – anything unusual last night or even in the last few days – they should call her on that number. Any time.

The flat they walked into looked tidy, pristine, *unlived*. Empty cupboards, beds with no bedding, two sumptuous, desolate bathrooms, neither of them containing towels or toiletries. And no food or drink of any kind – absolutely nothing – in the big, designer kitchen.

'It's like wandering around the bloody *Marie Celeste*,' Williams observed.

Emma Smith corrected him. The *Marie Celeste* was precisely what it wasn't like: no unfinished meals, no unwashed dishes, no traces of hasty departures. There was a plasma TV set just like Tracey Heald had said. But there was no sign of the video equipment she'd also said had been connected to it, none of the personal signatures you'd expect in an occupied living space. No CDs, no books, no newspapers, no clothes. The place looked exactly like what the neighbours claimed it *was*: a partially-furnished apartment, available for rent but not rented out in recent weeks.

Williams had picked up the pile of mail that they'd stepped over in the entranceway between the main door and the inner door. Junk mail, utility bills, charity appeals. All of it addressed to The Occupier or to B.S. Marshall, the former tenant who now, seemingly, lived on the other side of the planet.

'You don't think she just got the address wrong, do you, Emma? Or the number of the flat anyway?'

They were in the main lounge. Late September sun streamed through the wall-sized window, giving a false, warm impression of the bright, cold morning outside. DC Smith shook her head.

'It makes sense that there's no one around after what they're supposed to have done. And the neighbours – well, a place like this, you could be here months and not really be sure who's living next door – or whether anybody *is* living next door.'

She swept her eyes around the room. The problem with the theory was the neatness of everything. If someone had been living here recently, they'd done a very thorough job of cleaning up before they'd left. Although they didn't know yet whether a cleaner might just have been keeping an eye on the place or not. There were a few framed art prints and photographs on the walls and in odd corners. But all of them seemed carefully, impersonally, tasteful. None of them about to offend anyone under the age of a hundred and fifty. Exactly the neutral tone the TV makeover shows advised if you were thinking of the property-letting game. She approached the long, white sofa, looking for a crease, a wine stain, any indicator that could be stamped as of recent origin. Nothing. Or nothing that the naked, non-forensic eye could see.

DC Williams's mobile rang: the plod down in the parking bay. There were half-a-dozen beamers in residence, three of them were close enough to the girl's description to be worth taking a further look although none of them had scuff marks on the side panels and none of them featured 'SGN' on the registration plates. Williams asked himself what DCI Jacobson or DS Kerr would do in the circumstances. Answer: ask the plod to chase up the owner in each case, check out each vehicle's whereabouts in the last twenty-four hours. It didn't sound hopeful, but – in Jacobson's well-known phrase – *elimination is four-fifths of identification, old son.* The second uniformed would be needed here to keep the apartment secure, prior to a visit from the SOCOs and prior to a door repair, and for now – with no detentions imminent – the patrol downstairs would need to be released back to other duties. Which left everything else to CID – far too much of it, and most of it requiring authorisation at a level above the rank of Detective Constable. Which meant that DS Kerr would need his Sunday morning disturbing after all.

Chapter Eight

An hour later, Detective Sergeant Ian Kerr drove into the car park in the woodland clearing at the foot of Crow Hill and parked next to a patrol vehicle and the scene of crime van. He switched off the engine, used his mobile, waited for one of the uniforms up at the crime scene to come and find him. He didn't have long to wait. But it was long enough to observe a manic squirrel failing to gain access to a lidded litter bin and then giving up, darting towards the nearest tree in energetic defeat. The plod led him through the woods to the area where the SOCOs were working, but didn't go any further himself. Instead he handed Kerr a standard issue crime scene protection kit. Pull-over plastic body suit – white. Slip-on shoe covers – blue.

The outer cordon of the crime scene, marked off by police tape, extended all the way back to the car park. But for now the focus of attention was in the inner cordon, an area less than ten yards across. Lightning had felled an oak tree during a sudden, unexpected storm back in the spring and, some-time since then, the dead tree had been hauled away, leaving a tiny clearing which the briar and holly had only partially recolonised so far. In the centre of the clearing was a neat rectangle of freshly-dug earth which two SOCOs, watched by a third, were sifting through – inch by inch, or so it seemed. Kerr approached them carefully, making sure his feet didn't stray from the stepping boards. He was mildly surprised to realise that the third figure – the one apparently muttering to itself – was none other than Jim Webster, the

Crime Scene Manager or the Chief SOCO, depending on whatever vintage of official-speak you favoured. Usually it took a murder scene, and a complex one at that, to get Webster away from his family on any weekend – like this one – when he wasn't on formal standby. More or less the exact opposite of Kerr's own domestic situation. Someone on Webster's team had phoned him at home maybe, thinking that they were faced with a bad case. One that was too bad not to pull out all the stops.

Kerr asked him the obvious question:

'Found anything, Jim?'

Webster switched off the little voice recorder he'd recently taken to using at crime scenes before he replied. These days he seemed to like to make instant verbal notes, then write them up later into something fuller. There was an unkind rumour that he'd got the idea from watching some TV cop show or other. A case of life imitating art. Or imitating Channel Five anyway.

'Well, it's certainly been dug out like a grave – and we're lifting what might be human hair and human skin samples. So it could be that we can at least show that the *girl* was here. Whether we get anything that points to the culprits – well, that's another story at this stage.'

'So no trace of her clothes then?'

'Not so far. We think we've found the spot where she says she was brought in the car though. The other half of the team are over there right now. There's some ruts in the dirt right enough – but it remains to be seen whether they can cast enough for an identifiable tyre track. And, even then, who's to say it would be from the right vehicle?'

Somebody like me's to say, Jim, Kerr thought to himself. Somebody who gets to put all of the pieces of the jigsaw together. Somebody who gets to look at the final picture. You depended on the SOCOs every day – and, behind them, the backroom specialists in the forensic labs. But Kerr couldn't have hacked either job for a single minute. It was full of absorbing attention to detail, yes. But it could never be hands-on in the way that mattered to him, drove him. The boffins, geeks and scientists were never in on the final action, never made an arrest, never felt a collar. That was one way that real life definitely wasn't imitating the American imports on the telly – even if, officially, you were meant to refer to the SOCOs as Crime Scene Investigators these days (which nobody except the rawest new recruits ever did).

'But the hole's been freshly dug at any rate?' he asked after a moment.

'I'd say so. Quite a few cut-up roots and foliage that still look fresh and green. No more than a day or so, tops.'

Webster readjusted his microphone clip with just enough irritation to suggest that he really wanted to be getting on.

'Fine. Leave you to it, then,' Kerr said, beating a retreat.

Jacobson would probably have insisted – needlessly – on seeing the ruts that might turn out to yield tyre tracks from the vehicle that might have brought the girl out here. Kerr was happy enough to wait for the expert verdict, didn't need to rub it in the whole time that CID always had ultimate control of a case, that the SOCOs were only their auxiliaries, only sub-contractors. But that was Jacobson for you, he thought, the Zen master of rubbing people up the wrong way when he felt like it, of making life harder than it needed to be.

He used his mobile on the drive back through town, checked progress. Williams and Smith were back at base, chasing up the property management company. Item one: find out who precisely was or wasn't supposed to be living in the Hat Factory's penthouse level. Item two: arrange access to the Hat Factory's CCTV system. There were cameras in the main entrance and in the car park: last night's footage needed looking at urgently. William answered his call: they were on the case but hadn't quite got there yet. The property people weren't sure exactly which lettings agency was involved with number thirty-four, had suggested a list of a half-a-dozen possibles which they were just about to check out.

'One positive thing, guv. They're sending someone pronto to let us into the CCTV set-up. Mick Hume's already on his way over there.'

'Cheers, Ray. Any news, patch me in quickly,' Kerr said, ending the call and re-accelerating.

Finding Mick Hume's name on the weekend call-out list which had been pinned as usual to the disintegrating brown cork noticeboard in the CID Resource Centre had felt like an instant stroke of luck. He'd been thumbing down the list while Williams and Smith had brought him up to speed. It had sounded like a nasty case all right. One where you didn't want anybody corrupt or incompetent involved. The two categories tended to go together in Kerr's experience but neither of them attached to Hume.

The North Crowby bypass, when he got there, was still Sunday morning quiet. It was a road he used almost every day. On trivial journeys and on important ones. He'd taken the exit to the hospital on the day his wife had given birth to their twins. He'd taken the exit to the crematorium on the grey, rain-filled afternoon he'd witnessed his mother's body burning down to ash. He shoved the memory to one side, making a mental note that he hadn't talked to his dad in a few days, ought to pay him a visit whenever he could. The uniformed on the tail of the Hat Factory's BMWs called him. He'd only located one of the owners in person so far – he was taking a statement right now – but said owner was a Nigerian heart specialist who didn't remotely fit any of the girl's descriptions. Plus, in any case, he'd apparently been on call all night over at Crowby General.

Kerr drove on, nothing playing on the in-car, still getting his head around the basic situation. You pick up a harmless girl, bury her alive – but not enough to actually kill her – and film yourself doing it. Plus 'you' are two women as well as two blokes – and you don't seem to be really living where you appeared to be living. It wasn't a standard MO, that was for sure. And no standard motive either. Maybe not any comprehensible motive. When he reached the Woodlands estate, he drew up on the main drag – Shakespeare Road – for a moment, made another two calls. He told Mick Hume he'd meet him at the Hat Factory, just as soon as. Then he phoned his wife, Cathy, thinking she'd be up and about by now. She'd wanted to drive over to Homebase this afternoon, had ideas about redecorating their bedroom. He told her not to wait for him, she'd be better going on her own, if she definitely wanted to get there this weekend. He told her he loved her too. He often did that recently. Although he had no idea if it was true or not, if it ever had been true or not – or what the hell he meant by it. Along Shakespeare Road until the far end, he thought, somewhere not all that far from Shelley Court. The address was around there someplace. Cathy: something else he was relieved to shove aside, something else that would keep for later.

The girl lived with her mother. No brothers or sisters, father long since vanished. She'd two shoplifting convictions against her according to the PNC, but nothing serious and nothing for a year or so. Her criminal record had an upside to it – it meant that her fingerprints and her DNA details were already in the system, would make life easier, or at least speedier, for the SOCOs. Kerr thought he recognised the mother when she showed him in. But probably only because she fitted the bill as one of those gaunt, thin women who haunted the entrances and the lobbies of the magistrates court, waiting to see if a husband or a boyfriend was coming home today or where he needed his shirts sending on to if he wasn't.

Carole Briggs was still on the premises, working her magic – or trying to. She'd made them both tea, was still fielding Tracey Heald endless cigarettes. Tracey was sitting on the edge of the sofa in the front room, chewing her fingernails between draws, staring into nowhere. She was still wearing a rape suite tracksuit. The shopping channel, QVC, was quiet in the background: a guy with impressive muscles let down by an antique mullet hair style demonstrating the alleged benefits of a home exercise system.

'Well?' the mother asked.

That was it. *Well?* Meaning have you caught them yet? Meaning are you taking this seriously or don't you give a monkey's because we're from the Woodlands? Meaning I've hated coppers all my life, and I hate them even more this morning when there's no one else in the flaming world who can help my daughter.

Kerr told them as much as he wanted to tell them. They hadn't found anyone on the premises, they hadn't traced the car. But, please believe him, they weren't going to let this go, they were going to pull out every single stop. No one had asked him to sit down so he carried on standing. Tracey spoke up. Like a message beaming in from outer space.

'I said they had to go round straight away. I said it.'

'From what I'm hearing, Tracey, they might never have gone back to the Hat Factory anyway,' Kerr lied.

If the story was true the way the girl had told it, *somebody* must have gone back there – and cleared away the props. The video equipment. The glasses of champagne. The robes and the hoods. The coffin. He told her he'd like her to spend time with the e-fit unit as soon as he could set it up. If they could get images from CCTV that would be great. But e-fits would be useful too. It might have to keep until tomorrow though. Monday.

'Don't put yourself out,' the mother said.

Kerr let it go, knew better than to argue. It had been a courtesy call as much as anything anyway. The girl had told them all she was likely to for now and Kerr had already fast-forwarded through her video interview. The real reason he'd driven out this way was to talk to the boyfriend, Kevin-known-as-'Casper' Donnelly. Donnelly

44

would be able to corroborate the first part of her story, might also have got a reasonable look at three out of the four suspects.

He made his final excuses and drove on to the address: a flat on the fourth floor of Gerard Manley Hopkins House – GMH, as it was inevitably known locally. Donnelly's mother answered the door: Tracey Heald's mother's fatter, less attractive, even less healthy-looking sister.

'He ain't here,' she told Kerr, without asking why Crowby CID wanted to talk to her son.

Kerr told her anyway. They weren't after Casper for anything, not anything at all, but he might know something useful in connection with a serious incident. It was to do with his girlfriend, Tracey.

Kerr heard a door creak somewhere in the interior. Kevin 'Casper' Donnelly, who hadn't been here mere seconds ago, had mysteriously manifested himself in the vicinity.

'Casper, is it?' Kerr queried when Donnelly loomed up in the doorway behind his mother.

He was barely twenty and looked the part. Tall and lanky, a face that might be handsome if you weren't put off by acne scarring.

Casper Donnelly nodded.

'What's this about Trace?' he asked.

Kerr suggested it might be better if they could talk inside, reiterated that Donnelly wasn't wanted for anything – or not for anything new. Casper featured on the Police National Computer too. A few car thefts, a bit of drug muling back when he'd been usefully under age, a couple of drunk and disorderlies. What Kerr said was true enough though. There was nothing currently outstanding against him. No reason for him not to cooperate as long as Kerr didn't put his back up.

A kid of about fifteen or sixteen scarpered into the kitchen when the mother led the way into the front room. Donnelly's younger brother presumably. Another veteran of the juvenile justice system. Kerr gave Donnelly and his mother an edited version of what was alleged to have happened to Tracey after he'd been ejected from Club Zoo – no addresses, no explicit details about the coffin or the mock burial. Even so, Donnelly leapt off the edge of the shabby armchair he'd been sitting on, shouting out that he needed to go directly round to her place.

'Hang on a minute, son,' Kerr advised him, 'I'll give you a lift over if you like. But I need to get your side about last night first.'

Donnelly's version of the previous night's events, when he'd calmed down enough to give it, dovetailed closely enough with Tracey Heald's. He underplayed the significance of the argument – it was only a tiff to hear him tell it – and he claimed it had taken four bouncers to get him off the premises, not the two (one of them female) that his girlfriend had mentioned. Crucially, Donnelly said that he'd definitely noticed the 'poncy' bloke in the corner and the two young women who'd been with him: 'I could ID those twats no problem if there's CCTV or 'owt to look at.'

Kerr asked him for his mobile number, told him to expect a call in that regard.

Donnelly produced a packet of blue Rizlas from the pocket of his jeans, tore a strip of cardboard off the top and scribbled down the number with the busted chewed-end biro his mother had been using to fill in the quick crossword in the *News of the World* before Kerr had disturbed their Sunday morning. He handed the strip to Kerr who stuck it into the front of his notebook.

'Tell you what,' Donnelly said, standing up again, 'you'd better catch this lot before I do. That's a fucking promise.'

Kerr disturbed the cushions on the sofa that didn't match the armchairs, revealed the haul of assorted pill bottles he'd clocked Donnelly's mother covering up – a fraction too slowly – when he'd walked into the flat. Benzodiazepines, mainly, in a variety of the prescription drug formats – Valium,

Ativan, Centrax – except that Kerr was prepared to bet there wasn't a legal prescription anywhere on the premises.

'Better get yourself off this crap first then, Casper,' he commented, 'if you're planning on having a go.'

Donnelly shrugged, couldn't seem to think of a reply.

'Yeah, well,' the mother retorted, coming to her son's rescue, 'if you lived in this pigshit place, you'd need to get off *your* face an' all.'

Kerr let it go. He stuck a card on the mantelpiece in case Donnelly remembered something else later. He repeated the offer of a lift but the youth declined with a show of huffiness. He'd sooner flaming walk if Kerr didn't frigging mind.

Kerr told him that he didn't. Not one bit.

Brady had preferred the quaint external character of the place they'd been using in Crowby but he wasn't actually unhappy as such with their Birmingham base. They were holed up – Brady preferred the term *repositioned* – at Cambrian Wharf, directly overlooking the revamped canal side. Another fashionable in-town location. Unlike the Hat Factory, the building this time was regrettably modern, purpose-built. But the apartments compensated by being even more impressively spacious. Up here – on the top level, naturally – you had a cityscape view as far as the Bullring and even some way beyond that. They'd decided to do another girl tonight. Or, to be more precise, Brady had decided to do another girl tonight, would announce his decision to the others later, would present it to them as a given, a fait accompli. He crossed the room to the big table where Adrian was editing last night's material on one of his laptops. On the nearby wall there was a fatuous print of a well-known monstrosity by Lucien Freud. His usual, obscene gig of ugly, bulging, all-too-naked flesh. Freud showed human bodies the way too many of them really looked. A pointless act of bad faith for which he should have been taken out and shot, in Brady's view, not given every award, accolade and prize under the

47

sun. He stood right behind Adrian, up close, resting his hands for the briefest, patronising instant on his shoulders. Maria was through in the kitchen cooking up a late breakfast. And Annabel, Brady knew (since he'd only recently left her there), was still fast asleep in bed. Adrian was making slow progress by the looks of it. Brady had liked the idea of emphasising the noise of the girl banging on the coffin lid – head-butting it had sounded like – above the music and the chanting. But, for whatever reason, Adrian seemed to be having a problem with the overlay.

'Three years of Comp Sci, and a year at film school, Ade,' Brady said. 'This should be a piece of piss for you by now.'

Adrian didn't reply, didn't bother to look up. Brady was the boss, the overall kingpin. There was no argument about that. But the tekky stuff was *his* – Adrian's – domain and he had no intention of conceding an inch of it to anyone else. Besides, sound balancing was a fiddly task and he could live without an audience breathing smarmily down his neck. The trick, which needed concentration, was getting the levels right between the input tracks so that – in the finished product – the girl's desperate banging and muted whimpering wouldn't be completely drowned out by everything else. Adrian worked on doggedly until Brady got fed up, a matter of a few seconds really, and retreated to resume his previous activity – gazing out of the tall window into the heart of England's second city. If he was honest, and he always tried to be, with himself at any rate, Adrian was starting to get a little tired of the yuppie pads that Brady always seemed to insist on using. He could see the sense of it, how they suited some of the defining aesthetics of the project. But the plain fact was that they were all a little bland, all a little samey, all predictably much of a muchness. He'd be glad really when the job was done and he could pick his own kind of place to lie low in for a while, even settle into permanently. Somewhere in Portugal was a possibility, he'd been thinking recently, in the Alentejo for instance. Or maybe a rambling feudal relic in the old Eastern bloc. Bulgaria, Romania, Slovenia. One of those set-ups. Somewhere with a bit of land anyway. And an old well or two. He could see himself quite nicely strolling lazily down to a bar in a village, enjoying a lazy glass of wine, having a lazy crack with the locals.

'Grub's up,' Maria shouted through from the kitchen.

Adrian saved his latest edits and yawned as he stood up. It had been a long night followed by nothing like enough sleep. Plus what lay ahead was a long day at the computer *and* probably another live operation if he was any judge of Brady's strategy – which, by now, he reckoned he probably was. Still, he thought, walking through and catching the cooking smells in his nostrils, Maria had been as good as her word. A proper, traditional English – even if Brady had spoiled the effect with his insistence on organic bacon and free-range eggs, and his demands for grilling everything in sight.

Maria had laid the food out buffet-style. Adrian filled his plate and ate standing up, feeling the need to stretch his back after an hour or so bent over the keyboard. He watched Maria, who had sat down, picking at her plate. She'd restricted herself to a single piece of bacon, a single piece of gluten-free toast and a couple of tomato slices. She was wearing her usual morning outfit: a skimpy, barely adequate dressing gown. Adrian glimpsed the pinkish tinge of her nipples as she leant over her plate. She caught his look with a blank gaze of her own but didn't say anything. By now the game of sexual exclusion, although it was still played, was mainly – though by no means always – played in verbal silence. Brady and Annabel. Brady and Maria. Possibly, tantalisingly, Annabel and Maria. Unarguably and definitely, Adrian and absolutely nobody.

Brady came in and fiddled with the radio before he did anything else, managed to pick up a crackling signal from Crowby FM on its alternative AM frequency. They weren't expecting a news story this early but it was sensible enough,

49

Adrian supposed, to keep a check on the situation. He watched Brady walk over to Maria, stand behind her too, his hands on her shoulders now. Then he watched him reach down, pull apart the two sides of her gown until both her breasts were on full display. After that he helped himself to a healthy-enough amount of bacon and eggs, though substantially less than Adrian's own plateful, and then sat down opposite her.

'A beautiful sight first thing, wouldn't you say, Ade?' he asked, without actually looking at Adrian, without actually taking his gaze away from Maria, who hadn't done anything at all about her wide-open gown, but had carried on carefully cutting one of her two tomato slices into a series of tinier and tinier sub-slices.

Adrian didn't bother to answer this query either, just kept on eating. He would fuck her stupid – Annabel as well – if he ever got the chance. But he knew that he never would, knew that Brady would never allow it. No In-House Sex For Adrian had been one of Brady's key policy decisions from day one. It was back to the issue of aesthetics again, back to the fundamental nature of the project. Ade was a hired hand, not a true believer. Ade was only in it for the money. Ergo Ade was excluded from true communion, barred from ultimate union. Brady had spelled it out emphatically the only time that Adrian had got remotely close, one particularly drug-fuelled night back in Watford. *Fuck's sake, ladies,* he'd said, employing his irritating, phoney Mr Toad voice to its full extent – and digging at him, daring him to do something about it – *you can't shag the employees, I'm afraid. You really can't, you know, it really isn't done.*

Mick Hume was waiting for Kerr on the stone steps which led up to the main entrance of the Hat Factory. There was a woman with him. Late twenties-something. Tall, willowy. Dark eyes that probably sparkled when they hadn't been hauled out of bed with a hangover behind them on a cold morning. She introduced herself. Gwynne Roberts. The Duty Assistant Property Manager. Or, as she put it, the mug that got called out on a weekend if someone went away and left the bathwater running overnight. They followed her into the mezzanine and along a corridor which led to a door which led in turn to a stairway down to the garage level. There were two flights of stairs. At the bottom of the first flight there was another door into a cramped, windowless, CCTV control room. Gwynne Roberts tried three keys from the substantial bunch she'd produced from her bag before she found the one that fitted and was able to unlock the door. What she told them as she did so was disappointing.

The way Kerr heard it, the Hat Factory system was ancient and basic. Analogue not digital – and set to record at less than one frame every twelve seconds. A good deal, he supposed, from the property management point of view. They'd be cramming anything up to the old max – nine hundred and sixty hours – onto a single VCR tape; would only have to change it or rewind it every five to six weeks. It didn't look quite so good though from the CID standpoint. A recording speed that was about as non-real-time as you could get. Only three fixed-mount cameras hooked up to the multiplexer: one trained on the main entranceway, one each on the vehicle entry and exit ramps. All in all it was the kind of situation where things could get missed, could go unseen, could be left unrecorded.

The room itself spoke of the uninspired set-up. Bare walls. A bare, single light bulb. An office-surplus chair and table. And – in non-pride of place – an ageing L260 deck connected to an even older monitor.

'I thought they took security seriously in upmarket places like this,' Mick Hume observed ungallantly.

Gwynne Roberts scratched the tiny diamond stud on the right side of her nose, didn't seem to take it personally.

'I'd say they have done, pretty much. Video entryphone for the apartments, keypad entry for car parking. That's where

51

the money's been spent' – she switched the monitor on as she spoke – 'and anyway *recording* isn't really security, is it? Nobody cares *who* burgles them or nicks their car, do they? What they want is not to be burgled or have it nicked in the first place. So long as you've got a couple of visible cameras, you get the deterrent effect regardless, don't you?'

'She's got you there, Mick,' Kerr commented.

The logic was impeccable if you weren't police. And most people weren't, a fact that too many coppers, himself included, had a tendency to forget.

He picked up the black-covered notebook that someone had left sitting next to the VCR player. Apparently, tape-switching was a task for the building's part-time caretaker, and this was where he noted down his record of dates and times. He flicked through to the most recent page: the tape had been rewound – but not replaced – as recently as Thursday. That was something anyway. As well as the last few days, they could also take a look at a good chunk of the last month if they needed to.

Gwynne Roberts didn't want to hang around after she had the system up and running. She offered Kerr the room key and a business card which gave her office address. Kerr told her they'd arrange for the key to be returned when they were through. When she'd gone, Hume plonked himself into the uncomfortable-looking chair and pressed *rewind*. Kerr offered to go off in search of a couple of take-out hot drinks. There were a couple of little cafés further down the street if he remembered correctly, he told Hume.

'Yeah, great, two sugars please, guv,' Hume said, without looking up.

He'd sooner have been at home. But given that he wasn't, Hume wanted to get on with it. Even just working through the overnight footage would be time-consuming, he was thinking. Not to mention mind-numbing. A lot of systems now were motion-activated, conveniently missed out the tedious, empty stretches of time where there was nothing moving in the camera's field of vision. But this old set-up just ran and ran. Like the film that arty tosser had made years ago about the Empire State Building in New York. Hour after hour of bugger all.

Kerr took twenty minutes to come back with the teas. One place was closed and the one he'd used had a long queue of Sunday overtime building workers in – from the old Co-op building, another Victorian edifice undergoing profitable redevelopment into overpriced living space. He sat the drinks down on the corner of the table, was surprised to see Hume talking on his mobile instead of hunched over the monitor. Then he took a closer look at the paused image on the screen, understood *why*: a BMW series five, captured in rear-view as it was being driven under the raised barrier and into the Hat Factory's sunken car park. The number plate, clearly visible, ended in three letters: SGN.

'Quick work, Mick,' Kerr said.

'Up till now anyway,' Hume replied, not about to be beguiled into unguarded optimism. 'I started the tape running at midnight. It's only the second car that's come or gone so far. There's been nowt on the main entrance cam either. Totally sod all.'

They drank their teas, chatted idly, waited for the control room to call Hume back. Kerr committed the time display to his memory – one fifteen AM – but didn't bother about the fussy seconds and the even fussier fractions of seconds. When Hume's mobile rang, he repeated the newly accessed details out loud for Kerr's benefit: a rental car, the registered owners listed as Crowby Prestige Rentals. Kerr scribbled down the address, even although he reckoned he knew where they were located anyway.

'Great,' he said, 'I'll chase the car hire angle up, Mick, and you can stick with the footage. Assuming this is when they drove over from Club Zoo, we still need to know when they left again – and whether they came back for a second time later.'

Mick Hume nodded resignedly, sensing the afternoon he'd reserved for his newly installed home cinema and possibly a couple of chilled lagers mutating into a less-congenial viewing session. He'd joined the force for action as much as anything, had hated the idea of a job that might keep him cooped up behind a desk, counting the hours till lunchtime, then counting them again till quitting-time. But now – seven million security cameras in the UK later – there were days (and today was shaping up to be one of them) when he felt more like a professional couch potato than a detective. Kerr gulped down the rest of his too-milky tea quickly and left Hume to it before he had time to complain.

Kerr drove back through the town centre and then out again, ignoring the speed limits and the speed cameras, not wanting to waste any more time than had already been wasted. Ray Williams and Emma Smith had played it too much by the book initially, should at least have organised some level of surveillance on the Hat Factory from the first minute they'd heard the girl's story. But the fact was that they hadn't – and there was no point in recriminations right now. He shoved a John Lee Hooker compilation on to the in-car for the journey. 'Boom, Boom': more energy delivered to your brain and nervous system in the first ten seconds than from any cup of tea you'd ever get to drink legally. Crowby Prestige Rentals lived out on the old Copthorne Road industrial estate, just where'd he'd thought it did – more or less at the entrance to the estate, not far past the roundabout and the BP garage.

There was a portacabin office at the front of the site. Behind the office, the rows of hire cars were secured by a high, metal-barred fence. At the counter, the sole, visible employee was wearing the kind of Hi-You're-Welcome smile that would have made even an American tourist feel at home. Kerr flashed his ID, told him the registration number he was interested in, saved them both the trouble of pursuing the customer-friendly corporate routine any further. John A.

Gilbert – according to the name badge on his neatly-pressed white shirt – turned his vacuous grin down to medium volume and tapped the details into a nearby keyboard.

'It's one of the cars due back tomorrow morning,' he said, when he'd retrieved the rental agreement. 'A Weekend Special Deal.'

Another young boy-man barely scraping twenty, Kerr thought. Although his age was probably the only thing he had in common with Casper Donnelly. John A. Gilbert was slick of hair and smooth of chin, gave the impression that clerking for a car hire firm was definitely just his warm-up act for something bigger and better. Actual car sales maybe. Even an estate agent gig.

'I wouldn't bank on it,' Kerr commented, 'it's possible the car's been involved in a serious criminal incident. Whoever's hired it might've done a runner – or be thinking about doing one.'

Gilbert's smile vanished altogether. He swivelled his computer screen so that both of them could read it, clicked his mouse for a print-out.

'I took the booking myself. Friday afternoon – cash deposit.'

It wasn't clear whether 'cash deposit' was a good thing or a bad thing. Kerr asked him for a description of the hirer but John A. turned out to be better at smiling than remembering. *Male, in his twenties, height about five ten* was about as good as it got. That plus brownish hair: *not cut short – but not really long either*. Kerr couldn't completely keep the exasperation out of his expression. The description just about fitted the abductor that Tracey Heald had said had been called Brady. But only in a vague, imprecise way that would fit a million others just as well.

'He didn't have a local accent though,' Gilbert added, struggling to help, 'Posh, I'd've said. Down south – like his driving licence.'

'And his licence checked out?'

'Nothing came up on our systems anyway. Though we don't have the same access that you do, do we?'

Don't believe everything you've read about our access, Kerr thought. Not if you've read it's accurate and up-to-date anyway.

'No, I guess not,' he said diplomatically.

Gilbert handed him the print-out.

'Nothing else that struck you as memorable about this, eh, Mr Denbigh?' Kerr asked.

'Afraid not. He came out in a taxi – but lots of our customers do that. He said he was taking a girl away for the weekend, wanted to impress her with a decent car. That's hardly unusual, is it?'

Kerr agreed that it wasn't, wanted to know if he knew *which* taxi firm.

'No, sorry, I didn't really notice. Obviously, if I'd known—' Gilbert replied, with a look that intimated he'd be happy to make something up if that was what the War Against Crime demanded.

Kerr studied the print-out in detail.

'You weren't bothered by the discrepancy between his current address and the address on the driving licence?'

'No, that's not unusual either. I took a credit card imprint anyway. That's policy for a cash deposit. And that checked out OK too.'

Kerr gave him his police mobile number, told him to call if he did remember anything else later – and to call immediately if the vehicle *did* turn up, to be bloody careful too, if that did happen.

Back in his own car, he checked the information more thoroughly, called in the credit card and driving licence details to the control room. Alan Phillip Denbigh. An address in North London. A DOB that made him twenty-six next month. If Gilbert was accurate about the height, it definitely sounded more like 'Brady' than 'Adrian'. But Gilbert had probably been too busy smiling and schmoozing to pay any real attention to what his customer looked like. All you could reliably take from his testimony was that the hirer had been male, on his own, and – implicitly – hadn't looked wildly unusual in any way. Wasn't a Martian with two heads, for instance.

The control room rang back, a voice he didn't recognise – somebody new maybe. The credit card was in order as far as the credit card company knew. And so was the driving licence according to the PNC/DVLC link. His phone rang again the instant he ended the call. Emma Smith: they'd finally raised someone at the relevant lettings agency who'd been public-spirited enough to log into their computer system on a Sunday lunchtime. Ray Williams was still with the guy, trying to find out anything else he could. The upshot was that number 34, the Hat Factory, had been rented out since the beginning of last week. She read out the tenant's details for him. Another 26-year-old male. Another previous address in North London. But a different one altogether – and an entirely different first name, middle name and surname.

Chapter Nine

By late afternoon, Adrian was finally happy with the cut. He hooked the laptop up to the TV and all four of them settled down to watch the movie. There had been no nice big plasma screen provided by the landlord this time so they had to make do with the portable which they carried around with them in the van. The screen, at twenty inches, wasn't hugely bigger than the laptop's. But Adrian was a true geek, was never happy, technically-speaking, until he saw what the end result looked like *outside* of the computer system he'd created it on. He sat down on the big sofa as soon as he had everything sorted. Brady was already ensconced at the other end of it with Annabel. Maria, still in her scant dressing gown, was kneeling on all fours at his feet – she frequently was – but at least he'd allowed her to turn and face the direction of the screen so that she could enjoy the show just like the rest of them.

Brady had insisted on choosing the opening music: 'Danse Macabre'. Adrian had argued against it, considered the choice to be corny as fuck and unworthy of the project. It had a tendency to crop up any time a bored, hack director had a routine horror script to deal with. But Brady had his arse-hole heart set on it. And so 'Danse Macabre' it was. Blaring out over the titles and the opening sequence: the girl sitting unawares in the crowded bar, her deadbeat boyfriend beside her. Maria had shot the jerky segment with her mobile as discreetly as she could, had worried about the poor, blurry quality. But Adrian had reassured her that she'd done just fine, had made sure he'd told Brady that too. It was exactly what was wanted for starters, a little stylistic nod towards the old cinema vérité pioneers. In any case, Adrian had segued Maria's stuff with some nice creepy shots of moonlit wood-land – the girl's ultimate, narrative destination obviously – and some general clips of the Club Zoo interior which he'd pasted in from the nightclub's amateur-hour, ill-designed website.

He'd managed to talk Brady out of the coffin scene at least. It might have worked, he'd thought, if they could've filmed effectively from the inside – shown the girl's face, for one thing – but there had been too many practical diffi-culties involved. He'd mucked around with trying to rig up a webcam under the lid. But that had only led to problems with lighting that he hadn't been able to resolve. Filming from inside was a sound idea – you only had to look at what Tarantino had accomplished in *Kill Bill* and on *CSI*. But that had been Tarantino. Plus a team of industry professionals. Plus proper studio resources and kit. All you had otherwise, shooting from outside, was a wooden box to look at and a bit of low-audio banging and whimpering. No guarantee for the viewer that there was even anybody still in there, that you hadn't just done a bit of cutting and splicing on the QT. So the coffin bollocks had gone, the whole Grand-Guignol number in fact. All the cloaks and bogus chanting. Since day one, Adrian had being trying to educate Brady on that point. How what you had to do was play to your strengths, make a virtue of limitation and simplicity. *Think* Blair Witch *in reverse*, he'd kept saying, attempting to distil his big idea into a Brady-friendly concept. What Adrian *had* kept though was the girl's reaction when she saw them coming for her that first time, all of them hooded up. The precious, virginal minute when the fear first hits them – when they realise that they've fucked up just by being there, that instead of some-thing nice, they're in for something very fucking unpleasant indeed. The way he'd cut it you had poor little Trace drinking champers and gazing into Brady's handsome mush one minute and screaming blue murder the next; lunging out at them and getting nowhere. Or nowhere safe.

Annabel said she wanted a spliff and Brady told Maria to roll one and be quick about it. Onscreen, they'd reached the woods: Annabel shoving the girl out the car and then the girl making her hopeless, futile run for it, Annabel indulging her bitch-slapping tendencies when they'd caught up with her. Real moonlight by then, obviously, shining down through the trees. And a cloudless, smogless sky with the stars visible. The final sequence coming up now: Brady in his element – even Adrian would concede him that much – looming over her in the grave, bringing her all the way into the terror zone, breaking her, making her beg and plead, promising him anything for just a few more minutes of life. That was all a human being was in the last analysis: a piece of shit that didn't want to die.

Brady and Annabel applauded when the film ended. Maria finished building the joint. She lit it and offered it up to Brady who shook his head, told her to pass it directly to Annabel. Adrian disconnected the laptop from the television and clicked *Turn Off*. They'd agreed seven o'clock as tonight's start time. Or, to be more precise, Brady had suggested seven o'clock and nobody had contradicted him. Sunday was the last gasp of the weekend for the nine-to-five drones, Brady had said, a dog-end night where the clubs and bars would get busier earlier, if they got busy at all, and close earlier too. It was near enough five o'clock now and Adrian wanted to rest up for an hour before they got going. Especially since the other thing they'd 'agreed' was that tonight's pick-up would be a non-Brady operation – with Adrian taking the lead role in his place. When the shut-down was complete, he closed the lid and told them he'd see them later. Brady gave him a curt nod: the monarch acknowledging the retreating courtier.

Adrian took a leak in the elaborate bathroom and then

got his head down, setting the alarm feature on his watch for exactly sixty minutes later. He'd chosen the back bedroom for his sleeping quarters. It was the smallest room available and had the least interesting view. But Adrian had liked the fact that it was well away from the master bedroom which Brady had obviously selected for himself – and therefore also well away from the soundtrack of Brady's nightly fun with Annabel and/or Maria. He woke up a full ten seconds before the alarm, was proud of his unlearned, seemingly innate ability to catnap himself into proper sleep and back out again, more or less at will. He showered, shaved, pulled on some decent jeans and one of the smart new shirts Maria had picked out for him the last time they'd hit the shopping malls, armed, as usual, with half-a-dozen *magha* credit cards.

Maria was waiting for him in the lounge. She was properly dressed at last – although the tight leather trousers and the tit-hugging leopard skin top might have been Brady's choice, not hers – and she'd already finished her own refinements: a blond wig was evidently tonight's major feature. Maria had trained at the London School of Fashion – the BA degree in specialist make-up design – even had proper, paid industry experience behind her. Plus everything she did was subtle. Changes of hair colour and style, small but dramatic alterations to skin tone. Very occasionally, minor prosthetics that changed the shape of your nose or gave you a distinguishing blemish you didn't actually have. Plus, in his and Brady's case, there were all the endless permutations of shaved and unshaved: goatees, sideboards, moustaches.

Adrian sat down at the big table where the laptop had been moved to one side – carefully, he hoped – and let his mind drift while Maria got to work. What they'd realised early on was that you couldn't fight surveillance, couldn't avoid it: instead you had to make it work *for* you, not against you. If you poked your head out of your front door in the United Kingdom, you were caught on camera upwards of three hundred times a day. But quantity wasn't the same thing as quality. It was why street-kids loved hoodies and baseball caps and why lazy-bastard coppers hated them. Nine times out of ten, the images on shopping centre and fore-court cameras were crap, useless, *generic*: nothing like detailed enough to satisfy a jury or even a half-asleep magis-trate. All they'd done, pooling their different technical knowl-edge and skills, was to take the street-kids' strategy a stage further. It wasn't foolproof, no strategy could ever be that, but it could still provide the difference between success and failure. Over in Crowby, the police would be after them by now, would have the girl's descriptions to go on as well as whatever turned up on the local camera systems. But how Brady, Maria and Annabel had looked last night was *so* yesterday, *so* not how they looked today.

'Green's going to go best with that kind of complexion, Ade,' Maria said, ending his reverie.

She handed him the fresh set of contact lenses. Clumsily, though not as clumsily as at first, he slipped them on. It was something he still hated, still absurdly, illogically, resented (since he enjoyed perfect twenty-twenty vision), but it was another instance of her thoroughness, of her dedication to keeping all four of them out of the clutches of the system.

'Nice,' she said pleasantly, holding up the hand mirror so that he could see his latest incarnation, 'I could go for you myself.'

It wasn't really a sensible remark for her to make. Brady was absent from the room. Likewise Annabel. And Adrian wasn't any kind of a grass. But Maria couldn't know that. Not completely anyway, not for safe and certain. For that reason – for her own sake more than anything – Adrian didn't comment. He just smiled and stood up, let the moment go.

He switched on the TV, watched the regional news bulletin. Nothing. There'd been a bad crash on the M6 and the report of it, plus the afternoon's sport, had used up most of the available time. Earlier, Brady had said there'd been a mention on Crowby FM, but right at the end of their bulletin and hardly any details. Police looking for a vehicle in connection with a serious incident early on Sunday morning. They'd given the make and the reg no. apparently, but hadn't even mentioned any attack on any girl. *That's fine*, Brady had said, *the calm before the storm – just exactly how we want it.*

Annabel waltzed in, ready for her turn with Maria's skills. Brady was still in the kitchen, Adrian assumed. That was where he'd last seen him anyway, sat at the table with a cup of tea or coffee that he didn't seem to be drinking and looking engrossed – his nose buried in the review section of the *Observer*, his favoured Sunday read.

Adrian split back to his bedroom and did a quick line of coke on the back of an empty CD case. Each to their own, he thought. Brady had his extensive, natural, sociopathic charms to draw on. Adrian didn't. But he estimated that a tenner's worth of charlie just about equalised the situation between them when it came to the practical matter of going on the pull.

When all three of them were ready, they took the lift down to the secure car park. Annabel was tonight's designated driver. She drove them off in the new hire car (another beamer, but a series six convertible this time). They'd left the old one, the series five, in the Brunswick Street NCP for now but before they'd done that (before they'd left Crow Hill in fact), they'd stuck a set of false plates on it. Maria sat in the back seat and Adrian sat in the front passenger seat with the *A to Z* open across his knees since – for obvious traceability reasons – they couldn't use the sat nav system. Adrian didn't know the city other than what they'd researched prior to the operation. Now they were here, everything looked different on the actual ground. They took wrong turnings more than a few times – including an interesting but utterly useless detour through the Jewellery Quarter – before, finally, they were headed away from the centre in the right direction: south-west, out towards the university area.

They cruised around the likely parts of Edgbaston, Mosely, Selly Oak, until finally they found the kind of venue they thought they were looking for over on Bristol Road. A big Victorian relic of a pub, no more than ten minutes' walk away from the main campus, and with a loud guitar band warming up at full volume inside, spilling drum rolls and reverb out into the turning-dark night. They'd had to abandon any idea of doing something closer, even although there were endless, ideal opportunities virtually on the doorstep and there for the taking. The canalside, and Broad Street nearby even more so, formed the epicentre of the city's nightlife, were crammed with crowded bars, clubs and restaurants. The problem was the sheer volume of CCTV systems that had grown up and developed alongside them. Even when you were taking professional-standard precautions (because you were taking them in fact), you had to set sensible limits to the level of risk you were prepared to run. And the Walkabout, Ipanema, the Revolution and all the rest were definitely on the wrong side of sensible if what you were about was the non-legal business of kidnap, humiliation and fear.

Annabel parked the car two red-terraced side streets away. Before she got out, she sampled the joint at last which, aping Brady, she'd told Maria to roll for her while she'd still been struggling the wrong way along Hagley Road and watching for a break in the traffic to do a U-turn. Maria had used a mellow smoking mixture only, since Brady had banned them from skunk before or during a snatch. Adrian led the way back on to the main drag and towards the pub. Not hurrying exactly. But not slouching either, the coke still egging him on. The band had got properly going now, some kind of sub-White Stripes number with the amps maxed-up as far as they would go. They picked the room that didn't have the band in, needed a space where talk would be possible and where you could make easy eye contact. Adrian got the drinks at the long, brass and mahogany bar – nothing faux-retro about this one – and Annabel and Maria nabbed one of the few tables still unoccupied by noisy students and noisy ex-students. Nobody around much beyond twenty-five or without some kind of past or present connection to higher education. Brady was the true chameleon, swimming in any kind of current, but Adrian was only really at his best in a context he fully understood. It was a matter of common-sense again, of setting yourself up for success not failure.

He'd ordered a pint of Pedigree for himself, his old Student Union favourite, and mojitos for Maria and Annabel. He moved carefully through the crowd and deposited the drinks on the table. Annabel offered him a cigarette when he sat down and he held it left-handed while she lit it for him with an uncharacteristically cheap-looking lighter. Brady was left-handed too. An odd, statistically unlikely connection between them. *Meet the Sinister Brothers*, Brady had joked one time in a rare fit of good humour. He smoked his fag, sipped at his beer, studied the bar's female customers under the guise of a general, casual glance around.

The coke was helping but this still wasn't something he felt easy about, knew that Brady had given him the task as a challenge, as yet another test of his usefulness. The only way through it, he thought, was to act as if he *was* Brady, to approach the situation exactly the way Brady would. Adrian had always assumed that Brady's main interest was in the end result of a snatch – in the place, the state of mind, he finally brought them to. Maria and Annabel too maybe. Though both of them were still ultimately unfathomable to him, still inexplicable and mysterious. But then at breakfast time, Brady had made the comment that the beginning was a supreme moment too: the instant when you made the selec-tion, acted as judge and jury, played God. He turned back towards his two companions, started into the made-up riff he'd pre-rehearsed: how his 'job' was going, how old, purely fictitious friends were doing, how he wished they were all back in casual, dossing-around student days. It was as if the rest of the room didn't really interest him. But in his mind's eye, he was still seeing his two first-choice candidate victims, still evaluating them the way he knew Brady would. Identical, more-or-less classic circumstances in both cases: each on her own but in the (sole) company of what seemed very like a friend and a friend's boyfriend. Playing gooseberry. Looking like they felt left out of it. Both of them were eye-candy enough too, not so very much to choose between them. Adrian *would* be choosing though. He'd give them a couple of minutes before he'd re-assess them, make up his mind for definite. As a direct consequence of his choice, one of them would go home, would sleep soundly and unmolested while the other one would be made to regret coming here tonight for a long, long time – maybe for the rest of her life. He took another twitchy draw, another swift gulp. Eeenie meenie. The decision is yours, mate. All yours.

Chapter Ten

Detective Chief Inspector Frank Jacobson crossed the foot-bridge which led to the car park behind Crowby railway station. The pretty blonde woman beside him looked like she'd need fifteen years to catch up with him in age, although in fact she'd only need around ten. Every now and then Jacobson would glance at her as they walked, just for the sheer pleasure of looking. Both of them were carrying overnight bags. Jacobson had offered to carry Alison Taylor's bag but she'd insisted she could do it herself, that it wasn't really heavy. Maybe not, he'd argued, but there was the matter of her shopping too. She'd smiled at that, relented, offered him one of the big Printemps carrier bags to take for her.

The car park was quiet, less than a dozen cars in residence. They'd come in on Eurostar to Victoria and then caught the nine thirty-six from Euston, the last stopping train to Crowby on a Sunday evening. By now it was near enough a quarter to midnight. When they reached his car, Jacobson opened the boot and insisted on putting everything inside single-handed.

'Your place or mine?' he asked, opening the passenger door for her.

It was a joke of course really. Mainly they spent their time together at her flat in preference to Jacobson's. For one thing it was a lot more comfortable, a lot less spartan.

'There's more sex toys at mine,' she said, climbing in.

'No contest then,' Jacobson answered, trying to look dead-pan, not entirely succeeding.

Another running gag: the informal competition as to who could talk the raunchiest, the crudest. Jacobson tried hard but Alison nearly always won. She watched him taking his mobile out of his jacket pocket instead of starting his car engine.

'You're off-duty for the entire weekend, Frank,' she said, touching his arm lightly. 'That means until tomorrow morning, doesn't it?'

He looked at her again, his face creasing into a smile.

'OK, you're right. Let Greg Salter worry about it for now – whatever *it* currently is.'

'Exactly,' she commented, smiling back.

He held out his free arm and she leant close, kissed him on the mouth. A couple of minutes later, he put his phone away, started the car, drove off.

It had been a rare enough weekend for both of them. Most weekends when he wasn't working, Jacobson remained on potential call-out. It was an employment condition that went with the territory of senior rank. Which was why he'd booked this weekend as annual leave: the only official mechanism guaranteed to achieve pure, unalloyed time off. Even so, he put the radio on when they reached the Flowers Street junction. Crowby FM. But Alison knew that trick too – Jacobson hoping to sift the midnight news for something relevant to Crowby CID. She switched over to the CD player: Madeline Peyroux reinventing Hank Williams. *That's better*, she thought, lighting one of her own cigarettes to keep the music company, lighting a B&H for Jacobson.

Jacobson drove on carefully, the way he always did, his mind already replaying the highlights of the weekend, highlights it might go on playing for days to come. He'd booked them extravagantly into a hotel at the pricier end of the Boulevard Saint Michel – well, why not? – and they'd dined out expensively each night. Last night, Saturday, they'd tried an Indian restaurant near the Pantheon that was the current rage with Parisian foodies. Indian cuisine in general was, apparently, according to Alison. The French – always first with the news, Jacobson had commented sarcastically. Though he'd had to admit that the food was actually pretty good, if not quite up to Mr Behar's standard back in Crowby. They passed the Riverside Hotel on their way to Alison's place on Riverside Crescent. She was the hotel manager there but, setting her usual good example for him, she barely glanced at its imposing edifice as they cruised over the Memorial bridge and turned right along Riverside Walk. She fixed the nightcaps once they were inside. Glenmorangie times two. And if Jacobson demanded a bigger measure than she did, it was also the case that he liked it with far too much ice in it.

Jacobson slept like a baby, woke up recalling the view from the top of the Montparnasse Tower. They'd strolled over there, arm in arm, on Sunday afternoon. Jacobson had thought they'd have to join the queue for the lift up to the tourist viewing platform on the 56th floor. But Alison had a better idea: take the quieter, instantly-available lift up to the piano bar on the same floor instead, enjoy the same view but with a couple of decent cocktails thrown in. It was the kind of harmless, frivolous activity that normal people enjoyed on a regular basis. Some of them every day of the week. But until he'd met her – April last year – Jacobson had laboured under the delusion that he didn't really do fun any more.

He'd planned to sneak out and leave her to sleep on. Both of them needed to be at work by nine and Jacobson wanted to drive back to his flat in Wellington Drive first, pick out some clean clothes, look over his post. He also needed to persuade himself that he did still live alone, that however much he liked her, Alison wasn't *serious*, wasn't on her way to becoming anything remotely like a wife. That was a can of worms Jacobson had no intention of re-opening. No intention at all. But she'd woken up as he'd padded around her bedroom, looking for his socks. She'd pointed out that it was only half past seven, that it would be cold outside, that the traffic would be like shit.

An hour and twenty minutes later, Jacobson rushed from the police car park and into the rear entrance of the Divisional building, still adjusting a garish, bright pink tie that Alison had found for him from somewhere at the back of her wardrobe. It had belonged to her ex-husband, she'd said, and it was the only one on the premises, take it or leave it. Reluctantly, Jacobson had taken it. He decided to use the back stairs up to his office on the fifth floor. All the way, every single flight. Partly from his resolve to exercise more, mainly to minimise the tie's public exposure. He took a breather when he got to the third floor, examined his reflection in the narrow side window that gave a squinting view of the fire escape and not much else. He wasn't scruffy by modern CID standards – smart leather jacket, neat chinos, and a decent pair of brogues (at least) – but the absence, for once, of a sober-looking suit would add fire to the unkind rumour that he was becoming a less miserable bastard since his personal life had taken its unexpected upturn for the better.

He laboured up the remaining stairs, glad when he got to the top unseen. There was always the chance, even the likelihood, that nothing major had come in over the weekend. Detective Chief Superintendent Greg Salter's Senior Management Meeting wasn't until ten. His idea was to check his email, his voicemail, the latest incident sheets. Then he'd nip over to the shopping centre, grab a replacement tie that would feel less out of place around his personal neck. But when he reached the front corridor where his office was located, he saw DS Kerr pacing restlessly outside his door, knew that something *had* come up – and that his tie-replacement plan might be in jeopardy.

Kerr had carried two hot drink cartons with him from the canteen. Tea for himself, coffee for Jacobson. They stood over by Jacobson's window while they talked, taking in the unlovely vista – the library-cum-NCP car park, the Crowby Arndale Centre and the pedestrianised square where a team of refuse workers were sweeping away the relics of another town-centre weekend: cans, bottles, broken glass, fast food detritus. Only the Town Hall with its art deco flourishes and the sturdy row of oak trees which fronted it gave the heart anything to sing about. The canteen's coffee tasted as mediocre as usual. But at least it had saved Jacobson the trouble of fishing out his illicit kettle and brewing up an even worse cup of black instant.

Kerr brought him up to speed about Tracey Heald and her mystery assailants. They'd worked right through Sunday afternoon and Sunday evening but no suspects had returned to the Hat Factory apartment, there'd been no sign anywhere of the missing hire car – and, worst of all, there'd been no luck with either of the two North London leads.

'Identity theft then, old son?' Jacobson asked.

Kerr nodded.

'It certainly looks that way, Frank. The Met picked up both guys. They really exist at the given addresses but it's pretty clear they've never set foot in Crowby – and certainly not in the last couple of weeks. Seems like there's a couple of thous' worth of bogus transactions on credit cards taken out in their names – again all of it in the last fortnight.'

'So we can trace the spending patterns then at least, check where and when the frauds occurred?'

'Yeah, that's the theory of it anyway. The Met should be sending all the data on to us this morning. I was thinking Emma Smith and Ray Williams could work through it, they're pretty experienced in paper chasing.'

'I agree, old son. Assuming Smoothie Greg is willing to prioritise the case.'

Kerr drained the last dregs of his tea.

'But he will surely, won't he? I've got nothing more serious on, neither has Smith or Williams as far as I know. Mick Hume neither. And it *is* fucking serious surely? Four weirdos

71

frightening the girl out of her wits. The doc reckons she probably lost consciousness, reckons they waited for that to happen before they cleared some of the earth off her and scarpered.'

'I'd say it's serious all right, Ian. The lass could easily have died after all. But the fact is she didn't – and the fact also is that your four weirdos have vanished into thin air. Smoothie Greg likes cases we're likely to win, not difficult, time-consuming buggers with no guarantee of success.'

'And the lass *is* from the Woodlands, of course,' Kerr retorted.

'You know damn well that's not my point of view,' Jacobson replied, 'but she is – which again doesn't help where an idiot like Salter is involved. *He*'s going to see her as a lowlife all right, somebody without connections, nobody bending the Chief Constable's ear on her behalf.'

Kerr binned his empty plastic cup.

'But you are going to argue for it, Frank?'

'Of course I am. You're all designated as Serious Crimes Against the Person specialists. I'm supposed to be the Senior Officer with Special Responsibilities in that area. If all the official bollock-speak means anything at all, it means we're supposed to be more than just an ad hoc murder squad.'

'*Modern policing must be pro-active as well as reactive,*' Kerr commented, quoting a recent management memorandum.

'Exactly,' Jacobson said, 'let's see Salter wriggle out of that one. If these customers get away with it once, why the hell won't they try it again? What about the CCTV situation by the way?'

'The beamer shows up only twice overnight at the Hat Factory. Comes in just after one, leaves again after four. The other thing of interest is a Ford Transit that's clocked at six twelve and then at half-seven. Only the number plate's illegible. Mick Hume reckons it's a dodgy plate, deliberately non-readable. What I'm thinking is that they dumped the BMW somewhere after they left Tracey Heald in the woods and probably picked up the transit at the same place, used it as a getaway after they went back to the flat and cleaned up after themselves.'

'You mean getting their props out the way? The coffin and all that?'

Kerr nodded.

'Early days of course. But it's a working hypothesis anyway.'

Jacobson finished off his own drink. Then:

'What about Club Zoo? You've got footage from there too?'

'Mick Hume's still working on it, he's been clocked on since seven. We're going to get Tracey Heald and her boyfriend in here later this morning, see if they can ID anyone useful.'

'Fine,' Jacobson said, opening his window a discreet fraction. 'You can coordinate the effort for now, Ian. I'll catch up with the rest of the weekend news. Then I'll try and grab a word with Webster – see what the SOCOs are up to – before I go to Salter's prayer meeting.'

When Kerr left the room, Jacobson treated himself to his first proper B&H of the day. He'd attempted one on the drive in but the traffic had been as Monday-morning awful as Alison Taylor had predicted, and most of the cigarette had gone unsmoked as he'd braked, signalled, changed gear, braked again and generally crawled his way towards the town centre. He sat down at his desk and lit up with the silver lighter that had been a lifetime-ago present from his ex-wife, Janice. Super-sensitive smoke detectors had finally arrived earlier in the year, theoretically enforcing the Divisional building's status as a complete no-smoking zone – with certain exceptions, such as the interview rooms down in the custody suite. And even there – officially anyway – you were supposed to get the permission of the duty custody sergeant. But Jacobson, his own worst enemy as usual, had discovered that if he opened his window and regularly fanned the carcinogenic fumes towards it with an A4 writing pad or a document wallet, he could at least defeat the detector outside his own office door. He listened to his voicemail and skimmed through his IN tray as he smoked, found nothing more pressing – in his opinion – than the case Kerr had just told him about. Ditto for his email when, gingerly as ever, he booted up his PC and checked the electronic backlog that had accrued there over the weekend. The only new thing worth knowing was that Greg Salter had shoved his meeting forward to ten thirty. Jacobson clicked the infernal machine off, smiled briefly to himself. A rare-enough sight at any time, rarer still on a Monday morning. But, even allowing for his intended call on Jim Webster, the welcome fact was that he had time to replace the tie after all.

He bought exactly what he was looking for in Tie Rack: silk, no pattern, a discreet shade of pale blue. He put it on in the shop and stowed the pink ogre, which Alison Taylor's ex-husband had seemingly worn without shame or embarrassment, deep inside his jacket pocket. He walked back to the Divisional building feeling less sheepish than he'd exited it, cornered Webster in his fourth-floor 'office': a partitioned-off cubicle at the far end of the smallest of the two Scene of Crime labs. Barely enough room to swing an evidence bag, let alone a cat. Not that Webster was the type to swing anything of any kind within his hyper-neat, well-ordered domain. Jacobson squeezed into the only spare chair and waited until the Crime Scene Manager finished whatever he was doing on his computer.

'Tracey Heald,' Jacobson said, when Webster finally swivelled away from his keyboard – and not wasting any extraneous words where he knew they wouldn't be appreciated.

'Fibres and possible skin samples inside and within the vicinity of the grave,' Webster replied. 'We assume the girl's skin at least – which should be straightforward enough to check out from the Catchem DNA database, thanks to her

74

police record – but we *could* also have something from persons unknown. If so, Sod's law states that they won't be as easy to trace.'

Jacobson lifted both hands wide: I surrender.

'Plus – don't tell me – you need authorisation.'

'You can bet your pension I do, Frank. Nothing goes over to FSS unless Salter gives you the proper go-ahead.'

FSS was the Forensic Science Service's laboratories in Birmingham. Everything the force sent there *cost*. Jacobson didn't comment further. They'd both find out soon enough anyway precisely what Greg Salter's attitude was – and just how big or how small an operation he was prepared to approve. Instead he asked what else had been discovered out at Crow Hill.

'The team took a decent-enough cast of the tyre track – and they found scrapes of paint,' Webster said. 'Theoretically, there's enough material to establish whether the hire car was definitely at the scene or not. Again assuming someone's willing to pay out for the necessary work. And also assuming you're able to recover the vehicle at some point.'

Jacobson nodded. It was the kind of thing that would be crucial when they got to the stage of putting charges. Costings apart, the only other teeny-weeny, slight little problem-ette about reaching that stage was that they'd need to catch and arrest somebody first.

'Anything of interest beyond the inner cordon then?'

Webster turned back to his computer for a moment, executed something unfathomable with his keyboard and his mouse before he replied.

'The usual mass detritus, what else? Fag ends, sweet wrappers, old apple cores, a couple of used condoms. All the stuff you get wherever you let the great British public wander.'

'The girl was adamant there was nothing actually sexual,' Jacobson said, recalling Kerr's run-down but fixating on Webster's mention of condoms the way you did when you spent your life cleaning up society's dirty linen.

'We've seen no reason to doubt her, Frank. But we've bagged the Durex along with the rest just in case. It's the old story, I'm afraid. Probably most of what we've lifted is completely irrelevant – but we can't rule any of it out until you give us a suspect or two to test against.'

Webster was diligent, and keener than he liked to let on. Away from the job, he was a steady family man too, with a wife and a much-adored daughter at home. Jacobson liked him – or would have done, if the CSM wasn't so ultra-defensive that he could probably keep goal in the Premier League. He noticed the hands on the wall-clock above Webster's head. Smoothie Greg's meeting beckoned. And he hadn't asked him about the Hat Factory yet.

He mentioned it now.

'My guys still haven't got there,' Webster admitted – after a pause in which he seemed to be counting the number of pens currently stashed inside the pristine, unchipped mug he kept on his desk for the purpose. 'The duty team were on their way over there yesterday after they'd finished up at Crow Hill. Only that's when the news came in about the job out at the Waitrose complex – and that took priority, obviously.'

'Obviously,' Jacobson said, leaving the sarcasm definitely in.

He'd read about it in the incident sheet. Somebody had done one of the electrical goods warehouses after trading hours. A professional job. A serious amount of stock falling on to the back of a couple of nice, big, unofficial trucks.

'But you'll take a look today?'

Webster was looking fidgety now, probably wanted to get his reports together for Salter's meeting.

'Sure, Frank, of course,' he said warily, 'assuming you get your authorisation.'

Chapter Eleven

Casper walked round to the back garden at Tracey's mum's place and knocked on the kitchen window. It was what you did if you knew them. The front door bell was used solely by debt collectors, meter readers, bailiffs and all the various other forms of unwelcome human filth. The Old Bill for instance. Tracey's mother let him in. The expression on her face was definitely frosty but it was still an advance on yesterday when she hadn't let him an inch past the door. He'd tried three times but each time she'd told him to get lost and to stay lost – that the whole bloody thing was his frigging fault.

'Put the kettle on, why don't you?' she asked, shutting the door after him and then sitting down at her kitchen table.

It was an instruction really – and meant to be a fucking rude one, not a question, so Casper didn't say anything in reply, just did what he was told: filled the kettle then reconnected it, clicked it on. He found a couple of clean mugs drying on the rack next to the sink, extracted two teabags from the open PG Tips box that was sitting in its usual place on the shelf above the fridge. His hands shook a bit when he poured the water, added the milk, stirred in the sugar. He'd been staying clear of the benzos since yesterday morning, since right after he'd heard the news about Tracey from the copper in fact. He'd hated to admit it to himself but the swine had a point on that score. If he hadn't been off his face the other night then maybe he wouldn't've wound Tracey up quite as much, or might have kept a better eye out for her, even if he had.

He put one mug down in front of Denise, which was Tracey's mum's actual name. Casper had always called her Mrs Heald although he didn't really know why. She was old, sure, maybe even pushing thirty-five, but not totally decrepit. Mean to say: he wouldn't mind giving her one himself. Dirty Laura wasn't very much younger to be honest. And Denise was quite a bit sexier-looking than her (not to mention slimmer), a lot sexier-looking in fact, on the days when she made an effort. Or he wouldn't have minded anyway. Past tense. Before the last couple of days had come along, pulled him up fucking sharp. He sat down opposite her with his own mug, feeling his head and face sweating and itching, itching and sweating – but not wanting to rub or scratch, to give her something else to get irate about.

'Is Tracey about yet?' he asked her, keeping his voice a shed-load quieter than its normal bluster.

He could hear the noise of water running upstairs, guessed that Tracey was taking a shower or washing her hair. Denise shot him some more daggers and shook her head for emphasis.

'As if you flaming care. I could frigging swing for you, I really frigging could. Getting flung out like that, leaving her all on her own in the middle of the town on a Saturday night.'

Casper didn't try and defend himself, even though – a fair point in his view – he wasn't the one who'd started chucking the drinks about. Just take it, he was thinking. Just sit here and take it.

Denise gulped at her tea when she got to the end of her tirade, banged her mug down on the table afterwards. They sat in silence after that for a while. Denise smoked a Superking. She didn't offer one to Casper and Casper didn't ask her for one. He drank his tea with both hands, easier to keep the mug steady that way. Finally they heard footsteps descending the stairs and both of them looked anxiously towards the scuffed door into the hall. Denise had a semi-regular boyfriend of her own. But he stomped around like a fucking elephant when he was here so you could tell that it wasn't him.

Tracey walked in looking as pretty as ever. She was wearing her best CK jeans and a neat white top. Her blonde hair looked newly groomed and shiny. Her expression had a brave face etched precariously on top of it.

'You,' she said, then repeated herself, turning up the volume. 'You! Sobered up at last, is it? Or has Granny Laura got fed up with you cadging pill money off her and given you her frigging marching orders?'

Casper stood up, offered her his chair, even though there were two others vacant around the table to choose from.

'I've finished with that old trout,' he said. 'I mean it – I phoned her and told her yesterday. Straight to her face.'

Denise asked her if she wanted him kicking out. Tracey just shrugged for an answer, sat down in a different chair from the one he'd offered her. Without waiting to be told, Casper clicked the kettle back on, found another mug.

'The coppers phoned me up first thing,' he announced. 'They want me to go in and see if I can ID some of those bastards, said they'd asked you an' all. I was thinking – easiest if we went in together like. My old dear's subbed me for the cab fare.'

Tracey looked at Casper, looked at her mum, looked back at Casper again,

'Well you wouldn't have any frigging cash of your own of course – even though you was supposed to be working on Friday afternoon.'

Casper watched the kettle boiling, knew that his cheeks were blushing bright red, knew that he couldn't look either of them straight in the face. What little cash he'd had, he'd blown on Saturday night's binge.

'Everything's going to be different from now on,' he said quietly. 'I swear to flaming God it is.'

The taxi turned up for them late. The driver sounded his

horn curtly – three times only – and kept his engine running and the central locking engaged while he waited for them to emerge from the house. A lot of the cab firms would no longer set foot on the Woodlands estate, not even in daytime. The few firms that were still willing to risk it could afford to be snooty about it – and rake their fares up well above the odds. The driver dropped them off near the NCP car park – as close as a non-police car could get to the Divi's main entrance. Casper, sober, didn't bother with a tip, was prepared to swap insults if the fucker kicked off about it. But, as per the rest of the journey, the driver said exactly nowt, just handed the change over and made good his escape. Casper had a weird feeling as they walked up the steps towards the big, revolving doors. It wasn't his first visit here. You could say that again. But it was the first time he could recall walking in of his own free will – and without a pair of deliberately overtight handcuffs cutting in to his flaming wrists.

Some old cow who called herself Carole Briggs appointed herself to look after them, or Tracey anyway, while they did some more waiting and hanging around. She had a cosy office all to herself. Flowery posters on the wall, leaflets about counselling and advice and God-knows-what other do-gooding crap all over the shop. Eventually the big cheese from yesterday, Detective Sergeant Kerr or whatever, showed up, escorted them to another frigging office. Smaller this time but with a computer linked up to a big LCD screen. Casper had to sit on a chair outside first though. Something about they wanted them to take a look individually, make sure that Tracey didn't pick up what the big cheese called a 'cue' from Casper – or the other way round. Casper asked him if he could smoke – the Briggs cow had allowed it in her office, had even doled out the fags – but the cheese had said no, he couldn't, not in this part of the building, not out in the corridor. So Casper had kicked his heels, really frigging sweaty and itchy now, feeling worse than fucking death.

Thank fuck that he didn't have long to wait. And it didn't take him long himself either. There was another plainclothes copper in the room, working the controls. A big, burly customer, this one. What they were showing them on the screen were stills from the Zoo's security cameras. In particular, the one that filmed everybody as they queued up at the ticket booth to go in. Ten minutes was all it took and there they were: plain as daylight. The two birds – not bad-looking either of them, you had to admit that much – following behind the estate agent-looking twat. The big copper zoomed in on their faces and Casper clocked them one by one, then asked to see them again, told Kerr he wanted to be positive it was definitely them. Which was frigging true enough, he thought. He wanted to make sure he'd recognise any of the three of them again. Dead sure. Anytime. Anywhere.

Adrian had just grabbed his dressing gown for now. His last night's clothes were already stashed in a black bin liner in the corner of his bedroom, ready for disposal, and he'd been too sleepy, waking up, to think about what clothes he'd wear today. Brady and the two women were still asleep of course. Or still in bed anyway. Although in which configuration Adrian didn't know. He'd heard a resonant slap followed by a sharp, female moan as he'd padded along the hall past Brady's room, which led him to believe that Marla was in there with him – but which didn't mean or prove that Annabel wasn't. In the kitchen, he'd fixed himself strong coffee and then, still half-dozing, he'd burnt two slices of bread in the toaster. What the hell, he'd eaten it anyway – and washed the plate up carefully afterwards, porting every last crumb into another one of the ubiquitous black bin bags. Everyday life, the way they were living it, certainly had its tedious aspects. Carrying all your food, all your cooking utensils, all your plates and cutlery around with you. Ditto for your bed linen. Ditto for everything in the bathroom. And cleaning up obsessively every time you were ready to move on, trying to leave as few traces behind as was humanly possible. In theory, each of them had their specific areas of responsibility in that regard. But Adrian had taken to personally checking up that everything actually got done, that the other three, engrossed in their head games, didn't fuck up. Maria, for instance, was supposed to keep an eye on any post that arrived and put it back looking undisturbed when they did a flit. Yet she'd forgotten all about it when they were quitting the Hat Factory – and Adrian had to sort it himself at the last minute.

He walked through to the lounge, loaded up the laptop, ran the anti-virus program, verified the firewall settings. OK. Fine. He pasted in the target destinations from his address book, attached the correct file and then checked everything again. Great. Good to go. There was still a clear fifteen minutes left anyway before the time that he'd agreed with Brady – or 'discussed' with him anyway. Mid-morning, Brady had decided. *Elevenses in the drone-world, Ade,* he'd said, *plenty of time to put their cute little arses in gear, to get their act together for the lunchtime bulletins.* Adrian hooked the camera up while he waited, started to download last night's raw footage. As soon as he'd done the other thing, he'd need to get to work on that as well. So the sooner the data was copied into the machine the better. He mooched back through to the kitchen once the transfer was underway, poured out the last coffee dregs and swigged them down black. The kitchen had pretty much the same skyline view over the city as the lounge had. Adrian gaped out at it. But without really taking it in. His mind filled instead with the sounds, the sights and even the smells of last night.

They'd driven her off in the direction of Edgbaston, had told her it was for a party, had transferred her swiftly into the van out on Church Road, near the golf course. The back of the van was where she'd encountered Brady for the first time. She hadn't seemed all that pleased about it, funnily enough. Disappointingly she'd turned out to be a delicate little flower in the end, a bit of a drip quite frankly – she'd broken so much more readily and easily than the girl from Crowby had. She'd been a wimp really – sobbing and blubbering, literally pissing herself. The golf course had been a nice venue though: set in woods and parkland (originally laid out by Capability Brown no less) around the Georgian pile of Edgbaston Hall. There was even a famous artificial lake near the twelfth hole, which was where they'd finally staked her down – spreadeagled her – like a naked, human starfish. Maria, at Brady's suggestion, had used an indelible black marker pen to write *Property of Art* in big neat letters across her breasts and her front before they'd left her there. She'd probably caused quite a stir by now, Adrian thought, turning back to the sink and rinsing out the coffee jug, had probably made another cheap spectacle of herself when the early morning golfers had started to tee off.

Half-a-dozen senior CID officers and a couple of co-opted senior civilian managers tried their best not to loll in the low, comfortable chairs which had been arranged in a circle around the low, oval table on which a harassed lad from the canteen had perched a set of cups and saucers, two coffee percolators, a pot of tea and a full range of related items, including a tray of assorted chocolate and non-chocolate digestive biscuits. This was DCS Greg Salter's famous 'ambient' area, the corner of his spacious office, well away from his desk and his personal work space, where he liked to convene many of the meetings which comprised a hefty chunk of his working week.

Jacobson had positioned himself between Jim Webster, who'd caught the lift up to the eighth floor with him, and 'Clean' Harry Fields, the head of the drug squad: two of the less slippery individuals present in Jacobson's view. Salter as usual was trying to give all of them the run-around, playing the specialisms off against each other, manipulating personal animosities and ambitions to achieve the results he thought his department needed – or, much more likely, that he thought would go down well with the Chief Constable, the Assistant Chief Constables and the rest of the force's top-level hierarchy. Jacobson's previous boss, the now-retired Chivers, had just barked out his orders and expected instant obedience. It had been a crude, old-fashioned approach with a lot of faults. But at least Chivers had fundamentally understood policing, what the point of it was, had only rarely put spin before substance.

Jacobson munched through another digestive while the DI from the robbery squad gave his detailed report. The job out at the Waitrose complex had been the second of the kind this month, he reminded them – and he could really do with some extra officers on the case, if there were any available. Salter cast his eye conspicuously around the table. He'd already mentioned the PR disaster of large volumes of washing machines, dishwashers, home cinema systems and freezers going AWOL on a regular basis. The traders' associations, the chamber of commerce and the local council were all up in arms. It was bad for the local economy, he'd told them: national firms might pull out of the area if they were already here – or look elsewhere if they weren't. Jacobson had snorted mentally at that point – it wasn't a good thing, fair enough, but it wasn't burying somebody alive either, fucking with their mind and body.

Clean Harry kept his head down. Jacobson favoured staring blankly into the middle distance. Both techniques worked for about thirty seconds. But that was all. Although you wouldn't have given tuppence for him out on the streets, with his three-coloured agenda in front of him, and his sugarless cup of coffee balanced on a clean white saucer, Smoothie Greg could be as bold as Achilles.

'Harry? Frank? Maybe some of your lads – and lassies, of course – could get on board for a day or so, help rev up the impetus?'

Fields attempted an instant counter move, outlined again

the heavy-duty operation which according to him – this was par for the drugs squad course – had reached a crucial stage. Jacobson thought gloomily about his own pitch. The Tracey Heald case could mean a complicated liaison with the Met, and maybe with the National Identity Theft Unit as well. At the very least, it was the kind of thing where you couldn't guarantee a result, couldn't even state a likely time-frame. Plus, in Salter's words, there had been 'no real harm done'. *No real harm done.* That's what the managerialist, empty-headed cretin had really, actually, said barely half an hour ago, when he'd asked them for their initial workload summaries. *How sure are you about the girl's story, Frank? We all know what Saturday nights are like in Crowby, don't we just? Drink. Promiscuity. Fun that gets out of hand. Or drugs, Frank. Fantasies, hallucinations? Things that never quite happened the way they get reported to us?*

'I don't think that's a great idea, eh, *Greg*,' he started to say as soon as Clean Harry stopped talking. 'This abduction inquiry could just as easily have been a murder investigation. If the—'

There was a knock on the door and DS Kerr walked in, breaking Salter's protocol that nobody interrupted his Monday morning meetings unless—

'Sorry, Sir,' Kerr said abruptly, 'but I thought you'd want to hear about this straightaway.'

Chapter Twelve

Casper badly needed a drink after they left the cop shop. Just one, he told Tracey, just one to get his head straight. It had all taken longer than the cops, lying as per usual, had said that it would. After they'd looked at the CCTV images, they'd had to help with making e-fits as well. Casper hadn't been too impressed with the outcome. Those things never looked like real people as far as he was concerned. He decided on the Brewer's Rest in Silver Street. It was known as a coppers' pub. But they couldn't stop you drinking there. Your money was no worse than their money, after all. It wasn't lunchtime yet anyway, it would still be half-empty. Plus it was nearby. Plus it was about the last pub where they'd run into somebody they knew. Tracey could probably do without that right now, he reckoned. He walked straight up to the bar when they got there, ordered her a vodka with lime – although she'd said she hadn't wanted anything – and a pint of Stella Artois for himself. Exactly as he'd expected, there were only a handful of drinkers in the place. Retired old gits by the looks of them, drinking the day away, dodging their coffins. Nobody that resembled a copper in sight. Even so, Casper carried their drinks over to a corner table for the sake of privacy. Tracey followed him.

He convinced himself he felt better after his first couple of mouthfuls. He brought out his fag packet. Only one left. And he knew Tracey hadn't any on her, knew he couldn't light up and not offer her one. Not with the way things were right now. He fished out his wallet, counted out the remaining cash from his mother's sub. If they took a bus back to the Woodlands instead of another cab, then he easily had enough to buy a new packet. He put the suggestion to Tracey. She didn't disagree – didn't actually say anything – so Casper read this as consent, nipped over to the fag machine and came back with a Marlboro vending pack – eighteen cigarettes only. They were supposed to be banning smoking in pubs soon, he said to her, taking two out and making an attempt at casual conversation. Casper told her he couldn't see it working. Mean to say: a pub was about relaxing, having a laugh. It wasn't a fucking health farm. Tracey didn't bother to comment. She drank the vodka down in one, seemed to have changed her mind about not wanting it, then went off and bought herself a second. Casper realised that she must have money with her of her own, probably courtesy of Denise. Ever since she'd had a go at him in Denise's kitchen, she'd barely said two words to him. On the other hand, she hadn't tried to ditch him at any point, hadn't stopped him coming into town with her, had waited for him out in the corridor when it was his turn to ID the bastards.

He watched her coming back with her drink. She looked like Tracey, moved around like Tracey. But he was starting to think that she wasn't the Tracey he'd known before Saturday night. What he couldn't work out, though, was whether she was less than that – or more.

'I still don't know what really happened,' he said at last, somewhere between his first cigarette and his second. 'I mean – did they—'

Tracey gave the slightest shake of her head: *no*.

'I don't want to talk about it, Casper. I just want to get flaming even.'

'You'd need help with that, Trace,' he said, earnest, serious – but not doing anything daft, such as pulling his chair closer, such as putting his hand over hers – nothing that would set her off against him again.

She swallowed the last quarter inch of her second vodka

straight down. She'd ordered a double this time. And neat: no mixer, no ice.

'You'd *better* frigging help me,' she said. 'It's the flaming least you can do.'

Jacobson, Kerr and Salter crowded over a computer screen in the cramped, dangerous office which belonged to the civilian computer officer, Steve Horton. Jacobson and Kerr were no strangers here, were adept at finding standing room amongst Horton's dangling cables, half-dismantled mother-boards and piled-up terminals. But Salter had never set foot in the place before. 'Press', 'media' and 'television' were the magic words uttered by Kerr which had caused him to rapidly adjourn his meeting and descend from Mount Olympus all the way down to the second floor.

Kerr had taken a call from Henry Pelling, the chief crime reporter at the *Evening Argus,* who'd tried him as a second option when he couldn't reach Jacobson. Pelling had forwarded the file directly to Kerr and Kerr had forwarded it on to Horton. It looked like Horton's expertise would be needed in any case so Kerr's thinking had been that he might as well be roped in immediately. Horton closed the eye-jangling confusion of open windows on the screen until only one remained, repositioned the cursor then clicked *play*.

ART TERRORISTS
Series 1 Edition 1
FEAR IS FREEDOM

The film was fifteen minutes long, not counting the seconds. Jerky footage of Tracey Heald drinking in Club Zoo with Casper Donnelly and clearer, steadier sequences, which Kerr confirmed as taking place inside the Hat Factory apartment, took up the first five minutes. After that the scene shifted to Crow Hill. Tracey Heald trying – failing – to get away from her attackers. Her ordeal in the woods. Lingering close-ups of her pleading for her life while someone offscreen shovelled earth over her face. For the most part, though, her assailants weren't camera-shy. You could make out what sex they were, what height, what build. The only precaution they seemed to have taken was that their heads and faces were always carefully pixelated over. The film seemed to fade out at the end but came back with a coda: gloved hands clearing the dirt away from Tracey's face, indistinct, unseen laughter in the background. And then a slow dissolve to the final message:

Filmed on location in Crowby, Central England. Saturday 23rd September-Sunday 24th September. ART NEVER SLEEPS. MORE SOON.

Jacobson fidgeted with his collar, suddenly aware that he'd tied his new tie too tightly around his neck. He'd seen his share of murder victims over the years. Now he thought he'd just seen the look they might've had on their faces in the useless seconds when they knew for certain that the bad thing had come for them and that there was no way out. Steve Horton brought up the email which had been sent to the *Evening Argus* along with the movie file. For some reason, Pelling had forwarded them separately to Kerr. There was no subject heading and just two lines of text:

ONLY UK PERFORMANCES THIS YEAR. ADMISSION NOT FOR EVERYONE.

Jacobson guessed he already knew the answer but asked the question anyway.

'Any chance we can trace the sender, Steve?'

Horton shoved his chair back a fraction from his keyboard,

leaving even less cramped space to share out between Jacobson, Kerr and Salter.

'I'll do what I can, Mr Jacobson – and I can do a bit more if I'm allowed to liaise with ICU. But I'll be gobsmacked if the send details are genuine. These days, dodgy files and mail mainly just hitch a ride on a compromised system somewhere. There's not exactly a shortage of them now that everybody and their granny has a broadband computer connection – usually with sod all in the way of security in place.'

'I'm surprised Pelling even opened it,' Kerr observed. 'It must've looked like just another bit of junk mail after all.'

Horton treated all three of them to the trademark white smile which indicated that he was moving into his element: bringing secret wisdom to the illiterate masses. You smiled, Jacobson thought, you cracked jokes, you scored petty points over your colleagues. None of it meant that you didn't give a fuck. In all probability, it meant precisely the opposite.

'Except that the email's got a clever little script plugged in,' Horton said, 'which means that anything attached to it opens automatically the minute it hits your machine, regardless of any standard filters there might be in place. My guess is the *Argus* guy never had any real choice in the matter.'

Jacobson's mobile rang: Henry Pelling trying again. He stepped out into the corridor to take the call. Kerr and Greg Salter immediately repositioned themselves to grab a few extra inches of elbow room.

'Pelling reckoned this stuff's been sent out to about a dozen addresses all told,' Kerr commented.

Horton nodded, executed a click or two, brought a list of email addresses on to the screen.

'These are the ones they aren't trying to hide,' he said. 'But that doesn't mean they're the only recipients of course.'

Kerr and Salter studied the destinations they could instantly decipher. Local press, local radio and regional TV made up about 50 per cent. The national media – including the BBC and ITV – comprised the other half.

Jacobson squeezed back into the room.

'Just exactly as you said, Steve. Just downloaded itself and started playing, according to old Henry. The *Argus* tekkies are going ape-shit apparently, trying to find out if it's brought a virus or anything in that line with it.'

Horton smiled again: he told them he was confident that there wasn't – although, personally, he'd loaded Pelling's data on to his auxiliary system just to be on the safe side. Greg Salter asked Jacobson what the *Evening Argus* was planning to do with the story.

'Right now, they want to know how much they can spill without getting a rocket from the Chief Constable. I told Henry I thought you'd probably want to call him yourself.'

'Thanks, Frank,' Salter said, sincerely enough for once.

'I could do with a bit extra help if—' Jacobson added, leaving the sentence deliberately unfinished.

Salter brushed an imaginary fleck of dust from the right lapel of his immaculately grey Paul Smith suit.

'Of course. I'll need to recheck the rosters, see what we can do, who we can move around.'

Jacobson almost felt sorry for him. He only had to solve the case, Smoothie Greg was the one who'd have to deal with the media – if the media decided they had something nice and juicy on their hands. Which, frankly, it was difficult to see how they couldn't. Reality TV with a vengeance, old son, he thought. Especially if they do another one and film that too.

Chapter Thirteen

Adrian had showered and finally got dressed properly for the day after he'd emailed the Crowby production to the selected media destinations. He had the Cambrian Wharf apartment all to himself for the next few hours. Annabel and Maria were off on a spending spree in the Bullring shopping centre, armed with cash advances from fresh, previously unused credit cards, and Brady had taken a train over to Coventry to scout out potential venues for their next live operation. The peace and the solitude suited Adrian just fine. If he possibly could, he wanted to complete the Edgbaston film edits before any of them, and especially Brady, came back and tried to interfere.

He worked on steadily, absorbed in the technicalities, taking the occasional break to fix himself more coffee or, like right now, just to stare for a moment or two at the wide view from the lounge window out across the busy, workday city, picturing in his mind the drones, as Brady liked to call them, shut up in their office buildings as far as the eye could see, drudging and grubbing their way through the monotonous hours of the daily grind. Not to live like that, not have to do that for the next twenty, thirty or even forty years, he reminded himself, was what the project was all about. Or it was for him anyway. Even now, even after he'd proven himself (in their terms) on the Edgbaston golf course, Adrian knew he was still the outsider, the extra pair of technically skilled hands they'd hired out of necessity to get the job done. For them, the project – or, to be more precise, the *process* of it

– was an end in itself, regardless of the ultimate, long-term result. All of them, even Maria, loved hurting the girls, really loved making them believe that they were really about to die. Adrian had that stuff in him too, couldn't deny it after Edgbaston, but it was something he'd just as soon have left buried and neglected in the basement of his mind, just as soon not acted on. *Don't tell me you didn't enjoy that, Ade,* Brady had said to him when they'd finally finished with the girl at the golf course, *don't tell me that didn't make you feel fucking good.* Adrian hadn't replied, had been more concerned with getting the hell away from the scene in any case, but he knew what his honest answer would have been if he'd given it: OK, yes, I admit it, I bloody enjoyed it – but, unlike you, I could live without it.

He sipped his latest coffee, watched what might be rain clouds moving in over the city from an easterly direction. They'd been office drones themselves when they'd first met. Himself, Brady and Annabel anyway. It had all been a matter of chance really, or so Adrian wanted to believe, a random consequence of working at the same shitty place, even in the same shitty part of it. But he knew there was more to it than that. There was something about him that had meant they'd clocked him as a like mind, somebody they could do their unusual kind of business with.

Adrian had worked on the twelfth floor of the call centre. If you looked out of the window there, you could watch the ceaseless sequence of trains pulling in and out of Watford Junction station. Not that the call centre work routines gave you much time or opportunity for window-gazing. Adrian's gig had been in New Customer Enquiries, sifting the time-wasters from the genuine callers, talking polite bollocks into your mouthpiece while fast-keying the computer system, pulling up address details, credit ratings, CCJ histories if there were any, trying to sort the chaff who were stuffed already from the wheat who weren't totally stuffed just yet. The bulk of the business was about loan consolidation, chucking plastic card and overdraft debts into one nice big variable-interest egg basket. You were told to make a loan offer if you possibly could, even when it was obvious that the desperate stooge on the other end of the phone line would default within months or even weeks. So long as they still had a house or some other useful collateral that could be taken away from them later, nobody gave a fuck – or the company certainly didn't anyway. Adrian still had nightmares about the place, would wake up sweating that he still worked there, that he had to get up and get a move on or he'd be late for his next shift.

He still wasn't sure whether he'd become aware of Brady's and Annabel's presence there before they'd become aware of his or if it had been the other way around. He couldn't work out either if that mattered; if, for instance, it had the slightest bearing on the relative levels of culpability and blame. Everybody on the twelfth floor had a cubicle to themselves: desk, chair, telephone, computer terminal. For security reasons, the desks had no drawers and any personal additions to the cubicles had to be vetted by management. A lot of the women favoured cuddly toys or photos of their kids if they had any. The blokes had football calendars or tore scrappy pictures of a Porsche or something like that out of a magazine. You couldn't have pin-ups obviously, since they were officially regarded as sexist, demeaning to women and unacceptable in the workplace. Adrian had done precisely zilch of course to personalise his own rat hole. If you were going to be treated like an automaton, having all your calls recorded, your keystrokes randomly monitored and your toilet breaks timed, then, as far as he was concerned, you might as well be a total, full-on, hundred and ten per cent robot: no traces of personality – just come in, hit the phones, talk shite and go home again. That had certainly been one of the things that had first caught his attention about Brady and Annabel (apart from Annabel's fuck-me tits, legs and arse of course). Like his own egg box, A and B kept their cubicles completely devoid of any personal items.

Weirdly, in a sea of furry animals, giant fucking teddy bears and Premier League fixture lists, this made their cubicles stand out like sore, original thumbs. It was like hanging a secret sign up, a coded message: *I work here but I'm not fooled by it, I'm not taken in like the rest*. Brady and Annabel, evidently, had read the same signals in reverse about Adrian.

There had been other mutual intimations too. Every Monday morning, if you were on the day shift, there was a twelfth-floor team meeting, attendance compulsory. Gerry Black, the New Enquiries Manager, summarised last week's sales figures, talked about the targets for the week ahead, took the opportunity to commend the current sales person of the week and usually worked in a moan or two about absenteeism and the minority who didn't pull their weight, who were letting the twelfth-floor 'family' down. *There's always India*, he liked to recite like a mantra, implying that the company was practically engaged in an act of charity for not closing the entire centre and shipping the work out at a huge cost saving to Bangalore or Hyderabad. *No offence*, he'd usually add afterwards, scanning the room for anyone of a Hindu, Sikh or Muslim disposition, trying to reassure them with his bad-teeth smile that there was nothing racial about his comment, that he was only making an objective assessment of the situation. Adrian's technique for these Monday morning mind-control sessions was to grab a seat at the back and never ever volunteer an utterance of any kind. Brady and Annabel, he started to notice after a while, always did the same. One time, an unpleasant, loud, fat cow, called Michelle-something–or–other, had cried, actually *cried*, when Gerry Black had praised her for setting a new sales record and had called her out to the front of the meeting to receive her magnum of bargain warehouse champagne. Brady and Annabel had exchanged rapid smirks. Adrian had seen the brief interchange and contributed a smirk of his own which Annabel had caught. A couple of days later, Brady, standing behind him in the lunch break canteen queue, had invited Adrian to join him over at the table where Annabel was already ensconced. *Planet fucking Moron*, he'd added quietly, sarcastically, glancing around the room, *best for the intellectual element to stick together, don't you think?*

Chapter Fourteen

Adrian had been out of university for a year when he'd started work at the call centre, had been there two months when he'd started to hang around with Brady and Annabel. He'd gone away from home to study, had gone up North, had done all right academically. But neither his degree in computing and visual culture nor his postgraduate diploma in digital editing techniques had so far led to any worth-while job offers. Maybe he was crap at interviews or maybe he just couldn't act stupid enough to look like any serious employer's idea of a fully exploitable resource. He'd more or less slunk back to Watford, more or less slunk back to his old teenage room in his mum and dad's semi, more or less slunk into the call centre as a means of at least getting out of the house on a daily basis, of at least having some spending cash in his pocket. Brady had done Film Studies at Bristol, where Annabel had 'dropped out' from – ie, failed – the same course. But, despite even his glib self-confidence at interviews, he hadn't succeeded any better than Adrian had in the crowded graduate job market – or not in any of the cool media set-ups where he aspired (or was prepared to condescend) to work. At least A and B were still living away from home though, Adrian had thought enviously, when he was first getting to know them. Albeit that their place was a ridiculously overpriced 'flat' carved sloppily out of the top floor of a cramped, musty, terraced house. They'd moved back over from the West Country to be as near as they could to London, where most of the big media companies were located and where Brady had geographically positioned his giant ambitions for the future. He knew he had it, knew he could do it, he'd say over and over again. Although precisely what 'it' consisted in, was usually harder to pin down. He'd let slip one time that his family were from Guildford, but as far as Adrian knew, he never went back there, never seemed to have anything to do with them.

Adrian, bored senseless to be back at home, spent more and more of his free time chez A and B. There was always a steady supply of recreational drugs round there, there were DVDs worth watching, music worth listening to, conversations that weren't totally conventional, mind-numbing and dreary. And then there was the sex. Kinky, fetish sex – and plenty of it. Adrian, like everybody else, had seen that stuff on the internet but A and B – and Maria of course – actually lived it. One of several ironies in A and B's domestic arrangements was that Maria, who earned more than both of them put together, paid the lion's share of the rent and the bills for her 'owners'. Brady had actually wanted her to hand over her entire salary for him to 'administer' but it was the one thing she'd refused him, as if that would've been a step too far beyond any kind of remotely normal existence. Adrian couldn't take any of it as seriously as Brady's exclusive ménage à trois evidently did yet he was still happy enough to tag along when they went to their frequent fetish nights, especially as Annabel or Brady always seemed to find someone – usually female, usually highly attractive – who was more than pleased to personally 'serve' their guest for the evening. There'd been a married woman from Enfield that he'd met that way, that he'd ended up with more-or-less real, more-or-less sincere feelings for. But her husband had changed his job or got promotion or something and they'd sold up, moved away right out of the area. He'd even asked her not to go the last time they'd been together (in the bland Travelodge room she'd drive him to up at the Teddington services on the M1). He'd very nearly pleaded with her:

don't leave, tell him about us, stay with me instead. He'd had her tied across the bed, naked, vulnerable. But she'd still looked at him with sane, grown-up, hazel eyes. Eyes with pity in them maybe. *Don't be silly, love. This is just fantasy – fun – for God's sake don't go living your life by it.*

It had actually been an idyll of a kind, he realised now. Sleepwalking his way through a week of shifts at the call centre, dropping something or smoking something around at A and B's in the evenings, maybe with Tarantino or Almodovar blaring from the DVD player, then the fetish scene at the weekends. The only downer, perhaps, had been enduring Brady's constant stream of bullshit plans for his big, bright future.

Adrian walked through to the kitchen, put the coffee pot back on to heat. He really needed to get a move on if he really was going to get the edits together before one, two or all of the trio returned. He couldn't remember any more the precise occasion when Brady had first mentioned identity theft as a realistic, conceivable option.

Working at the call centre meant that ID theft was part of his, Brady's and Annabel's mental wallpaper in any case. Everybody there was meant to be ID Theft Aware, to use the management's term, had to attend regular staff awareness sessions, aimed at preserving the company's business from ID scams of various kinds. Plus there was a sacking every now and again: some inept sod or other getting kicked out for perpetrating a bit of low-level leakage. The company conducted random searches at the main doors and spot checks in the cubicles but the odds were still good for any half-diligent data thief. There was CCTV too, obviously – but to actually watch everybody for every hour of every shift would have required an entire army of zealous security staff and not just the two or three sleepy old geezers the company relied on. Besides it was the work of seconds to shove a tiny high-speed data stick into the nearest USB port and download a few thousand customer leads for whatever legal or illegal purpose your purchaser had in mind. And only the work of a few seconds more, if you had the bottle for it, to swallow the data stick along with your morning coffee and wait the twelve or so hours for nature to take its course.

So identity theft came into the mix alongside Brady's principal inflated dream: that he had it in him to be a real film maker – an *auteur*. If the industry wouldn't recognise your talents, if you weren't so-and-so's son or so-and-so's nephew, weren't plugged in to the old-boy and luvvie networks, weren't connected, then maybe there were new ways, twenty-first century ways, of making an impression, of catching the public's fickle attention. If nothing else, Brady had argued, ID theft could give you a 'quality lifestyle' without the tedious need to work your arse off for it, could generate capital for other purposes too, could free all four of them to do something worth doing with their lives. Adrian had told him he was mad at first, that the entire scheme was crazy. But Brady had won him round (or worn him down), had given him, additionally, certain crucial assurances. He'd used old-fashioned flattery too. Adrian's computer skills would be vital for this kind of project, they couldn't do it without him. And in any case, he'd said, reverting to the theme of assurances, nobody would really get hurt, not terminally anyway, not anything they wouldn't recover from. And in the final analysis, they'd be making a statement, making a point. When all was said and done, they'd be making *ART*.

Chapter Fifteen

Annabel and Maria came back around four o'clock in a flurry of upmarket shopping bags. Brady turned up about an hour later just as Adrian was saving what he considered to be the final cut on to back-up storage. True to form, Brady had all kinds of suggestions for changes that he thought were needed. Adrian accommodated just enough of them to keep him happy – and leave him with the illusion of his key creative role – without fundamentally ruining any of the sequences or spoiling the smooth narrative structure he'd imposed on the footage. The film was a winner in any case and both of them could see that it was a definite advance on the Crowby effort. Adrian kept to himself the obvious fact that the key difference was that he'd ignored far more of Brady's ideas this time than he'd included. Brady had seemed in a good mood anyway, had announced that he'd definitely chosen the venue for the Coventry operation. He would still need to take a *drive* over there tomorrow though, he'd added: knowing the pick-up venue in advance was useful, but it was even more important to know where exactly to take the next girl once they had her.

All four of them sat down to watch the six o'clock news on BBC 1. They were up against war, politics, economics, were prepared for only getting regional coverage at this stage. But at precisely twenty-two minutes past the hour, the story ran: a fleeting extract from the footage (blink and you'd miss it), a set of three e-fits that looked liked none of them and a dull, frankly pointless daytime exterior shot of Club Zoo with the shutters down and the doors firmly closed. The voice-over was the best part really. The police were said to be 'baffled' and the incident was described (three times) as 'bizarre'. So far though there was no mention of last night's Birmingham escapade. Maybe the police hadn't made the connection yet – or maybe they were playing their game of holding stuff back from the media.

'National TV,' Brady exclaimed, a genuine smile on his glib face for once. 'We're on national TV at the first attempt. I told you this was going to work – I *knew* it would.'

Annabel kissed him and sent Maria into the kitchen with instructions to fetch champagne.

In the end, they downed four bottles of Veuve Clicquot between them, endlessly replaying the tape of their first ninety seconds of public fame, and chain-smoking party-spirit joints as fast as Maria could roll them – Brady excepted of course, although even he drank a couple of glasses of the champagne. When they noticed that they were hungry, Maria put together a tray of imported Spanish tapas from Selfridges' food hall – and then another tray's worth after that. Annabel wanted to go out somewhere to celebrate but Brady said no, they should lie low tonight and, in any case, there was plenty excitement for her to look forward to over the next few days. Absolutely plenty.

Adrian left the three of them to it about ten o'clock, just as the situation in the lounge looked set to turn three-ways sexual, sloped off to his bedroom. The alcohol and the dope (skunk this time) had made him nicely groggy and he wanted to capitalise on that feeling in any case, give himself up to the good long sleep he felt he richly deserved. He'd put long, hard hours into film editing yesterday and today and the events of last night and the night before had taken their toll in stress, tiredness and post-combat exhaustion.

It was as if his head had only just hit the pillow one minute and that the very next minute there was Maria shaking him gently awake, telling him it was nearly lunchtime, telling him he'd slept right through breakfast and right through most of the morning. Brady stuck his head round the door in the next second, paranoid maybe about the proximity of Maria to the body of another man, sprawling and naked under a rich blue Indian cotton sheet.

'No problem, Ade,' he said. 'You take it easy for the day, get yourself sorted for this evening.'

'You're in a good mood,' Adrian answered, yawning and scratching the top of his head against his pillow.

'And why wouldn't I be? We've made all of the tabloids, plus two of the qualities. We're everywhere, Ade, just everywhere.'

Adrian pulled himself up to a comfortable, sitting level.

'Jesus, the time,' he said, thinking outloud. 'What about sending out the new film?'

Maria stood back from the bed, moving away.

'Don't worry. Annabel sent it out. There wasn't a problem, I double-checked all the steps with her when she did it.'

Adrian slumbered again when they left his room, dozed on for another hour or so.

When he finally got up, Annabel was just on her way out. She told him that Brady had taken Maria with him on his Coventry driving recce. She was heading over to the Electric Cinema on Station Street, she said. There was some kind of special matinee happening there apparently. Local independent films or something like that, although it was the cinema itself that she actually wanted to see. Adrian nodded, told her he was sure it was worth a look. He'd read somewhere that they'd built it back in 1909 and that it was the oldest working cinema in the country.

'Come with me if you like,' Annabel said.

She was wearing a short leather coat and a shorter leather skirt that showed her long legs off to their full advantage. Adrian pre-played sitting close to her in the semi-darkness, the idea of it catching in his throat.

'Thanks. But I've got stuff to do here,' he lied.

'Pity,' she said, checking her bag for her mobile, 'see you later then.'

Adrian watched her walk along the hall to the door, watched her open it, watched her go. Brady wouldn't have liked it, he reminded himself, might even have gone ape-shit. He definitely wasn't keen on unchaperoned contact between Adrian and the two women unless there was a project-related need for it. Plus Annabel was probably just prick-teasing him anyway, probably hadn't meant the invitation seriously.

The rest of Tuesday afternoon passed uneventfully. He ventured out himself after a while, grabbed a late pub lunch in the Pitcher and Piano, mooched around the current exhibition in the Ikon gallery after that. The plan this time was for Brady and Annabel to make the snatch using the Birmingham-rented BMW and to transfer over to the transit somewhere on the edge of town where Adrian and Maria would be waiting for them. By five thirty they were all back at Cambrian Wharf and good to go. Maria had worked her costume and make-up magic on each of them, Brady had shown them his selected location on the map, had made sure that Adrian, as well as Maria, knew how to get there. Brady and Annabel would head out towards Coventry first and Adrian and Maria would follow on later, but taking a different route. It was going to be their third operation, and everything had worked like clockwork up until now. Even so, and even after his solid day's rest, Adrian treated himself to another generous line of coke before he left the premises, needing another dose of ersatz, artificial confidence to bolster his nervously dwindling supply of the real thing.

Chapter Sixteen

They tuned the radios in both vehicles to BMRB en route, all four of them wanting to hear the latest coverage on the local news bulletin. They'd stuck phoney plates on the Birmingham beamer late on Sunday night, just as soon as they'd got the student girl out of it and safely transferred her, blindfolded by then (for disorientation reasons), into the back of the transit. Even so, Brady thought, big-girl's-blouse Adrian will probably shit himself, hearing the newsreader read out the letters and the numbers of the original plate in the correct order. The girl must have memorised them, must have passed them on to the police. He told Annabel to phone Maria on her mobile.

'Tell her to tell Adrian there's nothing to worry about. It's something we've already dealt with. We anticipated it, pre-empted it. Tell her to tell him not to lose it, tell him just to stick to the plan.'

The traffic was worse than shit most of the way, commuters crawling home in every direction. So that it was seven thirty, not seven o'clock as he'd intended, when Brady and Annabel walked into All Bar One in the centre of Coventry. He'd parked at the location he'd picked out yesterday: the patch of temporary wasteground created by the demolition and building work which was underway not far from the Cathedral. For the time being, you could park there all day at a fraction of the charges over in the NCP. Strictly At Owner's Risk, the sign at the entrance said. That had been the attraction for Brady of course. No CCTV, no attendant on permanent duty.

Brady bought the drinks while Annabel found a table. The place was A-one ideal. Hordes of after-work twenty-somethings knocking back wine, beer, cocktails, spirits. Unwinding. Relaxing. Out for a good time. There were at least half-a-dozen girls he liked the look of instantly, knew he could enjoy breaking the will of any of them. He sipped at his mineral water when he sat down, trying to refine his selection, narrow it. There was a male-female couple a few tables away whose voices carried now and again above the general din. An argument in progress or at the very least in the making. He nudged Annabel and they both started to take a discreet interest. Brady couldn't believe he could be that lucky, that the Crowby MO would magically repeat itself. But, on the other hand, there was no reason why not. Couples argued. It was virtually part of the definition of the term. Annabel had brought some holiday brochures with her, was flicking through the pages, occasionally pointing out something for Brady to take a look at. It was as useful a cover as any – and Brady found he actually liked the idea of some of the Caribbean options. There would be lots to do later, when their real lives could begin, and when Brady would be free to devote himself fully to exercising his creativity, but there was no reason why they couldn't take a break first, take it easy somewhere hot and sunny for a month or so. Provided they chose a good enough resort, of course, somewhere well away from the dreary hoi polloi.

The girl was getting seriously irate now, ticking her boyfriend or whatever off about a string of alleged failings. The nub of it seemed to be that they were meant to be moving in together, looking for a place. But half the time if she arranged to go and look at something he'd phone with a pathetic excuse as to why he couldn't make it – yesterday, apparently, he just hadn't showed up at all. The guy started to look embarrassed, a sheepish grin on his youth-blank face. He was – what? Twenty-two, twenty-three maybe. Still at an age where life hadn't written anything worth reading on his face, had barely written anything at all. He was nicely dressed though. Brady would give him that. A decent suit that hadn't just fallen off the nearest peg. Brady's best guess was car sales – but if not cars, sales of some kind anyway, he was certain about that much. The girl was actually borderline for looks. Not in the same league as Tracey Heald or the little student sweetie Adrian had picked up for him in Birmingham. But she was no cow pat either. What Brady really liked about her though was her temper, the flush it brought to her face and the sparkle it put in her eyes. That was what clinched it for him – the idea of personally stamping out all of that defiance, all of that natural self-belief, bringing all of it tumbling right down until it was nothing but empty, broken dust.

The guy gave up about ten minutes later. *That's it, I've had enough of this*, he'd said, almost politely. Then he'd downed his beer, shrugged his shoulders and walked out. The girl kept her gaze straight ahead, ignoring his exit as if it had nothing to do with her. When he'd gone, she took out her mobile, started casually texting someone. A girlfriend maybe, passing on the latest news about her man trouble. Annabel finished her happy-hour double gin and tonic, ordered a refill at the bar and a large glass of Chardonnay. She'd seen that the girl had been drinking white wine so she statistically maximised her chances, went for the common-or-garden choice. Approaching the girl's table, she tried for a rueful smile that she hoped would look friendly and not too pushy. She placed the full glass of wine next to the girl's empty one, waved the G and T she was holding in her other hand.

'I hope you don't mind,' she said, still smiling, 'but I thought maybe you could use another drink.'

The girl looked at Annabel, looked at the unasked-for glass of wine, looked at Annabel again.

'Do I know you? Have I met you before?'

Annabel tried to keep her smile going.

'No, no. It was just I thought that—'

'You thought what? I saw you and your friend gawping at us when you thought we weren't looking. All ears, the pair of you. Never heard of minding your own fucking business?'

She was standing up now, sticking her phone into her bag. Annabel watched her, lost for words. The girl took a quick sip from the wine glass Annabel had carried over, transformed her face into an exaggerated grimace.

'House white. I might have bloody known. You must think I'm a cheap shot for whatever you had in mind. What are you – a lezzie or something?'

Annabel wanted to hit her. Or to take her G and T, pour it straight over the bitch, then shove the rim of the glass right into her mocking face.

'Look, I'm sorry, forget it,' she managed to say – but her smile had vanished.

'You're forgotten all right – weirdo,' the girl said, sweeping past her, very nearly knocking her drink out of her hand. Annabel stood rooted to the spot, aware that she was the immediate centre of attention for several tables around. She watched the girl disappear into the crowd. and then reappear in the distance, exiting through the main doors.

Brady was by her side suddenly.

'Come on, love,' he said, in a loud, over-cheery voice intended for the benefit of Annabel's recently acquired audience. 'I think you've had enough, don't you? It's time to go home.'

He took the gin from her, put it down next to the two wine glasses. Annabel caught on, even feigned wavering on her feet a little as Brady put his arm around her shoulders, appearing to support her as they made their way out.

The street outside wasn't over-busy but the girl had already vanished in an unknown direction. They stopped at the third shop window down, a branch of HMV. Brady pretended to study the new DVD releases while he assessed the situation.

'Don't worry about it,' he said. 'We can't expect it to be super-smooth every single time. There's bound to be the odd failure.'

'But she made me look like a fool, she *humiliated* me, Brady. That's not supposed to happen.'

Brady felt for her but the project was beyond all of them in a way, couldn't be jeopardised for individual ego.

'Listen, you did the right thing, you kept your cool. What else were you going to do? Smack her in the face and get yourself arrested?'

He took her by the hand and they walked along Priory Street to where he'd parked the beamer. The makeshift car park had no lighting, only what little reached it from the nearest street lamps. It seemed quiet, deserted, but when they drew near the row where Brady had left the car, they saw that there was a slight figure ahead of them, fumbling for the keys out of her bag in front of an old-model Ford Fiesta.

Annabel was running towards her before Brady had even taken it in that it was the girl from the bar. The girl had quick reactions, put up a real fight, but Annabel was taller, stronger – and she had the advantage of surprise. She was bashing the girl's head against the bonnet when Brady caught up to them, pulled her off. He grabbed the girl in a neck-lock, kept his free hand tight across her mouth while he tried to think. No one seemed to be around, no one seemed to be coming running.

'The boot. Quick, take the keys,' he said quietly.

Annabel found the key-fob in his jacket pocket, ran towards the beamer which was maybe six cars away, unlocking the boot as she ran. Brady dragged the girl with him as rapidly as he could. He was nearly at the beamer, when she nearly struggled loose, nearly tripped him, managed at least one good, pain-delivering kick into his groin. She made a run for it, screaming blue murder, but Annabel caught her again, struck her on the forehead with the tyre lever she'd just snatched out of the boot. As far as was practical, they carried anything obviously suspicious bagged up in the transit to minimise the risk if they were ever stopped – but even a BMW could get a flat or a blow-out, could carry a few basic tools. The girl slumped and they carried her back, dumped her, unresisting, inside. Brady took a final look around before he pulled open the driver's door. The immediate area was silent, not a soul in sight. All you could hear was the distant roar of traffic out on the Ringway, the city's ring road. Your life was ultimately governed by chance, he thought, unless like him, you took control of your own destiny. The car park could have been busy or there could have been someone, even someone not afraid to get involved, walking past at the right (or wrong) moment when the girl was kicking at him and screaming *Fuck off* at the top of her voice. Ultimately, the girl could have met her boyfriend in another pub or parked her car somewhere else. But none of that had happened. Instead, Brady was the one climbing into the driving seat, and she was the one in the boot, his very latest guest star, en route to her role as tonight's star performer.

He tore a strip off Annabel on the drive towards the transfer point about the tyre lever. The blow had only dazed the girl, had only made it easier for them to subdue her again. But she could just as easily have knocked her out, rendered her totally useless for filming – or something even worse. Annabel took it, said she'd watch it next time. But he could tell what she was really thinking: *I enjoyed that, Brady, that bitch deserved it.*

The transit was ready and waiting at the correct spot, a quiet, suburban street where the BMW should be safe enough, parked there for an hour or so, and where detached houses were set well back from the road behind high walls or tall leylandii and at the end of long driveways. The only interval of risk was the moment of transfer itself. But it was something they'd rehearsed and practised for speed and efficiency.

Brady reversed the BMW into place behind the transit and unlocked the boot electronically. By the time he and Annabel emerged casually from the car, Maria and Adrian already had the girl securely inside the back of the van.

Brady had picked a scrubby area of woodland near to an under-construction housing estate situated out towards the M6 as suitable for their purposes. The estate was going to be a small-scale affair when it was completed. No more than a few streets. No more than, say, fifty or sixty houses all told. Starter homes: *little boxes for little minds*, he'd said sarcastically to the others when he'd told them about the location. There was probably a security patrol keeping an eye on the building development overnight but Brady had found a track that veered off before the main approach road and brought you straight to the edge of the woodland. It was marked with a dead-end sign but that hadn't stopped flytippers using the area to offload unwanted computers, busted television sets and wrecked sofas. If anybody like that happened upon the transit while it was parked there they wouldn't blink at it, would just assume that one of their own kind was at work somewhere in the vicinity.

Maria drove now since Adrian was needed in the rear of the van with the DV camera. They'd cuffed the girl and gagged her as soon as they'd got her inside but Annabel had tightened the cuffs and retied the gag more strenuously than was strictly necessary.

'Not so lippy now, are we?' she'd asked rhetorically, shoving the girl forcefully into the corner.

Brady let her have her fun but made sure she didn't do any real damage, wanted the girl conscious and physically intact for the night's main business.

Maria drove as close to the first trees as the track permitted. She cut the lights and killed the engine while the others dragged the girl out of the van. Brady made sure the girl saw him sift through the half-dozen black plastic sacks of equipment they kept stored inside and produce a stout length of rope with one end already tied into a convincing-looking hangman's noose. He slung the rope over and around his shoulder and then picked up a folding camping table which had been leant against one of the side panels.

'Not your lucky night, Jane, one way and another,' he said, stepping down and closing up the van.

He'd searched through her bag on the journey, finding out who she was and making sure her mobile was turned off.

Five minutes inside the wood, they found an oak tree with a solid branch at just the right kind of height. Maria and Annabel kept a firm hold of the girl while Brady got the rope into position and Adrian kept the camera running. When he had it sorted to his satisfaction, Brady walked over to her, stared into her face, made her his usual offer. They'd remove the gag but only if she kept quiet, only if she didn't shout or scream. Try anything in that line and she'd regret it: that was a personal, fucking promise. The girl nodded her head and Annabel removed the gag, a silk scarf in a modish green colour. Brady stayed right in her face.

'Not your lucky night at all,' he said. 'We're the Art Gang, by the way, that's what the papers are calling us. We're going to hang you from this tree just because we feel like it.'

The girl's legs nearly gave way, started to tremble beyond her control. Her voice was weak but there was still anger in it.

'I've done nothing to you. I don't even know you.'

Annabel slapped her. Brady shook his head with mock gravity.

'That's what they all say, Jane, but that's just it. Pointlessness. A pointless act of pointless violence. Pointlessness *is* actually the point.'

The girl let out a piercing scream, struggled against Annabel and Maria's grip, kicked out at Brady again He slapped her hard then, harder than Annabel had managed and told Maria to re-gag her.

Annabel and Maria stripped her after that, uncuffing then

112

recuffing her in the process. Annabel asked Brady if she could be the one to use the marker pen this time.

Brady nodded and Maria passed her the pen. Brady had decreed earlier that they should mark each one as *Property of Art* from now on. *It'll be our calling card*, he'd said, *our kitemark.*

When they were ready, they frogmarched her towards the tree. Brady put the camping table together and Adrian handed the camera to Maria. The way they had it planned, it would be her job to film the next sequences. The table was maybe two feet, definitely not more than two and a half feet off the ground.

'Don't worry about the lack of height, Jane,' Brady said, playing to the camera. 'You can drown somebody in a bath after all – and you can hang somebody in a cupboard if you have to.'

Brady and Adrian lifted her on to the table and Brady – with difficulty – managed to thrust her head through the noose. She was putting up a fight again, kicking out and wriggling. Adrian held her in place while Brady helped Annabel with the other end of the rope, hauling it downwards until the noose was tight around the girl's neck.

'The face, the face,' Brady exclaimed, gesturing to Maria, 'make sure you get the look on her face.'

'Definitely not so lippy now,' Annabel said, laughing.

Adrian stood just to the side of the table. He couldn't tell whether Annabel's laugh was real or acting. Maybe, he thought, it didn't make any difference either way. He set the stopwatch feature on his watch, made sure he could read it in the shafts of moonlight. He'd researched the topic on the internet, had guestimated the maximum number of seconds that were likely to be remotely safe, had recalculated in his mind when he'd seen the shape and size of the actual girl. He didn't want to be the one to do it, of course he didn't. But, on the other hand, he knew he could trust himself: doing it also meant that he was the one in place to catch her, to take her weight, to stop her dangling before it got too dangerous.

'Whenever you're ready, dear chap,' Brady said in his phoney, on-camera voice.

Mr Toad meets the Marquis de Sade, Adrian thought. He took a deep breath, hardened his eyes, kicked the camping table right over.

They did it three times. The girl passed out completely when Adrian caught her the third time. He undid the noose, undid the gag, laid her down on the ground, using her discarded clothes as a blanket layer.

'Jesus, Adrian,' Annabel sneered, 'you should have gone in for nursing. The uniform might suit you.'

'Shut it,' Brady told her, suddenly irritable. 'There's no mileage in hanging her if she doesn't know what's going on. We'll give her time to come round, see if we've broken the bitch yet.'

Adrian mentioned the fact that there was a bottle of water in the front of the van. Brady told Maria to go and fetch it. The girl was sitting up a little when Maria came back. Adrian helped her to drink some of the water down. She started to cry, sobbing that she wanted to go home, please, please, just let her go home.

'You'll go home all right, cow,' Annabel said, stepping forward. 'You'll go home in a nice big box.'

She pulled the girl roughly off the ground, started prodding and pushing her over towards the tree where the noose had been left dangling.

'Fuck's sake,' Adrian said, getting to his feet, 'she's had enough surely – and we've got more footage than we'll need.'

'You might be right, dear chap,' Brady said, still in Mr Toad mode, 'on the other hand the wench was rather rude to Lady Annabel when we first chanced to meet.'

Annabel turned her head, maybe to laugh with Brady, maybe to laugh at Adrian.

The girl saw her one, slim chance and took it. She twisted

her body around quickly, breaking Annabel's grip on her upper arm. A split-second only. But enough. Still naked, she made a run for it, desperately heading deeper into the wood. All four of them ran after her. The girl was cuffed, hurt and exhausted but she was smaller than any of them, less impeded by the branches that got in their way, catching them in the face and ripping into their clothes. Annabel fell behind, tripped up by twigs or creepers. Ahead of them they started to hear engine and wheel noise out on the motorway. The girl kept going, running for her life, gaining more and more distance.

Adrian thought his lungs would burst, forcing himself onwards. He was the first one of them to emerge from the treeline and on to the steep, grassy slope that pitched down towards the crash barrier and the hard shoulder beyond. The girl was already over the barrier. She looked behind her, saw Brady looming up next to Adrian and then saw him pushing Adrian out of the way and start to crab-run down the slope, still coming after her. Adrian didn't move, felt himself transfixed. The traffic was busy in the other direction but there was a lull on this side, apart from a solitary lorry throttling along the inside lane. There was no time, Adrian thought, for Brady to reach her unseen or unobserved. No time in the world. All she had to do was to stay where she was and make sure that the driver saw her. But Brady kept coming and in the final bone-crunching, body-mangling moments of her existence she panicked, got it wrong, made a doomed, reckless sprint for the central reservation.

Part Two:

Girls On Film

Chapter Seventeen

EVENING ARGUS***

ESTD. 1901   Thursday September 28   thirty five pence   **FINAL EDITION**

'Bizarre' video death gang snatch 4th victim Police issue new warning to women by our Staff Reporter

Police today stepped up their hunt for the gang believed to be behind a series of 'bizarre' abductions across the Midlands after TV stations and newspapers, including the *Argus*, were sent a new video apparently showing the **ordeal** of the gang's latest victim. On Tuesday night, a young woman, who police believe was fleeing from the gang at the time, **died** in a horrific road accident on the M6. A total of four young women have now been subjected to **terrifying** ordeals at the hands of the gang. Police have

119

so far refused to name any of the alleged victims but have confirmed that they are all young women and that three of them were abducted after attending popular night spots in the region. Their ages are believed to range from 18 to 24. The latest victim was **seized** in Wolverhampton last night but police are withholding details of the incident. The hunt for the gang began last weekend when a local teenager in Crowby was forced to undergo a 'mock **burial**' after an evening out at the town's Club Zoo venue. Similar attacks followed on Sunday night in Birmingham and on Tuesday night in Coventry where the attack is believed to have led to the road death on the M6. A total of four **'disturbing'** videos depicting the abductions have now been issued by the gang. So far the BBC, ITV and the other major television networks have -continued page two

Don't go out alone, police warn – turn to page three
Should TV show 'twisted' images? – turn to page four

January Shepherd studied the report in the local paper after she'd glanced at the coverage in the *Guardian* and the *Daily Mail*. In the old days, Dad would order all the papers wherever they happened to be living; wanting to keep up, he'd say, not just with the music business but with everything. Curiosity never killed any cat at all, he'd said to her one time: not one single cat. Now though these were the only ones he seemed to take. The *Mail* was for Kelly probably, Dad's current live-in. Kelly probably shared the *Mail*'s obsessions with show business gossip and the latest health fads. The *Argus* was the most up-to-date, the other two had obviously been printed before they'd known about the latest abduction and the latest video. January didn't usually follow the news all that much. Not in detail anyway. Bad stuff happened all the time. And, unless there was something you could personally do to help, then what was the point of knowing about it? The media spread fear and negativity like a cancer. It could seep into your bones if you let it, and you'd end up feeling small, useless, powerless. Just the way the system – the governments and the big corporations – wanted you to feel. It was just the fact that it was local, she supposed, and concerning women her own age. Horrible stuff like that happening close around you. Too close for comfort.

January put the newspaper down and blew across the surface of her peppermint tea – which had finally reached the perfect combination of strength and temperature. She stretched back in the big wicker chair and sipped at her mug, contemplated the sharp green leaves of a datura plant that, even in here, had so far resolutely refused to flower in the English climate. January liked the tropical plant house. Especially liked it on a late afternoon in autumn when the wind outside blew rustles of leaves against the windows. She loved the way the air always smelt of warm, sultry earth and the co-mingled odours of growth and decay. She loved the irregular creaks and rattles from the ancient pipe work and radiators. Dad had plans, he'd said, to gut them, to replace them with something modern, efficient, computer-controlled. He was having plans drawn up for an aerial walkway too. So that you'd be able to wander above the palm trees, take a bird's eye view of everything. January had started a quiet but steady campaign against these proposed innovations. The oldness, the inefficiency, the dilapidation, were the things that she liked. The peeling brittle paint on the arms of the uncomfortable, wrought-iron benches. The occasional cracked pane of glass. And yet nature still increased in here, still triumphed regardless. Her mobile beeped on the little wicker table. Another text from Nick. Well *that* can wait, she thought, taking a second sip and then a third.

It was great that Dad had bought this place. Really great that he'd come home at last. Fay, her mother, Dad's second ex-wife, the English one, had told her that she thought he was mad. That if she never set foot again in cold, poxy Britain she wouldn't lose a minute's sleep over it. *That country is so over, Jan, wound up, finished*. But January reckoned that it was him who'd got it right, that back here maybe he'd finally get himself sorted. When you'd travelled everywhere, seen everything, eventually all you wanted to do was to go home. Not that Boden Hall was precisely where Dad had come from. Though the council house he'd grown up in was still there on the other side of Crowby. You could drive straight to it in not much more than thirty minutes. And it was a real place. A real drab house in a real drab street. And real, drab people living in it.

Dad had acquired Boden Hall for a song anyway, pretty much. The previous owner had been a very naughty boy, had been caught with his hand in an extremely nasty till. With the result that he hadn't just copped a lengthy prison sentence, he'd been stripped of his assets too, Boden Hall pre-eminently included. If January knew her father, and she reckoned that she knew him just about as well as anybody did, the notoriety of the case had probably been an additional selling point, an added bonus. She finished her tea and condescended to read Nick's text message, although still not bothering to reply. Worrying about the set-list as usual, fussing like a wuss. If it had been left up to January, she'd only have fixed the order for the first two or three numbers. Then take her cue from the crowd, *sense* what to hit them with next. She decided she'd take a walk around a part of the grounds before she went back to the main house. She hadn't visited the gazebo since she'd flown in, which was another threatened ruin which had grabbed her imagination. So maybe she'd stroll over in that direction. Then she'd do her pilates and yoga, followed by a long, hot soak before she put some last-minute practice in. She shouldn't be so hard on Nick though really, she thought, gathering up the newspapers and the couple of novels she'd bought at the airport but hadn't started to read yet. She was serious about the gig, serious about the band. Of course she was. But not in the way that Nick and the others were. How could she be? How could anybody expect that from her? Nick was

122

maybe a bit like Dad was when he'd been starting out. Driven, determined, ambitious. But all of that was easy when you were coming from nothing, when everywhere you might go would be brand new, shiny, exciting. When you already came from there, when it was where you already lived, it was a lot harder to get really excited about anything.

Emma Smith drove the car. Jacobson, in the passenger seat, switched off his mobile and attempted to get his thoughts in order ahead of the meeting. The Regional Crime Squad had condescended to take a look at the cases and had swiftly declined them. Not big-scale enough. No obvious links to any of their current investigations. That had been on Wednesday, the day after the third abduction and the first death. Earlier today, Thursday, the top brass had finally made a decision: the investigations were to stay in the hands of the local sides in the relevant areas. Each SIO – Senior Investigating Officer – would continue to deploy their local teams but from now on they would liaise on a daily basis to share intelligence and coordinate progress. Jacobson had no illusions, knew that the reasons for the chosen strategy were all political. The government still had plans afoot to merge the existing police forces together into larger, so-called super forces. Virtually every Chief Constable in the country was vehemently against these proposals. Suddenly – surprise, surprise – inter-force collaboration was the flavour of the month. Particularly when it came to high-profile operations with a big media footprint, to use a current Salter-ism: four nutters whose idea of fun was terrifying young women out of their wits on camera fitted the bill very nicely. And, especially so, now that one of their victims had ended up dead under the wheels of a long-distance haulage truck.

County HQ was four miles outside of Crowby and close to the motorway. The ideal location – so it had been decreed on high – to bring the relevant SIOs together for the first time. DC Smith pulled up at the entrance barrier and, following the latest protocol, switched off the engine while both of them were security-checked. When they were done, she drove to the car park nearest to the main building. She killed the engine again, applied the brake and waited deferentially until Jacobson clambered out before she got out herself.

The set-up out here dated back to the 1960s just like the Divi back in town. The difference was that most of the HQ buildings were low-rise and the grounds had been nicely landscaped. It always reminded Jacobson of a small university campus. Or it would have done minus the high-security perimeter fencing, the helipads, satellite communication masts – and the rumoured presence of a nuclear-proof underground bunker which would supposedly house the emergency Regional Seat of Government on the day that civilisation finally packed up. They found the room easily enough. 103, up on the first floor. A corner location with long windows down two sides.

Jacobson and Smith were the last to get there, even though they'd travelled the least distance. It didn't matter too much for the outcome of the event since Jacobson had been designated as the chair and the meeting couldn't start without him. He had the seniority for one thing, and a decent track record. He'd also had a head start on the other SIOs since Crowby had been the scene of the first known attack. Emma Smith poured him out a coffee, managed to find enough left in the pot for a half-filled cup of her own.

Jacobson sat down on the conspicuously vacant chair at the head of the table. DC Smith and himself apart, there were four other officers in the room, three men and one woman. Jacobson knew all of them by name but only two of them by sight: DCI Nelson from Coventry and DS Barber from the City of Birmingham force. Nelson had been another one of the delegates on a memorable training course that Jacobson had attended down in London years ago. Memorable not for content – some weaselly Met drivel about

124

suspect profiling – but for several decent nights of boozing and general male bonding. DS Barber had been DC Barber until last year, had partnered Mick Hume on several Crowby murder squad operations before he'd got his promotion and transfer. Jacobson guessed from the way they were conferring that the guy on Barber's right must be his boss, DI Coleman. Jacobson had brought Emma Smith along for an important reason but his instant snap was that Coleman might just be the type who liked a bagman with him, maybe to bolster an elevated sense of his big city self-importance. Nelson hadn't bothered to and neither had the woman from Wolverhampton, a certain DI Monroe. No relation to Marilyn apparently, to judge by her unhandsome features. Not that I'm one to talk, Jacobson thought, drinking his coffee down in quick, extended gulps to get it out of the way.

As well as coffee and a room with two views, County HQ had even laid on a secretary with a laptop. She would type up blow-by-blow minutes of the meeting and file electronic copies afterwards to Jacobson, Nelson, Coleman and Monroe. To kick off, Jacobson summarised the latest state of play in Crowby: there'd been no more attacks since Saturday but there'd been no police breakthroughs either, just hard, plodding work that had still to produce a payoff. Then he sat back and listened as the others followed suit. The Birmingham victim had been a twenty-year-old Fine Art student who, since Monday morning, had been a voluntary psychiatric patient at the Queen Elizabeth hospital. According to Coleman, who'd visited her again this afternoon, her voluntary status might not last out very much longer. She'd tried to self-harm twice since she'd been admitted and she was now so heavily sedated that her accounts of the incident and of her attackers were basically useless from a police point of view. Jacobson wasn't surprised by the news. He'd seen the movie file from the self-styled 'Art Terrorists'. He'd thought Tracey Heald had looked scared when he'd seen the first film they'd sent out. But the girl from Birmingham had trumped her. There had been a lingering segment where an unseen hand had ran a long, sharp-looking kitchen knife inch by inch against her breasts and then against her throat. As close as you could ever go without piercing the skin. The expression on her face had read like an urgent telegram from hell itself. Pragmatically, though, her damaged mental state wasn't actually an immediate problem for the investigation. There had been good CCTV footage from the pub where she'd first encountered three of her attackers. The two friends she'd gone there with, on what should have been an ordinary, enjoyable Sunday night, remembered them – and there'd been no shortage of other customers and bar staff who'd also been willing and able to confirm the captured images. Plus there'd been one solid fact emanating from the girl herself: the registration number of the gang's BMW, which she'd obsessively taken to writing out over and over, as if the letters and numbers were tattooed permanently on her memory. The registration number had led Coleman's team directly to time, location, credit card details and descriptions from witnesses which related to the gang's second known hire of a BMW. Irritatingly, security cameras, which should have been working, weren't – so there was no accompanying visual record.

There was CCTV from Coventry too, according to Nelson. Although only for two of the abductors this time, one male, one female. The pair who, witnesses said, had taken an interest in the abducted girl when she'd been in All Bar One with her boyfriend. The girl's body had been a grisly mess, crumbled and broken. But the inked 'message', *Property of Art*, had still been legible. To their credit, the first traffic cops at the scene had grasped the significance straightaway. But, even so, that had still left enough of a time window for the gang to slip out of the vicinity before a full alert could be raised – and it had been an hour after that before the likely scene of the attack had been first located. Nelson was optimistic that the traffic cameras would eventually reveal the route and the vehicles the gang had used for their getaway. That might be some kind of help, might give some kind of indication as to where they were holed up.

'It looks like what happened on the motorway panicked them,' he added. 'The crime scene crew are finding all sorts of useful forensic stuff at the site. The victim's clothes, quite a few shoeprints. Even the rope it looks like the bastards were using on her. Most of it's probably going to be pretty useless of course until we've got some suspects in custody to match against.'

Jacobson sighed audibly, nodded his head. Bizarrely, despite the fact that there had been a death this time, the gang had still sent out a video of their handiwork: hanging their victim, Jane Thompson, a twenty-two year old legal receptionist, from an oak tree, and not just once but three times. Without the video, there would still have been significant gaps in the police understanding of the precise sequence of events.

'You identified the lass swiftly enough though,' he said, looking for something – anything – upbeat.

'True, Frank. We did have some luck there,' Nelson replied. 'She was still living at the parental home, apparently *never* stayed out all night without texting or phoning first to let somebody know she was safe. Not usual these days, but there you go. Anyway the mother reported her missing just after two AM – the only new misper that had come in all night. So it didn't take long to put two and two together and come up with some bad news.'

At twenty-four, the Wolverhampton victim, an assistant manager in Top Shop, had been the oldest of the four. Her experience also confirmed an alarming pattern of escalation. The Crowby and Birmingham victims had been more or less seduced into their predicament. In Coventry, the abductors had attempted a seduction and only secondarily resorted to force. The Wolverhampton abductee had been snatched without any prior attempt to hoodwink her. She'd been seized from a bus stop in a quiet, outlying street. She'd seen the white van pull up, hadn't liked the look of it, had made a run for it but had been outpaced, subdued, taken.

'No witnesses, then?' Jacobson asked, thinking outloud and cutting unintentionally across DI Monroe's lilting account in mid-sentence.

She wasn't just Scottish, he'd realised, but from somewhere up in the remote, frozen North. What the Scots from the more populous Lowlands referred to sarcastically as a *cheuchter*.

'I was just coming to that,' she replied pointedly. 'This was a suburban street at nine in the evening. We've a couple of folk who've admitted they might have heard something. But nobody seems to have been looking out of their front windows at the right moment. Or prepared to say so if they were.'

Jacobson nodded and waited till she'd finished this time. Hypnotised by plasma screens and deafened by surround speakers, homeowners nowadays regularly failed to register real screams from real people in the real world on the other side of their firmly locked front doors.

'The coffin might tell us something though surely?' he asked.

The young woman from Wolverhampton had been given the same mock burial treatment as Tracey Heald, except that she'd been buried *inside* the coffin. The Wolverhampton movie had included a sequence that had somehow been shot from the inside too: the victim fighting for breath and clawing at the lid. They'd driven her right out of the city beforehand to a small wood outside a village called Codsall. How the gang had seemed to work it was that they'd monitored her remotely from the camera until she'd passed out, then dragged the coffin back out of the ground, pulled the lid off and scarpered.

'The coffin should be with FSS by now,' DI Monroe replied, not exactly smiling but maybe slightly mollified.

'Plus two of my team are trying to trace the manufacturer. These do-it-yourself jobbies are all the rage apparently down here. Trust the English to want to save money on a funeral. But the useful thing is that there's only a finite number of firms making them. It might give us an idea as to where this crew are really originating from if we can trace it.'

Sexist considerations apart, DI Monroe instantly leapt up a couple of hundred per cent in Jacobson's estimation. The first hundred was for the possession of a sense of humour. The second was for probably being right. The Art Gang, as they were becoming known inside the police operation (thanks to a headline in Tuesday's *Daily Telegraph*) were strangers to the region, he was sure of it. It was why, despite a good supply of CCTV images and witness-assisted e-fits, no one had as yet come forward to identify any single one of the four unknown suspects. They never looked quite the same twice, it was true, seemed to have some kind of professional expertise in the area of make-up and disguise – yet if somebody really knew one of them well, he believed, they'd see through all of that, wouldn't they? The problem was that although the cases were being reported by the media nationally, only the local outlets were reliably carrying every detail that the police fed to them and reliably using every picture.

'That sounds like your cue, Emma,' Jacobson announced.

DC Smith and DC Williams were burrowing as far as they could into the forged driving licences and illegal credit card usage which had been associated with the gang. Again, Jacobson's hope had been that the patterns revealed might be geographical as well as financial. There'd been no luck so far. The detected credit cards had been used sparingly and only in Crowby and in Central Birmingham. Emma Smith connected her data stick to the room's computer unit, switched on the electronic whiteboard, talked them through what was known or what was at least probably known so far.

'As of an hour ago, we're aware of three cards used by the people we're interested in. But that's not to say that they don't have others, maybe dozens. As you can see, two are Visa, one is a MasterCard. Two made out in men's names, one female. All of them made out to real people who check out as innocent dupes, all with North London addresses, all with DOBs in the twenty plus age range.'

'But none of them actually made out to the real person's real address?' Coleman, the Birmingham DI, asked.

'Not exactly,' Emma Smith explained. 'Part of the scam seems to be an elaborate sequence of mail forwarding and diverting. Once they've known enough about their dupes to be able to pose successfully as them on paper, they've set up postal redirections via Royal Mail.'

She clicked the keyboard and the image of a young, fashionably dressed woman appeared on the screen in greyscale. A side-on shot: the woman waiting at a glass-protected counter, a good portion of her face hidden behind large sunglasses.

'When you unravel the trail, everything ends up at a post office box at the Watford sorting office, which is where this image comes from. The box is a month old and it's been emptied out twice. We think by this same female each time.'

'Impressive,' DCI Nelson said.

'Thanks. We're been getting good support from the National Identity Theft Unit. They were the ones who suggested running the dupes' address details against the Royal Mail computers. That's how we got to the box number scam. Plus most sorting offices operate CCTV recording and they all register the date and time when anyone accesses a PO box number.'

'The homebase for this crew has to be London then,' Coleman commented.

Smith looked doubtful but didn't reply, maybe not wanting to correct so lofty an individual as a Birmingham DI.

'Maybe, maybe not, old son,' Jacobson said, coming to

the rescue. 'There's a wide distribution for the North London addresses for one thing. No obvious pattern there. It could just be that however they're acquiring the dupes' details in the first place is via some scam that works better in the smoke. Don't forget there's eight million idiots prepared to live in that shit-hole so, whatever scam you're running, you've more chance of achieving results from there than from anywhere else in the country.'

DI Not-Marilyn Monroe did smile this time.

'Aye, I can see that. Like shooting fish in a barrel. The bigger the barrel, the more gullible fish you can cram in.'

DCI Nelson looked up from his notebook.

'Sorry to be dense, guys, but what you're all saying is that the way this works is that somehow the scammers get hold of enough details about somebody so that they can successfully apply for new credit cards in their name – and then when the cards are issued they get delivered to a diverted address?'

'That's exactly it,' Emma Smith replied, 'or some of their mail gets diverted in the first place – which could be part of how the scammer learns enough to submit a convincing-looking credit application. As well as getting hold of their DVLC drivers' numbers. The exact MO's something that we badly need to find out. We could be looking at something hi-tech and computer based. Or it could be down to somebody grubbing their way through dustbins and rubbish bags.'

Jacobson nodded again. Smith, Williams and Steve Horton had all treated him to advanced tutorials in identity theft over the last three days. Even after all his years in the force, he still wasn't above showing off newly acquired knowledge.

'The beauty of it, old son, is that the scammer ends up with a legitimate card and a legitimate pin number from day one – and usually has a month or so's grace before the mug whose details have been scammed off ever gets to hear about it. It's another instance of so-called tighter security measures actually making life easier for the crims.'

Emma Smith brought a new set of data up on the screen: a chronological list of the transactions on the illegally acquired cards. The gang had hired two cars that were known about so far and put down rent plus deposit on the Hat Factory luxury apartment. The same male gang member, they were convinced, had hired the first BMW and rented out the flat. A female had hired the second BMW, probably the same one who'd made collections from the Watford sorting office. They couldn't be totally sure because of the lack of camera evidence when the car was hired out. A different card had been used as collateral each time. What was interesting, DC Smith emphasised, was that otherwise the gang seemed to working with cash as far as possible. Each of the three cards had been hit for a hefty cash advance prior to any other use.

'The idea, we assume, is to keep the electronic trail to a minimum,' she concluded.

'So the bottom line is that we're dealing with a bunch of highly sophisticated, probably well-educated customers here,' DI Coleman commented, stating the blindingly obvious and confirming Jacobson's suspicion that the Birmingham SIO might be more style than substance.

'They certainly *think* they're sophisticated,' DS Barber said, maybe signalling a distance from his new boss. 'All this Art Terrorist crap dressing up the fact that they're a bunch of sickos who get they're kicks from hurting women.'

DI Monroe shook her head at the thought.

'And yet two of them are lassies themselves. It's a weird set-up right enough.'

'That's the second big question after where they've come from,' Jacobson said. 'What the hell is the motive for all this? We don't know how long they've been operating. But let's assume from the fact that they're pretty adept that's it's been a fair while. Not a bad little game of illegal soldiers really. Renting cars, property, other stuff we don't know about yet – generally leading the high life at other people's expense. So why jeopardise all that with these bizarre abductions? And why guarantee yourself maximum police attention by sending out a video record each time?'

Nobody looked tempted to answer. Jacobson discovered a second untouched coffee pot on the trolley, helped himself to a second cup. The others copied him until the second lot of coffee was gone too.

When they'd drifted back to their seats, Jacobson summarised his thinking so far.

'It might be that there isn't a motive of course – or not one that anybody outside the foursome will ever understand. All we can do is keep looking – and keep talking to each other. They've gone from persuading women into dangerous situations to *forcing* them inside a space of four days. Plus they as good as murdered the lass from Coventry. Christ know's what's coming next if we don't find them soon.'

'We'll find them all right,' Coleman said with an air of certainty that Jacobson, for once, didn't share. 'I've brought DS Barber along since he's got the latest information on the location front.'

So there was a reason for Barber's presence, Jacobson thought, conceding, although only to himself, that he might have assessed Coleman wrongly.

Barber had his data stick too – he moved over to the computer and brought up a map on the whiteboard which pinpointed every known location which could be connected with the four known abductions.

'We can do all sorts of shit with this new mapping software kit,' he announced. 'For instance if we correlate every coordinate we know about and then compute the dead centre' – Barber kept his eye on the screen while he clicked the mouse a couple of times – 'the answer, as you can see, is the ground floor of the Bullring shopping centre.'

He paused for effect. Then:

'Obviously, that's an unlikely hideout. But it could still be significant as a general indication of where they might be hiding out. Bear in mind that the second hire car was picked up on Sunday afternoon from a garage near Five Ways – and that the centre of Brum's chockfull of gaffs along the lines of the Hat Factory in Crowby. So there *could* be some kind of pattern there. What part of our team is doing now is looking systematically at the yuppie property market in the area. Particularly at properties which have recently been let out on short-term contracts.'

'So taking the Crowby let as the template?' Jacobson asked.

The uniformed patrols were keeping a regular eye on the Hat Factory apartment. But it was as a precaution only. Jacobson's assumption was that when the gang had vanished from the place on Sunday they'd vanished from it for good.

'That's right, guv,' Barber replied, 'unfortunately it's a pretty mammoth task – and with four customers as smart as this, it's probably unlikely that they'll use the same credit cards or references again.'

'Plus the fact that they look the part – smartly dressed and young,' DI Monroe observed. 'Ideal candidates for an upmarket rental. And not very likely to stand out in the memory of a letting agent.'

Barber looked glum for a minute but then he recovered, moved on to talk them through his other computer-assisted correlations: the timing of the abductions, the lengths of time the victims had been held for, the possible through routes that might have been used for transportation.

Jacobson found himself listening with only half his attention stream, letting the other half follow its own inclinations. The fact was that the gang had to have gone to ground somewhere. The Crowby abduction was the only instance where they'd risked taking their victim home. The other three times they'd dined out al fresco. And Barber was surely right that they were smart enough not to use the same details again if they had rented out another gaff. But the assumption that they were located in the centre of Birmingham was just that: an assumption. And even if they had been there, there was nothing to stop them from moving on.

DCI Nelson was the first to speak when Barber got to the end of his presentation.

'These references you mentioned, lad? I don't think we've been copied in on that aspect over in Coventry.'

Jacobson let Emma Smith deal with it. He understood the general principles involved but it had been Smith and Ray Williams who'd done the actual spadework.

'One of the four – we think "Brady" – arranged the apartment rental in Crowby, using the name Colin Lee Duncan, one of the credit card dupes,' DC Smith said. 'He claimed he was a company director for a public relations company, told them his company were looking to expand into the area. The letting agents made their usual standard background checks of course. But basically all that amounts to is sending out a letter and making a phonecall. The responses they got back seemed in order to the agents. But if they'd looked a little deeper, they'd have found that all they'd really done was make contact with a business address and forwarding service based down in Slough. As for the PR company, it's registered in the Isle of Man and it's pretty damn certain that it only exists on paper.'

'Plus you can set up both of those things on the internet in about ten minutes,' DS Barber added.

'So the problem is that if they do it again, they'll just use a different set of bogus details?' Nelson asked.

'You win today's star prize, old son,' Jacobson said. 'Four nutters in your haystack and all you've got to find them with is a needle the size of the Home Secretary's knob.'

'Now that's what I call wee,' DI Monroe commented.

Jacobson allowed himself a momentary smile, warmed a little more to Monroe's presence. He started to think that the meeting had served its purpose and that it was time to get back on with the actual investigation. It was a difficult set of cases all right. Daunting. Even when you had his level of experience to draw on. But Jacobson had still to grow out of the old-fashioned notion that you should try to do

135

something vaguely useful when you got up in the morning. Otherwise why bother to get up? There were more pointless occupations in the world than attempting to put a stop to at least some of its badness.

Chapter Eighteen

Brady stepped out of the van and sat the petrol carrier down on the ground. He found the screwdriver in his pocket and got to work undoing the non-detect number plates, front then back. They'd been hard to get hold of (so had the detectable but phoney plates they'd fitted onto the two BMWs) and there was no telling when they might come in handy again. When he was through, he stowed them in the boot of the Volvo. If his strategy was right, their use of the two rented beamers would lead the police down the wrong garden path, get them devoting valuable hours and personnel to a fruit-less trawl through the region's car hire outlets for other hires that matched the apparent pattern. The purchase of the Volvo, he reckoned, was a pure act of genius. Four years old, local registration, and in reasonable condition. The perfect, unob-trusive vehicle. Plus – this was the best bit – they'd bought it for cash via a small ad in the *Birmingham Evening News*. The seller had been hard up, facing a mortgage reposses-sion according to his wife, and too delighted to have a wad of crisp fifties shoved into his hands to notice that Maria and Adrian had walked off with the all-important tear-off at the bottom of the pink slip: the part which enables a street-wise owner to notify the DVLC that the car is no longer their responsibility.

He closed the boot and stood out of the way while Annabel reversed the Volvo a healthy fifty yards or so back up the dirt track. The next five minutes were crucial. There was no way that they could guarantee that an unwanted visitor mightn't turn up unexpectedly and stick their nose in the time it would take them to get the blaze going and then to get the fuck out of it. But managed risk was part of what the project was about. If you didn't want risk, you kept your head down, bit your tongue, did what you were told, lived by the rules. He picked up the petrol container, took the plastic cap off, took a careful look around. He listened carefully too. Silence – apart from a cawing bird above the tree-line. The disused quarry lay half a mile through the small woodland from the nearest B road. There was a conservation project underway according to the signpost at the turn-off. Drippy *Guardian* readers playing at coppicing, Brady had thought, futilely intent on saving the planet. Too little, too late in his view. But hopefully they'd only get out this way at the weekends, would be too busy making money or patronising the working classes on a weekday. According to his reading of the map, they were four miles away from Wynarth, another eight maybe after that to get to Crowby itself. By now, the transit had outlived its usefulness and, ideally, they'd have junked it somewhere back in Birmingham, thrown the police another useful blind. But physical isolation was harder to arrange in a city. Over here there was a reasonable-to-good chance that the burn-out wouldn't be found for days, maybe for longer. The coppicers would mainly park up near where they were working, might only rarely wander this far down the track to where there was nothing to conserve and nothing to save, except for a few lonely boulders that could probably look after themselves.

Moving swiftly now, he opened the van door, doused the interior with two gallons of high octane unleaded. He wound the window down, closed the door and walked back to what he hoped was a safe distance. He should have brought Maria instead, he thought now; he would've enjoyed ordering her to get the cigarette going for him, maybe even kidding her that she had to throw it in. It would have been interesting to find out if fire was one of the things that frightened her. Still, even a master should get his hands dirty on occasion. He took out the packet, found the lighter. He'd make one final visual check through the full 360 degrees. Then light the blue touch paper.

The cases had an official inter-force name now: Operation Icarus. There were approximately twenty officers available for tonight's local Crowby exercise. Most of them young uniformed constables eager for an opportunity to show what they could do on a plainclothes exercise. DS Kerr, assisted by Mick Hume, briefed them in one of the third-floor meeting rooms. The plan was for the officers to work the town's pubs, bars and night clubs undercover, keeping an eye out for anyone who resembled any of the known images of the Art Gang and potentially picking up bits and pieces of intelligence which hadn't got passed on when the town's drinkers and clubbers had been quizzed upfront by CID over the last few nights. Most of the venues that were of interest in the inquiry attracted relatively few customers over the age of thirty and neither Kerr nor, even less, Hume looked sufficiently youthful any more to be convincing in the role.

'How likely do you think it is, guv, that they'll show up in Crowby again?' a female PC found the courage to ask when Kerr had outlined the main components of the exercise.

'That's a fair question,' Kerr replied, 'the short answer might be not very. They haven't repeated themselves so far and they've covered a wide area within the region. But that doesn't mean that tonight isn't the night when they *do* repeat themselves. They could be banking on the idea that we'll rule out the venues where they've already struck. Plus don't forget that any one of you could be the one who overhears a snippet of conversation that leads to a breakthrough. A rumour or a bit of gossip that never got told to us officially but that ends up taking us somewhere. If DCI Jacobson were here, he'd tell you that detective work is all about banging your head against a brick wall – and not giving up before the wall does.'

'And besides it's not every bloody night you get paid to potentially get your leg over,' Mick Hume commented, amidst general laughter. 'I'd make the most of it if I were you.'

Kerr and Hume grabbed hot drinks in the police canteen after the briefing. Additionally, Hume ordered a plate of egg and chips. Half an hour from now he would be meeting DC Ray Williams in the Brewer's Rest. Hume and Williams were tonight's 'official' patrol. They'd move from pub to bar to club, talking to whoever would talk to them, looking for the elusive witness to last Saturday night's events in Club Zoo, the one who, probably unknowingly, had seen or noticed something vital. The other link in the operational chain was Sergeant Ince and his team in the control room. They would be the hotline to the young officers in the field, would forward anything requiring an urgent response to Kerr himself. Kerr was effectively taking over Jacobson's role for the evening. Time was when Jacobson would work round the clock on a serious case, would hog all the responsibility to himself. But these days, in the era of the lovely Alison, Jacobson would occasionally treat himself to a night off – although he always kept his mobile switched on just in case, hadn't been completely transformed into a non-obsessive, non-workaholic, non-miserabilist normal person. Not so far anyway.

Kerr was surprised to see Hume add a side order of green salad to his meal.

'Wife's instructions, mate,' Hume said, reading Kerr's expression. 'Got it into her head that we need to eat more healthily. I blame that doctor woman on the telly. You know that healthy eating show that's always on now?'

'I know it, Mick. Healthy for her bank book anyway,' Kerr replied on autopilot, his mind already drifting elsewhere.

He left Hume still playing with his lettuce leaves when

he'd drained the last dregs from his own cup of tea. What he did himself over the next couple of hours would be pretty much irrelevant to the operation – provided that he was instantly available at the end of his mobile. In the corridor outside the canteen he pressed the button for the lift, called up Emma Smith while he waited. Smith was certainly still young enough for tonight's pub crawl but her talents were needed back here at the Divi. The Met had sent on more details about the three London dupes and DC Smith would spend the next few hours sifting through the data. Something about them or their lifestyles might have made them particularly vulnerable to ID theft. If there was something, whatever it was, it could yield a useful lead. She told him she was on her way and that she'd just dropped Jacobson off outside his gaff in Wellington Drive.

Kerr exited the lift on the second floor, caught up with Steve Horton, the civilian computer officer. Horton was working with the only two pieces of video footage which were reliably believed to show the white transit which the gang had been using: over at the Hat Factory, Sunday AM, plus a fleeting sequence from the security cameras at the entrance to the Edgbaston golf course in Birmingham. The timestamp fitted the best estimates for the time and the route which the Art Gang must have taken on their way to pegging out a naked, terrified student on the neatly-trimmed fairway at the twelfth hole. Horton's immediate target was the registration plates which had been designed to outwit the surveillance cameras. It was the kind of technical challenge that Horton seriously loved, another opportunity to try out the beta software applications that he had a knack of acquiring from his geeky industrial and research lab contacts. One look around Horton's door however answered Kerr's question for him.

'No luck yet Steve?' he asked regardless.

'Not yet, Mr Kerr, but I'll keep trying.'

Kerr nodded encouragingly. The plates were most probably faked in any case as well as unreadable. But he knew from experience not to curb Horton's enthusiasm. Even when he was working down the wrong track, Horton occasionally threw up a result that was worth knowing about. Horton's main current focus was trying to trace back to its source the electronic pathway which the gang had used to distribute their videos. Apparently he was stalled in that task for the time being. He needed to access Russian server logs to get any further but only ICU had the necessary authority to liaise with their counterparts in Moscow. ICU was the Internet Crime Unit, a specialist grouping which had been inside the NCIS, the National Criminal Intelligence Service, until the NCIS in turn had been swallowed by the newer, bigger supercop outfit, SOCA, the Serious Organised Crimes Agency. If you want to get ahead, get an acronym, old son – as Jacobson was fond of saying. Greg Salter had given the go-ahead locally but there was nothing more that Horton could do until ICU first of all acquired the necessary data, and, second of all, sent it on.

Kerr took the stairs down the rest of the way to the ground floor. It was ten past seven and there was nothing to prevent him from going home for an hour or so, helping his wife with the twins' bathtime, maybe grabbing a bite to eat himself. He took the old Wynarth road out of town, shoving the Fall on to the in-car: *Live At The Witch Trials*, one of half a dozen CDs he'd picked out at random the other morning, too sleepy and in too much of a hurry to make a more careful choice. The John Lee Hooker compilation had been the cream of the crop so far but by now he'd played it and replayed it to the burn-out point. He turned the volume up for 'Rebellious Jukebox'. He doubted if he'd listened to this stuff anytime in the last decade. Yet they'd been Cathy's favourite band when they'd first met. As a matter of fact they'd met at a Fall gig. He could still picture her that night, still recall their sudden, instant, mutual attraction. Starry-eyed and laughing – and spilling beer down each other's fronts in the jostling, sweaty crowd. But all that seemed a lifetime ago now. Before the kids, before the Bovis estate, before his extended (and extensive) cheating with Rachel. Before real life – as some liked to call it – had kicked in. When he reached the turn-off for the estate, he played the game he always played in his head when he was in this kind of mood, slowing right down, even signalling left. Only there was no traffic behind him anyway, or up ahead, so nothing prevented him speeding up again, killing the signal, driving straight on. He reached Wynarth in less than fifteen minutes, drove around the market square and found a parking space. He drank a bottle of Beck's in the lounge bar of the Wynarth Arms and then a second one in the wine bar nearby. Neither place was all that busy and he didn't linger in either. The pub would get a lot busier in an hour or so of course thanks to the well-publicised 'secret gig' that was scheduled there for later tonight. There would even be a couple of Operation Icarus officers in attendance, just on the off chance. One of Rachel's friends – the one called Judy, he thought – was in the wine bar with another woman that Kerr didn't recognise. She'd seen him come in, he was sure of it, but she looked right through him whenever he'd cast a glance in her direction. Entirely as if he wasn't there. The oriental crafts shop where Rachel sometimes worked when she was short of cash was down at the end of the narrow alley next to the wine bar. It would definitely be closed at this time in the evening so Kerr risked a look when he was back outside. The window display had barely altered since the last time he'd seen it, maybe a month or so ago (another furtive after-hours visit). Half a dozen Tai Chi figurines in different shadow boxing poses. Fans. Lanterns. A kite shaped like a giant butterfly. Taped on to a corner of the window near the doorway was one of Rachel's business cards advertising her feng shui 'consultancy'. The card was a new development anyway. Kerr checked that she hadn't changed her mobile number, noticed that according to the wording she even had a website these days. Stuff was going on in her life, stuff that apparently didn't concern him any longer. He walked back to his car, fighting the impulse to take a walk down Thomas Holt Street where her flat was. A policeman could go anywhere and usually find some justification for being there. But the daft game he was playing came with its own daft rules. Thomas Holt Street was out of his self-imposed bounds; for him to be there would make him feel too much like a stalker for his mental comfort zone. What he *was* allowing himself to do – drive over to Wynarth now and again in odd free hours, browse in the antique shops or, as he'd just done, call in somewhere for a quick drink – wasn't that. Not in his opinion anyway. If he ran into her like this it would just be a matter of chance, coincidence, something she couldn't find fault with. Wynarth wasn't a big place and this way, sooner or later, they'd both be at the same spot and at the same time. Then, maybe, finally, she'd let him explain, at least listen all the way through. Just one chance, that was all he was asking for. She ignored him if he phoned her or sent a text, so what the hell else could he do? Other than forget her – and he hadn't achieved that yet.

Mercifully, he suddenly remembered something work-related that he'd forgotten. He called up Sergeant Ince in the Control Room: could somebody in Ince's team check progress on the car hire angle? There were three separate traffic divisions involved in that part of the operation and Kerr, like Jacobson, was concerned that information didn't get lost, or turn up late, due to the different, conflicting ways of working inside three separate bureaucracies. The Fall came back on when he turned the ignition: 'Futures and Pasts'. But he didn't listen to them for long, had to switch them off before he reached the outskirts of the village, heading back in the Crowby direction. Not all the music you'd ever liked stayed with you for ever. You didn't listen for a long time and then one day you discovered that some music didn't seem to have someone like you in mind any more.

January Shepherd dressed down for gigs. Tonight: blue jeans, biker chick belt, Day of the Dead T shirt. There was a wall-size mirror along one side of the big rehearsal room which Dad had kitted out in the west wing of the building even though he rarely picked up an instrument these days. He'd had a whole suite purpose-built over here in case the mood ever found him again. A recording studio. Video facilities. A full set of instruments. State-of-the-art sound-proofing. She clocked her image, pouted at the mirror over her guitar. *sotreuM sol ed aiD lE*, the T shirt read across her chest: *El Dia De Los Muertos*. Not quite yet actually, she thought. Still a month or so away. They'd be in London by then – or maybe off somewhere on the continental leg. She ran through the opening number again and then played a few jazz scales to stretch her fingers nicely although there was no need really: she was as practised for tonight as she needed to be, almost perfectly on the right side of under-rehearsed – the spot where the nervy adrenalin rush helped the music soar. When she felt ready, she put the Stratocaster back in its case, checked she had a spare set of strings in the side pocket. The guitar was vintage; according to Dad it had once belonged to BB King's cousin. He'd given it to her as a present on her sixteenth birthday. When he'd finally grasped that she was serious about learning, that nothing he could do or say was going to talk her out of it. She took out her mobile, called Nick up at last. The rest of the band were booked in at the Riverside Hotel. Dad had invited every-body to stay out at Boden Hall of course. But Nick and a couple of the others had been funny about it. When the best-known thing about a new, hungry-for-success band was its connection to a rock legend (or a rock dinosaur, if you took a different point of view), the standard advice was either to embrace the fact to the hilt or to completely play it down.

So far Alice Banned had tried for a middle path between those two extremes that was actually pleasing or suiting none of them very much. Nick listed the running order for the first six numbers. January's voice shrugged down the phone: *Yeah, OK, whatever, see you there*. She picked up her guitar case and stepped into the long corridor that led back to the main part of the house. It was only a warm-up gig anyway, she was thinking, not part of the official tour. All the same they'd got out some solid word-of-mouth publicity locally and via the internet. The gig would be the biggest thing the Wynarth Arms had seen in a long time, that was for sure, and there would be at least one London journalist in the crowd. Another thing that worried Nick of course was that apparently there was a rumour buzzing in the music chat rooms that January's dad was considering a guest appearance, that the fabled father-daughter workout would at last be replicated on a British stage. She'd told him there was no chance, no danger, of that happening. But Nick had worried about the prospect all the same.

Dad and Kelly were ensconced by the indoor pool. Dad could spend whole hours there. Alternating between bouts of his clumsy, precarious dog paddle and the endless telephone conversations to his business associates which he'd conduct from the poolside. Right now, he was stretched out on a recliner while Kelly dried his back with a big pink towel. Kelly was OK as far as January was concerned. Dark-haired and waif-like. Indistinguishable, pretty much, from her predecessors except that January suspected her of being brighter, more clued-in, than she let on. They'd been together six months or thereabouts. On January's calculations that meant she had another year, maybe another eighteen months, before she'd go the same way they did. A nice chunk of hush money would be paid into an account of her choice if she promised not to talk to the tabloids. And if she smiled sweetly while she was packing, he'd probably let her keep her car and the jewellery as well. She smiled non-committally at both of them as she passed.

'Break a leg,' Dad shouted encouragingly, holding up a glass and waving it at her.

Started on tonight's brandies already, January thought. It was supposed to be one of the things he was working on since he'd moved back to the UK – giving it up. But so far January had seen precious little sign of it. Kelly left his side for a moment, walked over and held a wrist band up to January's free hand. Wispy, bound strands of coloured cloth. January let her slip it on, knowing full well she'd discard it before she went on stage. Kelly told her it was for good luck and that she'd bought it in one of the New Age shops in Wynarth: they were supposed to be made by the monks in Dharamsala or something.

'Thanks, Kelly,' she said, wanting to get away really.

Kelly asked her if she'd be coming back to Boden Hall after the gig or whether she'd be partying all night with the rest of the band at the Riverside Hotel.

'Hey, we're Alice Banned, not Spinal Tap,' January replied, laughing. 'I'll probably just have a couple of drinks, unwind a bit, and then head home.'

Perry brought the Mercedes round to the top of the driveway. He offered to take the guitar for her but January insisted on placing it in the boot herself. Perry was OK too and likely to be around a lot longer than Kelly. Perry was six four, broad shouldered, ex-SAS and before that ex-minor public school. January could never remember which one. Minder just wasn't an apt enough description. Handholder, bribe payer, fixer, smoother of paths. Everywhere Dad went, Perry went too. Taking care of business, keeping problems at a distance, keeping trouble firmly out of the equation. She'd argued with Dad about it earlier. She'd be travelling with the band on the rest of the tour, taking no special precautions. So why put Perry to the bother for just one night? And in Wynarth of all places. What the hell was going to happen there? They'd be playing London next month – and Munich, Paris, Rome. Places where stuff did happen. There'd been the news story about the abducted girls of course. But in reality that had nothing to do with her or the way she lived her life. What were they going to do? Snatch her off the stage in front of two hundred people? Dad had just smiled in that stubborn way of his: *while you're under my roof, Jan.* He'd really said that! Playing at the Victorian pater familias and seeming to enjoy the pretence so much that in the end January had just gone along with it. It would be easier than driving over there herself anyway. And it wouldn't do Perry any harm to get off the estate for an hour or two instead of cooping himself up in the coach house with his martial arts videos or whatever else it was he passed the time with in the evenings. She phoned Nick again, stepping into the merc, checked what time the rest of the band would be arriving at the venue, told him that she thought she'd probably get there about the same time they would.

Chapter Nineteen

Kerr still didn't feel like going home, still didn't need to be anywhere near the Divisional building. He remembered his dad all of a sudden, the resolve he'd had to see him earlier in the week. He took the quickest route from his current location, cut over from the Wynarth Road to the North Crowby bypass, completed the journey inside twenty minutes. John Kerr still lived on the Beech Park estate in the ex-council house that had been the family home when his wife was still alive and his son and his daughter were still kids. He'd resisted buying the property ('stealing the assets of the people' in his words) until the council had been in the process of selling on the running of its dwindling housing stock to a private management company. He'd suffered a mild stroke last winter and, although the doctors had claimed he'd made good progress since then, both the father and the son were more worried about the situation than either of them was prepared to admit to the other. But at least there'd seemed to be no permanent damage to his speech or his mental processes. Kerr knew that the one thing his dad feared more than anything else was losing his mind, blunting the sharp intellect that had made him a life-long free thinker and dissenter.

Kerr parked up and rapped on the door, waited for the sound of no-longer swift footsteps shuffling in the hall. Kerr had tightened up the old man's security recently, had upgraded his locks, installed a fish-eye lens in the door and fitted a couple of safety chains. The Beech Park was still a nice enough area, full of the decent, everyday, hard-working families his dad had once believed would inherit the earth and make it good. But it still didn't make sense for an old bloke living on his own, and long past his physical prime, to take any needless chances.

He followed his dad through to the kitchen where, as ever, there was stewed tea ready and waiting. Kerr poured a cup for himself and topped up his dad's Che Guevara mug, one of a set which Kerr Senior had proudly acquired in the Museum of the Revolution on a trip to Havana a couple of years back. John Kerr had never approved of his son's choice of occupation but had almost learned to live with it over time. Or he had done until recently: the 'War on Terror' (always prefixed by 'so-called' in his usage), and the big increase in UK police powers which it had been used to justify, had reawakened a lot of his old anger and disappointment about his son.

'You're working on this video gang case, then?' his dad asked.

Kerr nodded.

'Jacobson's worried that the whole thing's escalating out of control. Each incident seems to be getting worse than the one before.'

'I'm surprised you haven't caught them yet, I must say. All that CCTV surveillance – and the buggers are even sending you their own film records.'

Kerr sipped at the over-strong tea.

'We'll get them all right. It's just a matter of time until they slip up somewhere. What beats me is *why* they're doing it – what the point of it all is?'

'When you live in a decadent, purposeless society, Ian, lad, you're always going to get bad people doing meaningless things – just to stave off the boredom of their empty, useless lives.'

Kerr didn't rise to the bait. I just wanted to see you, you old bugger, he thought. I am *not* going to have a political argument.

'There was that Leopold and Loeb case years ago in America, as I recall,' John Kerr added. 'A couple of rich, spoilt bastards carried out a motiveless murder – just for the experience of it, they said. Old Alfred Hitchcock made it into a movie.'

'Yeah, I think I've seen that one on TV,' Kerr commented neutrally.

He didn't mention the murder scenes he'd attended out at the Woodlands. One time last year a schoolkid over there had been torched to death for his trainers and his iPod. The old man would have his answer for all that anyway: if you herded people together like unwanted animals, told them they *were* unwanted animals, then you shouldn't be too surprised when they acted like it.

The conversation stalled for a while then turned to other, less contentious matters. Cathy. The twins. Kerr promised they'd all come over to see him soon, maybe all head out for a day together somewhere. He found himself staring at the old family picture which his dad had framed and hung on the wall behind the kitchen table. The beach at Minehead. His mum in her swimming costume, reclining on a beach towel; Kerr throwing a beach ball at his sister, Rosie. John Kerr was nowhere to be seen, had presumably been the one who'd taken the shot.

'Heard from Rosie recently?' he asked him.

Kerr's sister was a schoolteacher in Glasgow. The good child. The one who shared some of the parental world-view.

'Aye. She's taken to phoning me every week, wants to make sure I'm all right most probably. She keeps saying she wants me to go up there for a while. She says she's got plenty of room in her new place. A spare bedroom and everything.'

'Maybe you should think about that,' Kerr said, 'maybe just for a break anyway, treat it like a holiday.'

'I'm too busy right now, Ian. This campaign against ID cards? I've said I'll speak at the rally they're organising over in Birmingham.'

The old man poured himself out a refill, asked if Kerr wanted a top-up.

'No thanks, Dad. I should probably get a move on, check in at the Divi.'

He'd planned on staying another ten minutes or so. But no way was he going to get involved in a discussion about ID cards. For one thing, he wasn't even sure that his dad wasn't actually right on that particular issue.

'Aye, of course,' John Kerr said, 'good to see you anyway.'

They shook hands in the hallway. The old man came from a place and a generation where real men didn't hug, didn't embrace. But between a father and a son even a brusque handshake had its own eloquent meaning.

Jacobson opened an Australian Shiraz and poured out a generous glassful while his sad bastard meal spun around inside the microwave: Sainsbury's Rogan Josh, serves one to two. He checked under the grill for the progress being made by a recently-defrosted Peshwari naan bread. It looked very nearly ready so he set out a place for himself at his kitchen table. When everything was prepared, he sat down to eat with Radio 4 on a low volume in the background, some fairly tedious programme about the economic prospects for the European Union. The kind of thing you didn't really listen to, that you put on just for the sake of having the sound of human voices around you. Alison had phoned him practically as soon as he'd got through the door to cancel their planned evening together. There were sudden staff problems at the hotel and the only way she'd been able to solve them, at least for tonight, was to take over the evening shift at the reception desk herself. She'd mentioned that she'd be finished by midnight if he still wanted to meet her back at her flat then but Jacobson had declined the offer. He'd read the wariness in her voice as she'd made the suggestion, knew that she'd be exhausted after the extra shift, that probably what she'd really want to do later would be just to get home and get straight off to sleep.

He poured himself a second glass after he'd washed up and he carried it through with him to his lounge. He was looking into Daniel Dennett these days, trying to work out whether he was prepared to buy any of Dennett's theories about mental processes or not. He'd thought that maybe he'd spend another couple of hours with the philosopher's immodestly titled book, *Consciousness Explained*. If Dennett had been British, instead of a classically brash American, Jacobson always reckoned he would have called his tome something more along the lines of *Consciousness: A Few Tentative Preliminary Remarks*. But now, when it actually came to it, the whole idea seemed like an extremely poor substitute for Alison's blond, curvy, seductive company. He flicked through the TV channels for five minutes or so. None of them remotely grabbed his attention and most of them positively repelled it. Inevitably – so inevitably that he felt he was virtually watching himself as if he was a fly on his own wall – he mooched out into the hall and came back with his stuffed-full briefcase: copies of witness statements, Jim Webster's initial reports, his own notes, the DVD that Steve Horton had made for him containing the complete footage of the Art Gang's four movies. He shoved Horton's disc into his player, finally got it working at the third attempt, settled down to watch each film closely from beginning to end. He'd seen them before of course, as had all the key officers on the cases, yet he knew from experience that there was no such thing as over-familiarity with evidence. The gang obviously knew what they were about, had edited each film carefully – but that didn't mean that there wasn't some small detail somewhere that they'd overlooked or hadn't noticed; something that would bring Crowby CID down on them like a ton of bricks.

He watched the footage of the four incidents one after the other and then he played each film all the way through again in turn, pausing the screen frequently and more or less randomly – in the hope that in one frame or another, something would strike him that no one had noticed before. He still couldn't understand *why* the gang had wanted to guarantee maximum publicity for themselves in this way. They'd sent their handiwork to all the major TV channels and truncated versions of each film had been shown on all the national news programmes. So far the TV stations had cooperated with the police. They'd pixelated over the faces of the victims and hidden their naked flesh, had followed police advice about how much – and precisely what segments – of the footage to show. Nonetheless, the gang had made nationwide prime time when, if they hadn't communicated with the media, it was doubtful if the incidents would have been reported outside the region. He finished off his glass of Shiraz, contemplated a third, decided against it for now. He'd watch the films a third time, he decided, then recharge his glass, then reread his way through the paperwork. He'd started to notice that although the gang clearly had four members, three of them were onscreen far more than the fourth. The one called 'Adrian' – according to Tracey Heald's original testimony – was only rarely seen, suggesting that he was the main camera operator and maybe the technical wizard in other ways. Tracey Heald had also described how 'Brady' was the one who'd seemed to be in charge, doling out orders to the others. It was always worth thinking about the relationship between a group of lawbreakers, what their hierarchy was, who had the power, who didn't. It was something you could exploit to your advantage once it got to custody, interviews and potential charges. Right now, though, custody and charges seemed a long, long way off. Right now, the gang was still out there somewhere, unmolested – and probably preparing for their next attack.

He paused the screen again, changed his mind about delaying his third glass, padded back through to his kitchen where he'd left the bottle. He decided he might as well have a B&H as well while he was about it. Recently, Alison had floated the notion of them both seriously quitting, giving up together. Jacobson knew she was right, knew that his endless 'cutting down' was hopeless, ineffectual. One of these days they should just get up in the morning and go cold turkey; chuck both their latest packets away for good. But so far, that brave new morning hadn't arrived. He was out in the hall again, searching in his jacket pocket for his silver lighter, when he realised that something else puzzled him about the Art Gang. Each of their victims had been stripped naked, but otherwise none of them had been subjected to any kind of serious sexual assault. Yet the psychology displayed in the movies, particularly from 'Brady', seemed to be a lot about control, about bending someone completely to his will. It was a rapist's profile without actual physical rape. Jacobson couldn't see what that meant yet. But he made sure that he committed the thought to his memory. He was prepared to believe that it was a significant element: maybe the most significant he'd uncovered so far.

Brady sat back at his ease on an armchair near the bed while Maria unpacked his clothes and put them away neatly. Socks and pants into the chest of drawers. Jackets, shirts and trousers onto hangers and then carefully into the wardrobe. There was a right way and a wrong way with clothes as far as Brady was concerned and Maria had at last learnt (the hard way) the essentials of the approved method. Jackets arranged by quality, shirts by colour spectrum, trousers categorised and divided into suit, chino and jean. When she was through, he told her he needed a cup of tea, sent her down to the kitchen to make it. After she'd gone, he glanced through the window into the garden. Despite the half moon and the cloudless sky, there was no longer enough light to make out very much of the long, straight lawn or the floral borders, dead at this time of year in any case, or the garden's low, drystone walls. Just before the front gate, there was the ruin of what had once been a fishpond. The water, when you could see it, was a dark, unwholesome green and there was a crumbling, lichen-clad statue at its side. Pandora, from the old myth, with her box of troubles at her feet. He'd noticed earlier that the tip of her nose was missing and that the top slice had fallen off her left breast.

There'd been no kind of statue in the front garden at home of course. That would have been too fancy, not remotely plain enough. But that was Mum and Dad for you, with their mad religion, forever intent on über-drabness and anti-pleasure. He'd been a 1980s child, still learning to walk while Mrs Thatcher bashed the Argies and the miners. But his parents had been throwbacks. No television, no cinema, no Christmas idolatry, no bringing friends to the house who were non-believers: a category which ruled out every single other kid at school or in the neighbourhood. The sect was small, no more than a couple of hundred families scattered across the south-east counties and you only ever met other sect children in rigorously supervised circumstances. The fact that it was so small was probably what had saved Brady, if he *had* been saved. It couldn't run or support its own schools and his dad's pathetically lower-middle class income didn't amount to much. He'd clerked morosely for years in the borough housing department, couldn't remotely fund any idea of sending Brady off somewhere to receive a suitably austere private education. His mother *couldn't* work of course, couldn't earn, couldn't be allowed to parade around like a harlot in public. So Brady had escaped seven hours a day to the local primary and then to the local comp. That hadn't been easy either, excluded from assemblies and religious instruction, spat at and bullied as a weirdo until he'd grown big enough to fight back. But at least it had given him some kind of perspective, some kind of knowledge of how the rest of the world lived. He'd walked out of home for ever on the morning of his sixteenth birthday, a July day during the school holidays, his first day of legal semi-adult-hood. There had been a girl by then of course, a girl he'd had to meet furtively before he'd slung his hook. At the school gates, at dinner breaks, and on the sacred afternoons they'd bunk off together. She'd been a bit of a slapper really, loose, easy, and so had her mother and, probably, her mother before that. But that had been all right, hadn't bothered him. When he'd left home, they'd even let him move in to their council gaff for a while, where the telly was always on and you could eat what you liked, go to bed when you liked, drink, smoke and drop what you liked. It had been a heat-wave the first few weeks he'd stayed there but Brady had remained indoors, glued to the big TV screen, watching and re-watching every video on the premises, rewinding scenes, studying them and inching through them in slo-mo. He'd got junior Macjobs to pay his way of course and carried on with his studies, taking his A-levels via evening classes, forging his dad's crimped, spidery signature on his student-loan form when he'd got the offer of a place at Bristol.

He turned away from the window consciously, deliber-ately. He looked at the face of his genuine Rolex, courtesy of a non-genuine MasterCard, realised that it was a lot later than he'd thought. He hated it when this happened, when he ran into some unwanted association of ideas that kick-started his memory in the wrong direction. He decided to go downstairs himself, check up on the others, make sure they'd be ready on time. The ceiling out on the hallway was low and the floorboards creaked with nearly every step. So did the old wooden staircase. Maria already had his cup of tea ready. There was a full-size Aga up and running in the kitchen and it was a matter of seconds to boil the old-fashioned copper kettle. It was something the property agent had promised – that they'd fire up the Aga ready for them coming, generally get the place warmed through and rendered spick and span. Brady sat down at the solid oak table and asked Maria snappily where the hell Annabel and Adrian were.

'Annabel's having a bath. I think Adrian's probably still unpacking in his room,' she answered him, stirring in the milk and then placing the cup and saucer before him.

'Well go and tell them I need them down here inside ten minutes,' Brady said.

Maria nodded compliance in the exaggeratedly demure way he'd taught her – practically curtsying – then was gone again.

As far as possible, he never thought about his childhood. When you've already lived through crap, why relive it in your mind over and over again to no good purpose? But it still crept up on him in dreams and in odd, unguarded moments like this one. What he hated most of all was the dreary, tedious, *obviousness* of his case: how the way he acted now mirrored how he'd been treated then. He envied Annabel and her originality in that respect. Her parents had been laid-back, sandal-wearing old hippies yet she'd still turned out with tastes like his own. But at least he lived in the twenty-first century, when identities were fluid, no longer fixed; when you could deconstruct your past, reconfigure yourself, remake and remodel. The project was therapy ultimately. Live it, act it, be it. There had been a cellar under the hall. Not old or interesting or anything like that. More like a sunken box room really. There had been a single, naked light bulb dangling from the ceiling and neatly stacked boxes of old clothes and dismal assorted household objects lined up against the walls. It was where his mother sent him when he was 'naughty' – for any of a hundred and one weird and wonderful 'infringements' that had made no sense to him, that as often as not contradicted each other. She'd tricked him the first time she'd locked him in there. *Jesus is a poof,* he'd told her one day when he'd been six or seven, no idea of what he was saying, repeating something an older kid had told him at school (had told him while he'd been ducking his head violently into a sink full of cold, running water in the boys' toilets). She hadn't even looked angry, had just asked him to go into the cellar for her, had told him there was a box in there she needed to get something out of. He'd trotted in there happily, a little boy pleasing his mum, being careful to switch on the light before he'd gone down the few, narrow stairs – the light that you could only switch on and off from the outside. He'd no idea how long she'd kept him in there that first time. Or any of the many, subsequent times really. How can you measure time when you're a kid? A week, a day, even just an hour, can pass as slowly as a lifetime. All that Brady knew, and wished he could forget, was that he'd gone into the cellar as one kind of potential adult, had come out again as another kind altogether.

He sipped at his tea, forced his mind firmly back to the present moment. He studied the idiotic horse brasses the moronic owners had hung on the oak beams. They were living in Andalucia now apparently (probably in a house full of castanets and sombreros, Brady thought). Or at least that was what the agent had told Annabel and Adrian when they'd first viewed the place in their newly-married couple disguise.

Brady reckoned the cottage was another stroke of genius, just like the Volvo. A couple of overly-romantic newlyweds taking on a year's rental, not a solo yuppie taking on the six months he'd arranged in Crowby or the three months Maria had fixed up in Birmingham. Best of all was the fact that it *was* a cottage: a restored farm labourer's gaff at the end of a dirt track in the middle of bloody nowhere. The whole project, practically speaking, was about confounding expectations. Setting up apparent patterns and then breaking them, going off the wall, thinking outside the box, taking advantage of the fact that the police were simpletons. Fine when they could put the boot in to some hapless junked-out burglar in a hoodie. Totally out of their fucking depth whenever it came to anybody with sufficient class, imagination and intelligence. Knowing what was to come, Brady could almost feel sorry for them. Except, of course, that he didn't do empathy. Not for the longest time.

Chapter Twenty

Casper had his hunting party together at last – thanks mainly to help from Mad Billy Briers. There were six of them all told. Four blokes. Two birds. Casper had reckoned that having a couple of women involved was crucial. They could talk to any prat who was suspect, maybe act as bait where necessary. Otherwise you needed some lads who could handle themselves in a scrape. Casper was no fighter himself, not really. But that didn't matter when you had Mad Billy with you plus two of Mad Billy's closest mates, Kenny and Dave. Kenny in particular was a nasty piece of work to come up against in any kind of ruck. He was only skin and bones to look at but the guy was hard, completely fearless. He just didn't give a fuck about getting hurt himself and that was what always gave him the edge. Tracey had wanted to come out with them too. But Casper had pointed out two reasons to her why that just wouldn't work. One: she still needed to rest up, take care of herself, take it easy for a while. Two: it was possible that the bastards they were after wouldn't remember Casper too well, but they'd remember Tracey all right, would clear out sharpish from anywhere where she put in an appearance.

They cruised into town in Dave's work van. Dave had got a proper job recently, doing deliveries for a car spares outlet, and one of the perks was that he got to use the van in his spare time. It wasn't big – one of those little Fords with the short wheelbase – but the girls squeezed on to the passenger seat and Casper, Kenny and Mad Billy squeezed into the back. The main thing about the van was that it wasn't a stolen, wouldn't draw police attention to them. It wasn't the kind of consideration that normally bothered him but – as he'd said to Mad Billy earlier – this shit was serious; it meant taking precautions and measures, it wasn't about having a laugh as per usual. They were going to *get* these bastards, teach them a lesson they wouldn't forget in a hurry.

Dave parked at the top of Silver Street, where there were no parking charges in the evening if you were lucky enough to find a space. That was part of the plan too – a central location and, again, no danger of the van coming to the wrong kind of attention. They walked down to the corner of the High Street together and then split up as they'd agreed. The girls – Mad Billy's girlfriend, Leslie, and her mate, Stacey – were headed for Club Zoo to start off with. Kenny and Dave would try the new Wetherspoon's on Flowers Street while Casper and Mad Billy would basically pub crawl from one end of town to the other, concentrating on the ponce bars they'd normally avoid like the plague; places that fitted with the profile of the crew they were after. Casper had been pleased with that – 'profile' – had picked the word up from one of the TV reports, had used it when he'd been explaining the plan to the others. Billy and Casper headed into the Brewer's Rest. Casper didn't see it as the most likely venue but it was still one that they'd put on the list. Casper, obviously, had the most likely chance of spotting one of the gang if any of them were out and about in Crowby but the others had studied the e-fits and the CCTV images too. Plus they'd agreed to all stay in touch via their mobiles. Casper waded through the crowd of suits at the bar – as well as coppers the place was popular with all kinds of poncy, well-paid types – and got the first round in while Mad Billy grabbed a table which would give a good view in all directions. It was just exactly the way he'd told that copper on the Sunday morning: those bastards had better pray the police got to them before the boys from the Woodlands did.

*

January always liked a shot of Jack Daniel's before a gig. It was the corniest, retro-ist thing – she knew that – but it was also part of the great rock and roll tradition. Nick was drinking a half-pint of weak, English draught lager while the rest of the band shared a couple of bottles of white wine and a couple of mild, almost pointless spliffs. The Wynarth Arms' green room was on the first floor of the building, directly above the stage – so that the bass reverb of the support band thumped right under your feet. It also made the floor vibrate more than you felt it should – as if the whole structure was about to fall down at any minute. Nobody was saying very much, just sorting themselves out mentally for the gig, each in their own way. Perry sat on his own in a corner, nursing a glass of mineral water and listening intently to something on his MP3 player. Whatever it was, January thought, it probably wasn't Alice Banned and it probably wasn't anything by her dad either.

Nick started fussing about the set-list again, mentioned that maybe 'Screwed Up' wasn't the best opener after all.

'"Screwed Up" is awesome, Nick, it hits it every time,' January said. 'Just relax, the gig's going to be great. As always.'

'Yeah, but this is England now, Jan. And tonight's the first time the band's ever played here—'

'Jesus, Nick. You're English, I'm English. It's what's great about what we do. California meets English Cool.'

The rest of the band – bass, drums and keyboards – were listening to the conversation now.

'And you're sure your old man's not going to show up? Turn the whole thing into a circus?' Nick asked, reverting to his other current topic of anxiety.

'He was getting rat-arsed by the pool the last I saw him, Nick. He's not coming anywhere near the place, believe me.'

'Relax, man,' Randy the drummer said, 'January's right. They're gonna love us here.'

'I hope so,' Nick replied – but left it at that, swallowed down the last of his beer.

The door opened: Richardson, the ageing rocker who ran the place, personally bringing in the tray of cheese and pickle sandwiches Randy had asked for half an hour earlier.

'Sorry for the delay, mate. It's pandemonium down there. We're packed out solid, turning 'em away at the door.'

'No sweat,' Randy answered, hungrily picking up two sandwiches at once as soon as Richardson had put the tray down.

'See? I told you it's going to be fine,' January said to Nick. 'I just know it's going to be one of those gigs – the kind you don't forget in a hurry.'

Nick didn't reply but at least he didn't argue either. He picked up his guitar again, still working on the new song he'd told her about earlier. He'd got the idea for it on the flight over from LA, he'd said. January poured herself another JD, watched him bent intently over the fretboard, trying to hear himself over the other band's music from downstairs. Nick drove her mad with his obsessive perfectionism, drove everybody mad with it. But the stuff that came out of his head and fingers compensated every single time.

Kerr caught up with Emma Smith in the CID Resource Centre, the open-plan office space allocated to the basic grade detective constables. DCS Salter had imposed a hot desking system a couple of years back that just about every single DC loathed. At busy times of the day you could easily find yourself stuffed for any access to a working computer, a working phone line or even just for a desk and chair to park your arse on. Nine o'clock on a Thursday night wasn't a problematic time though. Most of the duty shift were out and about pursuing cases and there was only a handful of other DCs currently using the room.

'Anything relevant yet?' he asked her.

DC Smith looked up from her computer screen. She'd

waded through most of the data that the Met had sent on about the three known north London identity theft victims – but so far there'd been no eureka moment.

'Not much that we didn't already know, guv,' she said. 'Two males, one female. All in their twenties. One guy's a medical doctor, the other one's a plumber. The woman, believe it or not, is a prison screw, works in Pentonville apparently. No criminal records, nothing that links them to each other. They don't live in the same local areas either.'

'Which could rule out any kind of organised data theft from their rubbish bins, at least,' Kerr commented.

'I reckon so, yes – assuming the gang are doing the hands-on work themselves, which they might very well not be. Once data gets nicked, it gets sold on – they could be coming in as purchasers a lot further up the chain. Or else working a computer-based scam of their own.'

'The Met actually got off their behind to talk to the victims then?'

Emma Smith waded through the wad of paperwork on her desk, found the faxed copies of the three statements, passed them to Kerr.

'I see that all three of them have got home computers anyway,' Kerr said, once he'd read his way through. 'They're all claiming to be careful about what they do online of course, all saying that they'd never be stupid enough to give out their personal details anywhere dodgy.'

'Nobody likes to look like an idiot though, do they, guv? And down in London not even doctors are necessarily keen to help the police.'

Kerr looked at the doctor's statement again. The personal details on the front sheet included an IC4 code, denoting a male of Afro-Caribbean origin. The Met claimed to be 'addressing' racism within its ranks. But out on the streets the problems persisted.

'That's a good point, Emma. Wasn't he the one they'd actually nicked into custody – before he was able to prove that he was nowhere near Crowby when the gang were having their fun with Tracey Heald?'

Emma Smith nodded.

'He's the one all right. They picked him up at six o'clock, Sunday night, didn't let him go until after midnight.'

'What about this, eh, Julia Dove woman though? The prison officer? You'd expect her to be better disposed towards the Old Bill.'

'Except that she *really* wouldn't want to admit to her stupidity if she's been duped by a computer scam or something like that. It would be like you or me being taken in, wouldn't it? Serious big red face time.'

Kerr's mobile rang. Sergeant Ince in the control room with his scheduled hourly operational update: no change, nothing new to report, nothing useful coming in so far from the pubs and clubs.

'Too bad we can't re-interview them ourselves,' Kerr said, after Ince had rung off. 'But we'd need permission from the Met. And you know how long that can take.'

'And that's assuming we actually get permission, guv.'

Kerr nodded, heading for the door. Among the many things that the supercilious London police force hated venomously were provincial coppers intruding directly on to their patch. If they couldn't refuse a request outright, their usual response was to stall you for as long as they could in the hope that you'd eventually give up.

He took the stairs down the two floors to Steve Horton's office. No progress there either – and Horton was pulling on his jacket, ready to clock off. It was gone nine and he'd already put in several hours over the odds for a non-shift civilian worker. Kerr waved goodnight, phoned Mick Hume while he took the rest of the stairs down to the ground level. Still nothing much doing: Hume and DC Williams had managed to speak to a couple of witnesses who'd been in Club Zoo on Saturday night and who hadn't been there again until tonight; they'd confirmed seeing 'Brady' and the two females leaving the premises with Tracey Heald in tow but hadn't really added anything significant to the picture which the inquiry team had already built up. Kerr walked out to the car park, found his Peugeot and climbed in. Jacobson would be back in action tomorrow morning but until then he was the one running the operation. Big deal. Being at the top of the food chain, he'd started to realise over the last couple of hours, really just meant spending a lot of time hanging around waiting for something to happen somewhere else. The foot soldiers took their orders from you and you made the major decisions: but only when there was something that needed a decision, only if and when the guys in the field turned up something new. No wonder Jacobson liked to get out and knock on doors himself, always did his own legwork as far as he could get away with it, didn't seem at all interested in crawling any further up the greasy career pole that led to a life of confinement inside a senior management office up on the eighth floor.

He started the engine. All of which left the question of what the hell he was going to do with the next couple of hours. Drive, he thought. Just drive. Maybe cruise around town and then out to the motorway and back. The Art Gang's white van had never been located, neither had either of the rented BMWs. It wasn't very likely that he'd run into them by chance when so far they'd managed to elude three traffic divisions. But at least he'd feel he was doing something useful – that he wasn't just a bored, spare prick waiting on the end of a phone line – and at least it would keep him well away from Wynarth, stop him from snooping creepily around there after Rachel.

Chapter Twenty-one

Even Nick had been pleased with the gig. Three encores, two and a half hours on stage, the crowd loving everything they did. They'd driven back to the Riverside Hotel afterwards, Perry following the band's big U-Haul transit in the merc. January had conspicuously travelled in the van with the others. Alice Banned had one roadie (who doubled as the driver) and one sound engineer. The band usually lugged as much kit in and out of the van as the roadie did. Or Randy the drummer and Alvin the bass player did anyway. January and Nick looked after their guitars and that was about as far as their contribution went. Melanie, the keyboard player – and the band's only other female member – had never been known to lug anything. But she knew about electronics, was able to help with setting up the mixing desk, at least did her bit that way.

The Riverside's late-night residents-only bar was fairly mobbed out with the delegates from some business convention or other. Luckily, there were two adjacent free tables left. Randy and Alvin shoved them together while the roadie negotiated the drinks round with a run-off-her-feet, stressed-out barmaid.

'Very rock and roll,' Nick had sneered, taking in the room full of business types, but everybody knew that he didn't mean it. He was too elated from the gig for one thing – and besides he was the least rock and roll musician that any of them knew. No drugs, no ciggies, virtually no alcohol. Richardson, the Wynarth Arms guy, had obviously enjoyed the gig too, had evidently wanted to throw a party for them over there. But Nick in particular hadn't been keen. There was the first official gig of the tour coming up tomorrow night and there was still the jet-lag issue, he'd told him. None of them had been in the UK for more than a few days, none of them had fully adjusted yet to the time difference or to the absence of proper sunlight. All of that was true enough, January had thought, but she knew that the real reason was that the music journalist from London had hung around after the gig too. January and Nick had been happy enough to talk to her until she'd mentioned the performance they'd done in LA last year where January's dad had infamously shown up on stage – and had proved unwilling to get back off again. It had been his first public appearance in more than a decade. It was also a topic guaranteed to piss off Nick. January knew that, as far as he was concerned, Alice Banned was exclusively about his songs and her songs – and nothing at all to do with an old fart who he regarded as being over the hill and musically irrelevant.

Around about one AM, January decided to call it a night. Randy, Alvin and Melanie looked liked they were settled there for a while yet, swapping their seemingly endless stocks of George Bush jokes and generally unwinding. She kissed Nick before she left. A real kiss, full on the mouth. They'd been lovers for a while when they'd first met. Something that hadn't lasted. Except that sometimes she'd look at him and see what she'd first seen. An intense, un-tall, slightly built Englishman in a tanned sea of Californians. A feeling like coming home.

By the time she'd said goodnight to all of them, Perry had already brought the merc up from the Riverside's parking level, had it ready and waiting outside the main entrance. She got into the back, knew he hated it if she tried to sit in the front passenger seat. Perry drove off, politely silent behind the wheel as ever. You experienced a good gig three times, she thought. There was the anticipation before the event.

There was the actual performance – and then there was the memory of it replaying in your mind afterwards. 'Screwed Up' was becoming their anthem, she realised. They'd started the gig with it, had played it again for their final encore. It was eighty per cent Nick's number. Except that the thing that made it truly fucking great was the solid thunder of the riff and the chorus. *Her* riff and chorus. The kind where you could be completely drug-free and the music would still make you see a horde of manic green devils dancing on top of the amps and speaker cabinets.

Brady fidgeted with the Volvo's radio on low volume. He tried half a dozen stations, eventually gave up and switched it off. He admitted to himself that he felt nervous. Not about their ability to do it, to carry it through, of course. He *knew* that they could. What worried him was whether there'd be the opportunity.

A lot of things could still go wrong. The main one being that there was no guarantee January Shepherd would definitely return to Boden Hall tonight. The rest of the musicians were staying at the Riverside Hotel and it was always possible that she'd be spending the night there with one of them. There'd been a rumour about her and Nick Bishop for a while. And even if that connection had come to an end, females in bands were notoriously sexed-up and notoriously incestuous. Sooner or later, so Brady believed, they'd get around to sleeping with just about everybody they played with.

Obsessively, he rechecked that his mobile was switched on and ready for use. The time window was tiny and they'd have to work bloody fast. Yet at least they could be sure that they were in exactly the right place if the moment did arise. She *had* to come past here: regardless of whether she came directly from Wynarth or via the Riverside Hotel or via anywhere else. On the final stretch, there was only one way in and out of the Boden Hall estate. The route out from

Crowby took longer than the route from Wynarth but it was over a better road that would be more likely to appeal to the driver. Bigger. Well lit. Cameras at intervals. If the guy knew what he was about as a bodyguard, and there was no reason to believe that he didn't, then that would surely be his route of choice. Out in the open. Seeing and being seen. Yet once you were within two miles of Boden Hall itself all of that changed. The estate was high-walled and gated, was finally accessible only by means of a security-monitored, strictly private road. But before you could get that far, the only option was along this way: a twisting B road through a stretch of Forestry Commission woodland, all of it on open access to the public. Nature trails. Car parks. Picnic tables. Roadside pull-ins. Tedium of a high degree – but useful on this occasion.

Brady eased the mask away from his face for a moment, needing to feel the sensation of cool air directly on his skin. They'd all be masked up this time. His decision naturally. He'd told the others it would sow another seed of confusion for the boys in blue. He'd got Maria to run them up, adapting ordinary woollen balaclavas she'd bought in a branch of Millets. This season's new look, terrorist chic, he thought, laughing to himself at his own joke – but keeping his gaze focused in the right direction. He'd parked off-road near a sharp bend, had squeezed the Volvo as far back as he could into a gap in the trees where it looked as if intermittent logging had been taking place. The merc would have to slow down as it passed by the spot, enabling him to make a positive ID. Half a mile up ahead, Adrian, Annabel and Maria were already in position – waiting for the call. *His* call naturally.

Perry drove out of Crowby on full professional alert, automatically scanning every car that came near them for signs of anything unusual and anticipating the road ahead as far as he could see. He'd worked for John Shepherd for eight years now, had been thinking of resigning for most of them. But Shepherd's generous salary was difficult to give up. So was travelling the world in premier class. So was spending half the day maintaining his fitness regime at Shepherd's expense. Too bad that a lot of the job was what he classified as 'dirty': maintaining Shepherd in his rich man's bubble, shielding him from the bad consequences of his frequent bad judgement calls. Which was why he had no problem whatsoever with driving Shepherd's daughter to and from the Wynarth Arms, hadn't looked down on the task as something beneath his dignity. This was the 'clean' part of what he did. Security. Close body protection. Keeping people safe in an unsafe world. Something he could feel good about.

He clocked her in the mirror now and again. She looked lost in her own thoughts – but lit-up, happy. They were supposed to fuck you up, your mum and dad. Shepherd and his second wife had done their level best by all accounts: rows, histrionics, booze, drugs, adultery, devotion to bogus therapists and crazy cults. Yet for all of that, Shepherd's daughter seemed to have turned out just fine. Dedicated to her music but no kind of prima donna. A nice girl really. Far, far nicer than Shepherd deserved. Perry applied the central locking discreetly as soon as the car reached the little forest that meant they were on the home stretch. The twists in the narrow road slowed your progress, making this easily the most vulnerable part of their journey.

He saw something he didn't like on the third bend. What he thought might have been the glint of car metal in a clearing. He drove on carefully, calculating the odds. If it was a car – and if it wasn't trouble – then it was probably one of two things. A courting couple (albeit in an unusual location) or an accident. The latter possibility made it worth investigating. But only, he decided, as his second priority. He'd carry on for now, get January safely back to Boden Hall, and then he'd come back on his own, check it out properly.

*

Restlessly, Adrian transferred his mobile from his left hand to his right hand and back again. After the Coventry girl had been killed, he'd talked openly about giving up, about abandoning the project. Brady had dissuaded him. Or he'd let Brady dissuade him, which amounted to the same thing. *It changes nothing, Ade*, Brady had said. It had been an accident. That was all. Not their fault. And, besides, all four of them were in deep now, implicated. The only good way out for any of them was to see it through, to succeed. *It's sink or swim, Ade*. Adrian had agreed eventually, had told him he was right, had made sure that he'd kept his doubts to himself from then on. It wasn't so much what Brady had said as the tone in which he'd said it. The only good way out for *any* of them: but maybe, Adrian had inferred, especially in the case of the Johnny-come-lately, the sidekick, the technical add-on. Brady was an ambiguous friend, he warned himself, but he would make a completely unambiguous enemy. The mobile vibrated. He'd thought he was ready, entirely mentally prepared. But he still felt his stomach trying to leap through his throat. He pressed the answer key, was rewarded by Brady's terse instruction: *OK, that's it, you're on.*

He watched Maria rush the BMW out into the centre of the road, blocking it in both directions. She killed the engine, grabbed the keys, bolted behind the shelter of some kind of pine tree. She only just made it in time not to be seen. The brakes on the merc didn't screech but the vehicle was only bare inches away from the obstacle in its path when the driver managed to pull up. Adrian was hoping he would get out, take a look. That was the dream scenario, the one they'd all hoped for. But he knew that the driver might very well be smarter than that, might very well force them to use Plan B. And he was: Adrian saw the merc switch into sudden reverse, pulling smartly away from the danger zone.

Adrian already had the second beamer in gear, his feet over the pedals, only had to turn the ignition. He shot forward, knowing that there were only seconds left between success and failure. He was coming from the other side of the road to Maria so that at least the direct impact would hit him on the passenger side – plus he had the driver's door unlocked and open, ready for exit.

Bam.

Even when you were prepared for it, the noise of car on car stunned you, deafened you, was louder than you'd imagined it would be. He threw himself out into the road, didn't know if he'd reacted quickly or too slowly. The driver was out of the merc too by the time Adrian struggled to his feet. He was big, powerful – and running straight at him. Adrian sprinted towards the trees, telling himself desperately that he was lighter and faster, that he had the advantage in speed. The driver was on him of course before his back foot had even completely left the tarmac, grabbed him in some kind of skilled, painful, instantly immobilising hold. He felt a forearm like iron against his adam's apple and one single capable hand somehow controlling both of his own wrists behind his back. The guy marched him towards the first beamer, the one that had forced the merc to stop. He held Adrian at his mercy while he peered into the empty interior; then he marched him towards the merc just as January Shepherd clambered out of one of the bashed-in rear doors. She looked dazed but able to stand. No obvious cuts or bleeding. The driver pinned Adrian against the crumpled metal, turned his own face towards his shocked passenger.

'If you've got your phone handy, January, you'd best dial 999,' he said calmly, gently.

She was wearing a short leather jacket over a T shirt and jeans, started to fumble in one of the pockets. The driver grabbed the bottom of Adrian's balaclava mask, about to yank it off. Adrian, expecting them, heard the footfalls before he did. He looked beyond him and watched Annabel stepping out of the woodland. She was holding a Walther PPK in her right hand and pointing it straight ahead. She was holding it confidently: like she knew exactly what she was doing.

'You're phoning nobody, bitch,' she said. 'As for you, big boy, fucking take your fucking hands off my colleague.'

Chapter Twenty-two

January Shepherd looked terrified of the gun and her legs started to shake. The driver/bodyguard didn't. But he stepped away, let Adrian go. Annabel told them both to put their hands on their heads and to keep them there. She motioned with the gun for them to move into the woodland.

'You can still walk away from this – whatever it is – if you stop now,' the driver said, lifting his arms up but not moving from the spot, 'think about it.'

'She's telling you to move, fuckface,' Adrian said, standing next to Annabel now.

The guy was a professional all right, had probably worked out quickly that the longer they stayed where they were in the middle of the road, the more likelihood there was that they'd be seen or disturbed. The road didn't really lead anywhere in particular other than the Boden Hall estate and there wasn't very much chance of other traffic at this time of night. But there wasn't no chance at all.

'I'm betting you wouldn't really use that, love,' the driver said, ignoring Adrian, talking directly to Annabel.

Annabel aimed the gun ostentatiously away from him and turned it steadily towards January Shepherd.

'And I'm betting that you can't afford to take that bet,' she said. 'Now move it and keep it shut – both of you.'

The driver took a couple of slow, reluctant steps, indicated by a nod of his head that the girl should comply with the order also. But then they all heard the sound of an approaching car engine and he stopped in his tracks again.

Adrian looked anxiously along the road but the vehicle never materialised. Instead they heard it pull up somewhere just out of their line of sight, heard the engine switch off, heard the noise of a car door opening and then closing. Adrian was ninety-nine per cent certain that it was Brady getting out of the Volvo. His heart stopped pounding.

'Get a fucking move on,' he said, relieved. 'Who told you to stop?'

Now that there were two of them, as well as Annabel with the gun, no Kung Fu or SAS bollocks, or whatever the fuck it was, was going to help the bodyguard out of his predicament. Plus they had Plan C in reserve: Maria, still in hiding, with the second Walther.

Brady brought the cuffs with him. He snapped a pair quickly on to the girl and then Annabel grabbed her, shoving the gun barrel right into her back. No way could the fucker take any kind of risk with them now, Adrian reckoned. And sure enough, he lowered his arms, let Brady cuff them behind his back without any kind of struggle.

Adrian couldn't resist the impulse. He patted the side of the big man's face like an overbearing uncle. Then slapped him hard with the back of his hand.

Annabel shoved January Shepherd roughly forwards.

'Now fucking get into the fucking woods,' she said, still playing at exasperation.

Perry had been in tougher scrapes than this, he reminded himself. While you were still mobile, you still had a chance, still had options. He walked a little in front of January but not so far that he couldn't watch out for her. After a couple of minutes, the party arrived at an oak tree where a clean, new-looking rope had already been wound loosely around the trunk. The girl with the gun stopped maybe a foot away from him, pointed it at his head while the two males grabbed January and tied her to the tree. The one who'd turned up late picked up a roll of masking tape from somewhere on the ground, pressed a strip all the way across January's mouth. Perry noticed that there was still plenty of length left in the rope once they had her secured. This was it, he realised: last orders, put up or shut up. Otherwise, once they had him tied to the tree as well, he was finished – and, whatever they had planned, they'd be able to carry it out unimpeded.

He let the two males take him by an arm each. He couldn't think of them as *men*, they were too civilian for that, amateurish in some way that he didn't have time to define. The girl was behind him now, would still have the gun pointed in his direction. *Now or never*: he lunged to the left and then to the right, forcing then nearly off their feet as they struggled to keep hold of him. The girl knew something about guns – or was a very convincing actress – but he was gambling that she had neither the high skill nor the recklessness to take a pop at close range while her two cobastards were clinging desperately on to the target. He really swung them now, ramming one of them head first into the oak and flinging the other one effortlessly towards an extrahard collision with a near-by beech. *Go for the girl and the gun. Go for it now*. He dived low, underneath the aim she nearly had ready, head-butted her in the groin. She dropped the gun as she fell to the ground and Perry rolled towards it thinking that the cuffs wouldn't stop him from holding on to it at least. It was underneath his stomach when he rolled on to the spot. *Now turn on to my back, grab it.*

But then the first blow sent him into blackness.

Maria brought the butt of the Walther down three times on the back of his head, wasn't sure how hard you should do it, or how many times would be enough. She knelt over him warily. He was still breathing but he wasn't moving. You could see all right by the moonlight. But not details. She thought there was a trickle of blood through his neat haircut, didn't want to touch it and make certain though. When Brady and Adrian had recovered sufficiently they dragged him back across to the oak, sat him up against the trunk, tied a length of the rope around him. Brady and Adrian looked the worse for wear, Brady in particular. His jacket was ripped and he had a bleeding cut on the palm of his left hand where it had been torn by thorns. Annabel said she felt sick. She'd hurt her head too, had banged it on a stone when she'd been felled. Maria used the masking tape to bandage up Brady's hand as best she could, managed to stop the blood dripping any further on to the ground.

'Damage assessment later,' Brady said when he'd at last got his breath back, 'right now we need to complete.'

Adrian checked the masking tape and the cuffs on January Shepherd and Brady untied her. They passed her to Annabel and Maria who held her between them, one on each arm. Before they headed back to the road, Adrian brought out his torch and with Brady's one-armed assistance cleared what could be cleared from the scene: the tape, the two guns, Annabel's stick of lip gloss that must have fallen out of a pocket when she'd been felled.

When they reached the Volvo, Brady unlocked the boot. Annabel and Maria shoved the girl inside. There was just enough room for her once they'd forced her to curl up knees to chest. Brady left the masking tape over her mouth but passed his keys to Annabel, told her to undo the cuffs in case there was a circulation problem. They didn't wait to see the girl's reaction, just banged the lid shut as soon as the cuffs were off her.

Brady took his mask off. The others copied him.

'What about the bodyguard?' Adrian asked.

'We leave him where he is.' Brady replied.

'No, I mean do you think we should go back and tape his mouth as well?'

'No need – we'll be long departed before he comes round,' Brady replied again. *If he comes round* was on the tip of his tongue but he left it unsaid.

Annabel and Maria got into the back seats. Adrian and Brady walked back along the side of the road towards the two BMWs and the Mercedes S600. The second BMW and the merc were already in position, metal crunched into metal.

Adrian climbed into the first beamer, turned the ignition, did a smooth 3-point turn and brought it close alongside the other two. He unlocked the boot and switched the engine off again before he got out. Brady lifted the petrol carrier out one-handed and doused the contents liberally over all three cars.

They walked away in the direction of the Volvo. Brady halted when they'd reached what he felt was a safe distance based on his recent experience at the disused quarry. Still working one-handed, he took out the cigarette packet and the lighter, passed them to Adrian.

'Your turn, Ade, I believe,' he said. 'And don't forget to run as soon as you've thrown it.'

Chapter Twenty-three

Jacobson was at his desk by eight thirty on Friday morning. He'd been woken up abruptly just before seven by an early morning slanging match between the couple upstairs, complete with door-slamming and loud cursing. But at least it had meant he'd had time to fix himself proper coffee instead of the Fairtrade instant he usually made do with at the start of a working day. Alison had phoned him before he'd left home to say she'd missed him last night, that maybe he could call round tonight if he wasn't busy. Or even if he was, she'd suggested, he could still call round later. That idea had put a smile on his face too, metaphorically if not literally. Kerr was still driving in from the Bovis estate. He'd left a message on Jacobson's voicemail to state that as of eleven thirty last night, there'd been no fresh developments in the Art Gang investigation. Jacobson had checked with the control room just in case but had been given the same non-result: no reports of significant leads coming in from the trawl of Crowby's pubs and clubs – or from anywhere else for that matter.

He switched on his computer and thought about the idea of the day's second B&H while it booted up. Not yet, old son, he decided. Let it wait. For the first couple of years since it had arrived in his office, his PC had sat neglected and unplugged in a corner. But no more: these days even Jacobson had to bow before the electronic revolution, had to check his Inbox regularly to find out what was happening in the rest of the organisation. He logged on and scanned the contents of his latest emails. Greg Salter was planning a press conference about the investigation later in the day and wanted Jacobson there with him to – quote – field questions of detail – unquote. He made a mental note to wriggle out of the event if he possibly could. He skimmed through then deleted a whole swathe of unnecessary internal junk mail. A civilian worker in the records office was offering kittens free to good homes. The Chief Constable, Dudley 'Dud' Bentham, had accepted an invitation to lead a seminar on 'best practice' police budgeting at the autumn conference of the Association of Chief Police Officers. Apparently there were still tickets available for the rugby club's forthcoming Halloween Dance. Computers were supposed to have speeded up communications inside the force – but they also bogged you down in the kind of mundane trivia that used to gather dust, unseen and unread, on justly neglected noticeboards along justly obscure corridors.

He scrolled down the screen to the one other new arrival that might conceivably turn out to be useful. The control room's famous incident sheet, issued once every twelve hours without fail, had been Jacobson's bible since his earliest days in CID. The incident sheet (the Current Incident Log was its correct Sunday name) summarised police and criminal activity within the given time period, enabled you to look for crime patterns or spot possible links between different lines of inquiry. Right up until last year it had actually been a sheet – or, more usually, several sheets, A4 size. Now it existed only in electronic form; if you wanted a paper copy you had to print it out yourself, assuming you'd connected your computer up to a working printer. Jacobson's had been fine yesterday but when he'd switched it on this morning it had instantly developed a paper jam which he was technophobically nervous about attempting to unjam without the benefit of expert advice.

He opened a new window and studied the details of the latest report. Car thefts, burglaries (commercial), burglaries (residential), assaults (public), assaults (domestic), traffic accidents. There had been a bad incident not far from Club Zoo. A rough sleeper disturbed in a doorway and given a nasty-sounding kicking. Almost certainly, Jacobson thought, by someone with a roof over their own head and quite probably with a nice wad of credit cards tucked inside their wallet into the bargain. But it wasn't an unusual incident and it didn't really have the specific stamp of the Art Gang upon it. Otherwise, Crowby looked to have been reasonably quiet from the police point of view for a Thursday night. There'd been some kind of vehicle fire out in the sticks which did strike him as odd however. Odd for the location – a couple of miles away from the Boden Hall estate – and odd for the number of vehicles involved. Three of them. Jacobson wouldn't have thought that there would have been three vehicles in that area at that time of night let alone that all three of them would get involved in some kind of combustible collision.

He copied the incident number and closed the report, brought up the live incident program and gingerly pasted the number into the search box. This was the plus side of the force's new computer system as even he had to agree. Once something had a number, you could pull up its live status from anywhere on the network. Traffic accidents weren't his domain of course. But anything unusual was. The unusual had a long-established way of impinging on his investigations. And besides, he'd arranged to meet Kerr at nine, prior to the team briefing he'd called for nine fifteen, and he needed something to distract him for the next ten minutes. Preferably something that didn't come out of a gold-coloured pack with the cheery message SMOKING KILLS emblazoned on the side panel.

The incident had been phoned in just before two AM. An anonymous call claiming there was a fire in the Forestry Commission's woodland. The single rural duty patrol car had been dispatched and so had the fire service as soon as the patrol car had confirmed that the call checked out. There'd been some tree damage close to the roadside but the blaze looked to have been brought under control easily enough. According to the minimalist entry from the duty car, there were no signs of a human presence at the scene and the assumption made was therefore that the blaze had been started deliberately to destroy the vehicles. Jacobson yawned as he read on, thinking that if he wasn't going to have a fag, another coffee might be a good idea. Even if this time the choice would have to between black instant brewed up on his illicit kettle or an over-stewed takeout from the police canteen. Burn-outs were one of the banes of life for the uniformed and traffic divisions. Joyriders would torch the cars they'd nicked when they had no further use for them, partly to obliterate their traces – but mainly just for the hell of it. Burn-outs cropped up everywhere and Jacobson had hardly made a study of the phenomenon. Yet he still saw the rural back roads which led to Boden Hall as an unlikely venue. Why would a bunch of toerags from the Woodlands, for instance, drive all the way out there? And why burn three vehicles at once? Jacobson was scarcely a car crime specialist but he knew that three together was a seriously unlikely amount in the normal run of things.

He decided on the kettle. There was less walking involved that way for one thing. He fished it out of its hiding place – the bottom drawer of his filing cabinet – and checked the water content. There was just about enough left without a refill. He stuck the plug into the nearest socket and switched the kettle on. While the water boiled, he scribbled down the name and number of the solitary, rural patrol officer who'd attended the scene. For the sake of thoroughness, he clicked on the link that would bring up the plod's full incident report but wasn't surprised to see that the page was still blank. Out in the field, coppers still mainly kept records in the tried and tested ways: filling in forms and making entries in their notebooks. The gap between something actually happening

in the real world and all of the relevant details being tran-
scribed into the computer system was never measurable in
less than hours, was frequently measurable in days, weeks,
sometimes even months. He looked at what there was so far
again, noticed that, as well a crime number, the incident had
a vehicle workshop reference attached. Somebody higher up
the chain of command had evidently decided that the
wreckage was worth towing on to police premises for possible
technical examination. The workshop reference led him to
a brief description: *identifications pending, possible marques
include Mercedes-Benz and BMW.*

He spooned instant coffee into a mug that was badly in
need of a rinse-out. For some reason the dirty brown gran-
ules made him think of soil and earth. Beyond that, his mind
was trying to recall if there was anyone senior in the traffic
division who owed him a favour – or at least who he hadn't
been rude to for a while.

John Shepherd woke up to the warm, wet sensation of Kelly's
mouth around his already-stiff cock. Her tongue was as artful
as ever, even without the little silver stud the dental hygienist
had recently advised her to stop wearing. He dozed again
after he'd fucked her. When he woke up she'd gone and he
took a hot shower and then dried himself over by the faux-
Tudor window which had some vague, alleged connection
to an associate of William Morris. The gardening team were
already at work, clearing fallen leaves from the long flower
beds and sprucing up the topiary near the fountains. The
gardeners were contractors of course, hired for the purpose.
Back in the heyday of the house, the Bodens had employed
their own gardeners just like they'd employed a full cap-
doffing complement of servants, kitchen staff, grooms, farm
labourers and general grovellers. But times change.
Nowadays you could grow up on another kind of estate (the
Beech Park in his case) and still end up owning a pile like
this one.

The shower had only shifted some of his sweats and only some of his headache. No worries on that score though. He'd already spotted an unfinished bottle of Remy Martin on his side of the bed, ninety per cent concealed by the untidy mound of yesterday's discarded shirt, pants and jeans. He vaguely recalled carrying it upstairs with him at the end of last night. Kelly must've missed it when she got up. Either that or she was in too much of a hurry to get started on her breakfast to do a proper search. She was such a hungry piece in general. Sex. Food. Travel. Shopping. You name it – whatever it was, she was always up for more of it. He unscrewed the top and drank straight from the bottle, didn't stop until he felt he'd injected a good enough start-the-day lining into his stomach. He pulled on a fresh pair of swim shorts and a crisp blue polo shirt, left yesterday's clothes in their pile on the floor. One of the two lazy little Latvians who laughingly called themselves housemaids could deal with the bedroom later. They better had anyway – or he'd get Perry to get on to the agency about them again. He went back into the ensuite, brushed his teeth, even gargled with mouthwash. Today was a new day and he didn't want to ruin it first thing with another debate about his drinking over the breakfast table. The fact that she'd recently taken up nagging-lite over his booze habit was the one tiny little flaw-ette in the otherwise companionable Kelly. Jesus, he'd told her the other morning, most girls in your shoes can't wait for the rich old geezer to kill himself off one way or the other – and get their hands on some of the posthumous goodies. She'd looked really hurt at that, he thought now, had told him how much she loved him, how much she believed in him: she didn't ever want him to die. What a fucking actress.

He phoned down to the kitchen: Birgit, the Dutch mistress of the culinary realm, picked up but he cut across her – *eggs benedict, love, and tell Kelly we're having breakfast by the pool again* – and ended the call as soon as he'd spoken. He walked out of his bedroom and along the too-dark landing towards the broad, ancient stairway. Grade A Listed was a pain in the arse if you wanted a little twenty-first century air and lightness around you in your home environment. He had an architect working on the problem: ways to de-gloom the old place without giving English Heritage a heart attack. He caught up with Birgit on the way to the pool. She had a breakfast tray in her arms: coffee, orange juice, bread, croissants, jams, honey – though no eggs benedict yet obviously. She was tall the way Dutch girls often were and stunning after her own fashion. He'd thought about her once or twice and then rejected the idea. Too many possible complications and, anyway, he was happy enough with Kelly for the time being. There were fools who believed that wisdom came with old age. But all that really happened was that you slowed down, couldn't be quite as arsed any more about life's myriad possibilities.

Kelly was already at the poolside table, munching her way energetically through a bowlful of fruit muesli. The two pools, one outdoor and (this one) indoor, had been an innovation of the previous owner, greedy fool that he was – but at least he'd won that particular planning battle, had managed to bequeath something worthwhile from his time here. Birgit set down the tray.

'There was quite a commotion last night on the way back here, John,' she said in her impeccable English.

'Birgit thought she'd be stuck out all night,' Kelly commented, had obviously already heard the story, whatever it was.

John Shepherd sat down, picked up a glass of orange juice, dimly recalled that yesterday had been Birgit's day off. She'd gone to visit her boyfriend in Birmingham, who was some kind of postgrad at the university.

'There were police, fire engines, everything,' Birgit added. 'There'd nearly been a serious fire in the forest, I think. I had to give them a statement, who I was, where I was travelling to.'

'What time was this then, love?' Shepherd asked.

'Around about three thirty. The policeman told me that some cars had been set on fire. But I think they must have been cleared away before I got there.'

Usually she'd stay for the whole night, Shepherd thought, travel back at first light in her little Clio. He wondered idly if they'd had a row or something. Not that it was any of his business.

'You mean like deliberate?' he asked.

Birgit transferred the last contents of the tray on to the little table.

'I think so. Maybe. January may have seen something too perhaps.'

Shepherd put the glass of orange juice back down. January! He'd completely forgotten that she was here, forgotten all about her gig too. He wondered if he should call her on the extension in her room, find out how it went. But then he thought that she might've been partying afterwards, might not thank him for an unwanted early morning alarm call. He broke off the end of a croissant, something to keep him going until Birgit returned with his eggs. He decided he'd leave it for now. At the very least wait until after he'd had his breakfast.

Coming round again, the first thing that Perry noticed was how unbearably cold his body felt. As if he was turning to ice deep inside. All apart from his arms where he could hardly feel anything at all – thanks probably to the cuffs on his wrists behind his back and to the rope they'd used to bind him tightly to the tree. But at least they'd left his legs free; slowly, agonisingly, he tried to lift and stretch each one in turn, tried to ease the feeling of stiffness. His head hurt so much that he couldn't bear to move it or lift it, just kept it slumped. There were dark patches down the front of his shirt. Blood, he guessed (and maybe vomited sick too), although mainly he was keeping his eyes shut for the moment, had discovered that he experienced less excruciating pain across his forehead that way. Whenever he did lift his head or open his eyes, apart from shooting pain, he felt a nauseating illusion of sudden movement, as if he was falling quickly out of the sky. He'd been knocked out cold, he remembered, realised he was probably badly concussed, was probably lapsing in and out of consciousness.

Staying, only with effort, in this part of his mind – where what he was experiencing was the object of his attention and not its entire content – he started to piece back together the likely sequence of events. He saw at once precisely where he'd gone wrong, the embarrassing, elementary mistake he'd made. The guy who'd rammed the second beamer into the merc's rear end obviously wasn't acting alone. How could he be? Perry should have stayed on the lookout for his accomplices after he'd checked out the first car and found it empty. Instead he'd taken his eye off the ball, keen to make sure that January was OK, that she wasn't badly injured. Split seconds only. But on any kind of battlefield, split seconds are all a watchful enemy ever needs.

He lifted his head again, opened his eyes, damned the pain. All he could see around him were trees. They must have walked further from the roadside then it had seemed to him at the time. High up in the nearby beech, he recognised the unconcerned, disinterested song of a blackbird. They'd all gone now. Of course they had. Scarpered, vanished. He mustered what little strength he could find into his lungs.

'January!'

His voice sounded weak, hardly sounded like his voice at all – and there was no kind of answer.

They must have untied her after they had him under control then taken her off somewhere else, *snatched* her. They'd seemed like amateurs at first but they'd beaten him, the so-called professional, hands-down. He closed his eyes but kept his head up this time. It was pretty light now even under the canopy of the trees. It would be broad daylight out on the road most probably. He'd been here hours then, impossible to know how long. The blackbird swooped down close by then flew off again. The feeling of coldness was getting worse and he noticed that he'd started shivering violently in the parts of his body that he could move to any extent. What he had to do was to get loose or get help while his brain was still working. This time of year he could be here all day, or even days, and no one would come near. Unless someone came deliberately looking. And he'd no idea what they'd done after they'd defeated him. If they'd covered their tracks successfully and if they'd taken January, no one would know where the hell to start looking. He thought of the scrapes he'd survived in Bosnia and the Gulf War. Scrapes he'd been made to sign forms about. Gagging orders. It almost made him laugh that his life might terminate here instead: tied to the bark of a trusty oak tree in an English wood.

Chapter Twenty-four

Brady, Annabel, Maria and Adrian all sat around the breakfast table together. A rare event. Rarer still was that Annabel had been instructed to cook the breakfast. Maria had saved the day according to Brady and, although it wasn't really a treat for her, wasn't really something she actually wanted, he'd declared that she should be free of domestic duties this morning. Brady apart, they had a bottle of champagne on the go along with their bacon and eggs to celebrate last night's successful exercise.

Brady's cut hand was the only downer they were aware of. As soon as somebody forensicated the scene properly, Brady's DNA bands would become logged, itemised official property.

Annabel mentioned it again while she got his second cup of tea ready for him.

'Not enough milk,' he complained before he picked up her comment.

'Sorr-eeh. It's not my fault you've given your slave the day off,' Annabel said – but pouring in more milk all the same.

Brady studied the cup as if it was an exam he'd just set her.

'They don't have me on their database to find a match. They don't have anything about any of us. We had to split before we could tidy up properly in Coventry, remember? So the same goes for there. It's only a problem for me – or for any of us – if we get caught. And who's going to care about anything if that happens anyway?'

'Plus we're not going to get caught,' Maria said.

She was sitting opposite Brady in her usual morning dressing gown. Today, though, he'd allowed her to keep it fastened.

'Exactly,' Brady said, 'so there's no point wasting any more energy worrying about it.'

Adrian spread margarine on another half-slice of toast then dipped the cut end of it into the dark yellow yolk of his second egg.

'The look on that big guy's face when Annabel appeared with the gun. Fucking priceless,' he said before he bit off a corner piece.

'Yeah – but it was Maria who really settled his hash,' Annabel said, trying on graciousness for size.

Adrian nodded his agreement vigorously, still thinking that it was in his best interests to appear keen from time to time.

'So what's today's programme then?' he asked, looking towards Brady.

'We lie low basically. Let the general hysteria build up a notch or two before we take the next step. Film editing's still your priority, Ade, obviously. And Annabel and Maria could do with putting in another *magha* session.'

Adrian looked surprised.

'You think so? We're getting to the endgame now. Surely there's no need?'

'Yes, we're getting to the endgame all right, Ade – but we don't really know how long it's going to take or what unforeseen complications we might run into. It's not going to do us the slightest harm to have some nice fresh ID data on tap just in case.'

'But we've a good half-dozen cards we haven't touched yet. Driving IDs too, passports—'

Brady favoured Adrian with his glib smile.

'That's all very well. But this is a situation where you can't have too much of a good thing. Any one of those IDs

191

could become compromised at virtually any minute. You're the computer scientist, Ade. Always back up your system, yes?'

Adrian shrugged for an answer, redirected his attention back towards his plate.

'Anyway,' Annabel said, still experimenting with let's-be-nice-to-everyone-this-morning, 'Maria and I love slutting around in the chatrooms. It's practically our second favourite activity.'

She reached across the table, grabbed the champagne bottle, charged all three glasses with the remaining contents.

'Cheers,' she said, lifting her own glass high. 'Here's to us, *all* of us – and here's to success.'

After breakfast, Adrian set up a couple of the laptops for the two women to use in the lounge. He'd brought a set of four with him plus two high-storage super-encrypted external hard drives on to which, as Brady had correctly insinuated, he backed up copies of everything on a daily basis. For himself, he planned on working out of the way in his bedroom, wanted to avoid as much disturbance and distraction as he could. Brady wanted to 'consult' him about the content of the next film and Adrian wanted that discussion to take place with only the two of them present. Brady, he'd learned, was a lot easier to deal with when he wasn't playing to the gallery. Immediately he'd finished at the table of course, Brady had set off in the direction of the outhouse at the rear of the cottage. Today's other task was surveillance – and Brady had made it clear that he wanted to do the first stint all on his own.

Jacobson's nine fifteen briefing didn't take long. He assigned Emma Smith and DC Williams to process the reports from last night's undercover operation as they came in. All the officers involved were under strict instructions to file their reports this morning and to do so as quickly as possible. Smith and Williams would cross-reference the new reports against each other and also against the existing paperwork. Just because the officers in the field hadn't thought they'd made any kind of breakthrough didn't actually *prove* that they hadn't. Mick Hume landed another CCTV session: compare and contrast the best images from the various Crowby sources with the full copies of the footage from Coventry and Birmingham which had finally been sent on. Steve Horton had a software program which would allegedly sift the images into the best-available composite but Jacobson still wanted a skilled real-life detective to pre-select the data set that Horton would work on. Kerr and Jacobson meantime would pay a visit to the vehicle workshop. The possibility that two BMWs had been torched together as part of last night's burn-out incident was too much of a coincidence to be ignored. Jacobson had managed to raise Brian Fairbanks, a superintendent in the traffic division who wasn't totally brain-dead in Jacobson's hypercritical, misanthropic view. Fairbanks had agreed to use his contacts to get the technical inspection speeded up – and for proper forensic precautions to be taken in case two of them did turn out to be the vehicles that Jacobson was interested in. Lucky for you, Frank, Fairbanks told him, that the suspicion had been that all three burn-outs were upmarket models: making the kind of incident where the traffic division liked to look squeaky clean and thorough for the benefit of the insurance company investigators.

Kerr suggested walking over to the vehicle workshop which was only a couple of streets away from the Divisional building but Jacobson said that they should drive: if the wrecks looked promising, then it might be worth taking a look at the actual scene of the burn-outs afterwards. They picked up Kerr's Peugeot in the police car park and edged their way out into the last, dying wedge of Friday morning's commuter log-jam.

'If these are the Art Gang's beamers, Frank, how the hell did they get as far as the other side of Wynarth when there's supposed to be an alert out?' Kerr asked as soon as they were entrenched in their own three yards of the traffic queue.

It was mainly a rhetorical question but Jacobson answered it anyway.

'False plates could be one part of it, old son. We know they're using them on their van. Plus any vehicle search is as much a matter of sheer chance as anything. The same goes for aerial support. It doesn't do you any good if you've stopped a thousand cars unless or until you stop the right one.'

Kerr changed gear, edged forward a handful of yards.

'But it's not just the patrols is it? All the camera operators in the region are supposed to be on the lookout too.'

'I don't doubt it, Ian, but – point one – there's a lot more bloody cameras than dozy snoopers to watch 'em. Point two – half of said cameras aren't working half the time. And – point three – if you stick to the back roads carefully enough, there's still ways to get from A to B without being happy-snapped by Big Brother.'

'You sound more like my dad every day,' Kerr observed.

'Your dad's no fool, old son. Just because he's still in mourning for Uncle Joe Stalin doesn't mean that he's got it wrong about the modern world. All this bloody over-the-top surveillance – if I wasn't in the force, I might even join one of these campaigning anti groups myself.'

The car in front pulled away and Kerr accelerated into the gap. The morning influx was clearing at last.

'If you've nothing to hide, you've nothing to fear, Frank.'

Jacobson snorted more than laughed.

'It's what the effing government's got to hide that worries me, old son. It should worry you as well if you've any common sense.'

Kerr struggled for a reply but Jacobson's mobile rang as he did so (DS Barber with the news from Birmingham that there was no news from Birmingham) saving him from the immediate, difficult, probably futile trouble.

A second call came through as soon as Barber rang off: the backshift, rural patrol officer who'd been the first at the scene of the burn-outs. Jacobson had acquired his off-duty number from the control room earlier, had left him a voice-mail message. The guy sounded exhausted, probably just wanted to field Jacobson's nuisance query and then get his head down for some sleep. As it turned out he didn't have a lot to contribute anyway. The cars had been ablaze when he'd got there and all he'd really done was wait around for the fire service to show up.

One of Brian Fairbank's constables was waiting for them when Kerr pulled into the workshop. He had a pleased-with-himself smile on his face that Jacobson hoped related to the burn-outs and not just to some permanent, personal state of healthy self-esteem.

'We've had a piece of luck, guv,' he announced after Jacobson had clambered out of Kerr's passenger door, 'the technicians found a VIN virtually as soon as they got the first wreck up on the ramps. I've just run the details against Swansea.'

Jacobson looked at him with interest. 'VIN' meant Vehicle Identification Number. 'Swansea' meant the link between the Police National Computer and the DVLC's vehicle records computer.

'And?' he asked.

'Direct hit, guv. A BMW series five, registered owner: Crowby Prestige Rentals, Unit Seven, Copthorne Way.'

They followed the traffic cop to where the burnt-out beamer was under inspection. One of the vehicle technicians stopped work to fill them in on the rest of the news. The fire damage was bad: ninety per cent plus, even for the BMW with the intact VIN. If it was a case where they were hoping for forensic evidence, he told them, they were probably wasting their time. Nothing organic was likely to have survived – although only a qualified FSS fire investigator would be able to tell for certain.

The technician had placed the VIN plate on a side-bench. It was gnarled and bent from severe heat stress but the number engraved into the metal was still readable by the naked eye.

'If these toerags knew what they were doing, they'd unscrew these things before they set their fires,' the technician commented. 'You can never predict what will survive a blaze and what won't.'

Jacobson shook his head.

'You'd be right if we *were* dealing with normal toerags, old son. But we probably aren't. We're probably dealing with tossers who think they're smarter than we are – the kind who like to thumb their nose at us and leave a calling card.'

He took in the spectacle of all three upmarket burn-outs. One up on the ramps, the other two waiting their turn. Nearly quarter of a million quid burnt down to the metal. *Vorsprung durch technik* and all that.

According to the letting agent, the outhouse would originally have been used for storing fuel or food or as shelter for any livestock belonging to the farm labourer's own family. It had been in a state of disrepair for decades until, two recent owners back, it had been renovated and converted. The ageing timbers had been treated and strengthened and the stonework had been re-rendered and, where necessary, replaced. The result was additional living space on two levels: a ground-floor workroom with a guest bedroom overhead which was accessed via an internal staircase. The bedroom was tiny but ideal for the purpose. The door at the top of the stairs was substantial enough and had been easy to equip with a robust padlock while the window was small and had been easily boarded up. There was even a rudimentary ensuite up there: shower, toilet, hand basin. Brady crept slowly and quietly into the workroom. All in all it had the air of somewhere that had never been much used. A big architect's-type desk, an angle-poise lamp, a single office chair and a filing cabinet devoid of files made up four-fifths of the pre-existing contents. The fifth item was a modern wood-burning stove for use when the weather turned even colder than it had been recently.

He nudged the door delicately shut behind him. They'd secreted a miniature webcam near the light fitting upstairs. She'd probably notice it eventually but probably not straight-away. Down here, Adrian had set up his fourth laptop on the desk as a monitoring station. Brady slid into the chair and clicked softly on the keypad, brought the screen to life. The webcam broadcast back to the cottage also. But the point about monitoring it from here was that you were on the spot, instantly available if she found some unforeseen way to do anything stupid or dangerous.

Right now that didn't look very likely.

She was lying down on the bed, foetus-curled. He studied her as if she was a specimen, which was exactly how he regarded most of the so-called human race in any case. Good result, he thought, just stay like that and make my life easy. They'd blindfolded her when they'd lifted her out of the Volvo's boot, had kept her that way until everything had been properly organised. They'd put lightweight shackles around her ankles and attached them to a precisely meas-ured chain which limited the range of her movements to a risk-free arc. She could hobble from the bed to the ensuite and back again – but she couldn't get within three feet of the door or the boarded-up window or the light switch. They'd stripped her naked of course to induce maximum vulnerability and, for now, she still had the tape across her mouth and her wrists were still cuffed securely behind her back. That would be their first negotiation with her later. They'd remove the tape and the cuffs – and bring her food – provided she vowed to stay silent, to keep it fucking shut. The cottage was remote, which had been one of the reasons for choosing it, but ramblers, walkers, all that kind, got every-where these days. And Brady hadn't come this far to blow the project by taking any stupid chances at the last minute.

She sat up as he watched her unseen. She looked up too, unknowingly turned her head straight to camera. He examined the detail of her face. She was attractive enough if you liked that particular type, maybe even beautiful. But it was the expression that really did it for Brady. The expression that he'd put there. He'd learned to recognise it now: the way they all looked after he'd brought them the precious gift of fear.

Chapter Twenty-five

John Shepherd poured himself a third cup of coffee and decided to phone Perry. He'd let January sleep on, assuming that's what she was doing, but it had occurred to him that Perry would also know how the gig had gone – or at least he'd know how the band had seemed about it afterwards. He'd probably be out on his morning run through the grounds. But that wasn't a problem, he'd just have to stop and take a breather for a couple of minutes. The rule was that Perry stayed welded to his mobile twenty-four seven. Shepherd paid him completely over the odds and in return Perry ensured that his services were never more than a swift speed-dial away.

'He's not answering!' Shepherd exclaimed incredulously after the seventh ring.

Kelly looked up from her post-breakfast magazine.

'Maybe you pressed the wrong number,' she suggested.

Shepherd redialled, still didn't connect. He tried a third time and then shot to his feet.

He wasn't angry – Shepherd owed Perry in too many ways for that – but he wanted an explanation. Perry's whole schtick was reliability: or it had been until twenty seconds ago.

He grabbed a fleece from the cloakroom against the late September chill and set off in the direction of the coach house which Perry used as his accommodation. It was a five-minute walk via the quickest route: skirting the edge of the arboretum and then out past the stables. All the while he kept dialling Perry's number to no avail. Later, he was never able to recall the exact moment when the dread that there was something seriously wrong first hit him. But it might have been when he'd noticed that the merc wasn't parked on the gravelled turning circle outside the coach house's pretentiously castellated front porch. Perry *always* parked it there over night so that he had it instantly to hand for any unanticipated early-morning chauffeuring requests. Except that he hadn't. Not this time.

Casper knocked on the back door of Tracey's place, expecting Tracey's mum, Denise, to let him in. No response. He knocked again. A minute or two later the door opened on the latch: Tracey herself. She undid the chain and let him in. She looked sleepy. She was wearing one of her in-bed T shirts, the pink one that said Crack Whore on the front, and an old pair of worn, loose-fitting jog pants she must have pulled on to answer the door. He could have done with holding her, pulling her close. But he knew he was still on probation as far as Tracey was concerned.

He put the kettle on while she produced a packet of still-wrapped Superkings from a kitchen drawer.

'Denise's secret stash,' she said, breaking the packet open and fishing one out. 'She's gone into town if you're wondering. They're hiring for the checkout at the new Lidl's. Says she's going to try for it, says she's going spare stuck out here all day.'

Casper passed her a red Zippo, saw an opportunity.

'Good for her, Trace. I'm going to be in work soon an' all. Dave says he'll put a word in for me at this car spares place.'

'Dave ain't got a record, Casper – he's one of the lucky ones who's never been caught, same as Denise. But you have. They won't look at you. Not for something where they can't have thieving.'

She yawned then lit the fag. She still hadn't offered him one but at least she'd left the packet open on the table, hadn't

200

returned it to the drawer. Casper found the teabags, rinsed out two mugs.

'Well, I'll get something, Trace. I'm through with fucking about.'

She pulled out a chair, sat down, looked at him hard.

'You'd better be through with fucking *around* too,' she said.

Casper pretended he didn't get the reference.

'You're looking like you slept well anyway.'

'Not so bad. Denise talked me into a couple of spliffs before I went up to bed.'

The kettle clicked off as he spooned white sugar into the mugs.

'It was gone three before we gave up,' he said, finally getting to the point. 'We never saw anybody that we thought looked the part.'

She put the fag down on a crowded ashtray, still watching him for signs of truth or deceit.

'Yeah, well maybe tonight.'

He put the mug in front of her, fetched an open carton of milk from the fridge. He'd been pill-free for five entire days and nights now, had managed to stay sober most of last night into the bargain.

'I don't think Mad Billy's up for another night. But Dave said he would – and Kenny.'

'I'd love to see that bastard Brady's face if Kenny gets hold of him,' Tracey said, nearly smiling.

She was the kind of bird who could wear an old sack and she'd still look good, Casper was thinking, the kind you hung on to if you weren't a complete and total fucking fool.

'Just wait, Trace,' he said, leaning as close to her as he dared while he poured in the milk. 'You'll see it all right – that's a frigging promise.'

The panic came and went in waves. January tried to sleep again, didn't know what else to do for now. The cuffs cut into her wrists and the shackles restricted her movements to a circumference of four, maybe five feet. She was hungry and thirsty and her mouth was sore and itching like hell under the tape. She lay on her side on the bed and closed her eyes. She felt cold too. The bed was only a bare mattress, tediously striped in two shades of blue; there were no sheets to cover herself with, no pillow for her head. In the bathroom likewise there was only one small, meagre face towel. She'd worked out experimentally that lying down on her side hurt less, was the least uncomfortable position. It stopped the cuffs pressing into her back or the rest of her body pressing down on her pinioned arms. She pulled her knees up as far as the shackles allowed, knew how pathetic and foetal she must look. Maybe medieval too: an outcast nun walled up for sins against God or against the earthly power of the king. One of the worst things was losing track of the passage of time, not knowing whether it was day or night, or how long she'd been here – wherever here was. She wasn't even sure how long she'd been in the car boot. Not that long probably except that every minute in there had felt like a trapped eternity. At least she'd tried to struggle when they'd shoved her inside it, some kind of survival instinct kicking in at last. Up until that point, she'd felt frozen, paralysed: a deer about to be run over, helpless and mesmerised by the beam of headlamps.

The struggling hadn't done any good, had made them rougher with her, made them angry. One of them had slapped and punched her. The punch had really hurt, had made her gasp for breath – but she felt that it had been one of the women who'd done it, that a man's punch would have hurt more, winded her more. *At least she'd tried*. She repeated the phrase in her head for its meagre comfort value. When she'd been in the boot, she'd found a memory from somewhere – something on some TV channel she'd seen sometime or in some newspaper or magazine she'd read – about kicking out the rear lights from inside, about attracting attention and possible rescue that way. It hadn't worked of course. She hadn't been able to get the angle right or find enough leverage, had wasted too much energy in the useless effort. She recalled a new thought now – or she thought it was new, even that was getting hard to tell: in the minutes before the car had stopped, the ride had suddenly gone bumpy and wild. Either – this was the new thing – the road surface had deteriorated badly or they'd no longer been on a public road at all.

She opened her eyes. Sleep wasn't on the cards in the too-bright room lit by a single, powerful light bulb. Bare like the bed but illuminating every corner. The switch was out of her reach although she didn't know if she would switch it off anyway supposing that she could reach. Another thing she'd read in some other place that she couldn't remember was how the constant artificial light was one of the things prisoners really hated about prisons. The way it was beyond their control, always *on* – whether they wanted it on or not. She thought she could understand that. Yet here they'd boarded up the window by the looks of it and, without the light bulb, the darkness might be total, might be more than she could stand.

When they'd pulled her out of the boot, for a few seconds she'd sensed free, outside air before they'd bundled her into some kind of interior. There'd been stairs involved and more slapping. They'd prodded her, pushed her, shoved her wherever they wanted her to go. And all the time she'd been blindfolded, right up until they had her naked and shackled. One of them had groped her too when they'd ripped her clothes off. Not much. But enough for her to be certain it hadn't been accidental. She'd swear that had been a woman too. Since when – nothing. They'd locked the door and gone – and she'd never once seen their faces or heard their voices clear and unmuffled. She sat up again. I might as well if I can't sleep. What she should do, she decided, was just replay it all in her mind from the very beginning, get every aspect of it clear, find some rational element to cling on to. There were four of them, two men and two women. Plus they'd abducted her, taken her prisoner. So they must be the video gang that the media were full of – and that was good news, that was definitely good news. It had been frightening, sure, what they'd done to those girls, but only one of them hadn't survived it. And that had been something to do with a road accident, hadn't it? Maybe wasn't necessarily the gang's direct fault. Plus the others had only been held for a few hours each. That was all, just a few hours. They were sick these people. Sick fuckers. But they hadn't kept anybody for long. Not long at all really.

She tried to stay calm, tried to deep breathe, tried to believe. But the video gang hadn't worn masks and she hadn't seen her captors (when she could see them) filming anything. Also the way it had happened – like an ambush, like they'd been waiting deliberately for her and nobody else. And there was what they'd done to Perry too. Perry! He'd put himself on the line for her and they'd clubbed him like he was an animal, as good as left him for dead. The thought enveloped her like a cold, clammy sickness: *maybe he even was dead.* Think about something else. Anything. The medieval nun. No, not her. She bit her tongue inside her taped-up mouth, tried to distract her mind elsewhere. Not her. That isn't what this is. Some mad thing where they just lock you up and leave you. To starve. To go mad yourself. And then . . .

Chapter Twenty-six

John Shepherd scrolled through the address book on his nearest phone, found three numbers for the Chief Constable, 'Dud' Bentham: piggy home, piggy office, piggy private mobile. Celebrity was pointless if you didn't use it, didn't make it work for you. Since he'd moved back to the area, Shepherd had made an easy, painless habit of getting to know the local movers and shakers. Or, more precisely, he'd allowed some of them (Bentham had been an obvious priority target) to get to know some of him. Over in Santa Monica, he'd been just another rich fucker from the entertainment industry, one of hundreds in a town where only tourists blinked if J-Lo went shopping for groceries or Brad Pitt stopped off for a beer. Back in Crowby, his arrival at Boden Hall had been news, a big-time big deal. So he'd put himself out mildly, thrown a couple of boring dinners when he'd first moved in, turned out for a couple of mind-numbing charity events. The usual I'm-rich-but-I'm-still-a-good-bloke bollocks.

He tried the mobe when neither the home number nor the office number produced a result. Come on, piggy, pick up for fuck's sake. Bentham finally answered on the fifth tone.

'John, nice to hear from you,' he said, before Shepherd himself had said anything, 'how can I help you?'

So the chief piggy's a proper fame-groupie, Shepherd thought, evidently had Boden Hall's starry number pre-stored. He told him what the problem was, only half-listened while Bentham made the predictable soothing noises that there was probably nothing to worry about, that there'd almost certainly be some simple, harmless explanation. He kept the important bit to the last.

'I'll get someone senior to look into it, John. Straightaway – put your mind at rest.'

'Thanks, eh, Dud, I'd really appreciate that. My cook says there was some kind of incident out this way last night. Cars set on fire or something. I don't know if maybe—'

'I'll see that's passed on. Don't worry, John – we take the security of our prominent citizens seriously.'

Shepherd extracted a new, full bottle of brandy from the walnut chiffonier when he rang off, told Kelly to shut it when she raised her faint objection: was he sure that boozing this early would really help?

'My daughter's missing, Kel,' he added. 'I need a fucking drink and I'm fucking having one. In fact I'm probably having two or three – as many as it fucking takes.'

Perry and the merc had vanished. January wasn't in her room, her bed didn't look slept in and her mobile was turned off. He'd spoken to Nick Bishop who was up and about at the Riverside Hotel but all he'd had to say was that January had left there last night in the merc with Perry. They'd set off around one o'clock, the conceited, talentless little twat had reckoned.

He'd imagined how this would be too many times, had woken up anxious and sweating in the middle of too many nights from bad dreams about it. He found a set of Georgian rummers in the same location, filled one up to the brim. Bentham could be right of course. Maybe there wasn't anything to worry about. Just conceivably January was *with* Perry somewhere. They'd always got on well. Plus Perry was probably some women's dream of a muscled love god. He'd never have put January into that category (not when evidently she'd found Nick Bishop shaggable) but it was still a possibility, still a hope for him to cling on to.

*

Jacobson phoned Jim Webster en route: the scene of last night's burn-outs needed urgent SOCO attention – and if Webster wanted to claim that his team was too busy else-where, he could take it up with 'Dud' Bentham. He phoned the control room too: they needed to get the rural patrol car over there again, maintain security until the SOCOs actu-ally showed up. The recent new owner of Boden Hall had pulled strings with the Chief Constable who'd leant on Greg Salter who'd leant on Jacobson. But, for once, Jacobson saw no need to argue, no need to circumvent an order from on high that was meant to privilege yet another fat cat over joe public. When you put one (and probably both) of the Art Gang's beamers two miles down the road from the report of a missing 22-year-old female, you had a *situation* – as the Yanks liked to say.

John Shepherd was just a name to him, some rock star who'd started out in Crowby, had made it big – and then, for God-knows-what reason, had recently come back to rule the roost in the local stately pile. He asked Kerr to fill in the details.

'Not my cup of tea really, Frank,' Kerr said, slowing on another country bend.

'Big in the eighties, not big now – or not doing anything new now anyway. He's bigger in the States than he ever was here – which is the right way round for making the big bucks of course.'

'But not your thing?'

Kerr was well known as a music buff – and also well known for dismissing any taste that didn't match his own.

'Too bland for me, basically. A great player technically – but no real balls, no edge. I always thought he was just re-cycling stuff that had already been done better. I'd classify him alongside Dire Straits or something boring like that. You should remember them anyway surely – at your age.'

'Fuck off,' Jacobson commented affably.

'The daughter's supposed to be cool though. Alice Banned.

I've not heard them but Steve Horton's downloaded them, reckons they're going to be huge.'

The rural patrol overtook them just as they were approaching the scene of the incident. Kerr stopped the car at the spot and Jacobson climbed out, exchanged a few words with the rural dayshift before they drove on again, made sure she understood the potential seriousness. Officially there were only police *officers* in the force these days (and the force, strictly speaking, was now a *service*) but Kerr, letching via the driver's mirror, still instantly logged her as the kind of blonde police*woman* you hoped would bang her cuffs on you any day of the week. Jacobson finally lit up his second B&H, rolling down the window to minimise Kerr's anti-smoking antagonism. He finished it just as the road emerged from the woodland and Boden Hall loomed up in the distance. Jacobson had been out here on police business before – as part of the complex fallout from the Jenny Mortimer murder case. He did the arithmetic in his mind, calculated roughly that it must have been about four years ago by now. Time flew when you spent your days cleaning up after murderers, rapists and (in that instance) greedy, rich bastards.

There was an electronically-controlled gate across the entrance to Boden Hall's own private road which Jacobson didn't recall being here back then. Kerr held his ID up to a thin, elongated camera. A light flashed from red to green and the barrier lifted.

'How the other half lives, Frank,' he said, driving in and surveying the extensive parkland on either side of the narrow but smooth-surfaced approach road.

'How the other five per cent lives, old son,' Jacobson corrected him, 'the tossers right at the top who owned seventy-one per cent of your arse at the last count.'

Kerr ignored the comment, suspected Jacobson of winding him up again about his dad's politics. One of these days, maybe everybody would just leave the topic alone.

John Shepherd was waiting for them on the steps. They

followed him inside, talked in a dark-panelled library lined with old bookshelves full of old books, the kind that nobody had bothered to read in a hundred years. Jacobson noticed that some of them, the valuable ones presumably, were locked away behind glass. He caught the smell of expensive alcohol on Shepherd's breath. It told the same story as the full tumbler the ex-king of pop was holding in his right hand. He let Shepherd retell the sequence of events that he already knew – that had already been relayed to him via Bentham and Salter: Shepherd's daughter and Shepherd's bodyguard had both gone missing, hadn't been seen by anyone since one AM in the morning when they'd set off from the Riverside Hotel in Shepherd's Mercedes S600.

'You've passed on the log book details for the vehicle then?' Jacobson asked him when he'd finished.

Shepherd confirmed that he had. He'd looked them out and someone from the police control room had phoned him ten minutes ago, had noted down the relevant information.

Two young women walked into the room. The tall one was carrying a tray: two pots, a milk jug, sugar, two cups, two saucers. Shepherd introduced them as Birgit and Kelly. You could tell that Kelly was the girlfriend from the fact that Birgit declined her offer of help with the drinks – coffee for Jacobson, tea for Kerr – and from the way she inserted her waist snugly into the embrace of Shepherd's free arm.

'It's going to be all right, John,' she said, looking up at him, 'the police are here now.'

Shepherd took another slug of brandy by way of an answer.

There were Queen Anne chairs around a long mahogany table in the middle of the room but nobody seemed interested in sitting down.

'It's very early days,' Jacobson said. 'The whole thing could just be completely circumstantial. Your daughter could be on her way home right now, maybe just doesn't realise her phone's switched off.'

Shepherd mentioned the missing merc and the police suspicion about the third burn-out.

'It's the A1 priority for our workshop technicians now they've got your vehicle details,' Jacobson said. 'We'll hear from them just as soon as they've completed their checks.'

The idea that the workshop would strike lucky with the precise identification of all three fire-trashed wrecks – or even two out of the three – without calling on time-delaying expert forensic assistance seemed outlandish to Jacobson: but he wasn't about to pass his doubts on in public.

'And in the meantime my daughter could—'

'In the meantime, we've other tasks that are just as important for us to complete,' Jacobson cut in. 'I'm told you've only spoken to one of the musicians who're staying at the Riverside, for instance?'

'That's right. Nick Bishop. But—'

'Then my people need to talk to all of them, Mr Shepherd. One of them might know something that he doesn't – might even know where your daughter is.'

Shepherd looked at his brandy glass but didn't lift it to his lips.

'Please, call me John,' he said, attempting a full-on celebrity smile, 'I'm just worried obviously. Who the hell wouldn't be?'

'I've a grown-up up daughter, myself, er, John,' Jacobson replied but didn't offer his own first name, 'you can trust us to do everything it takes. Now I need to know something about Perry Harrison as well. He's worked for you for how long?'

'Eight years or thereabouts. Ex-SAS. The man is a hundred per cent solid and reliable. That's the other thing that makes me think—'

'I'll still need some details. Date of birth, full name. His mobile number. I'll want your daughter's number too.'

'Their mobiles?'

If what Jacobson thought could have happened *had*

happened, they'd need the phone records, need to pinpoint where and when either of them had last made calls.

'It's just routine, John, the standard procedure,' he heard himself saying.

He'd trotted the words out a million times – but the public carried on buying them, carried on always wanting to believe them.

Shepherd looked suddenly lost, helpless. His girlfriend rescued him.

'You'll have all Perry's details up in the office, John,' she said, still entwined inside his left arm. 'The payroll program on the laptop?'

'Oh yeah, course. I was forgetting. I've an accountant comes in, sorts all that stuff out for me. I could get the details for you now if you like.'

'That would be helpful,' Jacobson said.

Kelly went off with Shepherd and Birgit left the room too after she'd confirmed the details of where she'd been the night before, when she'd got back and when she'd last seen January (yesterday morning). Jacobson poured himself a second cup of coffee while they waited. He'd drunk it down to the dregs before Shepherd and Kelly returned. Kerr had passed on more tea, claimed it was too weak. Kelly handed Jacobson the A4 print-out of Perry Harrison's details.

'I've scribbled January's mobile number at the bottom,' she said.

There was something elfin about her face that Jacobson liked. He hoped Shepherd was nice to her when he wasn't too busy pickling his liver. He noticed that she'd attached two photographs to the print-out. What looked like the copy of a passport photo for Harrison and a publicity shot for Shepherd's daughter: smiling face, tight jeans, good legs, cradling a shiny guitar in her arms.

He asked the rest of the usual questions. Did January have friends in the area? Or anyone she might have decided to visit on the spur of the moment? Shepherd pointed out that his daughter had only flown in from LA last weekend – and he'd only been living in Crowby for the past year himself.

'OK. Fine,' Jacobson said, 'obviously if January does just turn up – and I hope she does – or if anything else that might be relevant occurs to you, let me know straight away.'

He handed Shepherd his card. Shepherd managed to say thanks, even managed his smile again. There were a lot more difficult questions for Jacobson to put to him, questions that he might find a lot more difficult to answer. But all of that could wait until they knew for certain that the girl was in trouble – and exactly what kind of trouble she was in.

They stopped at the scene of the burn-outs again on their way back towards Crowby. Both of them got out of the Peugeot this time. The sex-bomb rural patrol officer had set up a control point for the limited amount of traffic that would be likely to find its way out here on a cold Friday morning in late September. Police tape flanked off the blackened, fire-damaged trees on both sides of the road and there were four SOCOs at work. One of them seemed to be videoing everything in sight and the others were taking measurements from the scorched tarmac. The one with the camera stopped filming for a moment, told Jacobson that they'd only just got here – they were still making their preliminary assessment, they hadn't really got down to work yet. Jacobson nodded, decided not to push it, read the sub-text easily enough: kindly bog off and let us get on with our job.

Hey. Hello.

The voice was faint but unmistakably a voice. All of them heard it, all of them stopped what they were doing.

Help.

Even fainter the second time, a distant whisper. The rural cop – PC Helen Dawson – pointed in the direction she reckoned it came from. Jacobson and Kerr followed her into the woodland. They walked slowly, stepped carefully. Dawson indicated snapped branches on trees and signs of disturbance in the undergrowth.

212

'Someone's been through here recently,' she commented.

'So nobody scanned the area last night?' Jacobson asked.

'I expect they did the usual search for thrown passengers once they had the blaze under control, guv,' Dawson replied, 'but I doubt they'd have come anything like this far in. No reason to.'

Hel—

The voice trailed off but they could tell they were getting closer. Dawson changed direction and Jacobson and Kerr followed behind her in single file, still watching their feet, still worried that they could be trampling over a crime scene.

His head slumped as soon as they got to him and his eyes closed as if he'd made all the effort he was capable of, was leaving it all up to them now. Dawson spoke urgently into her radio, arranged the ambulance while Kerr started to work on the tight knots on the rope. He tried just to loosen them with his fingers but quickly gave that up as hopeless. He took out the sharp, unauthorised pen knife he wasn't supposed to carry on duty and began to cut steadily through them instead. When he'd dealt with the rope he turned his attention to unpicking the locks on the handcuffs. They were serious-looking cuffs, definitely not toys, but he didn't recognise the design.

They stayed with him until the ambulance arrived and the paramedics stretchered him out of the woods. He'd lost consciousness completely by then, hadn't even been able to swallow down anything from the plastic bottle of Evian water that PC Dawson had found in the glove compartment of her patrol car. By then they knew that he was Perry Harrison of course. Jacobson had found his wallet inside a zipped, security pocket in his cargo pants. Whoever had forced him off the road and, by implication, had done something bad and illegal to January Shepherd, hadn't had the least interest in Harrison's credit cards or his two hundred quids' worth of crisp, clean twenties.

Chapter Twenty-seven

Annabel was in the lounge of the cottage on her own. Snug and comfortable, tapping happily at the laptop. When Brady had come back from the outhouse he'd taken Maria off for another heroine's reward – this time of the bedroom variety. Annabel wasn't fussed. *Magha* was her thing anyway, something she enjoyed because she was bloody good at it. She was checking through the email accounts that 'Sabrina', one of her favourite sobriquets, was currently using. On this particular account, as there had been for the last few days, there were half-a-dozen emails from the same source, each one more desperate than the one before.

Sabrina,
I know what you've done and I don't care. If you've used my details to get money here then that means *you're* here. I forgive you, darling S, I really do. All I want to do is see you, hold you, do to you in r/l what I've done to you in cyber. Don't tell me you don't want it as much as I do. I may have to punish you since you have been so naughty. But I would never do you r/l harm. If you need money or a place to stay I can help you. Email soon or come to the chatroom.
Your loving mistress, Julia.

Annabel smiled to herself and clicked the delete key. Poor old Julia Dove. Her identity ripped off to the tune of five K and still offering more, still not willing to believe that the soulmate she'd met online was largely the product of her own imagination and Annabel's practised skill in reflecting her fantasies back to her. Julia was a bit of a special case really: Annabel's Mug of Mugs. Most of the sad inadequates you picked up in the chatrooms at least used aliases initially, at least kept some stuff back about their real-life, everyday existences. But Julia had always logged on using her real name, had never pretended to be anything other than who she really was, had been willing to hand over her National Insurance number, her tax code, her date of birth, her employment history and her address after barely a fortnight of chat, messaging and email. A whirlwind romance in Julia's mind that, for Annabel, had actually been the easiest false seduction she'd ever achieved.

She sat back from the keyboard for a moment, took a draw from the mild, working-hours spliff she'd had to roll for herself in Maria's absence. Maria had been professionally jealous about Julia Dove, Annabel knew. Both of them played every conceivable role online but Maria was the real-life submissive, probably thought that a gift horse like Julia should really have been hers, would certainly have derived more actual pleasure than Annabel out of Dove's prison officer scenarios (some of which, Annabel had come to suspect, were based on reality). Annabel's tastes with women, and not a few men, went in the other direction. The only one she truly obeyed was Brady. Lord God and Master Brady. Or so he thought anyway.

She ran the secure-delete utility after the ordinary delete, always made sure that what was no longer wanted on the computer no longer remained there. Adrian would check everything at the end of the session anyway and she liked to keep him impressed with her thoroughness. Always keep your local tekkie happy, even if Sir Brady wouldn't let you fuck him. She took another, deeper draw. It would have been fun to email Dove again, to see just how far she could push her. But their rule was strictly no contact once they'd extracted sufficient data. Not every mug was as desperate as Julia was,

215

although most were too embarrassed at their stupidity to make a noise about how they'd been conned. But not in every case. There were some that would go straight to the police, would even try and trace you, set traps. That was how you got caught. By being too lazy and too greedy. Trying to till the same old land, when there were fields and fields still waiting out there, all of them rich, fertile and unploughed.

She scanned through the rest of the new mail in the account. None of it looked too promising. After the hundreds of hours she'd put in, Annabel had a near-instinctive ability to distinguish the time-wasters from the true, potential marks. You played with some bored office worker in a chatroom, gave out an email address and never heard from them again. Or if you did it was because they still wanted to carry on the game-playing, involve you in some illiterate, masturbatory fantasy. The minute you asked them a thing about their real life, never mind spun them one of the yarns designed to coax them into handing over the details you needed, they were gone: over and out, vanished into total, permanent radio silence. But the joy of cyberspace was its infinite scale. All you had to do was keep going hour after hour after hour. Eventually – and often enough – you hit paydirt: the lonely and the gullible; the desperate cases prepared to abandon common sense and *believe*. *Magha* – meaning fool – was the word they'd borrowed and adopted from the highly organised Nigerian scammer gangs who led the world in the art of parting idiots from their cash or their identities electronically. *A Magha a day keeps wage-slavery away*: Brady's crap but true little rhyme.

She tried another account, immediately saw something she'd been waiting for.

Sabrina,
Of course I believe you, dearest one, and I hate to
sound so suspicious. I will certainly act as your
sponsor and I will definitely send the Russian authori-

ties the letter you need. But I don't see why you need my driving license number when you already have all my address details. Please explain again so that I can understand. I want to help you of course and look forward every minute of every day to the time when you are able to travel here and we can at last truly meet, my beautiful princess.

Your eager servant, Roy F. XXXXX

She called up Adrian's database, scrolled through Roy F's details. His name and address had checked out and so had his claim to be a self-employed builder. Adrian had added a comment that they could probably use him now even if he baulked at giving them anything more. Annabel hit reply. No need for that, Ade, she thought. Roy is just about ready to roll over and give us everything else we need. This is a numbskull who probably has to spell-check his own fucking three-letter name; a sap too stupid to know he could just sign up with a genuine agency, get on a jet, spend a nice weekend in a Moscow hotel, take his pick of genuine would-be Russian brides. One of the tricks, they'd realised, was to always err on the side of unbelievability. You hooked fewer catches that way but you knew that each catch was a fish worth landing, a true and utter fool. She put the spliff down on the ashtray, typed out her first two sentences:

Roy, so *hot* to get your email. I always thinking you when I take shower.

Upstairs, Adrian reached the end of what looked to him like a good-enough final cut. He was listening to the soundtrack on headphones, partly for the sake of accuracy, but mainly to shut out Maria's ecstatic cries from Brady's nearby bedroom. The cottage was an ideal location in several respects but privacy wasn't one of them. Brady's idea this time had been for a 'Best-Of' compilation that could be sent out as a stop-gap to prevent the media interest from flagging before they made their next public move. Not an especially difficult task. Adrian had simply copied over some of the key footage from the three previous films and re-sequenced it for heightened dramatic effect. The only problem had been with the new text that Brady had wanted mixing in between the scenes. Brady had called it his 'manifesto' but to Adrian it just looked like more of his stock-in-trade, off-the-peg film studies bollocks, the kind of lazy stuff that, quite rightly, had meant that Brady had only scraped a pass for his final year dissertation. The *problematic* of modern visual culture, according to Mr B, was its *inauthenticity*, its inability to *break out* from itself, to capture actual experience. By putting *real* fear and *real* terror onscreen, the Art Terrorist project brokered an escape from the prison of self-referential artificiality and returned film to its true purpose. And so on. Christ knows what they'll make of that on the newsdesk at the *Sun*, Adrian had thought, but he'd put it all in anyway. Word for pretentious word.

He fast-forwarded through from the beginning again, checking for errors. Everything looked fine except for a spelling mistake on the very last frame.

ART NEVER SLEEPS.
FEAR MAKES FREE.
MORE REALTY SOON.

He corrected it then saved the file. When he'd closed the film editing application, he brought up the webcam for a few, brief seconds. The girl was still curled on the bed, still looking like she was trying to sleep. He didn't really enjoy watching her, even though he was as responsible for her predicament as much as the others. Not quite true. He did enjoy looking at her as such. What he didn't like was imagining what was going on in her head, the stuff they – him – were making her feel. But it's not for ever, he reminded himself. What they were doing wasn't the worst thing in the world, didn't equate to what a battle-hyped soldier might get away with in one of its war-torn trouble spots, for instance; that was the other thing he needed to remember, needed to keep in the forefront of his mind. He'd had another bad dream in the night about the girl from Coventry. But Brady had been right about her in his own twisted way. It *had* been an accident, hadn't it, not something they'd meant to happen. It had been the girl's own fault as much as anybody's, if he looked at it the right way – the way that meant he could survive this, get through this. And it would be over soon anyway, not much point getting cold feet about it now. This new girl, like the other girls, was only a pawn, only a means to an end. He watched her for a few seconds more then closed the webcam window, took off the headphones. Silence around him at last. Not even muffled conversation. Maybe Brady and Maria had finished then, maybe they'd even gone downstairs.

From the beginning, Maria was the one Adrian really couldn't figure. He'd asked her about it all late one night (this had been back in Watford) when Brady and Annabel had gone to bed and Brady had curtly told Maria that her 'services' wouldn't be required until the morning. *Why do you do it,* he'd asked, *take all that crap?* And it was a question that puzzled him even more now. At least she'd still had her career prospects back then, had actually been lined up to work on a big-budget American production over at Elstree when she'd jacked it all in and signed on instead for Brady's 'project'. He'd been hoping for some kind of real answer, something personal. But no. Maria had just come out with all the usual theories you heard in the bar at any fetish night. It was a lifestyle choice, a legitimate preference. Who was to say where desire came from? Genetics or potty training. And who cared anyway if it was what you longed for, craved, needed? She'd tried vanilla sex, of course she had – and had thought she'd die of

219

boredom. Brady gave her what she wanted. It was as if he had a window directly into her soul. He'd asked her again on Wednesday, the day after the girl had died, when Brady had sent them out to buy the second-hand Volvo. Why Brady and Annabel, though, of all people? Didn't she think they took it too far? *They really hurt people, Maria,* he'd said to her, *they make you really hurt them too.* They'd been sitting at traffic lights, somewhere in Aston, Adrian still getting used to the pedals and the unfamiliar angle of the steering wheel. *That's just it,* she'd replied, *it's real, they're not amateurs playing around, that's why I'll always serve them. Always. No matter what.* She'd said other stuff too, downright crazy stuff. That Brady was a genius, that one day the world would realise that. But he'd stopped listening by then, had shut her voice out, concentrated just on driving. I'm alone, he'd thought, completely alone with three demented strangers for company.

He needed to check with Brady next, in fact, get his executive approval before he sent the new film out. But he decided not to rush it, decided to stop up here on his own for a few, more precious minutes of solitude. None of them knew how long film-editing took anyway. And certainly not Brady. Brady could quote tedious chunks from Barthes, Baudrillard and Derrida till the cows came home but the areas he'd studied had been marked out by a scrupulous avoidance of anything practical or hands-on. Brady never ceased to remind them that he was the theoretician, the visionary, while they – meaning Adrian and Maria in particular – were merely technicians, the backroom gofers who translated his ideas into actions. It was the purest bullshit of course, had been ever since day one. Adrian had let it go, like he'd let all the sex games and head games go also, because he had his own agenda, his own reasons. Annabel never figured in Brady's I'm-the-ideas-man rap of course because she actually had few prior skills, theoretical or practical, other than being Brady's long-term twisted-head girlfriend (if a sociopath could truly be said to have anything as ordinary or everyday as a girlfriend). To give her due credit though, Annabel had developed a real talent for *Magha*-hunting, was at the very least Maria's equal online. The fact was, Adrian suddenly realised (or realised more fully than he'd ever done before), that there was only one person that the project, now it was up and running, could easily do without. He tapped the keyboard idly, preoccupied with his new thought. B- R- A- D. He let his finger linger too long on the final letter, watched it fill the notepad window at the bottom of the screen. BRADYYYYYYYYYYYYYYYYYY YYYYYYYYYYYYYYYYYYYYYYYYYYYYYYYYYYYYYY YYYYYYYYYYYYY.

The problem was that, out of the four of them, Adrian knew he was the only one who'd remotely grasped the fact.

Brady opened the door to the outhouse and walked in. Maria followed him, carrying the tray in her arms: a carton of orange juice, plastic knife and plastic fork, a paper plate of food – cottage cheese, salad niçoise, French bread. They were both wearing black jeans and black shirts, an appearance which – Brady's intention – transmitted the suggestion of some kind of uniform. Brady wasn't trying to keep quiet this time, wanted her to hear them, wanted her nerves to fire with adrenalin. He checked her on the webcam/laptop link. She was sitting up, looking like she was listening intently. He motioned to Maria to follow him and then climbed the stairs, his feet thudding against the wooden steps. The padlock was a complicated affair which involved triple-locking and always took him a couple of attempts to undo. When he had it unlocked at last, he undid the bolt and pushed the door open, ushered Maria to go in first. She put the tray down on top of the tiny bamboo table at the foot of the bed. It was a hideous, cheap item they'd found in the attic. The guest room had actually looked fairly cosy when they'd first taken over the cottage but they'd stripped it down to the bone, hadn't wanted to leave her with anything beyond the basic necessities, with anything resembling a comfort zone.

She stayed where she was on the edge of the bed, not moving but staring at both of them, maybe trying to notice something about their eyes or the narrow segments of their mouths which were all that was visible of their faces through the balaclava masks. Maria had questioned why they needed to go on wearing them now that they had her securely imprisoned up here. Brady had explained to her how it introduced another element of uncertainty into the equation: she might have seen their e-fits and video images on TV but she couldn't know for sure who had taken her – the famous video gang or somebody entirely different.

Brady ran through his pre-rehearsed speech.

'Something to eat, something to drink. All yours. My associate will undo your handcuffs and remove the tape from your mouth provided you keep quiet. That means no screaming, no shouting, no trying anything stupid. Do you agree?'

She looked at them for a second or two longer, still without moving. Then, slowly, she lowered her eyes, nodded her head.

Maria had difficulty getting the tape off until she managed to work her fingers underneath it at one end and gained enough leverage that way to rip it straight across. The girl let out a fierce whimper which Brady chose to ignore. Maria unlocked the handcuffs and clipped them on to her belt.

'Who are you? What's this all—'

Maria slapped her, though maybe not as hard as Annabel would have.

'He told you to be quiet. He meant it. Understand?'

She rubbed her face where Maria had struck it. The movement was slow, clumsy, jerky – probably something to do with how stiff her arms must be after their hours of immobility. Her wrists looked red and painfully swollen.

She nodded her head again.

'That's better,' Brady said. 'Keep it shut and you might get out of this in one piece.'

Maria shoved the little table closer to her so that she'd be able to reach the food without the effort of moving.

'See,' Brady commented, 'do all right by us and we'll do all right by you.'

He retreated towards the door and Maria followed him. They turned and looked at her again before they left the room. She hadn't touched the food yet, was still gawping at their every move. Brady scanned her face, thought he saw a question forming on her lips, one of hundreds that might be burning inside her brain. He fished the padlock key out of his pocket with one hand and held a single finger to his own mouth with the other.

'Please don't,' he said. 'Don't even talk out loud to yourself' – he drew the hand away from his masked face, ran it flat across his neck – 'please don't *or else*.'

Chapter Twenty-eight

Jacobson did what, ideally, he always tried to do whenever one of his cases suddenly accelerated in seriousness: he made an excuse to be in his office on his own, he shut his door, he sat down at his desk – and he tried to think. His excuse on this occasion was that he needed to check up on whatever was happening in Birmingham, Coventry and Wolverhampton. Between the four forces involved, there were now a total of twenty-four officers dedicated to Operation Icarus. Plus, as of his uncongenial conversation with Greg Salter ten minutes ago – or, more precisely, as of Salter's probably self-serving talk with 'Dud' Bentham five minutes after that – any requests he made for additional, ad hoc help in his investigation were now officially designated as the current A1 priorities for every duty shift in Crowby: CID, Scene of Crime, Uniformed and Traffic. He made the three calls in turn, wanting each of them out of the way as quickly as possible. The Birmingham team were pursuing the location angle. The pattern of renting upmarket accommodation with bogus credit cards and references could in principle lead them to the Art Gang's latest whereabouts. Coventry meanwhile were focusing on transportation. One: evidence from the car-hire companies of any further potentially relevant hires. Two: the whereabouts of the white van associated with the gang. Three (connected to two): analysis of the hours of regional motorway camera footage that might yet reveal at least part of the journey the two BMWs had made en route to the site of the burn-outs and the ambush.

Coleman, the Birmingham DI, was unavailable when Jacobson tried all three of his numbers but the last one diverted to DS Barber.

'Barber, old son, your boss gone AWOL, has he?' Jacobson asked him.

'No, guv. He's in with the Super, trying to get him to free up some more resources.'

'Any useful news at last at your end then?'

Barber told him that the short answer was no. The long answer was that they were still wading through the massive list of letting agents who rented out upmarket properties in the city, were still focusing on central locations. Jacobson tried Coventry next where at least DCI Nelson answered his own phone: nothing new doing there either although they still had hours of camera footage to look at, Nelson commented, and might turn up something yet. Which only left DI Monroe in Wolverhampton. Monroe's team were fielding all the calls from the public that came through on the dedicated Operation Icarus phone line. The idea was that Wolverhampton would make an initial assessment on each call and then farm it out for fuller investigation if the contents of the call checked out as worth pursuing. The line had been up and running since yesterday afternoon but so far the majority of calls had been easily classifiable in the all-too-familiar Looney Tunes category: the lost and the lonely who saw high-profile police investigations – and the special telephone numbers that went with them – as an open invitation to make hoax calls, malicious calls (frequently seeking to stitch up personal enemies), and barking mad, downright crazy calls.

DI Monroe confirmed the usual pattern when Jacobson got through to her. Already this morning, she told him, they'd had a call claiming that the Art Gang were aliens who'd been abducting their victims for the purpose of scientific experimentation and another one claiming that a next-door neighbour (who'd turned out to be a septuagenarian church warden with an unruly dog) was involved.

'Par for the course,' Jacobson commented.

'Too true,' Monroe replied, 'we might be getting some-where with the coffin at last though.'

'What? The forensics are back on that already?'

Jacobson sat back in his chair with surprise. On TV, the most complex forensic analyses were completed in hours and minutes. In real life, even high-priority work took days, even weeks.

'No, not at all,' Monroe said. 'I'm talking about its prove-nance. There's not as many of these off-the-peg companies as you might think. Certainly if you're not happy with re-cycled cardboard or wicker and you want to use something that resembles a traditional wooden coffin anyway.'

Jacobson stood up now, carried the handset over to his window, looked down into the lunchtime-crowded pedes-trianised square while DI Monroe filled in the details. The coffin the Art Gang had used for the mock burials of Tracey Heald and the Wolverhampton victim turned out to have been customised from its original design. It had been lined with red satin and painted on the outside with a dark veneer. But on closer inspection, these had looked to be home-made additions (so, more obviously, were the breathing holes and lock fittings). Underneath the alterations, the coffin was made of plain, unvarnished pine, a character-istic, apparently, of the low-budget, DIY variety. Its other distinguishing feature was its four rope handles, two on either side.

'My DS thinks we might be able to narrow the possibil-ities down to maybe less than half-a-dozen suppliers,' Monroe concluded. 'That could be a useful lead, don't ye think?'

Jacobson agreed that it could be, said thanks politely – and rang off. It was nearly one o'clock and, down in the square, office workers and shoppers were strolling at leisure in the late autumn sunshine. The weather had been bitterly cold overnight, the way it had been all week, but in the last hour the wind had suddenly died down and, for now, it almost felt warm outside.

He sat back down at his desk, took out his notebook and the personalised Parker pen his daughter, Sally, had presented him with last Christmas. The computer was all very well, but when he really wanted to get his thoughts down in some kind of order, Jacobson's first recourse was still to pen and paper. A number of things worried him about the case – cases, really – and most of them could be summarised under one heading. He wrote the word out in capitals – ESCALATION – then just looked at it for a long minute. The first couple of victims had been duped into their predicament, had gone off willingly with their abductors. The next two had been forcibly seized. And now the latest victim had been car-jacked and her paid-for protector had been as good as left for dead. That was one side of it. The other was the issue of who the latest victim was: the daughter of a rich and famous man who thought it worth his while to employ a full-time body-guard. Plus, according to Kerr and Steve Horton, the victim was near enough a celebrity herself, maybe only a rung or two away from the top layer in the music business. The manner of her capture was worrying too. There seemed little room for doubt that it had been pre-planned and carefully orchestrated. But there was an even bigger worry than that, another way the MO was different from the first four attacks. The girl who'd died apart, none of the previous victims had been abducted for more than a few hours; all of them had been found – or had been able to free themselves – at first light. But January Shepherd had now been missing for around twelve hours, there was no sign of her in the vicinity of the burn-outs, and there'd been no further communication from the Art Gang. Jacobson wrote down a summary of his concerns then re-read what he'd written.

ESCALATION:

SEDUCTIONS - FORCED RANDOM ABDUCTIONS - FORCED NON-RANDOM (?)
ABDUCTION WITH EVIDENCE OF PRE-PLANNING.
ALSO ESCALATION OF LEVELS OF VIOLENCE:
  MOCK BURIALS - MOCK HANGING - SERIOUS ASSAULT ON BODYGUARD.
ALSO ESCALATION OF TIME ABDUCTEES HELD.
BIG WORRY:
J SHEPHERD MISSING 12+ HRS, WHEN WILL SHE BE SET FREE?
WILL SHE BE SET FREE?

Jacobson closed his notebook. More and more, he was also getting the feeling that the Art Gang considered themselves to be playing mind games with the force, some kind of you're-too-thick-to-catch-us routine. There was CCTV footage of every member, there were the gang's own films – and now there were also the conspicuously burnt-out BMWs and the hospitalised bodyguard. Without the last two items, January Shepherd would only be filed, if she was filed at all, as an ordinary, low-priority misper – a sane, adult, missing person, no further action mandated for at least forty-eight hours. He felt that he was dancing to someone else's tune and it was a feeling he didn't like in the least. Williams and Smith had been processing last night's reports, Mick Hume had been working on the CCTV images. But now all of that necessary work had been disrupted. He'd put Hume on stand-by for the moment at Crowby General, waiting for some definite news from the medical team who were assessing Perry Harrison. Harrison had remained unconscious all the way to the hospital and had been rushed to the intensive care unit on arrival. Hypothermia had been mentioned and so had concussion and the possibility of actual skull damage. But so far the doctors were being cagey about their full diagnosis and even more so about their prognosis. Until Jacobson knew exactly what was what he needed someone immediately on the scene in case there was the chance of a sudden recovery and the bodyguard became able to speak about what had happened. Williams and Smith were on their way to Boden Hall. There were other staff working there who Jacobson and Kerr hadn't spoken to earlier. What Jacobson wanted now was a comprehensive list of everyone on the premises (plus a similar list of recent visitors). He also wanted to know when each of them had last seen January Shepherd.

He grabbed his coat on the way out, not trusting the sudden improvement in the outside temperature to last. Besides, he could sling it in the back seat of Kerr's car if he didn't need it. They were headed for the Riverside Hotel next on the trail of the other members of Alice Banned who Jacobson had decided he wanted to interview himself. So far they only had John Shepherd's word at second-hand that his daughter had been there until one in the morning – and Jacobson didn't evaluate a bloke not actually all that much younger than himself, who'd been half-drunk in swimming trunks and Gucci slip-ons at eleven o'clock in the morning, as the world's most reliable witness.

He took the lift down to the rear exit and made his way across to the car park. Kerr was waiting for him, munching on a canteen cheese sandwich.

'If I'd known your were going to be this long, Frank, I'd have had a sit-down meal,' he commented, handing Jacobson the brown paper bag that contained a second canteen takeaway: a BLT and a scotch egg.

'Affairs of state, Ian,' Jacobson replied, 'Salter told me he was surprised we hadn't cleared this up yet by the way. He said we needed to think outside the box – and I don't think he was referring to the Art Gang's coffin.'

Kerr laughed, unlocking the car doors.

'We'd better step up to the plate and push the envelope then.'

'You've got it, old son. A raft of blue sky thinking all the way to the next level.'

Jacobson climbed in and fell deliberately silent. Extracting urine from Smoothie Greg was an amusing enough hobby. Or it would be on a day when January Shepherd wasn't missing in evil-seeming circumstances – or when DCI Frank Jacobson, for all his famous past successes, and for all his recent thinking and scribbling in his famous notebook, hadn't just realised that he didn't actually have the first, slightest idea where to start looking for her.

Chapter Twenty-nine

Jacobson and Kerr walked along the renovated, pine-floored corridor that led to the gardens of the Riverside Hotel. Jacobson was a regular visitor at Crowby's most prestigious hotel since he'd taken up with Alison Taylor but this was the first time since he'd met her that he'd been here on police business. On a night when he wasn't working and Alison was, he might spend a relaxing hour in one of the quieter bars while he waited for her shift to end. Kenneth Grant, the retired English teacher who lived ten minutes' walk away in Riverside Terrace called in sometimes too, if he was out walking his dog, and Jacobson liked to pick Grant's library-sized brain about books and ideas and the kind of topics that, generally speaking, didn't feature highly in the everyday routine of a CID inspector. Jacobson had first met Grant the same way he'd first met Alison: as a circumstantial witness in investigations which, otherwise, had nothing at all to do with his peaceful, well-ordered, civilised existence.

Ultimately, Jacobson's self-concept was that what he did for a living he did on behalf of people like Grant and Alison. People who didn't need to kill or steal or cheat or bully their way through life. People who needed protecting from those who did. The Riverside, he realised, had become a kind of oasis for him recently, a place where he encountered light more frequently than he encountered darkness. Though maybe, he thought, not today.

Kerr slid the glass door open and they stepped back out into fresh air. Alison wasn't actually here right now, had been called to a meeting at the hotel chain's regional office in Leamington Spa. On balance, Jacobson decided that it was probably a good thing – since it minimised any tricky interface between his private life and his public occupation. He'd still shown his ID at the reception desk even though the staff there knew perfectly well who he was.

The Alice Banned party were expecting them, were sitting around two tables near an ornamental pool in a remote corner which was well out of the way of any potential eavesdroppers. Jacobson and Kerr grabbed the two vacant chairs at the second table. The gardens were one of the hotel's best features, had been laid out in Victorian times and maintained, more-or-less, to the original design ever since. He counted six of them. Four musicians. The roadie. The sound engineer. Kerr took their details including their dates of birth and their passport numbers. None of them objected. The story from all of them, when Jacobson moved them on to it, was unanimous: January had come back here after the gig at the Wynarth Arms, had left about one AM in the merc driven by Perry Harrison since when none of them had heard from her. No phone calls. No text messages. Nothing.

They were all Americans apart from the Englishman, Nick Bishop. He was slightly built and dwarfed by the five tanned Californians, even by the woman who said she played keyboards, Melanie Clayton. Yet if there was a group leader present, it was clear that he was it. Like the others, he was looking anxiously at Jacobson and Kerr – as if being police gave them some special insight into what the hell to do next.

'You're supposed to be playing in Birmingham tonight?' Jacobson asked, scanning all of their faces, directing the question at no one in particular.

Only Bishop picked it up.

'That's right,' he answered. 'At the Birmingham Academy. It's the first proper night of the tour. Last night was a late addition, an unofficial warm-up.'

'And you've all been in the UK since when?'

'We flew into Heathrow, Monday. Apart from January, she flew over on her own a couple of days earlier.'

'And she's been staying all that time at her dad's place, Boden Hall.'

'As far as we know,' Bishop said.

The others nodded.

'January left LA on Friday,' Melanie Clayton added. 'Caught a connection to Birmingham via Paris, France.'

Jacobson didn't bother to comment that he already knew where Paris was. She produced a packet of Marlboro from an expensive-looking leather bag, took one out and lit up. Jacobson mirrored her, mentally tallied it as his third today.

'Coming back to England like this, maybe there's just some old friend she wanted to see in the area,' he observed.

He knew the suggestion was dead in the water, knew in his guts that January Shepherd was in trouble. But he also needed all the background information he could get.

Nick Bishop shook his head.

'January hasn't lived permanently in England since she was ten. And even before that her mum and dad lived all over. Touring and then travelling around between tours.'

'I thought she went to high school here though?' Melanie Clayton asked.

'Yeah, she did,' Bishop said, 'but at a boarding school. I think she mainly flew back to the States out of term time. Plus the school was down in the south-east. I doubt if she's set foot in Crowby before this week.'

'And you're from down that way too originally?' Kerr asked, looking up from his notes.

'Yeah, Guildford. But don't hold that against me.'

Bishop looked awkward after he made his joke, probably thinking this was no time for levity. But Kerr and Jacobson both knew from long experience that there was more than one prescribed way to behave when the police were bringing you bad news.

'We'll try not to,' Jacobson said. 'What are you going to do about your, er, gig?'

Nick Bishop looked at the others but none of them seemed keen to displace him as Alice Banned's official spokesman.

'We're going to call it off, what else can we do? January's going to be in no state to perform when she turns up, is she? I mean, look at the kind of thing that happened to the other women these weirdos abducted.'

'Everything's circumstantial at the moment, Mr Bishop. We don't actually know yet that January's connected in any way to the other incidents,' Jacobson lied.

He'd wondered how much to reveal to the musicians but it was clear that they'd been in communication with John Shepherd who, at this stage, knew almost as much about what had happened as CID did.

'Tonight's the real get-go for the tour,' Randy the drummer said from the far end of the other table. 'No way is January taking off on her own right now. Someone's grabbed her, man. Some evil, twisted fucker.'

He was a blond giant with tattoos rippling down both arms and a T shirt that proclaimed Rage Against The Machine. He was also, Jacobson felt sure, a hundred and ten per cent correct.

'We're doing everything we can, believe me,' he said as convincingly as he could.

'The gig last night though – you said that it was a last-minute thing, er, Nick?'

Nick Bishop nodded.

'So when exactly was it set up? And how did your fans get to hear about it?'

'It was January's idea, really. Because her dad's living here now and because this is where he started out years ago. I think she saw it as paying dues somehow. I wasn't too fussed – but she had her heart set on it so I gave in,' Bishop replied. 'We fixed the date up a couple of weeks ago, put the news up on our website as soon as it was agreed with the venue.'

'I don't suppose you know exactly when that was?' Jacobson asked.

He was thinking about the fact that the car-jack must have been carefully planned. As an absolute minimum, the Art Gang needed to have known that Alice Banned were playing at the Wynarth Arms last night and that January Shepherd would be likely to drive back to Boden Hall after the gig.

Bishop looked doubtful but Melanie Clayton came to his rescue. She produced a Blackberry from her bag, scrolled through a couple of screens until she found the relevant information.

'We posted the word about the gig on September 12, 07.59 hours Pacific Time. It's the way Nick says – just over two weeks ago.'

'Plus we plugged it in our radio interview,' Bishop said.

'Radio interview?' Jacobson asked.

'Yeah, January and I did a phone interview from the States for the BBC – Radio 6 – ahead of the tour starting.'

Melanie Clayton had those details in her gizmo too.

'The broadcast went out here last Thursday night, just after seven. You're thinking how did these fuckers *know* where January would be last night, right?'

'Like I say, everything's mainly speculation at this stage. I take it you're all staying on here for now?'

Nick Bishop said that they would be. Jacobson stood up to leave.

'Fine. If there's any change to your plans please let someone on my team know.'

He gave Bishop one of his cards, added that all of them could contact him personally any time if something – anything – that might be relevant occurred to any of them later on.

Bishop said thanks then stuck the card in his pocket. Melanie Clayton stubbed out her cigarette and immediately took another one out of the pack. The others stayed exactly where they were, not moving, not speaking, not bothering to look up. Jacobson had thought that he knew next to nothing about how it would be to work in a rock band, playing together, travelling together. But suddenly he realised that he knew one really important, really fundamental thing already – and that he knew it, surprisingly, from the inside. A functioning band was exactly like a close-knit family or a close-knit police team: whatever hurt one of them, hurt all of them.

He checked with Mick Hume on the drive back to the Divisional building. Perry Harrison was still unconscious, the medical team were still investigating what could be done for him. His phone rang again before he could consign it back into his pocket. Henry Pelling, the *Evening Argus*'s chief crime reporter: the Art Gang had sent out a new film to their media distribution list, which Pelling was looking at right now.

'The good news from your point of view, Frank, is that there doesn't seem to be any sign of a new incident. It just looks like a rerun of what they've shown us before. Their effing greatest hits. Plus what they're calling their Art Terror Manifesto.'

'Manifesto, Henry? What the blazes—'

'Just what I say. The Art Terror Manifesto. It comes up like subtitles all the way through – and they've even sent it out as a text file in addition.'

Jacobson pressed his phone closer to his ear as they passed under the railway bridge.

He asked Pelling for a representative sample.

'Try this then. *Consumer society lies and stultifies. Consumer culture makes us all inmates inside its falsifying open prison. Only fear brings freedom. Only fear restores us to reality. Only—*'

'Thanks Henry,' Jacobson cut in, 'I think I get the flavour. No doubt you'll pass on full copies to us?'

'Already done, mate. I've emailed the lot to Boy Wonder Horton. And your exclusive tip-off in return is?'

'There's no new developments I can tell you about yet, old son,' Jacobson answered, choosing his words carefully. 'Like you say, even their own film is just a recap.'

The news that January Shepherd was missing – and was probably in the hands of the Art Gang – would send the media into overdrive when they found out. And find out they would, one way or another way. The Riverside Hotel staff would be wondering why the police had wanted to talk to the rock band staying there. A hard-up hospital employee might work out who Perry Harrison was connected to. Most of all, the Birmingham Academy (one of the city's premier music venues, he'd just learned from Kerr) would want to know *why* Alice Banned were pulling out of a gig they'd crossed the Atlantic for. That, Jacobson reckoned, would be when the shit would actually hit the fan. But he still had a few hours' grace before then. Nick Bishop had agreed to hold off contacting the Academy until five o'clock, probably as much in the vain hope that January Shepherd would turn up safe and well before then as anything else. Jacobson thanked Pelling for his call, rang off.

They were approaching the Divisional building now and the traffic had slowed to a post-lunchtime crawl. His phone rang a second time: DCS Greg Salter.

'Frank. I'm postponing the press conference until things are clearer. Good idea, you agree?'

'It's a good idea all right, *Greg*. The media will go apeshit once they know about January Shepherd and the car-jack. So there's no point facing them before we have to.'

'That's what I thought,' Salter replied, ending the call.

Jacobson at last managed to return his phone to his pocket. Greg Salter, he realised, had just made a sensible decision. He'd never been sold on the old theory about the monkeys, the typewriters and the works of Shakespeare. But now he wondered if he needed to reconsider his opinion. His phone rang again just as Kerr finally pulled into the police car park. He checked the display, saw that it was Henry Pelling calling back – and probably wanting a clue as to why the press conference had just been put on hold. This time Jacobson just let the damned thing ring, didn't bother to press the answer button. Pelling was very nearly a mate but he was also a journalist. If he couldn't put the latest story together for himself, it wasn't Jacobson's job to do it for him.

January ate every last crumb they'd given her and drank every last drop of the orange juice. She'd even hobbled into the tiny bathroom, filled the empty juice carton with water from the cold tap and drank some of that down too. When she'd finished eating and drinking she'd gone back into the bathroom and tried to get the shower started but it had produced no more than a minute trickle of cold water. The hot tap at the basin likewise. Undaunted, she'd turned the cold tap on again and splashed cold water on her face and down her body then dried herself patchily with the rough, non-luxurious face towel.

Having her hands free didn't extend her overall range of movement which was still restricted by the shackles on her ankles. What it did do was give her more opportunity to fully explore her restricted environment. She'd been looking for a tool mainly, or something that could function as a tool, thinking that maybe she could get out of the shackles somehow. But she hadn't found anything. Not even when she'd looked under the bed and under the mattress. Not even when she'd lifted the top off the cistern in the bathroom. Her wrists were still hurting like hell and now she was sitting on the edge of the bed again, rubbing them and massaging them – and trying to ease the stiffness out of her fingers. She wasn't sure what she'd be able to do next anyway in the remote circumstance that she managed to remove the shackles. The door was locked from the other side and the board on the window looked solid and securely nailed in place. And even if she could get out of here, meaning this room, she had no idea of what lay beyond it or how seriously they'd meant their threat about her keeping quiet and not causing them any trouble.

Stay positive, she tried to tell herself. At least she hadn't just been abandoned somewhere. And she'd been given food and drink, wasn't being left here to starve. Also, although she couldn't be sure exactly how long she'd been here, she was sure that it must be long enough by now for her to be *missed*. Dad would miss her, even Kelly and Birgit. And so would Nick and the rest of the band. They'd have tried to reach her on her mobile. Dad would have phoned the hotel and the band would have phoned Boden Hall. Between them, they'd have pieced together that something was wrong. Somebody would probably have contacted the police. If she knew her dad like she thought she did, he'd be pulling strings, calling in favours, making sure they were doing everything to find her. This was just this mad gang from the TV and the newspapers surely, pulling another mad stunt. But they'd let her go, of course they would. They'd let those other women go, after all, hadn't they?

She picked the carton up from the little bamboo table, took another deep mouthful of water. The main thing – the only thing – was not to panic, not to lose it. If she believed she could get out of this she would get out of this. The summer of the year she'd turned fourteen, Dad and Mum (they'd still been together then) had been living at an ashram out in Sedona. Every morning at sunrise everybody who was there – residents, guests, adults, kids – practised meditations and affirmations. The one that had appealed to January, that she still used from time to time, had been meant specifically for travellers or for anyone who found themselves in a strange, unfamiliar place. *The world is my home. And I am always welcome here*. She tried it now, *breathing* each word, making each word her own, affirming to herself that this really was the case – that wherever she was, was somewhere she belonged and where no harm would befall her.

She kept her voice low, barely a whisper, but she kept the affirmation going, turning the rhythm towards a chant.

Rattling. Then the door burst open. One of the women standing in the doorway. But not the one who'd been here earlier. This was the other one, the taller one. January noticed, without immediately grasping its significance, that she was holding something that looked like a thick leather belt coiled in her free hand.

The woman strode into the room.

'You were told to keep your mouth shut,' she said. 'You were warned not to say one fucking word out loud.'

Chapter Thirty

There were two parking spaces unclaimed in the staff car park. One unmarked and one marked 'Deputy Head'. Kerr chose the latter, unable to resist the impulse of his inner schoolboy. He parked up and walked towards the main entrance. The Operation Icarus phone line had thrown up a lead that hadn't been instantly rejected as bogus or bananas. A clubber had phoned to say she'd thought she'd spoken to one of the Art Gang at the Wynarth Arms all-nighter last Saturday night. The description she gave had sounded like 'Adrian'. By day the clubber worked as an art teacher at the Simon de Montfort Comp and Kerr had arranged to talk to her during the afternoon break. Jacobson had stayed put in the Divisional building: coordinating and 'thinking'.

A tongue-tied lad was dispatched to lead Kerr through the corridors to the teacher-stroke-night-owl's classroom. The teacher, Ruth Sutton, was daubing at a large, abstract canvas that reminded Kerr of the exhibitions of Tony Scruton's paintings which Rachel used to drag him along to, insisting that Scruton was only her friend and definitely not (or not any longer) her lover. Kerr tried to put the association to one side. Whoever was to blame about Rachel and him it was hardly this stranger's fault. Sutton turned out to be as young as Kerr had guessed she would be given her choice of weekend entertainment venue.

He showed her a couple of e-fits and Ruth Sutton repeated her claim that the one she'd spoken to had been 'Adrian'. Kerr liked her dark hair and hazel eyes and the curve of her breasts under her paint-splattered man's shirt. But A) she was even younger than Rachel had been when he'd met her, B) he'd had enough of arty women to last several lifetimes and C) he had a wife and two kids at home. Item C hadn't stopped him up until now yet he knew he'd been bloody lucky not to get caught, wasn't sure he wanted to go on running the kind of risks he'd been taking. He asked her to fill in the background to the story she'd already given to the hotline.

'I was standing at the bar, which was crowded as usual, trying to get a round in,' she said. 'And this guy started smarming me, offered to help me get served – all that business.'

Kerr studied his notebook.

'And this was around midnight?'

'Yeah, I think so. My friends and I had just driven over from Crowby so I don't see how it could have been any earlier.'

'You think he was trying to pick you up then?'

'Sort of. I don't reckon he was too serious about it. More like he was on auto-pilot. Oh look, there's a pair of tits – better move in.'

Kerr wasn't sure whether to smile or not – so he didn't.

'You said you thought he was on his own.'

'That's how it looked to me. I clocked him a couple of times after I was back with my friends. And he was still standing in the same place at the bar nursing a drink. It really creeps me out now – I mean, what if?'

Kerr nodded.

'He didn't mention who he was, where he was from, anything like that?'

'No, he didn't even say his name or ask mine. That's what I mean about not being serious. He wasn't local though. I know the accents well enough by now. Apart from wanting to get my drinks for me – prat – he mainly banged on asking what the place was like when there was live music on. It's all DJs on Saturdays by the way.'

Kerr thought about Item A again – clearly he was no longer expected to know this kind of detail at his advanced age.

'What it was *like*?' he repeated.

'Yeah. Was it easy to get a clear view of the stage when the bands came on? Stuff like that. Weird really – not exactly an award-winning chat-up line.'

The period bell sounded out in the corridor. Even years later, it still grated, still made you wish you were somewhere else. He asked her if she'd seen when he'd left the place but she said she wasn't sure. She'd forgotten about him well before one AM, hadn't noticed him again after that, hadn't thought about him again until she'd seen one of the news reports on TV last night.

'Thanks anyway,' Kerr told her, 'what you do remember's been helpful.'

'But you still have to work out where they are now though,' she objected, clearing her brushes away, maybe preparing for the onslaught of the next lesson.

'I'm afraid you're right there – but the more help we get from the public the better,' he said lamely – and thinking that not chatting up could be more difficult than chatting up.

Back at his car he looked on his mobile for messages: nothing. He thought about phoning Cathy, who'd just be about setting off now to pick up the twins from the infant school. But to say what exactly? Some mundane question about how her day was going? Or something profound – such as I've been cheating on you for five years now, it might be over at last – but if it is, I probably wish that it wasn't. Instead he phoned Jacobson to check in, returned Cathy and the twins and Rachel and Tony Scruton to his over-used mental compartment labelled 'DIFFICULT – DEAL WITH LATER'.

The return drive to town took fifteen minutes. He caught up with Jacobson in person inside Steve Horton's cramped second-floor office. Mick Hume was still on stand-by at Crowby General but it turned out that, before he'd left, he'd substantially completed the task Jacobson had set him earlier in the day: pre-select the best available images of the Art Gang before Horton ran the software program which would sift and meld them into the best-possible composites. Jacobson had interrupted Horton at work (not a rare occurrence) with a new request: what he wanted now was to look *chronologically* at the images which Mick Hume had picked out.

Kerr squeezed into the room next to Jacobson just as Horton started to bring the images consecutively onscreen.

'I'm trying to build up the time line, Ian,' Jacobson explained. 'We don't know whereabouts or how long ago these four customers started out in their line of work. We don't know where the hell they are right now. But there is some stuff that we *do* know.'

Kerr studied the first two images: stills from the CCTV cameras at the Royal Mail's Watford sorting office. The same young woman each time. Despite the sunglasses, and the careful angle she'd moved at, as if hyper-aware of being filmed, they'd tentatively identified her as 'Maria'.

'The Watford box number has been functioning since the twenty-first of August and emptied out just twice – on the sixth of September and then again on the fourteenth,' Jacobson said, his eyes darting between the screen and his notebook. 'This means we *know* the gang's been in business at least since August and we can reasonably *infer* that some or all of them were in the vicinity of Watford just less than a fortnight ago. Not only that but, according to Emma Smith and Ray Williams, the incorporation documents for the phoney public relations company that the gang used as a reference for the Hat Factory rental were also set up in August – Thursday the tenth to be precise.'

He indicated to Horton that he should bring up the next image.

'And here's "Brady" caught on the entrance cam at the Hat Factory a week ago on Monday – the eighteenth of September,' he said, pointing. 'The guy next to him is the letting agent. This is when "Brady" at least moves into Crowby – along with the white van which shows up several times over the rest of the week entering and exiting the Hat Factory's underground car park.'

Kerr took in the details of the face, wondered if the smug contempt for the human race he detected on it was really there – or whether he was only reading the expression that way because of everything else he knew about 'Brady'.

'This is the only shot we have of any them from the Hat Factory's entrance cam, isn't it?' he asked.

'It looks that way, old son. Hume thinks there might be a shot of "Adrian" as well but apparently the quality's too poor to be much use – mainly because whoever it was shielded their face with their hand. Otherwise they've obviously been careful to enter or exit the building by vehicle as much as possible while they were based there.'

Kerr nodded. The building's vehicle entrance and exit barrier cameras, he recalled, had been set up to capture registration plates only.

Steve Horton clicked through the rest of the images and Jacobson outlined the sequence of events that each one confirmed. Saturday night: 'Brady', 'Maria' and 'Annabel' in Club Zoo, Crowby. Sunday night: 'Adrian', 'Maria' and 'Annabel' in the student pub in Birmingham. Tuesday night: 'Brady' and 'Annabel' in All Bar One, Coventry. Always there were differences in each appearance. Changes of hair colour and hair style. Changes of eye colour, complexion and skin tone. Glasses and not glasses. Facial hair and not facial hair in the case of the two men. But there were underlying similarities too: the kind of thing that Horton's computer program promised to identify and enhance.

'So they hit Crowby sometime last week, probably the Monday, probably from down South. They're here as recently

245

as Sunday morning and they show up in Birmingham Sunday night,' Kerr commented.

'Except that we know that one of them – probably "Maria" according to the witness descriptions – hired the second BMW in Birmingham at twelve minutes past two on Sunday afternoon so the chances are that they were all in Brum by then.'

'Of course. I was forgetting that, Frank. The garage where the security cameras were down.'

Jacobson fidgeted with a broken hard drive until Horton asked him not to touch it – told him it was something he was planning on fixing.

'Sorry, Steve. Yep, that's the one. But we still *know* that she was there. The girl they pegged out on Edgbaston golf course remembered the number and Barber and co. were easily able to trace the precise time the hire went through the garage's computer.'

'Which is why you think they've been using phoney plates ever since.'

'Either that or every traffic cop in the region is blind as a bat, old son. And that can't be true of all of them.'

Jacobson apologised to Horton for the interruption and squeezed back out into the corridor. Kerr followed him.

'Now we've found out that "Adrian" was probably in the Wynarth Arms on Saturday night, we might be able to get an image of that appearance as well, Frank.'

'Yep, that'll add nicely to the collection. It also confirms Tracey Heald's story that the fourth gang member turned up *after* she'd already gone with the other three to the Hat Factory apartment. I'm seeing them as in Crowby until Sunday and then somewhere in Birmingham until last night.'

'And now they're back here?'

Jacobson walked towards the lift and pressed the going up button.

'Or somewhere within striking distance of here, old son,' he said. 'But there's something else comes out of all this.'

'Which is?'

'I checked back with Melanie Clayton again while you were over at Simon de Montford Comp. According to her, the band's UK tour was first publicly announced on their website on Monday August seventh.'

'And the earliest date we can connect to the Art Gang is August tenth – when they set up their phoney company?'

'Exactly, old son. Plus the letting at the Hat Factory was a last-minute affair. "Brady", that's who we're assuming anyway, makes his initial call to the letting agent on September twelfth – and actually moves in, or at least picks up the keys, on the eighteenth.'

'Hang on. Wasn't September twelfth when Melanie Clayton said they'd posted the news about the extra gig at the Wynarth Arms?'

The lift arrived – empty – and both of them stepped in.

'Yes it was,' Jacobson replied. 'Allowing for the time difference between here and California, he phoned the letting agent inside an hour of the website being, er, updated.'

'So what you're thinking is that—'

'Is that we could be looking at a highly targeted operation here, Ian. We've been thinking the Art Gang came to Crowby and then went to Birmingham. But it could be that it was Crowby that was the late addition to their plan – something they slotted in once the band's last-minute extra gig was announced.'

Kerr pressed the buttons for floors four and five.

'And their ultimate target was always January Shepherd, you mean?'

Jacobson half-smiled, half-frowned.

'That's the way it's looking to me. Why else was "Adrian" checking out the Wynarth Arms on Saturday night? There could be some kind of method in their madness after all – as the poet nearly says.'

Mick Hume was finally granted an audience with a junior

consultant. They talked in the office which belonged to the doctor's boss. A faded travel poster on the far wall showed a cruise ship moored in the bay at Santorini.

'It's bad, I have to tell you,' the doctor said. 'Epidural hematoma. The prof thinks it's operable – just. It's hit or miss, frankly, whether he pulls through.'

'Hematoma? You mean a blood clot on the brain basically?' Hume asked.

Like anyone who'd served on a murder squad for a few years, he had a working medical vocabulary for the kinds of life-threatening conditions that could be easily inflicted by hand, boot or weapon.

'Technically, it means a clot between the skull and the dura mater. Theoretically and statistically that's not as dangerous a condition as a subdural clot. But in this case . . .'

The doctor's voice trailed off while he flicked through the pile of X-rays he'd brought with him.

Hume kept his face looking appropriately grim. He knew what a lot of lay people didn't: that between the brain and the skull there was a thick leathery layer known as the dura. It functioned partly to further protect the brain, partly to nourish it with supplies of blood and spinal fluid. But if you hit somebody's head hard enough, you could actually make the brain bounce inside its casing with the result that some of the blood vessels around the dura could tear. Left untreated, the victim would lapse in and out of consciousness for several hours – but eventually the accumulation of blood in a space where there shouldn't be any would result in fatal swelling of the brain.

The doctor placed an X-ray photo on one of those light-up wall display things that Hume must have seen a hundred times but had never actually found out the name of. By contrast, the doctor's name was neatly printed on his lapel badge: J.E. Macpherson, although his irritating Oxbridge accent suggested to Hume that it was a long time since he'd visited the land of his ancestors, if ever.

'There are other problems too,' Macpherson said. 'The

248

prof thinks there might already be signs of cerebral contusions. And quite apart from the concerns about his brain, his core body temperature was moving into the hypothermic range when he was found. He's a big chap. Tough. Strong heart and lungs. But even so.'

He pointed a light pen at the X-ray, flashed a red dot onto the parts of the image he wanted Hume to look at.

'This is from the CT scan. This high-density area here is where our problem lies.'

Hume pretended to study it closely. The technicalities weren't really his concern – just the outcome.

'So you're operating soon?'

'Just as soon as the team's ready,' Macpherson replied, tapping the pager clipped to his tunic pocket.

'And he's still out?'

'Yes, he's out all right. Another hour or so in the woods and he would have been the pathology department's worry, not ours.'

Hume asked him about the actual surface damage to the skull. Macpherson replaced the first X-ray with a second one, flashed his light pen again.

'Pretty localised as you can see. Whatever was used wasn't a large object – or the area of it that impacted wasn't at any rate.'

'So you couldn't say what exactly—'

'That's definitely not our department, I'm afraid. If he doesn't make it, I dare say the pathologist will be able to enlighten you.'

Cheers, mate, Hume thought, this is only a man's life we're talking about. Then he reflected that Macpherson was just doing his job, probably had to check in his emotions at the hospital doors if he was going to be any use at it – and that there was no shortage of coppers who could leave him standing in the hard-nosed, callous bastard stakes. On a bad day, he knew, he could give him a decent run for his money himself.

*

January couldn't stop crying. Crying silently, terror-stricken that she'd make some kind of too-audible sound. She hated herself for it but the hate wasn't enough to stem the tears. Nobody, it came to her, had ever hit her before. Not even, she thought, when she'd been a kid. Certainly not her dad or her mum. Certainly not any adult. And she couldn't remember any playground incident either – or not one serious enough to have lodged itself in her memory. Most of her life people had liked her, had liked to keep her in her warm, safe bubble of wealth and talent and beauty. The pain was only part of it, although it was a big part. The other parts were psychological: fear and powerlessness and some kind of weird sense of shame. That was the part she couldn't figure. It wasn't her fault that this stuff was happening to her. She'd even tried to struggle when they'd been forcing her into the car boot. She'd put up a fight, tried to get away. And she was shackled now, trapped. She hadn't stood a chance when the woman had burst in. So what was it that she felt ashamed about? *I'm naked and they're not.* The thought took her by surprise. She repeated it to herself, amazed by it but recognising its truth. She'd never in her life worried about nakedness before, had no hang-ups about her own body or anyone else's. But this was different, she realised. Another element in the sordid little power game they seemed to be playing. Another aspect of keeping her under their control. *I haven't even seen their faces and they've seen all of me.* She'd mainly been lying face down on the bed since the woman had gone, just letting the tears flow. She decided that she'd try sitting up now, maybe even stand up – try and get some kind of grip on the panic that kept threatening to overwhelm her.

She leant over the edge of the bed and picked up the orange juice carton from the floor. It must have got knocked over during the assault but it was a detail she couldn't remember. She got up onto her feet and hobbled to the bathroom, refilled the carton from the cold tap and then gulped down several greedy mouthfuls of water. You could go a long time without sufficient food, she knew, but dehydration was a different matter entirely, could affect you within hours. There was a tiny square of mirror above the sink, cracked and peeling along one corner. When she'd drunk her fill, she turned her back to it and squinted at her reflection over her shoulder. She had to bend down a little to get the best view. The tears started again while she studied the damage that had been done to her – and she had to bite hard into her tongue to keep from crying out at the visual shock of it.

The woman had come at her like a whirlwind, spinning her round and pushing her down onto the bed, pinning her to it with her weight. She'd lashed at her back mercilessly, had used the belt buckle as well as the belt. January had screamed at her to stop but the woman had acted like she hadn't noticed, had just carried on raining blows down on her as if she was in a frenzy. When she'd finished, she'd grabbed January roughly by her hair, had forced her head up and sideways at a painful angle.

'See?' she'd shouted in her ear, pointing at the light fitting on the ceiling with her belt hand. 'It's called a webcam, you thick, stupid bitch. We can see and hear everything you do in here. Understand? Everything.'

January had nodded docilely. She'd moved her lips to speak but what came out was the barest whimper, a tiny, frightened voice that she barely identified as her own: *yes, I understand*.

The woman had released her after that, had stood back like a conqueror and watched January lift herself up from the bed, afraid to even touch her back and yet wanting to know how badly she'd been injured. The woman was masked and January could only see her eyes and a pink fraction of her mouth. But she still knew for certain that the woman had been smiling and elated as she'd stood there watching her. It felt to January as if the thing the woman had just

251

done was something that she'd wanted to do for a long, long time. Not necessarily to January personally. But to do to someone, maybe just to anyone. To hold them down, to beat them till they begged her to stop, to really, really hurt them.

Her back actually looked as if it had stripes: they were red and swollen, crusting over now where they'd been bleeding. Time was fading as a useful concept. Yet not that long ago, probably still not a day ago, she'd been January Shepherd, John Shepherd's daughter, singer and guitarist with Alice Banned, someone with her own fan club, someone who only read about bad stuff in the newspapers, someone with a rich, full life. But now when she looked in the mirror what she saw was someone she scarcely recognised. A scared, tired, naked, battered, shackled woman. A woman defined and limited by this shitty little room that held her prisoner. She picked up the mean, undersized face towel from the rail next to the basin and slowly wiped away her freshest tears.

Chapter Thirty-one

John Shepherd had his personal mobile, his personal/business mobile, his business mobile and one of the Boden Hall landline handsets laid out in a neat row on the poolside table. If he was in a mood for not answering a particular caller, he'd sometimes listen to their progress up or down this hierarchical chain of access as they tried – and failed – to get through to him. The landline number was theoretically ex-directory but that didn't seem to stop strangers on the make from getting hold of it, from chancing their luck with requests for interviews or charity appearances or pleas for investment cash connected to all kinds of ludicrous schemes and so-called business and/or creative ventures. All last week, he'd been plagued by a series of calls from some PR minion in the Geldof/Bono circus, wanting to sign him up for some anti-hunger gig or other. As if the problems created by rampaging global capitalism could be solved by a few musos bashing out a barré chord or two and patting each other's egos on the back. He got less time-wasting calls on the mobiles but even they weren't a foolproof barrier to the world's hustlers, dreamers and crazies. Kelly had told him that there were websites and discussion boards on the internet these days where 'celebrity' telephone numbers – and other details – were shared, traded and exchanged. There wasn't a lot that could be done about it apparently other than to change your numbers frequently. He'd sobered up since this morning, or just about, had finally taken Kelly's advice on the subject. If January *was* missing or in some kind of trouble, she'd argued, he wasn't going to be in too much of a position to help her if he was staggering about Boden Hall blind-drunk on French brandy. *You need to be in a good place till it's sorted, John,* she'd said. And somewhere into the second half of a bottle of Fussigny XO, he'd finally listened to her, had showered again, got dressed properly, downed a couple of ibuprofen and forced down a litre of still Malvern water.

Kelly was in the kitchen, cooking something up with Birgit. A hangover special, she'd described it as, adding that he needed to get something solid inside him. *As the bishop said to the actress, Kel,* he'd replied – and then felt crap with himself, playing the joker on autopilot when his daughter's life might be in danger. Might be: he had to keep thinking like that. Only might be. Not definite. Not certain. He was on coffee now, although with hot milk: he didn't think his stomach could stand it black yet. He poured out a refill and stared across the pool. The house was big, grand, but he always gravitated towards this spot or to the outdoor pool if the weather was warm enough. A consequence of too many years in Southern California, he sometimes thought, where you could live your whole life poolside. He tried to think about how much he really knew about his daughter these days; whether there was anything she'd said or hinted at recently that would give him a clue to what might have happened or where she might be. There wasn't, he realised. She hadn't lived with him for a few years now, even before he'd quit the States and come back here. He'd bought her own place for her on her eighteenth birthday. An apartment on the north side of Ocean Avenue with a view out over the bay. Red sunsets. Soft sea-breeze mornings. He'd still see her from time to time (although not as much as he would have liked), she'd still drive over to his house in the canyon on a whim. Especially if she wanted to mess around in his recording studio or talk about Zen Buddhism with Susanne, the live-in before Kelly, the one who'd buggered off the minute he'd helped her get her first record company deal. He'd been burnt out on his own quest for enlightenment by then of course, had rejected all of his gurus as liars, charlatans or fools. He'd settled on booze instead as the easy, always-reliable way to blur the edges of the unavoidable fact that, no matter how cool or how rich you were, one day you'd grow old and die. Fuck rebirth, fuck higher planes of existence: none of that esoteric shit could keep you *here* – in the only lifetime that mattered to him, with the only people, places and things he actually cared about.

The personal/business mobile rang: 'Surf's Up', the old Brian Wilson number he'd fixed up as a ringtone for Nick Bishop on the sarcasm grounds that although Bishop had spent a couple of years out in LA, his skinny, retarded English body was about as unfit for surfboard duty as it was possible to imagine. Bishop came into the category of callers he wouldn't automatically speak to (not that Bishop had ever phoned him more than a couple of times in any case). But not today. Today anybody who knew January even slightly had been promoted on to his must-answer hot list.

'Nick, any news?' he asked him straightforwardly.

'No. I was hoping maybe you'd heard something.'

'Nothing. The police have gone dead on me, all they'll say is that as soon as they know something they'll be in touch. Even Bentham, the chief constable – who's been in my house, who's sampled my fine fucking wines and spirits – won't deviate from that fucking clap-trap bollocks. It's been hours now, Nick.'

'What about Perry?' Bishop asked him.

'They're about to operate as far as I know. I've told them no expense, get the top experts in, all that. But they say the guy who's doing it's good. That it would still be his team in any case.'

'I was thinking maybe some of the band should go over there. His mother's on her way up from Kent apparently.'

Shepherd swallowed a mouthful of coffee, switched the

phone on to broadcast so he didn't need to hold it up to his ear.

'Yeah, it would be good if she's not on her own at the hospital. Birgit is going to meet her at the station, drive her straight there. I'd wondered if Kelly and myself should go over – but I'm weird about leaving this place in case January just walks in the door somehow.'

'We should keep in touch anyway,' Nick Bishop said, 'share information.'

'Sure. You bet. That's what we should do,' Shepherd answered.

The call was petering out and they both knew it. Neither of them liked the other one particularly and Shepherd was aware that Bishop had no time for him as a musician, no respect for what had gone before. But right now they had a common bond that put them temporarily on the same side.

'OK. Talk later,' Bishop said.

'OK. Later. Oh and Nick?'

'Yeah?'

'Thanks, mate. Thanks for calling.'

Brady (the great intellectual) was watching *Richard and Judy* from an armchair and only periodically switching the TV to the signal from the webcam. On the sofa, Maria was painting Annabel's toenails a rich, dark purple. Nobody, it seemed, was on 'official surveillance' in the outhouse. Adrian had tried his best to let what had happened go. It wasn't important and there was probably no permanent damage done. He'd seen the whole thing in his bedroom via the laptop, had told himself to ignore it. But now here he was, marching straight into the lounge, grabbing the TV remote right out of Brady's hand and cutting the sound, making sure that he had their attention.

'Ade' – Brady shot him a surprised look – 'what the fuck?'

'Annabel, that's what the fuck,' Adrian said, standing right in front of the TV screen.

'You're supposed to be the control freak, Brady. You could start with controlling this mad bitch.'

He pointed the remote control in Annabel's direction. Maria stopped what she was doing, inserted the little brush back in the little bottle, placed the bottle carefully on a side table. All three of them were looking at him.

'Calm down, Ade,' Brady said, still stretched out comfortably in his chair. He was keeping his voice relaxed, entirely as if there was no sudden crisis, no sudden big deal. 'Annabel likes that kind of fun. We all do, that's why we're here, isn't it?'

'There's supposed to be limits, Brady. You know that. No sex, no serious physical injuries.'

'Exactly – and we've stuck to that, haven't we?'

Adrian switched the TV to the webcam channel but kept the volume on mute.

'Her back doesn't look too good to me,' he replied, 'not good at all.'

'Relax, Adrian. Maria will pay her a visit in a little while, patch her up – a bit of antiseptic, maybe some bandaging, a spot of TLC.'

'It's not the first time though, is it? Don't forget Coventry. That girl had taken all she could take – but Annabel tries stringing her up again. That's how come she ended up escaping, ended up dead in case you've forgotten.'

Annabel took a cigarette out of the nearest packet and held it to her mouth.

'Adrian,' she said, after Maria had lit it for her, 'it's a bit late now for an attack of bourgeois guilt, isn't it?'

Adrian ignored her, kept his eyes on Brady. This was the confrontation he'd warned himself to avoid, yet he was provoking it, even relishing it.

'All the way through it's been the same. You say no sex – but she's had her hands all over every one of them.'

'I'd hardly call a quick feel in passing *sex*, Adrian,' Annabel said, affecting her smile. 'Although I suppose from your point of view—'

'Shut it, Annabel,' Brady said, his voice hardening. 'Adrian has a valid point. You *have* been bending the no sex rule – a rule which is there for a very good reason.'

'For a negative reason, surely,' Annabel countered. 'Who cares what kind of charges they can or can't bring if we get caught? We're *not* going to get caught.'

Brady got to his feet now. One dissenter in the ranks seemed to be regarded as an armchair matter, Adrian thought, but not, evidently, two. He faced Brady when he stood up, aware of his own superior height, maybe weighing him up in that regard for the very first time.

'Look, I'm just saying there was no need, that's all. I watched the whole thing on the webcam. Annabel was out of control. If January Shepherd had put up more of a fight, Christ knows what might've happened.'

'That cowed bitch,' Annabel sneered from the sofa, 'fat chance. She'd kiss my arse if I told her to – and if it wasn't against the famous rules.'

'I said shut it,' Brady said, not bothering to look at her, keeping his attention fixed on Adrian. 'From now on, nobody goes in or out of there without my explicit say-so. That especially goes for Annabel. That good enough for you, Ade?'

Adrian looked from Brady to Annabel then back again.

'Fine,' he said, 'just so long as everybody sticks to it.'

He threw the remote neatly on to the vacant armchair and walked out of the room without saying another word.

He fixed himself a coffee in the kitchen, took it back upstairs with him, felt he'd pushed it enough for now. But he *had* pushed it, there was no doubt about that.

He surfed the web idly for a while, didn't even look at the webcam feed. He'd decided to make none of it his problem for the moment; to take a little time out. Not all of the plumbing in the cottage had been modernised they'd discovered after they'd moved in. While he sat at the laptop reading the *New York Times*, the Melbourne *Age* and then the technology section of the *Guardian*, he could hear some of the geriatric pipework rattling in the background. Down the hall, he assumed, one of them must be running a bath or taking a shower. Engrossed in what he was doing, he didn't notice when it stopped. He was drinking the last dregs in his coffee mug when there was a sudden, quiet knock on the door. He looked round from the old-fashioned writing table he was using as a workstation in time to see Annabel waltzing in. She closed the door behind her and sat down on the edge of his bed as if it was her everyday habit and custom.

'What does he want now?' Adrian asked, assuming Brady had sent her as a messenger for one reason or another.

'I'm sure I've no idea,' Annabel answered, 'he's gone over to the outhouse with Maria. They've taken the first-aid kit with them. Acting as per *your* instructions.'

Adrian brought up the webcam window: January Shepherd lying on the bed, Maria ministering to her, Brady standing to one side, holding what looked like a pile of blankets.

'You really hurt her, Annabel,' he said, turning away from the screen again.

'Hurt or be hurt, Adrian. That's reality. Brady's right about that – we're providing a much-needed service: dial-a-reality-check. These women are finding out what they're made of, what they can take, *who* they really are – all thanks to us.'

She stood up, walked towards him.

'And take you, Adrian. Facing down Sir Brady – you're finding out what *you*'re made of too.'

It was too corny. Stand up to the monster and steal his woman. And what she was saying about the project was just more Bradyesque nonsense, not worth listening to, not worth considering. But none of that, he realised, mattered in the slightest to him right now. He undid the single silk cord of her bathrobe, told her to take it right off if she wanted to stay.

Chapter Thirty-two

Jacobson caught up with Jim Webster, the Crime Scene Manager, in the latter's cubicle-sized 'office'. He'd called a briefing meeting of his A team for five thirty, wanted to know the latest state of play with the forensic side of the investigation before then. He sat down in Webster's one, solitary visitor's chair and sank his weight on to grey, uncomfortable, moulded plastic.

Webster abandoned his computer with splendid reluctance – as if Jacobson was tearing him away from the discovery of penicillin or a cure for the common cold. 'Some of the preliminary FSS results are just in for Saturday night at Crow Hill, Frank. Also from the search at the Hat Factory apartment,' he said, after his ritual period of unnecessary delaying tactics had passed: on this occasion straightening a pile of paperwork and then unclicking a couple of clickable ballpoint pens.

'Anything useful?' Jacobson asked, entirely undeterred.

'Pretty much as expected. A few clothing fibres match across both locations. Plus there were enough skin cells inside the mock grave site to provide a DNA sample after all.'

'Tracey Heald, I assume?'

Jacobson was thinking that even Webster would have betrayed slight signs of mild excitement if the result had been more unanticipated or more interesting.

Webster nodded.

'Correct. A clear match to her Catchem database record.'

'But at least it confirms her story.'

'There's no doubt about that. We've confirmation all over the shop really. The paint samples we lifted where they'd parked the BMW are absolutely right for the year and the model that we know they hired from the car rental company.'

'So they de-forensicated the scene at the Hat Factory fairly thoroughly then?' Jacobson asked, his mind taking a new tack.

'That's how it looks. Like I say, we lifted fibres – there's no way you can fail to leave some kind of trace – but they've certainly been careful all right. And well informed. I reckon they've even taken their bed linen with them when they've moved on. Plus we've never found where they disposed of Tracey Heald's clothing – assuming they have disposed of it – which is another sign that they're forensically literate.'

'What about last night, Jim?'

'Well that could be a different story – although the courier's only left for Birmingham in the last half-hour so we won't find out for a while.'

'Everything's being fast-tracked though surely?'

Webster fidgeted with another ballpoint: non-clickable this time, one of those green ones Oxfam sent out in the hopes you'd write them a cheque straightaway and bung it back to them in the handy reply-paid envelope.

'Yeah, yeah, fast-tracked. Also known as not quite so painstakingly slow. This is the FSS HQ we're talking about. Wall to wall with too few scientists and too much crime-scene evidence.'

Jacobson laughed conspicuously – complaining about the Forensic Science Service's turnaround rate was about as gingerly close as Jim Webster ever crept towards the dangerous business of humour.

'But a different story maybe, you say?'

Webster nodded again.

'Quite a few blood samples from the area where you and DS Kerr found, er, Perry Harrison. Our own basic lab results suggest that Harrison is the most likely source – but certainly not for all of it. We could be looking at a DNA result for at least one of his assailants.'

Webster paused, looked down at his notes. Then:

'Oh yes – and we found a lipstick, nicely covered in prints. Could've been dropped if there was a struggle. Although it might not be related of course.'

'And too much to hope that there's a match to said prints on the NAFIS computer, old son?'

'You're right, Frank. We ran each comparison twice just to make certain.'

Jacobson wasn't remotely surprised. To turn up from a comparison check on the national fingerprint system, you had to be *in* the system in the first place. Whereas the whole nose-thumbing style of the Art Gang screamed out that none of them had a prior criminal record. No fingerprints, no mug shots, no previous addresses, no known associates. No DNA tests either, most probably – so that the blood traces Webster's SOCOs had taken would only *confirm* that Jacobson had caught the right suspect if and when he did, would do sweet Fanny Adams in helping him to *get* to that desirable state of affairs.

He shifted his weight on the uncomfortable chair.

'Any sign of the white van?'

The Art Gang had ambushed John Shepherd's Mercedes with the two rented BMWs and then torched all three vehicles. Ergo they must have used a third vehicle to depart from the scene. Jacobson's assumption was that they would have used their white transit.

'The team found some recent tyre tracks off-road near a bend about half-a-mile away,' Webster replied. 'They're still working on them, trying for the best fit of vehicle size and type. But we're already confident that it's not a transit or anything remotely like one.'

At last, Jacobson thought, something non-predictable.

'So you think that maybe they used a different vehicle altogether this time?'

'You're the thinker, Frank. My job's just about what's possible and what isn't. We've found no sign of a transit but we have found these signs. So all I'm saying is that this could be another possibility for you to consider.'

Jacobson said his thank-yous and left Webster to it. Another colleague you might ask after the wife and kids or the pet dog but Webster never seemed entirely at ease with non-work-related topics. Which made him, Jacobson realised, a bit like himself. He took the lift up to the seventh floor, grabbed a takeaway coffee from the canteen, and then took the lift down again to the third floor where the meeting rooms were located.

Kerr, Mick Hume, Ray Williams and Emma Smith were waiting for him. Only Barber's replacement was missing – for the simple reason that he hadn't yet been replaced. The room was small and windowless. Somewhere Jacobson couldn't risk lighting up in. So he contented himself with taking out his B&H packet, rechecking his running tally for the day, and putting it back inside his pocket. Jacobson's officers ran through their reports while he scrawled what he took to be some of the key headings on to the whiteboard. The process, as he'd anticipated, didn't take long.

Emma Smith and Ray Williams had gone back to cross-referencing after their trip out to Boden Hall. Neither activity looked to have brought anything vital to light. Birgit Kruijsdijk and Perry Harrison apart, John Shepherd didn't seem to employ any kind of traditional country-house retinue. Two young women from Latvia (on completely legal work permits) worked as live-in chambermaids but otherwise Shepherd used local employment agencies to supply cleaning staff, gardeners and extra catering workers as and when required. Cleaners visited the Hall twice a week and there was a gardening team on site currently.

'We've been on to the companies concerned, guv,' Emma Smith said. 'They're getting back to us ASAP with names and addresses for anyone who's been on the premises in the last fortnight. We could ask them to go further back if you like.'

'No, lass, that should do us for now. I dare say there'll be somebody with a record for something on the books somewhere. But that doesn't mean they're involved in this can of worms. Probably just the opposite in fact.'

'So you don't think there was inside involvement, Frank. A tip-off?' Kerr asked.

'Well, it's a possibility,' Jacobson replied. 'But I don't think January Shepherd's movements would have been too difficult to predict in any case. If she was doing a gig in Wynarth, where else was she going to stay except at her dad's place? Just a matter of laying in wait – which is exactly what they did in fact.'

'They'd need to have known that she'd be travelling in Shepherd's merc though, surely?' Kerr persisted.

'Agreed – but I doubt if the Shepmobile's too much of a secret locally – probably the kind of gen you could pick up in just about any pub in Crowby without drawing too much attention to yourself. Shepherd's made a bit of a splash since he's been back here. People are keen on celebrities these days – or so I'm told.'

'But we should still check out the staff lists when we get them?' Ray Williams asked.

'Oh yes, old son. Unless we have other priorities by then. Ninety per cent hard slog plus ten per cent harder slog – that's detective work. I take it you actually spoke to the, er, Latvians?'

'Ray spoke to them all right, guv,' Emma Smith said pointedly, 'both of them are blondes after all.'

Mick Hume started to laugh, then faked a cough to hide the fact.

Jacobson let the personal history subtext go.

'And?'

'They confirmed what Shepherd and his girlfriend told us,' Williams said, his face reddening slightly. 'She left last night in the merc with Perry Harrison driving – and they haven't seen her since. Her room was undisturbed this morning and her bed hadn't been slept in.'

Kerr went next, recapped on his and Jacobson's conversation with Alice Banned and with his own visit to the art teacher, Ruth Sutton. Mick Hume gave his report from the hospital: Perry Harrison was in the operating theatre right now but the prognosis didn't look brilliant.

Jacobson pulled the lid off his takeaway carton, drank down a couple of by now lukewarm mouthfuls, and then elaborated on his current thinking.

'As I see it, the Art Gang are holding on to January Shepherd for a reason we don't yet know – or something went badly wrong again and her body's out there somewhere waiting to be discovered. Either way, the task remains the same: find them – and find them fast.'

'I'm hopeful that she's still alive and they're holding her, Frank,' Kerr commented. 'The whole MO last night looks pre-meditated. If they just wanted to snatch another girl, there's a lot of easier ways they could have gone about it.'

'Agreed, old son. And I hope you're right. But, like I say, it doesn't alter our priorities either way. The pig is we've got nowhere near them so far if we're being honest. Steve Horton still hasn't traced their internet and email footprints, even with the help of the ICU. And even when he does, that's still leaves him a long, long way from physically locating their computer. Plus there's been no further activity on any of the credit cards we can associate with the gang. We're not dealing with fools here, that's for certain.'

Kerr put the question the others didn't feel their rank allowed them to.

'So what do we actually *do* next, Frank?'

Jacobson took another sip of canteen 'coffee' and found a square of blank, unused whiteboard.

'Boden Hall's remote – but it's not that remote,' he said, sketching out a (very) rough map with a red marker pen.

'Which suggests two immediate ways forward. One: our old mates, CCTV and security cameras. There's nothing in that line on the B road that goes nearest Boden Hall – or on the B road that gets you to that B road. *But you still have to get out that way in the first place.*'

He finished the sketch then drew an approximation of a circle around the clumsy dot that was standing in for Boden Hall on the whiteboard.

'We're talking late at night here and non-busy roads. If we can map every camera within say a five-mile radius then one of them just might have the kind of image we're looking for. And I don't just mean official cameras. What we want could come from a garage forecourt or even from somebody's home driveway.'

'They've driven the beamers and the transit van all over the region without getting caught, guv,' Mick Hume objected.

Jacobson updated them about the tyre tracks the SOCOs had found up the road from the car-jack location – and the theory that they weren't from the white van.

'The beamers are scrap metal and there's no sign of the white van at the crime scene. It's possible that we're looking for another vehicle altogether' – he tapped at his uneven circle with the marker pen – 'anything with wheels in this area after midnight last night, we need to know about it.'

'You said two ways, Frank?' Kerr reminded him.

'That's right. Though the second's not unconnected to the first. Again this is the rural hinterlands we're talking about – but it's not frigging Mongolia. We need to knock on every single inhabited door inside the radius. It only takes one rural drunk sneaking home late from the pub at twenty-nine point nine miles an hour – or one elderly insomniac who remembers spotting an unfamiliar car out their front window – to give us the lead we need. And don't forget the report of the burn-outs came in *anonymously*. Some bugger out that way's definitely seen something.'

Kerr clocked the expressions on the faces of Hume, Smith

and Williams. It was written all over them that the anonymous caller was a detail they'd completely forgotten. Himself likewise. Jacobson smoked when he shouldn't, absented himself down the pub when he shouldn't, sat around with his feet arrogantly up on his desk when he shouldn't. All of which, evidently, played its part in making him the best detective on the force. Hands down and no contest.

'So we're talking overtime, guv?' Mick Hume asked.

'And then some, Mick,' Jacobson replied. 'As long as the job takes.'

Annabel left Adrian's room with only minutes to spare when they heard Brady and Maria returning to the cottage. She crept down the hall into the bathroom, got back under the shower. Adrian resumed the *Guardian* feature he'd been reading, a review of commercially available firewalls for private computer users. Amusing stuff really; even the best of them you could slip in and out of completely unnoticed if, like him, you knew what you were doing. He took a shower himself when Annabel had finished, even treated himself to a leisurely shave. Brady was waiting for him when he came downstairs again. All smiles and wanting to discuss the all-important next film.

They talked it through at the kitchen table. Adrian on more coffee, Brady on black Earl Grey from the second pot which he'd got Maria to make for him, having rejected the first pot she'd brewed as insufficiently close to his favoured strength.

'Don't you ever get tired of bossing her?' Adrian had asked him when she'd withdrawn – at Brady's instruction – from the room.

'Second nature, Ade,' Brady had replied. 'And, besides, she loves it – goes wet at the slightest hint of a command.'

Adrian didn't bother to argue too much when Brady outlined his suggestions for the film. All that really mattered to him now was getting the basic message across and to hell with the aesthetics. The project, as once grandly conceived, had turned into bollocks somewhere along the line. Adrian wasn't sure where or when exactly. Maybe when the girl had gone under the lorry on the M6. Or maybe it had always been bollocks and it had just taken him too long to finally wake up to the fact. All he wanted to do now, he realised, was to get to the planned, successful outcome as quickly as possible.

'What about the timescale then?' he asked Brady when they'd scripted most of the new sequences out.

'Shoot tonight – release tomorrow. Let John Shepherd enjoy a nice, long, sleepless night.'

'You don't think we should just maybe *go* for it – do it all tonight?'

'Adrian, dear chap,' Brady said, adopting his mock Mr Toad delivery, but maybe not as ebulliently as in times past, 'anyone would think that you were growing tired of our exalted company. Tomorrow's best, believe me. More time for panic to set in.'

Adrian stood up, walked over to the sink and rinsed out the coffee percolator as well as his own mug.

'Think what you like,' he said evenly. 'I'll be ready with the camera whenever.'

Chapter Thirty-three

They stayed on in the windowless meeting room, used it as an ad hoc incident room. Steve Horton joined them, jacked up a laptop to a projector and a printer so that they could see everything they needed to see and get hard copies of anything they'd need out in the field. Jacobson took his share of the work along with the rest. By seven thirty, they had itemised every route to Boden Hall within the five-mile radius and had details of every address along each route, whether public or private, home or farm. Then they divided the terrain into equal segments, balanced (thanks to Horton's software) for population density and other relevant factors. Jacobson made his telephone calls after that, made use of the authority he'd been given to pull in as many duty CID and uniformeds as were needed for the purpose. By eight twenty they were ready to move. Twenty-two officers all told, two per vehicle (some marked, some unmarked), each car taking its own slice of the routes and habitations within the designated radius. Hume and Ray Williams worked together. Emma Smith was joined by DC Phillips, a new-ish CID recruit she didn't really know. Jacobson and Kerr headed out to a desolate sector of the map which lay to the north of Wynarth. A country pub, three farm spreads and an old watermill site that had been converted into half-a-dozen upmarket apartments. Jacobson had selected this segment mainly because of the pub. In his experience, pubs, whether urban or rural, meant late-night activity and tongues nicely loosened by the consumption of alcohol.

They worked systematically along the route, taking the farms and the watermill first, saving the pub until last. The farms were a dead loss for camera recordings. Two of them had security cameras in the vicinity of the actual farmhouses but, since in both cases these were located more than half-a-mile from the nearest public road, even a detective as thorough as Jacobson couldn't see any operational necessity to study their recent footage. *I shouldn't be telling you this*, the third farmer, who seemed to live on his own, declared – and then told them anyway: he didn't need any bloody security cameras, thank you very much, not when he slept with a loaded shotgun next to his bed every night. Jacobson warned him about the laws on proportionate response and the correct storage of firearms. Farmers weren't Jacobson's thing as a general rule – especially if they were also would-be vigilantes who thought the law of the land didn't apply to anybody wearing a tweed jacket or wellington boots. Right now, though, this one was the least of Jacobson's problems.

The watermill site brought them the same disappointment as the first two farms: a camera set-up that only functioned in the immediate locale of the properties and didn't record anything out towards the public road. Not all the householders were at home but those that were gave them the classic polite but unhelpful response. They hadn't seen anything, they hadn't heard anything, they'd all been law-abidingly tucked up under their non-allergenic duvets well before midnight. Ditto two out of the three farms. Only Mr Shotgun admitted to having been up and about, chatting on his computer to his son in New Zealand until two AM. He'd even taken 'a bit of a walk outside' before he'd gone off, armed and dangerous, to his bed. Like the others, he'd told them that he hadn't noticed anything that had seemed out of the ordinary.

En route to the Bideford Arms, Jacobson checked progress with Mick Hume and Emma Smith. They'd made no breakthroughs either but he clung on to the fact that it would be tomorrow morning before he'd know for certain whether tonight's operation had achieved anything. The co-opted duty CID and uniformeds understood a lot less about the investigation than Hume, Smith and Williams did; they might easily stumble across something crucial and not realise that it *was* crucial. His core team would need to sift through and cross-reference the other officers' reports before Jacobson would find out definitively whether something useful had been uncovered or not.

It was pushing quarter to eleven when they pulled into the crowded pub car park. The Bideford Arms had acquired new landlords since Jacobson and Kerr had last called in on a police matter (during the Darren McGee and Paul Shaw case). Jacobson thought he recollected Alison Taylor saying something about the place having been given a significant makeover. A proper chef had been brought in, apparently, and the focus had shifted from the bar trade to the potentially more profitable restaurant side. Alison had suggested that it might be a nice destination for a country drive some evening but so far Jacobson hadn't taken her up on the idea. At least there was some CCTV potential this time. The upgraded pub now had a moving camera that swept across the car park in a broad arc. What this meant was that, every ten minutes or so, the camera inadvertently recorded any traffic which happened to be passing out on the nearside lane of the road.

The new landlords were a cheerful young couple who looked run off their feet. In theory, they could insist on authorisation before allowing access to their camera system but Jacobson quickly got the impression that they were in awe of his official rank and keen to enter his good books. They weren't to know after all that he scarcely kept any. They set Kerr up in their back office with his requested mug of tea. While Kerr fast-forwarded through the relevant time window (one AM to three AM), Jacobson talked to customers, bar staff and kitchen staff – and hit his next piece of bad luck: the Bideford stayed open till two AM, Fridays and Saturdays, but the rest of the week, including last night, it stopped serving food at eleven and was closed by midnight. The upshot was that all of its customers had been gone by twelve thirty and most of its staff by one, nearly all of them heading back in the direction of Wynarth and Crowby.

Jacobson concentrated on the three bars. It seemed unlikely that anyone who'd dined in the restaurant last night would also be there again this evening (although he checked with the waiters just in case). He'd accepted the single malt he'd been offered on the house but had insisted on paying for it. When he'd finished it he ordered another one in the main bar and carried it along the low-ceilinged corridor to the smallest bar of the three. The Bideford was genuinely old and the new refurbishment had left its creaking floorboards and sagging timbers reassuringly unmolested. He entered the room that had probably been little more than a snug once upon a time but which now functioned as an overcrowded approximation of an old-style public bar: smoke filled (for the moment), more men than women, more over-forties than under-forties, even a few ruddy, beer-bellied characters in soiled overalls. The last redoubt, by the looks of it, for the kind of customers who didn't remotely fit the gastropub marketing profile. He raised the issue of the burn-outs near Boden Hall with several different groups of drinkers but none of them claimed to know anything beyond the limited reports that had so far reached the local media – none of which had made the connection to the Art Gang investigation. Any or all of them could be lying of course but none of them gave him any immediate reason to think so (and all of them looked like highly unlikely collaborators for style-conscious identity thieves). When he was through, he caught up with Kerr in the back office.

'Any luck, Ian?'

Kerr shook his head.

'I've gone through twice. But there's not a single vehicle

captured after the last car pulls out of the car park at one twenty. The chef in an SUV.'

'That doesn't mean that the road was empty though,' Jacobson commented.

'No, it doesn't – just that nothing went past when the camera was pointing in that direction. I expect if we just *listened* to the footage we could pinpoint the time when anything did go past.'

Jacobson fidgeted with his empty whisky glass, finally put it down next to a pile of brewery delivery slips.

'Yep, and that's going to lead us straight to them, old son,' he replied.

Two-thirds sarcasm, one-third despair, he thought – or somewhere thereabouts.

Kerr drove him back to his flat in Wellington Drive. Nothing else came in, there was nothing else to do. Dead or alive, January Shepherd was out there somewhere and Crowby CID still didn't have a clue as to where. He phoned Nick Bishop at the Riverside Hotel after he'd slung his jacket on the rail. A courtesy call he'd promised to make – if it wasn't too late – but also clutching at the straw that somebody in Alice Banned had heard something or remembered something after all. Bishop disillusioned him on both counts but at least he confirmed that the Birmingham Academy had bought the revised explanation (OK, lie) that Jacobson had advised him to sell them earlier, namely that January had succumbed to sudden laryngitis and was having to rest her voice on strict doctor's orders. John Shepherd had offered to reimburse the venue for any loss of profit – so that, for now, at least, the Academy was one less source to worry about in terms of the story hitting the news. It was the kind of case where the media had a useful role to play – but ideally Jacobson wanted them to dance to his tune and not the other way round. Bishop also had the latest news from the hospital but it turned out to be the same news they'd given Jacobson earlier: Perry Harrison had survived his operation but remained unconscious, still wasn't out of danger. Jacobson ended the call, thought about phoning John Shepherd at Boden Hall, decided not to – not when he had nothing useful to tell him. The two malts had put him badly in the mood for a third. He'd work a case round the clock if he had to and as long as he had something to work with. Right now there didn't seem to be anything more that could be done before the morning. He checked his watch – almost twelve thirty – wondered whether Alison's general invitation for tonight still held good after the witching hour.

Kerr had hoped that getting home to his semi-detached house on the Bovis estate after midnight would at least mean that they'd all have gone and he'd have avoided them. A glance at the non-resident cars parked nearby in the street told him otherwise: no such luck. At least they hadn't blocked him out this time. He squeezed on to his short driveway where there was just enough room left for a second vehicle behind Cathy's new car, a year-old Yaris. The cat was in the hall, exiled maybe, when he walked in. She gave him her plaintive meow and got under his feet while he slung his jacket onto the only available peg. The hubble of voices from the front room floated over the clink of glasses and a Robert Johnson CD: *his* Robert Johnson CD. He walked on into the kitchen and fixed himself a beer. The cat had fresh food in her bowl and clean water so he ignored her attempts to wheedle some kind of treat out of him. He stood by the sink, drank a couple of deep mouthfuls and then thought fuck it – it's my house too.

There were four of them ensconced in the lounge. Five if you included Cathy herself. An elderly bloke called Benny-something who Kerr didn't actually mind, the one he regarded as the best of the bunch. Two women about Cathy's age whose names Kerr could never remember. Cathy said this was because neither of them was very much to look at. Kerr suspected that was the complete truth of the matter although he had no plans to admit the fact to Cathy. Finally there was Edward – or Ed as he preferred to be called. Late twenties, shaved head, weedy, an earring on his left earlobe. Kerr thought he looked gay but Cathy said that he wasn't. Not that Kerr cared less either way. *That* wasn't remotely his problem about Ed.

Benny vacated the armchair where he'd been sitting.

'Make way for the workers I always say,' he said. 'I ought to be making a move anyway.'

'Me too,' one of the women said, 'I'm planning an early start on my essay tomorrow, now it's the weekend at last.'

Kerr thought she was probably the one called Dorothy but he didn't want to chance it and get it wrong.

'Please don't rush for me,' he said, sitting down – and sounding a lot more civil than he felt.

Cathy told them there was no need when they were nearly finished their discussion anyway: they should both stay to the end. Benny squeezed on to the sofa next to Ed and the woman who might be called Dorothy stayed where she was.

'So what Orwell's saying is that you can't rely on the proles to rise up against Big Brother. So long as they've got work and cheap entertainment they're happy,' Ed said.

He was waving his wine glass precariously as he spoke and he had an air of resuming some kind of important, urgent task which had been needlessly interrupted. Inventing nuclear fusion maybe – or writing the sequel to *Hamlet*.

'Except now the cheap entertainment actually includes Big Brother. Now that's what I call a real historical irony,' old Benny suggested, affably enough.

The others laughed and the conversation ran on. Kerr drank his beer and tried to concentrate on Robert Johnson: 'Stones in my Pathway'. Both the voice and guitar sounded darkly majestic even at background volume. Cathy had been 'restless' – her word – ever since the twins had grown old enough for her to go back to her office job part-time. *I'm sinking into a rut* was the other way she liked to put it. Her latest attempt to deal with her feeling of restlessness was signing on for a course with the Open University. That wasn't a problem for Kerr either. Nor the fact that recently some of the students from her course at the local study centre had formed themselves into a self-help group, meeting a couple of times a month at somebody's house or flat to discuss matters relating to their studies. No, all of that was fine. Kerr's only problem was with Eddie-boy. He was a graphic designer apparently, worked for one of the regional advertising set-ups. And Kerr didn't even mind that. It was just that Eddie was one of those half-educated middle-class types who considered themselves anti-police without actually knowing the first thing about policing: what the job was actually like, who the people really were who actually did it.

Cathy had signed on for an Arts degree and the introductory course she was taking was currently looking at George Orwell's classic, *Nineteen Eighty-Four*. It was a book Kerr had been unable to ignore in his youth. For years, it had been one of his dad's stalwart good reads. Then the news had broken (or been spun) about Orwell's death-bed 'treachery': allegedly passing on the names of 'covert' Soviet sympathisers to a public-school type from MI5. Kerr Senior hadn't just disowned the book, he'd ceremoniously burnt it in the back garden along with every other Orwell book he'd possessed. Later on, he'd had second thoughts, had gone out and bought replacement copies – but the incident had stuck in Kerr's memory.

'If only there were figures like Orwell around nowadays,' Ed was saying, 'all this surveillance and ID cards and everything. He'd've had a field day.'

I've already had all this shit from my dad, Kerr thought, except that he actually knows what he's talking about. He put down his beer, told the story about Orwell and the security services, could see that it was news to Ed and the others.

'Well that's a different thing,' Ed said, 'I mean communism, nobody wants that.'

'So it's OK to snoop on some groups, but not on others?' Kerr asked him.

He could see why Eddie-boy wouldn't want communism anyway. For one thing, the commissars might've assigned him to a proper job down the local tractor factory, might've forced him to get his soft hands dirty.

'He's got you there,' Benny said, 'if you say you're for free speech, it has to be for everyone.'

Ed swallowed down the last dregs of Cabernet Sauvignon. Kerr's Cabernet Sauvignon. He didn't look very happy and shortly after that he said that it was time he got going, time he went home. One by one, the others left too until finally Kerr was alone with his wife.

'You know-all,' Cathy said, when she'd waved the last of them off from the hall doorway. 'You know-all and show-off.'

She sat down on the sofa and picked up her unfinished glass of wine.

'Look, I'm sorry,' Kerr said, 'I didn't mean to spoil the party. It's just types like that Ed guy. They rub me up the wrong way. They assume I'm thick as shit because I get paid to keep them safe in their poncy beds, to do their dirty work for them.'

'You meet a lot of people like Ed in your line, do you? Designers, artistic people – people with flair, creativity and imagination?'

She still had fire, spark, despite the kids and the mortgage. He'd thought she hadn't for a while but maybe he hadn't been thinking straight back then.

'I meet all sorts, love,' he said.

Love was risking it in the immediate context, pushing his luck, but she let him away with it. He got up from the armchair, joined her on the sofa. Ed reminded him of Tony fucking Scruton, that was all – but he couldn't tell Cathy that. He didn't look like him but he was virtually a person-ality clone. Even when an affair was over (if it was over)

277

its repercussions carried on, its secrets held you ensnared in deceit and omission.

Cathy drank the last of her wine and put the glass down again.

'Well, I suppose he is a little bit pompous,' she said, leaning back, her head close. She'd had her hair done some new way that he liked. He smiled at her. Another successful risk taken. All he had to do was to forget about Rachel. That was all. Just let her go.

January couldn't sleep, didn't know whether she should be asleep or not, whether it was daytime or night time. They'd let her keep the orange jumpsuit and she'd carried on wearing it even although she'd wondered if her cuts and weals might heal more quickly if they were left exposed to the air. They'd given her supper too (she decided she might as well call it supper as anything else, at least try and distinguish one meal from the next): a dish of unappetising pasta, a banana, a couple of apples and a raspberry-flavoured yoghurt drink. She'd consumed all of it greedily. All except the second apple which she'd decided to hold on to for the moment. The idea that she still had one food item left that she could eat whenever she chose to eat it seemed important somehow. She'd 'dined' using only her left arm as much as possible. Her right arm still really hurt if she tried to move it even slightly. It had been one of the men who'd assaulted her this time. Not the tallest one, the other one. He'd twisted her arm behind her back to the point where she thought it would actually break. The other one had pulled him off, told him to stop. She'd more or less fainted at that stage. This had been after they'd stopped filming her and she'd thought they were about to leave her on her own again. But then they'd wanted to know something, and she couldn't remember it at first, couldn't give them an instant answer. She'd remembered when she'd come round and just told them, just wanted them to stop hurting her. It was an odd detail to want to know anyway, completely useless to them as far as she could see. Nothing to do with anything. Not like the other stuff they'd asked her about earlier which had made sense to her. Unless . . .

She looked at the apple which she'd placed on the little bamboo table like an unconvincing still life. Maybe if she ate it now then she could lie down for a bit, try and rest at least. This is what life collapsed down to when you became a prisoner, no longer free. Sit up or lie down. Close your eyes or keep them open. She wouldn't eat it yet, she decided. She closed her eyes, lay down on her pain-free left side. The film was a good thing anyway, she reminded herself. Maybe a step towards getting out of here. Good things were what she needed to concentrate on. Anything positive, anything not hopeless. Perry for instance. She didn't know for certain that they'd left him in the woods. She'd been thinking that he might be here too – somewhere near her and hatching a plan; that would be like him, always coming through, always delivering. And there were other good things to hope for. She'd definitely be missed by now, the police would have been called in for sure. No way that wouldn't have happened by now. Her dad would have seen to it – or Nick.

You met someone and you never knew where that might lead you. Without Nick the band wouldn't have happened and without the band there would never have been the tour. And without the tour . . . She kept her eyes closed tight, sick in her heart of the ceaseless, artificial light. She didn't believe in karma, never had done really, not even when she'd been a kid during the Sedona interlude. Karma was a distortion, an oversimplification. Stuff happened randomly. It was only afterwards that it seemed inevitable – and only because a million other possibilities had never found their way into existence. Good things, she told herself, keep thinking about good things.

Nick had been playing illegally in a bar band down in Venice the first night she'd run into him. Covers and crowd pleasers. A cartoon musclehead on lead vocals and a bass player who missed more notes than he hit. But Nick had something from the get-go. Runs high on the fretboard that could find stillness one minute and delirium the next. And his voice (when the musclehead shut up): English, quirky. He could take something safe and antique, some old number by Green Day or even REM, and turn it into something strange, new and dark. The cloth ears in the place hated it but January *knew*. She'd bought him drinks after the second set, had made herself *so* available. He'd come out from the UK on the faded half-promise of a record deal, was running out of cash and credit, had a month left on his visa waiver and unofficial floorspace in a skanky crash pad off Pico Boulevard. No way was he saying no to the blonde rich girl with the looks, the contacts, the (silent) air-con apartment and the two Cadillac convertibles (one pink, one black, depending on mood).

They practised all day every day, shared songs, ideas. All of it worked, all of it was great. When they weren't doing music or putting the band together, January showed him California. He'd been there months and barely got out of LA. The first weekend he moved in with her properly, they drove up Highway One to Big Sur, checked into the River Inn Resort. January had Nick on film somewhere, running along Pfeiffer Beach at sunset, dancing in the shallows while the waves crashed and swirled through the rocks reminding you that the biggest, wildest show in town was always Nature's: wholly alive and never asleep.

Despite the pain it cost her, she brought her right hand up to cover her eyes, sank deep into the memory of it. Remember this, he'd said to her, when the sun had almost gone and the rocks were black shadows. Remember this, Jan, for whenever you need it.

Part Three:

Cut Her Dead

Chapter Thirty-four

Saturday morning, just before eight, Jacobson crept out of Alison's bedroom. She had the day off and she was still fast asleep. Jacobson had kept her up late and could easily have slept on too if there wasn't January Shepherd and the Art Gang to worry about. But there was. It had been a long time, right back to the viable years of his marriage, since he'd enjoyed female company late into the night when he was in the middle of a bad case and badly needed to exorcise a few demons – to talk it all out or to let it all go for a few hours. He dialled a cab to take him over to Wellington Drive, paid the driver to wait while he went inside his flat, picked out a fresh shirt and checked his landline for new messages: nothing.

He ate a canteen breakfast (eggs, bacon, defiantly white toast), washed it down with orange juice and then took a large-size coffee with him to his fifth-floor office. His mobile started ringing as he was unlocking the door. By the time he'd got into the room, placed the carton down safely on his desk and flushed the mobile out of his jacket, it had stopped ringing – but a couple of seconds later his desk phone interrupted the brief silence. He grabbed the receiver and put the mobile back in his pocket. Henry Pelling at the *Argus*: there was a new film just in from the gang, he was sending a copy to Steve Horton straightaway, he didn't think that Jacobson would like what he was about to see.

The fully-equipped incident room Jacobson had been promised since Thursday afternoon had finally materialised.

Since it was located only one floor down he took the stairs in favour of the lift. Kerr, Hume, Williams and Smith were already there, already at work. Ten minutes later, Steve Horton had the footage ready to run on a projector twice the size of the one they'd made do with last night.

ART TERRORISTS
Series 1 Edition 5
SCREWED UP FOR REAL

There was no doubt that it was January Shepherd. Jacobson had studied her photograph, had even watched the Alice Banned promotional video Horton had downloaded from the internet for him yesterday. It was the same girl all right except that she wasn't smiling now, didn't look vibrant, confident, the way she'd done with her guitar in her hands and her body swaying to the hard, pounding rhythm.

The film was short this time: no more than three minutes long. For most of it nothing really happened. January kneeling on the ground in an orange jumpsuit, head bowed. Two figures in camouflage fatigues standing behind her, both masked. One of them was holding what looked like some kind of automatic rifle, the other one held up a handwritten message on white card: *Terror For Art's Sake*. The camera angle was static except for one brief sequence where it tracked to the right, showed how January was shackled to a wall. The whole thing seemed to have been shot inside a stark interior that could have been anywhere or nowhere. In the last minute, January looked up at the camera and spoke haltingly, as if she was reading from a faulty prompt.

'My name is January. I am the property of art. Instructions will be given for my resale to interested parties. They must be followed to the letter.'

The image dissolved at that point and then there was a thirty-second montage of atrocities from around the world: firing squads, beheadings, rotting corpses in a mass grave.

The final frame (as Jacobson had come to expect) concluded with slogans.

NOBODY IS REAL.
DO AS WE SAY.
IDENTITY IS THEFT.

'Sick fucks,' Mick Hume spat out when the film finished. Nobody in the room disagreed.

John Shepherd was sober and not enjoying it. He hadn't touched anything that Birgit had put together for breakfast, seemed to be surviving on black coffee and anxiety. Kelly phoned the hospital for him: no change in Perry Harrison's condition overnight. He'd moved his base of operations into the library. He wasn't sure why. Maybe because lounging by the pool was his normal state of affairs and what was happening right now was anything but. When your daughter was missing you couldn't carry on with your normal routine, you had to abandon it, give all your attention to that one, overriding problem. When Kelly came off the phone, she raised the issue of Fay again, his second ex-wife, January's mother.

'You ought to let her know,' she said, 'she has that right, surely?'

Shepherd nodded.

'Yeah, true, she has. I haven't forgotten about that. But I'd thought I'd wait until the time zones get into synch. It's going to be one thirty in the morning or something over there – and it's a fucking monastery or a nunnery or what-ever they call it. I don't really think they sit up late watching Home Box Office.'

'Even so, you should try, they must have a way of dealing with emergencies and stuff.'

'OK. OK. You're right. Can you find the info for me then?'

'Of course, darling.'

Shepherd drank more coffee, watched her zap the keys of the laptop she'd brought down from the office. He hated it when she called him that, like the thing was more than it was, more than it could be.

'The Diamond Sutra Haven, 410 Central—'

'I don't need the address, Kel,' he said testily. 'I'm not about to write her a letter.'

Fay was still riding the New Age vibe evidently. He'd tried to reach her last night with no luck. She was living up in San Francisco these last few years, running a women's restaurant – whatever that was. Eventually he'd made contact with a (slight) mutual acquaintance who'd told him she'd flown to Montana for a week or two. Some kind of tantric retreat event. Fucking Montana, he'd thought, where the fuck is that? *Can* you even fly there?

'Got it,' Kelly said, reading out the telephone number.

Shepherd tapped the numbers into his nearest phone and pressed dial: nothing.

'You must have keyed them in wrong,' Kelly said, 'give it here.'

He passed her the phone, drumming the two-hundred-year-old table that he'd never really liked with the fingers of his free hand. Agitation. Irritation. Something not far off panic. Another one of the phones started to ring in the meantime: the Motorola – his personal mobile, the holy of holies. The screen told him it was an unknown dialler, number withheld, but he picked it up anyway.

'John Shepherd,' he said.

'We know who you are' – the voice was glib, male – 'now listen carefully if you want to see your daughter again. Do you have online banking, John Shepherd?'

'What the—'

'It's a serious question,' the voice cut in. 'January certainly thinks it's serious. Don't you, January?'

A pause. And then January on the phone. Unmistakably, definitely.

'Dad, Dad! Listen to him. Just do what they say, OK? Just—'

He shouted out her name, didn't know if they'd taken the phone away from her before she'd heard him.

Another pause. Some kind of jerky noise he didn't recognise. Then the voice came back on.

'Online banking. Do you have facilities?'

He had to fight for a calm breath, his heart pounding in his throat.

'Yes,' he said simply.

He was sure he had, he had a dozen fucking banking accounts. He thought maybe Kelly had helped him to set it up.

'Three o'clock this afternoon. You'll be sent an email at your AOL address. You'll log in to your online account and you'll transfer out eight million pounds following the instructions in the email. In return, your daughter will be released unharmed.'

'But how do I—'

'No buts, John Shepherd. Transfer the money and your daughter lives. Fuck us about and she doesn't.'

'If you harm—'

'And one final thing. Don't involve the police. Involve the police and we hurt her before we kill her.'

The call went dead. And for a long second Shepherd just held the phone in his hand and stared at it blankly.

Casper watched Tracey sleeping. Mainly she seemed to sleep on her front. Usually they'd both sleep naked but last night – well, three in the morning, really – she'd got into pyjamas before she'd got into bed. He hadn't touched her or anything, knew it was too soon for that, too soon to push his luck. But he was getting there, wasn't he? He was here anyway.

She'd phoned him around about two, wanting to know if there was any news. There hadn't been. Still – Dave and Kenny had been up for it at least. He couldn't fault either of them.

287

They'd gone into town in Dave's van, had looked everywhere they could think of. There was hardly a venue they hadn't called in to. OK, he'd drunk more than the night before but he was still off the benzos, still pill-free. Six nights in a row now. Totally nothing doing though. Nobody that looked like any of them anywhere. Except for that one guy in Wetherspoon's. Kenny and him had followed him into the gents. The guy had bricked it, thinking they were about to gib him for his cash. Kenny would have done an' all but Casper had reminded him they were on a mission, not just fucking about. And the guy looked different up close. Plus which he was Polish or something, not English anyway. And whatever they were, those video-gang fuckers definitely weren't foreign.

Tracey turned on to her side, gave a soft yawn but still didn't wake up. They'd been more or less ready to call it a night when she'd phoned him. *You could come round if you like,* she'd said, *I'll wait up, let you in once I know it's you.* All he'd done was hold her really, hold her and tell her he was sorry about Laura and everything. Although he'd only told her that inside his head, hadn't thought she'd want to hear it right then. She turned the other way now, away from him. He snuck slowly out of bed, pulled on his jeans in case Denise was up and about, although he hadn't heard her if she was. He used the bathroom as quietly as he could then went down into the kitchen, clicked on the kettle. Dave had said he could borrow the van for the day, if he wanted to keep his eye out like. Dave didn't need it anyway, was taking a train over to Coventry for the football with a few other lads. Casper hoped that he'd meant it, he'd phone him in a bit to check that it was still OK. He was starting to think that maybe he'd never catch up with those bastards after all. Maybe they'd already gone and that was that. But so what? Tracey had come through it, you could tell that already. And it had drawn him up an' all, made him take a good look at himself. The best thing could be just to forget about them, not let it affect them.

He found a couple of clean mugs, wondered whether she'd want tea or coffee. She seemed to drink either as the mood took her. The thing about the van was he could take her out for the day, get her off the Woodlands anyway. Not Crow Hill obviously. But maybe somewhere else where there was a nice bit of peace and quiet. Or if she didn't fancy that, they could drive into Birmingham, fuck around in the big shops or see a movie or something. It was shit what had happened. But both of them were young, both of them had years to forget about it in. To fill their heads with better stuff, to build a future a lot better than their shitty past.

Chapter Thirty-five

An hour after the press and media had been sent the film featuring January Shepherd, and twenty-five minutes after John Shepherd had phoned Jacobson personally with the news of the Art Gang's ransom demand, Jacobson, DCS Greg Salter and the Chief Constable, 'Dud' Bentham, conferred in comfortable chairs in Salter's eighth-floor office. Bentham was out of uniform and wearing casual trousers and a pale blue Pringle sweater. He'd cancelled his Saturday round of golf at the last minute in order to be there. Salter had decent coffee on tap as usual but Bentham declined the offer. He needed to reach what he termed 'an executive decision' and he gave the impression that he wanted to reach it quickly. Salter took his cue from the most senior rank around as usual but Jacobson grabbed a cup anyway. Bentham could go home and put his feet up again after the meeting, Jacobson couldn't – or hoped he couldn't.

'Ordinarily, we'd automatically hand this over to the Regional Crime Squad lock, stock and barrel,' Bentham said when they were settled. 'That's the established protocol. The RCS have their procedures in place and they've a cohort of officers trained in the relevant disciplines. Hostage release negotiators and so on – as we all know.'

Bentham paused, possibly for effect, possibly just to clear his throat.

'This case however is anything but ordinary – and there are already four separate CID teams involved in what's become a complicated manhunt. In my view, therefore, vital time could be lost bringing the RCS up to speed at this stage.'

Jacobson nodded, relieved. He suppressed the comment that the RCS careerists had been offered the investigation on a plate earlier in the week and had turned their collective noses up at it.

'The other thing that's out of the ordinary is the publicity-hunting angle,' Bentham added. 'The last thing a kidnap-for-gain criminal usually wants is media attention. I really can't figure that one out. But I've got the press office working on a standard news blackout for the moment in any case. We're promising the media an ongoing hourly review of the embargo to keep them onside in lieu of a press conference – and to keep our own options open.'

'I don't think we'll know why until we catch them,' Jacobson said when it was clear that Bentham had finished speaking.

'Maybe the RCS could still send us an adviser though,' Greg Salter suggested. 'I was thinking especially on the release negotiation side.'

'Fair enough,' Jacobson conceded, 'so long as it *is* just advisory. There might not be an opportunity anyway. All the communications so far have been strictly in one direction only. Don't forget they're not planning to phone John Shepherd back, just email a set of instructions to him.'

'Can't we email *them*? Try and get a dialogue going?' Bentham asked with the naivety of a senior officer who relied on a personal secretary to handle his electronic correspondence for him.

'Every journalist they've emailed has tried that one, Sir,' Greg Salter said, keen as ever to impress the Chief with his minimal grasp of the situation. 'The replies just bounce straight back from whatever compromised system the gang happens to be using at the time.'

'And they never use the same one twice,' Jacobson added, leaving it at that.

If Bentham wanted the technical details he could ask Steve Horton like everybody else did. But later please – time in general might be infinite, according to the prevalent scientific theories, but the hours and minutes between now and the three o'clock deadline definitely weren't.

'Do you think Shepherd can get his hands on that kind of money in time, Frank? Supposing paying up becomes the recommended option?' Bentham asked, thankfully moving on.

'Apparently he can. He's on that list of the UK's fifty wealthiest fat cats that comes out every year for one thing.'

The standard protocol was to play for time, to trace or triangulate telephone conversations, to give yourself a chance to be at the scene when any exchange took place. The successful police outcome for a kidnapping was defined by three markers: safe rescue of the victim, recovery of any funds, and arrest into custody of the kidnappers. In this case, unless luck or hard slog changed the situation, Jacobson knew he would be happy to settle in the short term for marker one – get January Shepherd out alive and relatively unharmed.

Bentham had a follow-up question.

'And he can transfer eight million online at a few hours notice?'

Jacobson nodded again.

'He says he'll have to make some calls to set up the authorisations but yes, he reckons that, come three o'clock, he can click his mouse to the tune of eight mil if he has to.'

Bentham still ignored the coffee but leant across the table and poured a small amount of water into a glass. He sipped all of it down before he spoke again.

'I suppose it's something to be grateful for that he did let us know, Frank.' he said.

'He took his time about it. They phoned him at nine thirty but he didn't phone me until five to ten. He talked to his lawyers first, took advice,' Jacobson replied.

He hoped that Shepherd had made the right decision. Kidnapping was a growth industry and there were an unknown number of cases each year where the police were kept firmly out of the picture. Families paid up, victims were released on the QT and the criminals pocketed the ransom cash.

'The rifle in this latest video – you're confident it's just a replica?' Bentham asked.

'Fairly confident. Steve Horton enhanced the image – sent copies over to the senior firearms guys. They came back with an identification of what it's supposed to be, some kind of American assault rifle, plus a list of eighteen comparison points where the replica deviates from the real thing.'

'We still need to be careful though, Frank,' Salter commented. 'A gun butt could have been used on the body-guard after all.'

'Or the doctors won't rule that out anyway,' Jacobson corrected him.

Salter wasn't wrong (amazingly). If they got so far as locating the gang, they might have to think about whether to involve the Armed Response Unit. But it was something to worry about later, not right now.

Bentham stood up: executive consultation over.

'Fine. Greg will keep me up to date with progress but the ball's basically in your court, Frank. All the best.'

'Thanks,' Jacobson said, 'we're doing everything we can.'

He drank his coffee while Salter escorted Bentham through the full three yards to his office door and then pulled it open for him entirely as if the Chief Constable was a departing Maharajah. *All the best*. Jacobson would strongly have preferred the phrase that actors used: break a leg – break a leg in several hundred places.

There was a development when he got back to the inci-dent room. Kerr sketched in the details for him. The Birmingham team had located the property the gang looked to have rented in the city centre. DS Barber had hit on the idea of trawling the details of employment references provided to letting agencies for the kinds of property the gang had seemed to be using and had eventually got a result. The Isle of Man registered public relations company which they'd used as a phoney reference source in connection with the Hat Factory had been used previously to secure a three-month rental on a luxury apartment on Cambrian Wharf. The letting agency even had a record of associated credit card transactions – on a Visa card that hadn't featured previously in the investigation.

'We're getting details of any other activity on the card, I assume?' Jacobson asked.

'Definitely. The credit card company are on the case. And the Birmingham SOCOs are forensicating the property as of ten minutes ago.'

'Any idea *when* they were there?'

'Not so far. Barber reckons the place looks pristine – a rerun of the Hat Factory in that regard by the sounds of it. They're going door-to-door through the building as well so that might become clearer later. There's nobody there right now that's for sure.'

Jacobson half-smiled.

'That's hardly a surprise. But this is still good news, old son. It's a mistake they could have avoided easily enough, which shows that they do *make* mistakes. They're smart but they're not infallible – they can fuck up just like anybody else.'

Kerr had a half-finished cup of tea in his hand but the rest of the team were heads-down busy, scouring every report from last night with a fine tooth comb, hoping against hope for the one overlooked item of information that could lead to a breakthrough. One of the phone lines rang. Emma Smith, who was the nearest to it, picked it up, answered it, but carried on reading the report in front of her as she did so.

'DI Monroe, Wolverhampton,' she said, indicating that the call was for Jacobson.

Monroe told him that they had a caller on the dedicated Operation Icarus number who was insisting on speaking directly to him – and only to him.

'Better put him through then,' he said, resigned to one of the fifty-seven varieties of head-banger the freephone line was attracting.

'You that Jacobson then?'

The voice was a nasal whine masquerading as human speech.

Jacobson said that he was.

'The one that was down the Bideford Arms last night?'

'That too.'

'Then you should listen close. I got something you'll want to hear.'

'Go ahead,' Jacobson said, feeling as if he'd just agreed to buy a job lot of DVD pornography from a slimy oddball in a grubby pub car park.

'There'll be a drink in it will there?'

Jacobson reminded the talking nose that he'd phoned a serious inquiry line and that he (Jacobson) was in no mood to play silly buggers.

'Only kidding,' the nose whined. 'Here's what it is. I'm the one as phoned your lot about them burning cars in Boden wood the night before last. I had a little business out that way at the time. Involving wildlife shall we say? Pheasants and such. I heard how you was asking around the Bideford about other vehicles that might have been seen in the vicinity?'

Jacobson, with a little difficulty, put the call on to broadcast so that his team could listen in.

'If you've got something to say, old son, then just—'

'I'm getting there, I'm getting there. Patience is a virtue, my old ma used to say. Anyhow, I was driving out that way when I saw the burning wrecks and turned back, phoned your lot on the way. The thing is when I was headed out there in the first place, I only passed one other vehicle – travelling back in the Wynarth direction it was.'

'And?'

'I didn't get no number, why would I? But it were a Volvo, mate. A Volvo saloon, one of the old models. I think they stopped making them a year or two ago. White or off-white, that kind of colour. Youngsters in it – or younger than me, any road. Two blokes, two females.'

'I could be doing with your name and address, Mr, er—'

'No names, no pack drill. That's all I know. Volvo heading back to town, no more than a mile or so from where the burning cars were. Nice talking to you, Inspector Jacobson. Bye now.'

The call ended.

Kerr phoned through to the control room, requested the log data on the caller's details. The result was quick but non-illuminating: an unregistered mobile on the Vodafone network, untraceable in most circumstances. Emma Smith waded through a pile of paperwork, located a small padded envelope with a cassette tape inside. All 999 calls from the public were stored and recorded and this tape contained the conversation between the control room and the anonymous caller who'd phoned in about the burn-outs. She shoved it into a tape deck and pressed play. The call lasted barely twenty seconds and the caller barely said ten words. But the nasal whine was definitely there.

'I'd say it's the same customer, guv,' Mick Hume said, expressing the consensus.

'Agreed, Mick,' Jacobson said. 'In any case we haven't time to hang around waiting for a proper voice comparison. I suggest we factor this in straightaway. Any reports where anybody saw any kind of vehicle, we go back and ask them if it could be a white-ish Volvo that they saw.'

'The description's a bit vague though,' Kerr objected.

'Agreed too. We need to research models, come up with a photographic list of the possibles.'

'I'm on it already,' Emma Smith said, volunteering for the task.

Ray Williams raised another objection.

'Some old Volvo though. I thought this lot liked nice loft apartments and shiny new BMWs.'

'Up until now, old son. But it could be that was all just part of their set-up. They're certainly clever enough for that – establish an MO and then deviate from it. And, in any case, don't forget the white van they've been using. There's nothing upmarket about a Ford Transit.'

Jacobson's mobile rang: John Shepherd. He'd wanted to speak to him anyway but he'd wanted the peace and quiet of his office to take the call in. Not to mention the opportunity to grab a quick B&H. He told Shepherd he needed five minutes, told him to call back then, wondered idly how often in the average year anybody ever told Shepherd to do anything.

He took the stairs, trading off the exercise against the cigarette he'd just promised himself. Once inside, he closed his door and opened his office window to defeat the smoke detector. Down in the pedestrianised square, one of the regular town centre rough sleepers was sifting painstakingly through the litter bins and not seeming to find anything worth finding. Jacobson thought he knew exactly how the dosser felt. He lit up, took his first draw, didn't answer John Shepherd until after the sixth ring tone.

Shepherd was sitting on a bench near the knot garden. He'd hoped the fresh autumnal air might clear his head, might help him to think straight – and might also help keep him well away from his next, inevitable bottle of Fussigny. The policeman, Jacobson, was an unusual character, he was thinking. Bluff, even fucking rude actually, but you also got the picture that he was the obsessional type who lived for his job. If someone could sort this for him, maybe he was the man.

He was about to redial when Jacobson finally answered his sodding phone at last, asked him if there'd been any further contact from the kidnappers.

'No, nothing,' Shepherd replied. 'Not a bat squeak here. Any news for me at your end?'

The preamble was bland – but the follow-up had meat on the bones.

'We're pulling out all the stops, following several lines of inquiry. What I need you to help me with right now is *background*. You're a wealthy man. An obvious target for a ransom crime. But I need to know whether there could be any more specific reason behind this. Anything at all.'

Shepherd watched the rose bushes shudder against a sudden gust of wind.

'You mean do I have enemies? Somebody with a grievance?'

'That's it exactly, John. Not everybody employs a bodyguard. Not even every *rich* everybody.'

'It's a precaution, that's all. When you've lived in the public eye like I have, you're a target for all kinds of nutters and maniacs. And Perry's been useful to me in all kinds of ways. He's a mate – somebody I owe.'

'What kinds of ways exactly?'

Shepherd turned the collar of his fleece up against the wind. Someone else and he'd be tempted to say go fuck yourself – or look me up on the scandal blogs. But this was the one man who might be able to find his daughter.

'It's all past history now – and it's not a secret history either. After my marriage to January's mother broke up, I did the tedious rock arsehole thing big-time for a while. Hard drugs, whores, all that. Perry came on board to take care of business basically. He'd score whatever I needed to score, pay off whoever I needed to pay off. But, hey, none of that's connected to what's going on now surely? I'm only into two things these days: booze and Kelly – both of which were completely legal the last time I looked.'

'People can hold grudges for a long time, John.'

'Yeah, but there *aren't* any grudges. I was always generous. Generous to a fault. And these are small-time LA operators

I'm talking about. This video gang crew are all English, aren't they?'

Jacobson agreed that they were, reminded him that all his phone lines were being monitored now. If he did get any more calls from the kidnappers, the most important thing he could do was to keep the conversation going for as long as he possibly could.

When Jacobson rang off, Shepherd stood up and walked back towards the main house. He'd told the copper the truth and he felt good about that – he just hadn't told him all of it. And especially not the thing he'd only just remembered himself. He'd feel foolish really, mentioning it, didn't know why it had sprung into his mind at this specific moment.

Chapter Thirty-six

Annabel had spent the night in Adrian's bedroom, hadn't made the slightest attempt to conceal the fact. After breakfast, Brady had told her to help Maria load the dishwasher and she'd blanked him – just looked right through him and then carried on dipping the final remains of her chocolate croissant into her coffee cup. She was still there now, lying on his bed and flicking through the pile of old *Country Life* magazines she'd found in the loft when they'd first moved in and had been exploring the cottage's nooks and crannies. Adrian didn't like her, didn't like her history with Brady, didn't like the real, unambiguous pleasure she took in inflicting real pain whenever the opportunity presented itself. But her near-perfect body was difficult to resist when she was offering it to him on a plate – and also, by implication, denying it to Brady.

Adrian was using his laptop to check that all the bank accounts were up and running properly. He stopped for a moment and studied her long and undeniably shapely legs; her toes, courtesy of Maria, were still painted deep purple. Ever since the breakfast incident, Brady had gone into aloof mode, as if all of it was beneath his dignity and as if none of it mattered to him in the slightest. Adrian hadn't been fooled – and wasn't fooled. Even if you kept Annabel out of the equation, he knew that from here on in, he needed to cover his back. He'd faced him down twice. The first time had only been about Annabel, after she'd belted January Shepherd. But last night he'd gone the whole way, had interfered with Brady's own little slice of fun, pulling him off the girl before the idiot ended up breaking her arm or something. He'd expected consequences – and although they hadn't yet arisen, he'd gone on expecting them.

That was why, about four in the morning, he'd snuck downstairs, taken one of the two Walthers out of its hiding place, reloaded it and relocated it to the back of his wardrobe, shoving it out of sight behind a laptop carrying case.

He read the time from the bottom of the screen. Eleven twenty-three. All the accounts were in order. There was still the website to sort out. But they'd agreed twelve thirty on the nose for that. He sensed her watching him with her dark, jaded eyes, realised there was time for a quick fuck before then if he felt like it. Maybe with the door ajar this time – for added amusement and wind-up value.

Jacobson took the stairs back down to the incident room. Mick Hume pointed a telephone receiver towards him as he walked through the doorway.

'DI Monroe for you again, guv.'

Jacobson took the phone from Hume, found some wall space near a photocopier to slouch against.

'You remember the coffin we retrieved from Codsall woods?' Monroe asked him.

'Of course. Most probably the same one they used over here. Your team were trying to trace the manufacturer, weren't they?'

'Aye, they were – and now they have. They've also come up with a delivery address in Crowby.'

Jacobson abandoned the wall, found a desk where he could scribble the details into his notebook.

'You'll recall that the coffin was the pre-buy, DIY kind that a lot of folk are using who don't want traditional burials and so on,' Monroe said. 'Except that at least it was a proper pinewood coffin, not the full-on cardboard or wicker variety that the real eco-freaks go in for. That narrowed it down a lot for us.'

'And you said something about the rope handles being another distinguishing feature,' Jacobson prompted her needlessly.

'That's right. So eventually we were focusing on just this one company. They're located down in the south-west but they sell all over the country by mail order. You can purchase your last resting box direct if you're so inclined – but they also supply to any funeral directors who're prepared to act as resellers in their local areas. We asked them to email us all their order details back to the beginning of August. And, lo and behold, last Friday, they dispatched a delivery of one coffin to a funeral parlour in Crowby.'

Jacobson wrote down the address, read it back out to her as a double-check before she rang off. It could just be a coincidence. And, even if it wasn't, it mightn't lead the investigation anywhere new. But you followed up everything, ignored nothing, he reminded himself – or you weren't doing your job.

The rest of the team had their hands full with last night's reports. He decided to visit the funeral directors on his own. The address was out towards the Waitrose complex, anything up to half an hour's drive away through the Saturday morning shopping traffic – or ten minutes in a rapidly commandeered patrol car using its blue lights. Ray Williams phoned him en route. The credit card company had just sent on the full transaction records for the Visa card that had been linked to the Birmingham property let. The result was disappointing. The card had been used once and once only: to pay the full three months rental in advance plus the security deposit. Another set of data that led nowhere beyond itself, Jacobson thought, gripping his seat-belt on a tight corner.

He got the patrol car to wait for him, had to wait a few moments himself at the reception counter while the receptionist finished dealing with her two customers. A distraught elderly man and a middle-aged woman, maybe his daughter, who seemed to be as cheery as if she was booking the next family holiday and not a gloomy half-hour at the crematorium. He was sure he'd been here before on police business but his brain couldn't immediately access when or to what purpose. When the old man and his companion had gone, the receptionist found the details for him, swivelled her computer screen so that he could read them. The delivery of the coffin kit had been logged at ten twenty-five AM and the buyer had called to collect it at two fifteen in the afternoon, had paid up in cash. The buyer's address was listed as number thirty-four, the Hat Factory but the (male) name wasn't one of the aliases they'd previously associated with the gang.

'They paid cash. Pity,' he said, thinking out loud.

The receptionist was maybe his own age but her eyes were bright, lively.

'The customer placed the order by telephone. We'd have asked for a credit card number as confirmation,' she commented.

He watched her quick fingers bring up another screen: the new alias, the Hat Factory address and a MasterCard number. He dialled the incident room, passed on the details. Mick Hume called him back thirty seconds later: the card number, like the alias, was another brand-new result. He asked her if she'd been here when the delivery had been taken or when the purchaser had turned up to collect.

'Sorry, love. I was in Fuengirola last week. We always like to get away in September. Less crowded, isn't it? They always get a temp in when I'm not here. You could ask around in the workshops though. They might remember if—'

Jacobson tried. But no one he spoke to seemed to have been around when the purchaser had called by. He thanked the receptionist before he left, noted down the name of the agency that she said would've supplied her replacement.

Someone from duty CID could chase it up, he was thinking, see if the temp could give a description that sounded like 'Brady' or 'Adrian'.

He used the drive back to the Divisional building as thinking time. The body of evidence was building up nicely. Already they had the makings of the kind of solid case that even the thickest CPS dunderhead would have to try really hard to botch in the court room. Even Jim Webster was confident that the completed forensic tests would match fibres across the crime scenes and would probably finger at least some of the gang from DNA sources. The problem was that they hadn't *caught* anybody, didn't seem to be close to catching anybody, didn't know any of the culprits' true identities. The trails the inquiry teams were following were days-old at best and every fresh lead so far had turned out to be no lead at all. The poacher who'd called the hotline had sounded genuine but there seemed to be no other reports of a Volvo saloon in the area for instance. Not a single one. He tried to fix his mind on the gang's one known fuck-up: using the same phoney employment reference twice. If the gang could make one mistake then that meant they could make other mistakes, *QED*. That was an entirely logical, philosophically respectable inference. Plus every single credit card which had been uncovered was being monitored live on the banking systems. The gang only had to use one of them once again and – in theory, anyway – the transaction and its location would be instantly flagged up. Most of his cases were about persistence, about keeping going, about shovelling all the shite there was to shovel. Reluctantly he studied the face of his watch. Ten seconds past twelve noon. But most of his cases had a more generous event horizon than this one: barely three hours left and counting.

Brady watched January Shepherd sitting on the edge of her bed and staring blankly into space. He'd been tempted more than once to switch the light off up there, leave her in dark-

304

ness for an hour or two, give her a taste of real confinement. But he'd rejected the idea as unprofessional, the kind
of self-indulgence that could lead to unforeseen, unpredictable errors. He was watching her from the laptop downstairs in the outhouse, couldn't abide to be too near the
vulgar spectacle unfolding in Adrian's bedroom. Adrian had
pushed him close to the edge. But that was all. Close, not
over. The project was too near completion now to worry
about a tedious infidelity on Annabel's part. Adrian would
be parting company with them after the pay-out – that was
the deal – and there were lots of exquisite ways he could
punish Annabel later in any case. He might even switch their
roles for a while, make Annabel serve Maria, teach her about
life on the other end of the leash. It was weird how they'd
got used so quickly to their stage names, he thought; he
could hardly think of Annabel by her 'real' and so much
duller name (Susan) any more. The same went for Maria to
an extent. It was only Adrian's case, frankly, where he couldn't
see that there'd been the slightest improvement over his given
name. The reverse if anything. But using the name-changes
amongst themselves had still been a good idea, had made
them all continuously aware of the project's central premise:
identity was a fluid concept, impermanent, non-static. Your
family tried to fix an identity for you, then your school, your
education did the same – and later on so did whatever arse-
tonguing job you managed to get, or failed to get, whatever
status level the system decided to slot you into. But you
didn't need any of that, didn't need to be constrained in any
of those ways. Ultimately, you were whoever you'd decided
to be, whoever you said you were.

   In a way he almost took pride in Adrian's mini-rebellion.
Ade had at least learned something by being around him. If
you wanted something you took it. If you waited to be asked
you could go on waiting your entire life. Sidelined, irrelevant, a non-combatant. The outbreak of morality was
worrying of course. Adrian had enjoyed himself well enough

on their various forays, especially out at Edgbaston, had probably left it a bit late to start up an ethics committee. It was one thing staying within certain boundaries as a precaution in case the legal system caught up with you. Ade had learnt that lesson well, probably had a point in those terms. But it was another thing altogether actually giving a fuck who got hurt or to what extent. People, and especially women, needed waking up, shaking up, needed their zombiefied, complacent stupidity knocked out of them. If they learned the meaning of fear in the process, so much the better. Morality, as he'd pointed out to Adrian on more than one occasion, was pre-modern not post-modern.

She was bent down now and shuffling about, up to something. Ah, the shackles – that was it. Playing around with the chain links, looking for a flaw. No chance, sweetheart, not with only your bare, talented little fingers to work with. By rights, he should go up there and give her a good slapping for her trouble. Maybe he would in a minute or two, maybe wait and let her tire herself out first.

He was glad he'd come up with the website idea. The media were censoring everything they'd sent out, showing only the tiniest, mildest fraction of each film. This way, even supposing their handiwork only survived up there for a few hours, the entire world would be able to see the full, magnificent extent. More importantly, thousands of cyber-geeks, Adrian's legions, maybe tens of thousands of them, would have the presence of mind to download everything while they had the chance, make proper, unadulterated copies. Before the day was out their achievements would have passed into legend, would live on as underground classics for years to come. The Art Terrorist movies would become as cult-famous as the *Zapruder* footage or *Cocksucker Blues* or *Scorpio Rising*. The fact that they'd be eight million pounds better off between them was almost a side-issue, a minor bonus.

He watched her pulling futilely at the chain on her left

shackle. Even last night, Adrian had raised his whingeing doubts once again. They could have just staged the kidnap on its own, discreetly – not have bothered with any of the preamble. Well, of course, we could have, Ade, if we were just greedy, petty criminals. But we're not. And even if we were, the Art Terror project would still *rock*. The failure rate for kidnappings was high, around about eighty per cent. Mostly what went wrong was down to delay and obfuscation. The police would convince the victim's family that the kidnapper's threats were exaggerated, would encourage the relatives to play for the time the police needed to close in, grab you. Well that definitely wasn't going to happen on this occasion. All week they'd given a demonstration of what they were capable of and how the moronic clowns in blue couldn't get anywhere near them. John Shepherd wouldn't hesitate, wouldn't be swayed by the police agenda, would pay up on time. On the nail.

Look, just stop that you irritating fucking bitch. I really am going to come up there right now and make you cry. And then they'd be out of here as per their carefully planned pre-arrangements. Two million each wasn't a fortune these days but it was enough. Enough to set you free. Enough to start you on the life you wanted, dancing to your own fucking drum beat. They could even take their old identities back after a while if they really wanted them, if they still had a use for them when the heat died down.

Those identities were ticking over quite nicely, thank you. What could be more ordinary than four recent graduates (or near-graduate in Annabel's case) taking themselves off backpacking and casual-jobbing it around the world for a year or two? Especially when three of them had jacked in their shit-for-thanks call centre serf gigs in order to do so. It wasn't a difficult disappearing-act to maintain. All it took was the occasional email purporting to be from Bangkok or Machu Picchu or the occasional, untraceable, rerouted 'long-distance' phone call. That way, even if the piss-poor e-fits or the blurry CCTV images of them in disguise which were all over the tabloids jogged somebody's memory, they were just as likely to dismiss the thought as to act on it. Everybody knew that Susan and Brian were in Kerala (or was it Mumbai?) – and why would they be hanging girls in woods anyway? The other shackle now, pulling at it and pulling at it and pulling at it. Right, that's enough – you can stop that right fucking *now*.

Chapter Thirty-seven

Another call on his mobile detoured Jacobson to the hospital before he could get back to the Divisional building. Perry Harrison had regained consciousness, was probably out of immediate danger. The patrol car driver had used his blue lights again but Jacobson was still too late by the time he got there. Harrison had lapsed back into recovery sleep and the medical assessment was that he needed to be left strictly undisturbed. Jacobson asked the nurse if he'd said anything when he'd come round. She said that he had – but that it had all been gobbledegook, more or less raving. That wasn't uncommon or unexpected, she told him. The next time he woke up, he might be more *compos mentis*. Or the time after that. Jacobson smoked a B&H on the fast drive back across town, cleared it with the patrol guys first, made sure he didn't tip any ash on their commendably pristine interior. He walked into the incident room just as the website storm broke.

'Take a look at this, Frank,' Kerr said, practically shoving him towards the nearest computer screen. 'They've taken over the Alice Banned website – and they've sent an email to the media to make sure the media knows about it.'

Kerr talked him through the relevant web pages. All the films the gang had sent out were available for instant viewing and for full, instant download. The 'manifesto' that had been sent out with the Thursday afternoon film could also be downloaded as a PDF file.

'Anything else?' Jacobson asked.

'Oh yeah, there's something else all right,' Kerr replied, clicking on to a new page.

Jacobson gaped at what appeared to be a live image feed: January Shepherd, still shackled, still wearing an orange jump suit. She was sitting on the edge of a bare mattress and sobbing loudly. The feed zoomed to a close-up: wet tears streaming down January's face and a bruised, cut eye that was swelling up nastily.

'Is this stuff live?' Jacobson asked.

'Better ask the expert,' Kerr replied, deferring to Steve Horton.

Jacobson hadn't registered Horton's presence but now he saw that he was ensconced behind the incident room's main computer terminal, keying frantically.

'No, it isn't,' Horton said, looking up from the keyboard. 'That would be far too risky for them. The image feed's actually on a pre-loaded loop, repeats itself every four minutes. What they've done essentially is to go into the site, upload their data and then bugger off again sharpish. They'd've probably changed the system administrator password while they were about it – and they've anomysed their access paths as usual.'

'How did they get there in the first place?' Jacobson asked, hoping that Horton's reply would utilise some vague approximation to the English language.

'Either they got the system password from January Shepherd, if she knew it, or they managed to de-encrypt it themselves one way or another.'

Jacobson thought about the kidnapped musician's black eye, decided that the first route was more likely than the second.

'Once you're into a site with admin privileges, you can do what the fuck you like there basically,' Horton concluded.

Jacobson phoned Nick Bishop on the mobile number Bishop had given him.

'I was just about to call you,' Bishop said, his voice

unsteady, bordering on panic. 'They've got hold of our website somehow—'

Jacobson cut across him, needed to get to the point.

'Yes I've seen it, Nick. Do you know if January would know the, er, system password?'

Bishop told him that she did.

'We all do,' he added. 'There's a message board on there for the fans. We tend to take turns at posting answers to questions or whatever.'

Steve Horton scribbled something on a scrap of paper, passed it to Jacobson: *Ask him which ISP company hosts their site – and do they have a main contact there?*

Jacobson relayed the questions, grabbed a pen and jotted the answers down.

'So you haven't even found out where they are yet—'

'We're doing everything we can, Nick. *Everything*. I'm sorry. I need to go now.'

Jacobson ended the call, handed Horton's note back to him.

'What are our options on this, Steve?'

'Limited, basically, Mr Jacobson. The site's hosted in Palo Alto – where it's going to be about four forty-five AM right now, roughly speaking. They might have an overnight support guy or they might not. Depends how big their set-up is.'

'No, I meant what can we *do*? What can the ISP do?'

'If you mean immediately then there's really only two things – leave the site running as it is or take it off the host server, shut it down completely for the time being.'

The door opened while Jacobson was still ingesting the news. Just what he needed: DCS Greg Salter, adjusting his Armani tie as he walked in and looking flustered.

'The press office are being swamped with calls, Frank. I'm worried that the papers and the TV will use this internet site business as a lever against the news blackout.'

'I'd say the blackout's effectively dead in the water, *Greg*,' Jacobson replied. 'There's not much point to it if the public from Tipton to Timbuktu are gawping at January Shepherd shackled to a wall.'

Evidently this wasn't the reassuring answer that Crowby's chief of detectives had actually wanted to hear.

'But if the media stays silent, how are the public even going to know?'

Jacobson looked to Steve Horton, giving him his cue.

'They'll know all right. It only takes one obsessive fan to visit the site to start the ball rolling. He tells his mates. They tell their mates – and from then on it's exponential. You can't keep schtum on the internet, Mr Salter.'

'So we should try and get the site shut down?' Salter asked, seeming to be addressing the entire room, worried enough for once, maybe, to take advice wherever he could get it.

'It's a gamble in either case,' Jacobson said. 'But I'd say let it run on. That way there's a chance they might post something else – something that might give them away somehow.'

Something. Somehow. The vague leading the blind, he thought. But when you only had straws you clung to them.

Greg Salter readjusted his tie.

'OK. And I'll set up the press conference I've been promising. If we can't *stop* the news, we can at least influence how it gets reported.'

'You won't need me for that,' Jacobson said.

'Well as the senior investigating officer, I was expecting that you'd—'

'It wasn't a question, *Greg*. Nobody on my team's available. We're battling against the clock here.'

'This is important too, Frank. The force's public image is at stake.'

Jacobson snorted his disbelief out loud. It was almost a relief to have Smoothie Greg firmly back in total unpleasant idiot mode.

'A young woman's life is at stake,' he said quietly.

'But we'll advise Shepherd to pay the ransom if it comes to it, surely?'

'Yes we will, *Sir*,' Jacobson replied, deliberately using the epithet which Salter had declared infra dig for his senior officers. 'But we've no guarantee that this bunch of twisted little fuckers won't still kill her anyway – just for the sake of "art", just to see what it feels like.'

John Shepherd asked Kelly where to find the best pictures of the Art Gang. He was back kicking his heels in the library. Kelly dug out yesterday's *Daily Mail* then she remembered that the police had released what they'd claimed were 'enhanced' images last night. She switched the laptop away from the Alice Banned web pages, which Shepherd had been compulsively asking her to refresh every minute or so, and found the BBC news site. Shepherd looked hard at the latest image of 'Brady'.

'This is crazy shit, Kelly,' he said, 'but when I was talking to that policeman, I suddenly had a flash of that tosser who made a nuisance of himself at the Brits. You remember, last year?'

'I think so,' Kelly said, not really sure.

Last year's Brits – the British Music Awards – had taken place not that long after she'd started 'seeing' Shepherd, not long after he'd moved back to the UK. He'd been automatically invited to the music industry's annual bash and, untypically, he'd accepted the invitation. A couple of up-and-coming bands had been showcased at the awards event and Kelly thought she vaguely remembered him saying something about wanting to check out the competition that January was up against.

'Hang on. You don't mean that plonker who had the female in black leather with him – on the end of a dog lead?'

Despite the desperate situation January was in, Kelly gave an involuntary little smile at the returning memory.

'That's the one,' Shepherd said. 'He claimed he was some

old mate of Nick Bishop's from school or something. It turned out he'd blagged his way in – forged invitations, false names, the lot. He had some fucking daft idea for a film or something, interrupted us bang in the middle of the pudding course.'

'*The Story of O*, John, that old French porno thing. I'm remembering this now. He was pitching it as an urban musical, wasn't he? Wanted to set it in London or New York. Something like that anyway – *seriously* naff. You were a bit rude to him actually.'

Kelly studied the image on the laptop screen. Shepherd had been more than rude to be honest. He'd been well oiled, had told the interloper loudly to fuck off and when he didn't take the hint quickly enough, he'd proceeded to empty a bowl of raspberry roulade right down the front of his shirt. Security had arrived by then: no interest, professional or otherwise, in the rights or wrongs of it, just speedily extracting the non-celebs from the building.

'But now I look at this bloke, Kel – I don't think it's the same guy. His hair was different and his nose. And nobody's going to go to all this trouble, are they, just because of a bit of bog standard celebrity rudeness?'

'Not a normal, law-abiding person, John. I don't recognise him either. But you should always listen to your intuitions, keep your head open to your heart.'

'Very Santa Monica Canyon. But I should give Nick Bishop a call, shouldn't I? See if he really did know that guy – then maybe give the copper a ring after that.'

Kelly handed him his personal/business mobile.

'Do it, John. We've got to try everything, haven't we?'

Chapter Thirty-eight

Jacobson rallied the team after Greg Salter left the incident room. Not every property in the five-mile radius of Boden Hall had been successfully ticked off after last night's operation: residents not at home or not answering their doors to strangers after dark, not even strangers claiming to be police. Jacobson wanted a list. As soon as it was compiled, he intended to send out the duty CID and duty uniformed patrols, revisit every one of those addresses.

'And what about us, Frank?' Kerr asked, speaking on behalf of the others again.

'We carry on cross-referencing and we hope for a lead. I'm sorry but that's the reality of where we are. There's no point running around like a bunch of headless chickens just for the sake of it. We stay calm, we stay prepared, we do what we can.'

One of the phone lines rang and Jacobson picked it up: DCI Nelson in Coventry. At long last, the Coventry team had found a relevant camera image: two BMWs out near the Crowby exit from the motorway on Thursday morning, moving in tandem, both with phoney plates. The image could have been crucial at the time when it had been taken, Jacobson thought, but now it was only one more piece of evidence for a solid case against persons unknown that might never see a courtroom. It was more or less useless for any immediate purpose. He thanked Nelson anyway and studied the print-out which Mick Hume handed him. The MasterCard that had guaranteed the coffin kit order at the funeral directors had never been used any other time. Neither before nor since.

It took half an hour, all of them working on it, to put the list of unchecked properties together. When they were ready, they used Steve Horton's mapping software to plot routes and sectors and then DS Kerr relayed the details to the control room. It was down to them to divert as many duty patrols as it took to get the job done urgently.

Jacobson couldn't bear to look at his watch but he knew that time was running out. Time, the bringer of death and decay, was the enemy of every single living creature. But right now the enmity felt personal, like a needle match. His mobile went off and he pulled it out of his pocket, answered it gruffly. Nick Bishop told him the story about John Shepherd and the raspberry roulade. When he'd finished he added that he'd offered to phone on Shepherd's behalf. Shepherd was too agitated, he said, too close to losing it.

'But you can't remember this character yourself?' Jacobson asked.

'No, I'm afraid I can't. I've been looking at the "Brady" picture myself. It doesn't ring any bells. Looks like a hundred guys to me. Melanie says he's handsome but I wouldn't know. The thing is, since I've become a tiny bit famous, I do get the odd person coming up to me at a gig and saying they used to know me from here or there. Usually, I just smile politely, act as if I remember even when I don't.'

'You'd better tell me where and when you went to school anyway, Nick. The exact dates if you can.'

Bishop gave him unexpectedly accurate details. Jacobson scribbled them down. It was always possible a list of names might jog his memory or might jog John Shepherd's memory. Apparently, neither he nor his girlfriend could remember the name (presumably the real name) of the ligger who'd tried to buttonhole them about financing a hopeless music film project. There was an outside chance, too, that somebody connected with security for the awards event might have some kind of record of the incident. But both those possibilities would take some tracing – and neither of them was likely to tell him what he needed to know immediately: where the hell 'Brady' and company were right now.

Nick Bishop wasn't finished.

'Something else,' he said, 'we're all checking out of the hotel next. There's press everywhere here, trying to pap us for bloody interviews. John Shepherd's invited us to stay at Boden Hall. So we'll be driving over there just as soon as we've packed up.'

'Fine, Nick, bye,' Jacobson replied curtly, ending the call.

He updated Kerr with the Brit Awards story.

'There's probably hotel chambermaids and music business types from pole to pole who've got similar grudges, Frank. This guy's been a major prima donna arsehole in his time,' Kerr commented.

'Agreed. But let's assume that "Brady" and the raspberry roulade victim are the same man for the sake of argument. The fact that he *impersonated* his way into the event could be significant, surely? I'm not saying that's *why* he's kidnapped Shepherd's daughter, of course not. Yet maybe when you put a plan together to kidnap the offspring of somebody rich for ransom cash, then the one rich person you know who's treated you badly – even just trivially badly – then that might be the target that jumps out at you first.'

'You mean Shepherd put himself on Brady's radar?'

'Exactly, old son.'

Jacobson became aware of Emma Smith hovering in the vicinity. She was holding a report form in her hand and evidently waiting for a gap in the conversation.

'Sorry to butt in, guv,' she said. 'But I think you should definitely take a look at this.'

Dave had been genuine about the van, had even driven it around to Tracey's mother's place for them, handed Casper the keys personally. It had been after eleven before they'd got going though. Tracey had wanted to have a bath first, wash her hair again, then she'd wanted more tea and another cigarette. Casper didn't hassle her, was still walking on egg shells around her. She didn't seem to have any definite idea of where she wanted to go or what she wanted to do. So Casper drove them out towards Crowcross. It wasn't much of a place in itself and it was stuck in the middle of frigging nowhere. What you called a hamlet because it wasn't big enough to be called a village. All that was there was a few crappy old-fashioned houses, a bus shelter, one of those snobby country pubs full of snobby country wankers and a two-pump petrol-station-cum-shop that was only open during the hours of daylight. But none of that bollocks was why he'd come here. The point about Crowcross was that it was directly on the river and there was a car park off to the right, down by an old, abandoned jetty.

His dad had brought him out here a few times when he'd been a nipper, before he'd fallen out with his mum and buggered off somewhere north (Manchester was the last Casper had heard). But at least it was something to remember him by. They'd make up sandwiches and his dad would pack a couple of beers for himself, then get his fishing gear together. What you did was park at Crowcross and then walk a couple of miles or so along the riverside. Most of the fishing rights were private or else you had to fork out for a poxy day licence. But Casper would keep a lookout for the permit Nazis while his dad fished. Later they'd eat their picnic and Casper would skim stones out across the water, counting the splashes, trying to beat his record.

He didn't know what Tracey would make of the idea but she hadn't complained when they'd got there anyway. Seeing as how the van was legal and was on loan from a mate, Casper had stuck a pound coin in the ticket machine and stuck the little white ticket earnestly onto the inside of the windscreen. He told her there was a wood if they walked far enough along and farmland as well. Peaceful like. A breath of fresh air.

It was one of those days you could get in autumn when the clouds moved on, the wind dropped and a bright sun came out. After a mile or so, Casper took his fleece off and used the sleeves to tie it around his middle. An old couple, heading back towards Crowcross, had passed them as they'd walked on. The bloke had one of those poncy straw hat things on his old, bald head, had smiled warily at them – and then actually tipped it, like in some old-fashioned film. *Nice day for it*, he'd said. Casper had nodded straight back, polite as anything: *Yeah, cheers, mate*. That had been a laugh that had, a real laugh.

They'd gone past a field with cows in it and then one with sheep: fat lambs born earlier in the year. Tracey had leant on the fence for ages, watching them. *You'd think you'd never seen one before, Tracey*, he'd said. And she'd told him she hadn't really, or not many anyway: *The Woodlands and Crowby, Casper, what the fuck else do we ever see?* He'd started talking about jobs again, about getting his act together, putting his arse in gear. She was right about Dave's car spares number of course. They probably wouldn't touch him with a barge pole for something like that. But there were other ways to earn good money. The building trade for instance. He was serious about it, he told her, he'd get something.

If you kept going the Crow widened out again, got deeper, and then you came to the weir. Casper could have watched the water torrenting for hours those times his dad had brought him out here. He'd dreamt about it sometimes too as a kid, he reckoned. And in the dreams he could swim like a fish in the fast, dangerous currents. There was a car park here too and another pub. The Jack o'Lantern. The Jack was a different gaff altogether to the Crowcross Arms, had a little bit of non-snooty life about it. There was a field back of the pub set out for caravanners and campers. Brummies mainly, big families of them, who'd come out here at weekends. The pub would do pig roasts on a Sunday and sometimes there would be a band, though usually a crap one. All that yee-haw country stuff Denise liked and he and Tracey laughed at her from behind her back. He'd been out here on the QT with Mad Billy Briers more than once and they'd liberated more than one vehicle from the vicinity – but that was another story.

They'd been hungry by the time they'd walked that far so they'd treated themselves to a pub lunch. The woman behind the bar had been the friendly type, down to earth. She looked a bit older than his mum, but not much. Forty maybe.

'I don't know. Young love,' she said, smiling, when Casper went up to the bar for their second round of drinks.

'So what do you need? Bar staff?' he asked her, the words falling out of his mouth before he'd really thought about them.

There was a black-markered note taped on the serving hatch behind her: *Staff wanted*.

'Well, more than that really, sweetheart. There's all sorts needs doing here. The bar, the cellar, the kitchen – and then there's the campsite to keep in order over the winter. We can get student-types easily enough in the summer months but now it's coming up to October—'

He talked it out with Tracey. She wasn't sure, he could see that, but she wasn't saying no either. It would be just the thing, he told her. There was a caravan went with the jobs. It would be just like having their own place. The money wasn't great but it wasn't that bad either. Plus they'd be learning skills: cooking, catering, the bar trade. Once they had those under their belts, they could get work anywhere, go anywhere they wanted to. And the beauty of it was they'd be right out of Crowby, right out of the Woodlands. It would be a brand-new start. It would be frigging great.

She drank a mouthful of Red Bull and vodka, said nothing.

Then she smiled at him. A smile that started out small and grew bigger.

'OK,' she said.

That was all – and then she put her glass down and kissed him.

Chapter Thirty-nine

John Shepherd had stood all the sobriety he could stand. He was drinking Fussigny straight from the bottle, swigging it down in full, rapid gulps.

'Jesus, John, that's not going to help,' Kelly said.

She'd actually tried to grab the bottle away from him but he'd shoved her away. She'd even thought for a fraction of a second that he was going to hit her.

'When we get this email at three o'clock you're going to need all your wits about you,' she tried again.

Shepherd had managed the difficult task of slumping in a Queen Anne chair by pulling another one in front of him and sticking his feet up on it. He pulled a folded sheet of paper out of his shirt pocket and chucked it at her.

'It's all there, Kelly. All the authorisation codes. Every little detail you need. You're the computer whizz anyway. It's going to be a lot easier if you take care of business.'

The sheet landed at her feet. She bent down and picked it up, unfolded it, studied the contents. He was probably right about that particular aspect. If the money had to be paid out, it would be better to pay it out correctly, following all the instructions to the letter. She sat back down at the laptop, placed the sheet of paper next to it. He could be such a useless arsehole. But there were other sides to him as well. Good sides. Even if she was the only one who seemed to see them. Even if everybody else assumed she was just the latest emissary from Gold Digger Central.

Birgit was in the library too, pacing near the bookshelves.

It was well after two o'clock now and all three of them were on the edge of panic or something very like it.

'I should never have come back to this fucking country,' Shepherd said to no one in particular. 'They envy you your wealth here. Petty, mean-spirited bastards. In the States they say good on yer, mate, well done.'

'What has that got to do with anything?' Birgit asked.

'What's it got to do? Everything, Birgit, fucking everything. They don't play my music here. They don't—'

'You haven't made a record for twelve years, John. What do you expect? And what has this got to do with your daughter?'

Shepherd took another deep swig before he replied.

'Because I always lose everything, don't I? The music's gone, my fucking lesbian Buddhist ecological fucking wife's gone – and now they've taken my daughter from me.'

Birgit shook her head, lowered her voice instead of raising it.

'You are the most selfish man in the entire world. It's your daughter you need to be worrying about, not your fragile teenage ego.'

She walked over to where Kelly was sitting.

'I'm sorry, Kelly. I have to go. I can't stand this. I'm going to drive over to the hospital. I think maybe we can get in to see Perry now.'

'But—' Kelly said.

'Don't worry, Kel,' Shepherd interrupted. 'Let her go. Who needs her? Dutch dyke, get it? Bloody Dutch bloody dyke.'

January listened intently but she couldn't hear anything. Which didn't mean they weren't somewhere near, weren't watching her every move. She'd been around webcams before but now she wished she'd paid more attention to the technicalities: what they could do, what they couldn't do. Her captors had taken the door off the little bathroom but now she was wondering whether the camera's range actually extended all the way inside. That time she'd taken the lid off the cistern, looking for any kind of potential tool, there'd been no comeback at all from them while the least thing she'd attempted in the vicinity of the mattress and the bed had brought them down on her like a ton of bricks. She shuffled through there anyway, inspected the cut around her eye in the square of mirror above the sink. The cut itself had stopped bleeding but the swelling was getting worse. She looked at the rest of her face, felt she'd aged a hundred years since she'd been here. The words they'd made her say when they'd filmed her had sounded like some weird kind of ransom demand. And then there'd been the stuff they'd wanted to know: her dad's email address, his telephone numbers. But she was still here, still shut up in this shitty room. Even if you only watched the news bulletins about twice a year the way she did, you knew that kidnappers fucked up and panicked – or they killed you anyway just to keep you quiet. When that fucker had burst in that last time, and hurt her, really hurt her, he hadn't been masked. That really wasn't a good thing. That was maybe because her seeing him didn't matter any more. Didn't matter any more because . . .

She splashed water on her face, avoiding her bad eye, then patted it dry with the face towel. *So I've got nothing to lose. Nothing.* She looked at the top of the square of mirror where it was cracked and peeling. A little bit of leverage there and most of the glass would come away from the wall easily enough. Her hands were nearly shaking but somehow she kept them under control. She had no idea how sensitive the webcam microphone might be, how much it could pick up, so she used the face towel to muffle the sound. *Easy. Steady. Don't rush.* The top third of the mirror broke off into two long, tapering pieces, the rest of it clung precariously to the wall. She sat one piece down on the lid of the cistern, used the piece with the sharpest point to cut into the face towel. Then she put that piece down too, concentrated on tearing the towel into strips. When she had enough of them she wrapped them around the flattest end of her chosen piece of mirror glass. She held it in her hand when she was done, got used to the feel of it, made a few practice thrusts. The jump suit had two zip pockets. Still with her back to the non-existent door, she fitted the makeshift weapon into the right-hand pocket. The fear was still inside her and so was the hopeless sense of despair. What was strange was that there was a lake of calmness too if she chose to dive into it. She'd never fought anyone in her life, never had to. But there had been a time when she couldn't hold down a simple E Major chord either, couldn't hit a clean, pure note.

Brady, Annabel, Maria and Adrian were sitting around the kitchen table. Annabel, Maria and Adrian were sharing a spliff, wanting to take the edge of their nerves. Brady, predictably, had declined. He wasn't drug-free, everybody knew that, but none of them, not even Annabel, had ever worked out exactly what it was that he was on – or how regularly he was on it. This was the last conference, the final briefing. Whatever tensions there'd been, whatever fallings-out, had been pushed to one side for the moment. This was *it*. Do or die.

Brady asked Adrian if he was sure the money transfers would work, if there really wasn't anything that could go wrong.

'The email we're sending to Shepherd is idiot-proof,' Adrian said. 'I've set out the instructions step by step. All he has to do is follow them one by one. Remember, he doesn't try and send us eight million straight off. He sends it to us a hundred K at a time at strict one-minute intervals.'

'So that you transfer out each bundle of a hundred thousand before the next one arrives?'

'Exactly, and don't forget I'm sending the cash on to the

next layer of receiving accounts split down into nice, little ten K bundles that won't trigger any "unusual transaction" alerts. And I'm using two more layers after that. We've got accounts set up in virtually every time zone.'

Brady waved his hand. He'd heard enough to reassure himself again. But Annabel, who'd never really grasped the point, asked where the famous *record-locking* concept fitted in.

Adrian nearly smiled, warming to his theme. Brady half-smiled too. It was reminiscent of the hours the three of them had spent around a canteen table in that fuck-awful Watford call centre. Three underachieving graduates (or two and a half anyway) going nowhere fast, ambitions turning into dust, and wondering how the fuck they could get their lives sorted.

'The first account is the most vulnerable one, Annabel,' Adrian explained. 'The police won't have any difficulty in tracing Shepherd's transfers to it. If they're smart enough, and if they've moved quickly enough, they might even route Shepherd's outgoing data through their own servers in the first place. But the point is that even if they trace the account instantly, they won't be able to *see into* it until I log out of it. It's just like when you book an airline seat or a hotel room online. Once you've accessed a specific seat or a specific room it's *locked out* to any other user until you either buy it or quit your selection. Otherwise you'd turn up at the airport or your hotel to find that ten thousand other customers had made exactly the same purchase you had.'

'So by the time they access the first receiving account,' Maria said, passing the spliff back to Adrian, 'all the money will be long gone.'

Maria got it without any difficulty, of course, Brady thought. She was razor-smart, the only one of them who'd packed in decent career prospects for the sake of the project – although there were other considerations in her case. She was the third live-in slave he and Annabel had accommodated. But her predecessors had proved unsatisfactory, had quickly revealed themselves as superficial, fetish-night poseurs. Maria was the real deal, somebody they both treasured.

Adrian took a deep draw. Then:

'That's it exactly. I'll leave the laptop logged in to the first account until the automatic time-out kicks in. That could be anything up to twenty minutes or even half an hour after I transfer out the last bundle of cash.'

Brady stood up and – amazingly – fixed himself a glass of tap water.

'Which brings us neatly to the getaway,' he said, sitting back down and opening up his *A to Z* map book: *Birmingham And Fifty Miles Around*. He traced the route with his forefinger over several pages.

'Adrian's double-checked the route on the anti-speed and surveillance camera websites. It's going to take us nearly sixty miles to travel thirty but we won't hit a single camera on the way.'

He brought his finger to rest in the middle of a page.

'And here's where we pick up the train. An unmanned platform on a branch line that'll take us all the way into Birmingham New Street. No cameras, no station staff, probably no other passengers if we're lucky.'

Adrian passed the spliff on to Annabel. Brady picked up the four white envelopes that were laid out in an orderly row next to the *A to Z*. Each one had one of their names ballpenned elegantly on the front by Maria. Brady had told her to do it for the usual reasons but also because nobody could ever read his own illegible scrawl.

'Local tickets into Birmingham. Long-distance rail tickets. And of course e-ticket confirmations for the flights.'

He handed them round and everybody checked the contents of their own envelopes.

The plan was that each of them boarded a separate carriage into Birmingham and then took separate trains to four different airports for four different foreign destinations. The meeting point would be in Northern Cyprus, four weeks from today. The temperatures were reasonable in late October and there was still no messy extradition treaty with the UK to worry about. The plan was overkill, had been refined and refined and then refined some more. But overkill was how you got away with it. How you didn't get caught.

'And we just leave Blondie here?' Adrian asked, meaning January Shepherd.

He wanted to hear Brady confirm the point one last time.

'No, Ade, I thought I'd nip up and slit her throat just before we head off,' Annabel said.

Nobody laughed. Brady took a sip of water.

'Very droll,' he said. 'But what's really happening – as Adrian fucking well knows – is that John Shepherd will get the address in a text message from me as soon as I'm safe in my departure lounge and as soon as they start boarding the first-class passengers on to my flight.'

Annabel passed the spliff to Maria – or tried to; Maria didn't seem to be paying the slightest attention.

'Maria?' she asked, puzzled.

Maria took the spliff on auto-pilot, didn't do anything with it, didn't speak.

'The fuck is it, Maria?' Annabel persisted.

Maria pulled the ashtray across the table towards herself, abandoned the spliff onto the grooved edge.

'I can't believe this,' she said finally. 'But I think there's a problem. I think there's something we've forgotten to check.'

All three of them stared at her. The only noise in the room came from a piece of wood sparking somewhere in the bowels of the Aga.

'What?' Brady asked, 'What is it?'

Maria looked straight at him, every sex-game protocol forgotten.

'Fucking petrol, Brian,' she said. 'I don't think we've got enough petrol in the tank for the journey.'

Chapter Forty

Jacobson and Kerr sat in the rear passenger seats of the patrol car as they waited for the traffic lights to change. They were out near the Waitrose complex, heading back into town. The uniformed officer in the front passenger seat was Gary Bose from the Armed Response Unit. Like him and the driver, Jacobson and Kerr were still wearing bulletproof jackets – mandatory kit in any scenario where firearms were even remotely suspected or possible. Jacobson was in constant touch with the incident room on his mobile, had told the driver that there was no real point in speed-driving back.

It had been another dead end. Emma Smith had found a report worth taking further right on the periphery of the five-mile radius. A farmer out that way had told the uniformed patrol who'd got him out of bed last night that there was an abandoned shepherd's cottage a mile or so beyond the edge of his property. Dilapidated, not far off falling-down dangerous. A few times recently he'd seen lights there if he was driving past after dark. One time he'd seen a car outside and maybe three or four young people getting out of it. *I reported it to your lot, you can't get involved any more yourself, but I expect you did sod all about it*, he'd told the patrol officers. When they'd asked him if he could identify the car he'd said that it might have been an old-style Volvo. He wasn't completely sure about the make but it was definitely an old saloon of some kind.

Last night's patrol had checked the building from the

outside but hadn't found any signs of life. Jacobson hated lack of thoroughness, had seized on the report as an opportunity to ignore his own advice, to get out of the Divisional building, to do some desperate, last-minute running around. The report had also fitted his theory that the gang were smart enough to alter their MO, setting up patterns and then confounding them. But all they'd found when they'd got there, and gingerly shoved in the door, had been beer cans, pizza boxes, discarded condoms, bits and bobs of soft drug detritus. Kids using the place as a draughty, uncomfortable fuck-pad basically. Rather them than me, Kerr had said, putting Jacobson's own thoughts into words.

The driver accelerated smoothly, turning his wheels at the absolute point of transition between amber and green. Jacobson tried – and failed – not to look at the dashboard clock: two forty-two plus ten seconds.

Brady took Maria with him to get the petrol. They'd used up the contents of their fuel cans on the burn-outs but there was a garage-cum-shop only a couple of miles away. Maria was right: it *was* a fuck-up, one of them should have been keeping an eye on it, monitoring the fuel gauge. Yet it was a minor one surely, easily rectified. Adrian, untypically, had said it wasn't even worth bothering about. If the gauge was on red, he'd argued, there was probably still twenty miles or so in the tank – they could refuel en route once they got going. Brady hadn't liked that idea one little bit. The issue had come to light now, so *fix* it now, take care of it now. Besides, they'd be back at the cottage before Adrian had even sent out the email, never mind started the money transfers. Not that it mattered anyway. The transfers were completely Adrian's domain. All the rest of them could do would be to stand around, or sit around, and watch him.

They'd been keeping the car out of sight behind the outhouse as another precaution. Not that they'd been troubled by any visitors. It was an irritation in the sense that you had

330

to open an old gate to drive the car out into the 'delightful country lane' (according to the letting agent's house details). In actuality, the way out was along a lengthy pot-holed dirt track, high-hedged on both sides once you were clear of the cottage and the garden. That was no bad thing either when seclusion was one of your key priorities.

The drive to the garage was straightforward, so was filling up. Maria went into the shop, ready to pay in cash just as soon as he'd finished at the pump. There was no point wasting a new, unused credit card on thirty quids' worth of unleaded. They were well out of Crowcross and coming up to the second of the three junctions they needed to nego-tiate in order to get back home before Brady started to worry that somebody might be following them. He turned left instead of right, away from the cottage instead of back to it.

Casper and Tracey had walked back along the river hand in hand. Tracey had been animated now, making shopping plans for stuff they might want to take with them to the caravan. Casper had driven out of the car park at Crowcross feeling that he didn't have a care in the world and that he was thinking straight about things for the first time in God knows how long. Maybe for the first time ever. The little exit road from the car park brought you out in the middle of the place, directly opposite the forecourt of the shop/garage. Tracey had spotted them first: the bloke and one of the two fit-looking birds who'd been in Club Zoo. Casper hadn't been so sure. The woman's hair was a different colour from how he remembered it for one thing. But Tracey had seen them close up after all. If she said it was them, then that was good enough for him. The woman had just been climbing into the passenger seat and, in the country-quiet, they'd heard the tosspot Tracey said was the ringleader, the one called Brady, turning his ignition.

Casper had screwed the nut, had let them drive on a good,

few hundred yards before he'd pulled out into the main road and set off in the same direction.

'They're fucking following us all right,' Maria said, watching behind them in the wing mirror. 'It's that fucking girl in the passenger seat, I swear it is. The one from Saturday night.'

Brady kept his speed fast but steady. The engine was in good nick for the age of the vehicle but the van kept on coming, matching him rev for rev. There was no room for uncertainty any more. He'd taken four turns by now, criss-crossing the countryside. Each turn took them further and further from the cottage. And the van followed them every single time.

'Why don't you just stop? Force them to go past or something?' Maria asked.

She thought she knew where they were now. Jesus Christ, she was thinking, isn't this the road that takes you out to the wood, the one near Boden Hall?

'I'm going to stop OK, Maria,' Brady answered. 'Soon as we get to the wood, soon as we get somewhere nice and quiet and familiar. Stick your hand under the seat.'

Maria looked at him as if he was mad.

'Do it, girl, get on with it.'

She did as she was told. Her fingers touched hard metal: one of their two Walther PPKs. She lifted it up carefully, examined it, found that it was fully loaded.

'I told Annabel to sleep with him,' Brady said, totally lying about that part of it. 'I thought he needed watching. She saw him creeping downstairs in the middle of the night then hiding it in his wardrobe. So she re-hid it out in the car, thought that would be safer for the rest of us.'

'We're going to shoot them?' Maria asked.

'If it comes to it. The main thing is to neutralise them. Keep them out of circulation until the job's done. Fuck—'

Brady took a bend on the sharp side, left off speaking until he had the car back under fragile control.

*

'Watch it, Casper,' Tracey shouted as Casper swung the van around the bend, not wanting to lose sight of them.

Instinctively, she pressed her feet into non-existent, imaginary pedals, felt her heart pounding.

'We've got to phone the coppers,' she said, 'at least let them know the number plate.'

Casper swayed in his seat, trying to get the van steady again.

'I told you I ain't got a licence, Tracey, you know that. What if—'

It was their third time around the same circling conversation. Tracey felt that she was done with it.

'These are what they call mitigating circumstances, Casper. You'll be a frigging hero in any case.'

Casper's wallet was on the dash. She took the card out of it that the CID sergeant had given Casper on Sunday morning, switched on her phone.

'OK, OK,' Casper said, his hands tight on the wheel. 'You're right. Go ahead.'

The TV news in the pub at lunchtime had been the only downer on their day up until that point. These bastards had got hold of a rich lass now, wanted cash or they'd kill her.

Tracey started to dial the number but then they hit another bend and the phone jerked out of her hand, landed on the floor.

'Casper!' she shouted again.

Casper veered into the other lane, very nearly skidded, only just made it around the bend with the van still in one piece. He slowed his speed down, checked that Tracey wasn't hurt. The road had straightened out again by the time he re-accelerated. There was another crossroads up ahead but already the Volvo was out of sight. Casper drew up when he reached the junction, banged his fist on the steering wheel. Whichever way he chose, he had a two out of three chance of getting it wrong. Tracey picked up her mobile from the floor, completed dialling this time. The copper answered instantly. She told him what they'd seen and precisely where they were, reading out the four directions and distances from the old black and white road sign.

'Let's just forget about it, Casper,' she said when the copper ended the call. 'The police can deal with those bastards. We've got better things to think about now.'

She touched his arm lightly. Casper looked at her.

'If you're sure,' he said.

'I'm sure.'

'OK.'

He turned right, taking the quickest route back to Crowby as far as he knew.

Chapter Forty-one

There was an immediate piece of luck. The Air Support Unit's helicopter was already airborne on a routine snooper flight along Crowby's stretch of the motorway, wouldn't need to lose vital seconds in pre-flight safety checks and take-off. Plus it could travel at 150 mph, cover two miles a minute. The patrol car headed for the same target area, lights flashing. The driver told Jacobson and Kerr he could do it inside fifteen minutes at top speed. Jacobson nodded, his head welded for the time being to his mobile. The helicopter team's rear police observer was in live contact with the control room and the incident room. Somebody back at the Divi who knew how these things worked had patched Jacobson's number into the conversation. It could still be a false alarm, he was thinking. Tracey Heald and her boyfriend were just kids after all, might easily be mistaken. But two items made him hope otherwise. One: the vehicle description, a white Volvo. Two: the fact that it had been spotted at the garage in Crowcross, just outside the radius he'd drawn up last night, barely six miles from Boden Hall, if that.

Brady hadn't realised that he'd lost the van at the crossroads until it was too late. He'd even thought about doubling-back, trying to find it. In the end, he'd just driven on towards Boden wood, trying frantically to work out his next move. The plan had been made on the hoof, mightn't have worked, but at least it had *been* a plan: find a quiet stretch in the woodland, stop, wait for the girl and her companion to draw up, get them under control with the Walther. He'd known that just getting away from them wasn't enough, that they'd get on to the police, raise the alert one way or another. They weren't in Birmingham or Crowby or Coventry now. The roads out this way could be easily sealed off, isolated, battened down.

Maria said nothing. She'd thought she'd seen Brady in all his worst moods, fucked-off and angry. But this was new. This was scarier. Brady looks panicked, she thought, Brady looks afraid.

'It's Saturday. There's got to be ramblers or birdwatchers or something out in the woods,' he said finally, 'we can pick up another car, get the hell out of here.'

'What about Annabel and Adrian?' Maria asked.

'They'll have to take their chances. There's no time to get back for them.'

Maria felt the panic herself. Brady was just raving. They'd never stolen cars, didn't know the first thing about how to go about it. And if he was thinking hostages, he was just as mad. Annabel was the only one who'd learned to use the guns properly for one thing. It was no good, it was all too wild, all too unpredictable. She'd wanted Brady to be a God she could worship and he was failing her. Right before her eyes, he was dissolving into a shitting-himself mortal.

She heard the helicopter a fraction of a second before Brady did. They were in open farm country now, maybe half a mile from the woodland. In the fading September sunlight, she could see it as well as hear it: a black silhouette over the ploughed field on her left, shadow-puppet blades whirling. Then it was right above them, its engine roaring, and some kind of amplified human voice blaring down on them. The only word she could make out was *police*.

Brady kept going, foot to the floor. There were a couple of bends ahead and then you reached the shelter of Boden wood. If they turned off the road when they got there, the helicopter couldn't follow them. It would buy them some thinking time at least if they could get that far, would leave them with some kind of desperate, final chance.

The mobile they'd brought with them rang. Maria picked it up. The display told her it was Annabel. Brady told her not to answer it, told her to switch it off. It was too risky, he said, the 'copter might have monitoring equipment on board, the call might lead them straight to the cottage. And anyway, fuck those two he was thinking, if he wasn't going to get away, why would he want Annabel and Adrian to?

The helicopter stuck with them, loomed over them, the engine even louder now, drowning out every other noise. They had to bellow at each other to be heard. Maria experienced the weird fear that it would pick them up somehow, sweep the Volvo clean off the ground and into the air.

Brady saw it after he'd driven around the first bend. A tractor. Up near the second bend. Big and slow-moving.

'No!' Maria shouted, as he closed the gap. 'You can't see far enough ahead. If there's something coming—'

Brady nearly managed his sneer, interrupting.

'There won't be, there never is. Hold tight.'

He swung the Volvo out into the narrow, opposite lane, still gunning the pedal to the floor. They were past the tractor and swinging around the apex of the curve when Maria saw the red blur in front of her. Then she saw nothing.

The patrol car delivered Jacobson and Kerr to the incident scene just after the first paramedics arrived. Jacobson let the patrol driver do his job, setting up the traffic barriers, establishing a cordon. The helicopter team had already put through the urgent call for the fire service, and now the paramedics were stretchering Birgit Kruijsdijk into one of the ambulances for the journey to Crowby General. Her escape had been fairly astonishing. She'd managed to turn her car side-on somehow so that the Volvo had impacted well behind the driver's seat. The Clio had been ripped in two. She had multiple broken bones and bad whiplash injuries. But she should make a recovery, the paramedics were saying, she should *live*.

'Brady' still had a faint pulse so the fire crew worked on him first when they got there. They needed oxyacetylene equipment to get him out of the wreckage. He was unconscious but still breathing when the paramedics stretchered him carefully over to the helicopter. The girl was already gone, had probably died instantly. They cut her out dead, laid her mangled corpse on the tarmac while a paramedic went to fetch a standard-issue body bag.

Jacobson and Kerr still had their own job to do. The crash had sprayed wreckage and interior detritus across the road and into the fields. They scrabbled through it, looking for something that might yield a clue to the gang's hideout. Jacobson was confident now that they'd relocated themselves somewhere out this way. But somewhere wasn't good enough unless you could ditch the some and keep the where. Kerr found the leather bag that might be the girl's, shook out the contents. Lipsticks and make-up, a pink MP3 player, a purse containing fifty quid in fivers and a thousand quid in fifties. There were four credit cards too, all in different names. But nothing with any kind of address on. They were about to give up when Jacobson found a two-day-old copy of the *Evening Argus* lying next to a tyre foot pump. Nearly fell over it would have been a more accurate description than found. He'd caught his foot against the side of the pump, had nearly tripped, nearly lost his balance. The newspaper lay open at the Sudoku puzzle page where someone had sketched an un-neat drawing in the top left-hand corner. A series of arrows and interlocking parallel lines that might have been meant as directions. There were a few scrawled words too. But Jacobson found them illegible. So did Kerr when he showed them to him.

Half-a-dozen police vehicles were lined up along the roadside now. Any patrol that had been remotely in the area had a made a bee-line for it. Jacobson and Kerr noticed Helen

Dawson, the sex-bomb rural patrolwoman close by, deep in conversation with a burly-looking fireman.

'This mean anything to you?' Jacobson asked her, approaching her and holding up the newspaper page.

She peered at it attentively for a long minute.

'I'm sorry, sir. I can't read the writing,' she said. 'But I don't know, maybe if—'

She pointed to an 'X' near the centre of the drawing.

'It could be, I suppose—'

Jacobson suppressed his impatience.

'It could be what?' he asked.

PC Dawson spread the newspaper out on the nearest patrol car bonnet, pointed to the 'X' again.

'If you assume the "X" is the church at Crowcross and you follow the direction of the arrows, I think you end up here.'

Jacobson watched her tracing the route with her forefinger. There was another 'x', smaller this time, where her finger came to rest.

'It's a farm labourer's cottage. Or it used to be anyway. It got converted into something posher years ago. Well off the beaten track though.'

Adrian had already eliminated the hard disks from the three other laptops. He'd run his secure-delete utility against the root directories and then he'd physically destroyed them, burning them down to nothing inside the Aga. He was using the last functioning machine now, transferring the fourth hundred K bundle out to the second layer of receiving accounts. He was sitting at the big table in the lounge, hunched over his keyboard. Annabel was in the room too, staring anxiously out of the window.

She was listening for the sound of the car, listening for the sound of anything really. They should be back by now. It was no more than a ten-minute drive each way. What the fuck was Brady playing at? And why weren't they answering the mobile? She thought maybe she'd go and look through one of the upstairs windows where you could see a lot further along the lane towards the main road. She didn't want to disturb Adrian anyway, now that he'd started his work.

She decided she'd go into the kitchen first, though, fix herself a cup of tea. Camomile maybe, something soothing.

She was pouring the hot water into the cup when she heard the rumble of car wheels at last. She put the kettle down on the draining board of the sink, not sure whether to top it up with more water, not sure if it was worth it when they'd all be leaving soon. Absurdly, the first thing she thought was that Adrian had put the TV on in the lounge for some reason, had put it on bloody loudly.

Armed Police! Place your hands on your head and step outside slowly.

They must be using a loud hailer or something. Nobody had a voice like that, undistorted. The part of her that took it in, that actually processed the information, led her to the kitchen drawer where they'd secreted the Walthers. Brady had loaded this one as well while she'd removed the other one from Adrian's wardrobe out to the Volvo. Just to be on the safe side, he'd said.

Adrian was already in the hall, already walking towards the ghastly, dimpled glass door which had been somebody's tasteless, lowbrow idea of a home improvement. He had his hands right on top of his stupid head, reverting to type, doing exactly what he was told. Annabel had time to wonder to herself how the fuck he proposed to open the door *and* keep them there. Poor Adrian. Better in bed than she'd expected. But still a geek loser, still a wuss. His solution appeared to be to stoop down, one arm reaching for the handle and pulling the door open, the other one still resting on the top of his head. She pointed the gun barrel at the back of his neck and told him to stand still, to stop moving. There was a second when she couldn't work out why there had been a shot when she hadn't pulled the trigger. And then there was another second when she saw the hole in her chest. It puzzled her that it didn't really seem to hurt. She did pull the trigger then just for the hell of it. Then there were no more seconds.

Gary Bose, looking shaken, stayed with the bodies while the patrol driver spoke to the control room. He'd played it entirely by the book, followed all the directives, Bose told himself over and over. The woman had pointed the gun straight at the bloke's head, there was a definite intent to shoot. He'd fired himself only to save life. It had been the bloke's personal bad luck that her gun had gone off somehow as she'd fallen – and that her bullet had found him.

Jacobson and Kerr took five minutes of room-searching to reach the outhouse. Kerr noticed the padlocked door at the top of the stairs first but Jacobson was the one who spotted the bunch of keys on the middle of the big architect's desk. He handed them to Kerr when they reached the top of the stairs. The fourth key Kerr tried was the one that fitted the lock. He undid the bolt and stepped into the room.

January Shepherd had positioned herself in front of the bed. In her right hand, she was holding a sharp piece of glass. She waved it at him defiantly, still standing her ground.

Chapter Forty-two

Coda

Jacobson told the (male) Sister that he was finally going, that there was really no point in hanging on there endlessly. The Sister agreed, reminded him that they had his mobile number in any case: someone would phone him immediately if there was any kind of change in the situation – any kind at all. Jacobson thanked him, pressed the switch at the side of the intensive care unit's sliding, electronically-controlled doors. He'd started to feel like a hospital volunteer, somebody with Sunday afternoon time to kill on his hands, visiting a patient that nobody else in the world wanted to see. He exchanged a few words with the young uniformed constable who was stationed in the corridor outside. The plod had to be there because of the local protocol which demanded a police custody presence whenever a 'dangerous' prisoner was hospitalised. The arrangement was completely unnecessary in this case. But no doubt it would enable one of the force's bureaucrats to tick the right boxes on the right forms with the right kind of pen. In reality, 'Brady' was no longer a danger to anyone. Twenty-two hours after he'd been admitted to the hospital, he was still unconscious, was only breathing because he was attached to a ventilator. Jacobson would have enjoyed interviewing him, taking apart his undergraduate pretensions one by one, confronting him with the reality of what he'd done. But the medical facts were against that happening. According to the latest prognosis from the consultant, 'Brady' had only the slimmest chance of survival and, supposing he did pull through, he might be paralysed, he might have permanent, extensive brain damage. If it was me, Jacobson told the young officer, I'd sooner they just called last orders and pulled the plug.

He walked along the yellow-painted corridor and took the lift down to the ground level. It was maybe time to be going home, maybe time to salvage some of the weekend for himself. With January Shepherd safe and the bodies of the three other gang members lying cold in the morgue, there was nothing else he needed to do that couldn't keep until Monday morning.

He'd looked in on Birgit Kruijsdijk earlier. She was still heavily sedated, still with all her limbs in traction. It would be a while, the doctors were saying, before she was back on her feet. What was important, Jacobson supposed, was that they were also saying that she'd definitely get there, definitely make it. So would Perry Harrison. He was able to sit up in his bed now, his body on the mend and his mental faculties unimpaired, according to all the initial tests. He wasn't permitted ordinary visitors yet but DC Williams and Mick Hume had been allowed to take a brief statement from him last night – around about the same time that Jacobson and Emma Smith had interviewed January Shepherd. She'd taken some knocks, not all of them physical, yet Jacobson had read resilience over every inch of her bruised face.

Suddenly weary, he wandered into the visitors' café near the entrance to the main building. He should probably give Kerr a call. Kerr was out at the gang's cottage, acting as CID liaison to Jim Webster's extensive scene of crime operation. But Kerr knew what he was doing, would get in touch if he needed to. Maybe Steve Horton then. Horton had taken forensic possession of the gang's surviving laptop, was scanning its contents for traces of their true identities and any links he could find to John Shepherd's money. Jacobson – along with Kerr – had visited Shepherd again that morning out at Boden Hall. Shepherd had said that he actually couldn't care less about his transferred cash. That makes two of us,

Jacobson had thought. But at least Shepherd had been clean-shaven and sober – and he'd thanked Jacobson for finding his daughter with what had felt like true sincerity. He'd been sitting at his pool with his girlfriend, Kelly. Normal service more or less resumed. They'd caught up with January Shepherd and Nick Bishop in the tropical plant house, already engrossed in plans to reschedule the Alice Banned tour dates, get back out on the road.

Jacobson found a table by the window, drank his coffee. He decided he'd phone Alison instead of Kerr or Horton. He hoped he wasn't too late, hoped that she hadn't already made other, more reliable plans for the remains of the day.